SHADOWS & SURRENDER

A Snarky Urban Fantasy Detective Series

DEBORAH WILDE

te da media
vancouver

Publisher's Note: This is a work of fiction. Names, characters, places, and incidents are a product of the author's imagination. Locales and public names are sometimes used for atmospheric purposes. Any resemblance to actual people, living or dead, or to businesses, companies, events, institutions, or locales is completely coincidental.

Book Cover Design by Croco Designs.

Issued in print and electronic formats.

ISBN: 978-1-988681-45-0 (paperback)

ISBN: 978-1-988681-59-7 (epub)

ISBN: 978-1-988681-46-7 (Kindle)

Chapter 1

Lying to the cops wasn't generally something I advised, but it's a woman's prerogative to change her mind.

The man in the photo possessed that specific shade of forgettable light brown hair generic to many a white boy and his facial features were unremarkable, but he was saved from obscurity by a purple birthmark shaped like a comet under one eye.

"I've never seen him before." I handed the photo back to Sergeant Margery Tremblay of the Mundane Police Force and the closest thing I had to a friend among cops. "Who is he?"

"Can you confirm your whereabouts two nights ago between the hours of midnight and 3AM?" Despite her flawless makeup and cute silver pixie cut, her eyes were steely, and she asked the question with no trace of familiarity.

I leaned back in the plastic chair. "I was asleep."

"Alone?"

"Shocking, I know. My roommate was home."

"There's no one to confirm you didn't leave your place?" she said.

"No." I crossed my arms. "What's this about, Sergeant?"

She tapped the photo. "Yevgeny Petrov was shot dead."

My questions were legion, but I hurriedly crossed off the ones it would seem odd for me, a total stranger and supposed Mundane, to ask. Questions such as: "Why are Mundane cops investigating this when Yevgeny is Nefesh?" Or, "How was he shot when he can turn his skin to rubber? A fact I knew because that's the form he'd been in when he attacked me, and I accidentally tried to rip his magic from his body. A girl never forgets her first time, don'tcha know."

"My condolences," I said. "I'm sure his mother loved him. What does this have to do with me?"

Margery massaged her temples. "He's the one you allegedly attacked in that anonymous assault charge. When you were undercover as that old woman."

Yevgeny had never seen the real me, just the Lillian persona who I'd been illusioned to look like. However, when I went for his magic he'd recognized I was a Jezebel, enemy to the shadowy religious organization that he worked for called Chariot. Jezebels were a special breed.

"You think I found out and shot him? Bit of a leap, no? The assault complaint was bullshit. I don't have magic, so what's my motive in taking him out, Sergeant?" I said coldly.

Continuing to be listed as Mundane on public record had its uses.

Margery made a sound of disgust. "All right. Quit it with the 'Sergeant.' I'm just doing due diligence. I don't think you're involved and you're not being charged with anything, but you might know something. You're sure his name doesn't ring any bells?"

I shook my head. "Where was he found?"

"One of our squads took down a dogfighting ring. They found his body and called in the Nefesh homicide unit."

Last time I'd seen him, Yevgeny was laying on the floor, a whimpering wreck believing that ants were swarming him, an illusion courtesy of my partner in crime that night. Guess

2

Yevgeny'd gotten over the trauma enough to continue being a productive member of the criminal fringe.

"Yevgeny has magic?" I put the right amount of curiosity into my voice. "Is House Pacifica involved?"

"No. He's registered with House Ontario. He was just here visiting his sister. She's been notified already as next of kin."

What a load of crap. Even if the sibling part was true, my investigations had revealed that he'd been in Vancouver working for Chariot, kidnapping marginalized teens in order to sever their magic. It was then sold at an auction where he'd also provided security.

"Are we done?" I said.

As I didn't have anything more to add, Margery cut me loose with a sigh and instructions not to get in any more trouble until she went on vacation in the fall.

"I light up your life," I called and left.

I legged it back to my car, Moriarty, and logged into the House Pacifica database. Look at that, Yevgeny did have a sister. Tatiana Petrov, a level five Weaver. Yikes. There weren't a lot of people with level five magic in any specialty. What were the chances that she'd been the Weaver hired to set the security ward on House HQ, only to later null it and enable a German Chariot assassin to take out a person-of-interest?

There was one way to find out.

Getting her address was a piece of sleuthing cake. Starting my damn car was not. It had sprung a leak in the radiator hose. I went into my trunk and retrieved the relevant supplies from what I'd dubbed my "evil nemesis" kit.

Wearing rubber gloves and sunglasses, because safety first when dealing with coolant, I dried the hose, then wrapped the leak securely in several layers of duct tape. Ah, duct tape, was there anything it couldn't do? Lastly, I refilled the coolant reservoir. Add in bonus fun points for doing it all in the piss-pouring rain.

I got behind the wheel, wet hair plastered to my forehead. "I don't have time to take you to a mechanic right now and get the hose changed, so you're going to be grateful for my MacGyvered fix and work properly, or I'll drive us straight to a scrap metal yard. Got it, car?"

With my day off to a grand start, I cranked the heat and drove to Tatiana's place, situated in a rural area of Langley, about an hour away from Vancouver. I made one brief stop, a much-needed Starbucks drive-through jaunt for a mocha latte with extra whipped cream and a chicken wrap, both of which I consumed long before I arrived at my destination.

Parking on the side of the road next to a neighbor's driveway, I engaged in some gold-medal skulking around Tatiana's good-sized acreage. There were no buildings other than the ranch house with its sweeping maple tree in the front yard. An SUV with a cold engine was parked on the square of dead grass to the side of the dirt lane that served as a driveway. Her property wasn't within walking distance of anything interesting, and as only Brits and masochists appreciated a ramble about the woods in the soaking rain, unless she had another car, she was at home.

The house was far enough removed from the country road that the only sound was the wind in the trees, so the squeak of the back door easily carried to my position. Keeping lower than window height, I snuck around the side in time to see a car with muddy plates peeling away—not the SUV—the tires kicking up tiny whirlwinds of dust. The driver wore a baseball cap, obscuring them from identification.

I made my way up the stairs of the back porch, my Sherlock senses on high alert and a sharp red dagger made from my blood magic gripped tightly in one hand. Ready with a cover story about my car needing a jumpstart, I knocked on the kitchen door, but no one answered. There were no signs of a struggle visible through the glass, but her

4

brother was dead and her visitor had been in an awful hurry to leave.

A few minutes later, I once more approached the kitchen door, slipping on the thin gloves and toque that I'd retrieved from my car. I carefully tucked my dark wavy hair inside the knit cap and pressed my fingertip to the doorframe. No magic. I frowned. Wards weren't as common on private residences as they were on major public buildings, but Tatiana was a high-level Weaver and at the very least, her brother, who had been crashing here before he died, was involved with some dangerous people. There should have been a ward to sense hostile intent and then hold potential attackers. It would freeze them in place and neutralize their magic, if they had any.

Since wards didn't deactivate when the Weaver who'd cast them died, an active ward would have effectively gift-wrapped the visitor for the cops to apprehend.

Cautiously, I tested the knob, which was unlocked. No siren blared when I opened the door. There was no keypad inside, so a silent alarm seemed unlikely. All of this made sense if Tatiana had been relying on a ward to guard her, but she wasn't. I'd met a lot of recklessly trusting people and they didn't tend to be the ones with mad magic. Maybe Tatiana thought that living in such a rural area meant that her only visitors would be well-intentioned neighbors.

Somehow I doubted it.

If the person in the car had been an innocent visitor, then why had they raced off?

"Hello?" I called out loudly. When there was no answer, I slid off my motorcycle boots, leaving them on the outside mat so as not to leave tracks, and tiptoed inside, eyes darting around for anything obviously out of place.

I crept into the hallway and gasped.

Tatiana Petrov lay face down, limbs splayed crookedly in a puddle of still-congealing blood from the hole blown through the back of her skull. Probably instantaneous death, so that was a mercy. Had she known what was going to happen to her or had it caught her by surprise? The naked violence of the scene didn't yield answers, but my mind kept circling back to gunshot angles, and the image of a woman smiling to meet a guest and then faltering for a second as she realized what was about to happen.

I gulped down air, bent over double with one hand splayed on my tight ribcage. Suddenly, that Starbucks run's added trip time made me incredibly grateful. I was a professional, sure, but the reality of how close I'd come to having a front row seat to a murder prickled along the back of my neck. Had the person I'd seen race off been Chariot, or connected to them?

Was this a preview of my own fate?

Trembling, I stuffed my haywire emotions into a very deep box until I was able to regard this situation with a cool head. The smart thing to do would be to call the crime in anonymously to the Nefesh cops. On the other hand, if Chariot was behind this, a golden opportunity had just dropped into my lap. As a Jezebel, I'd take any edge on my enemies that I could get.

I called Miles Berenbaum, Head of Security for House Pacifica.

"What?" he growled. Wow. Grumpy really needed to perfect his phone manner with me, especially since we were going to be working together for a good long time.

"I have good news and bad news. The good news is that I'm 99 percent certain how the German hitman got past House wards to kill Yitzak." I gnawed on my thumbnail. How many more times would the price for answers be death?

Standard procedure dictated that I couldn't touch the body, but something in me needed to see Tatiana's face. Why? I'd seen death before. But this was different. Like

Yitzak's empty stare, it would remind me exactly what was waiting if I didn't keep my wits about me.

"What's the bad news?" Miles said.

"You're gonna need a new Weaver if you want to set up any more wards."

I appreciated a good old-fashioned bout of "fucks."

"Where are you?" he demanded. I gave him the address. "Where's the body?"

"In the hallway."

Miles made a pained noise. "You broke in?"

"No." The truth was so freeing. As were lies of omission.

"Uh-huh. Why must you always ruin my day?" Miles said.

I methodically searched the kitchen for any evidence tying Tatiana or her brother to Chariot. "Think of it as broadening your horizons."

"Get out of there and call it in."

"Give me an hour."

"It's a crime scene," Miles growled. "You'll contaminate it."

"Who do you think you're talking to? Gloves on, hair covered, shoes off, no touching the body. No grasping any handles or knobs directly so as not to smudge any prints." The kitchen yielded nothing more than kitchenware. Even the ancient address book tossed in the junk drawer was blank. I shoved the drawer shut. "You might have Chariot informants on the Nefesh force and if they get their hands on anything of note before we do, I guarantee it won't make it to the evidence locker."

"If Chariot did this, they would have swept the place already."

"I don't know, they didn't seem too keen on lingering." I shivered.

"You saw the murderer?" Miles sounded like he wanted

to reach through the phone and strangle me. "Did they see you?"

"No." I was confident about that fact, though it had been way too close for comfort. "I couldn't identify them, either. The plates on the car were muddy and the person wore a baseball cap, which I only glimpsed from behind."

"Levi is going to freak the fuck out."

"Then be creative with your report so that he doesn't," I snapped. Like this was my fault. Chariot was bent on acquiring immortality; they weren't playing by a rule book, and they definitely weren't playing it safe. Neither could I.

"If it weren't for the known Chariot connection to Tatiana's brother, who was killed a couple nights ago, I wouldn't have come in the first place." I searched the freezer in a last-ditch hope that the kitchen would yield something useful, but it, too, was a bust. "My Jezebel duties take precedence. I accepted the Mantle and I don't get to run away because it's scary. I'm checking the place out." I hung up on him, ignoring the persistent buzzing in my back pocket for the next ten minutes.

Tatiana was an interesting woman. She didn't own a TV, but she did have a CD tower full of classical music. While she had Weaver magic, she also enjoyed the good old-fashioned kind of weaving, as evidenced by the large loom with the unfinished tapestry that dominated the living room. Her house brimmed with artistic expression and no sign of religious conviction, so what had drawn her to Chariot? Had she been promised immortality or did it come down to cold, hard cash?

And why wasn't there a damn ward?

Her unprotected laptop on the coffee table failed to yield much beyond the bookkeeping records for her ward business and emails from clients.

Unlocking a phone with a dead woman's thumb wasn't my finest hour, but I kept my promise to Miles and managed to do it without touching the body. I airdropped her contacts list to my phone to go through later, so that was something. The texts were mostly social plans with friends. I left her phone where I found it.

Miles must have run every red light because he got here in a scant forty minutes. He and Arkady Choi, my friend, fighting mentor, and new neighbor, piled out of a pickup truck.

I met them at the back door.

Arkady not only worked for the House on hush-hush jobs, but he was part of the Nefesh Mixed Martial Arts League and was a thrill junkie. Their high-speed race here should have elated him, but his face was grim.

"What's wrong?" I said.

"Go fast, go hard, pedal to the metal. Would it have killed him to stop for a coffee?" Arkady's dark eyes flashed. "Make conversation?"

"It was a drive to get from point A to point B." Miles, a six-foot-four mountain of a man with muscles that begat muscles, slipped off his black shoes and left them next to mine on the doormat. "You knew that getting into the car."

"I guess my understanding of a ride is different than yours," Arkady said.

"That bad, huh?" I said, dying to call Priya about how these two had totally slept together.

They turned to me with identical expressions of surprise, like they'd forgotten I was there.

Arkady flung an arm theatrically across his forehead. "My life flashed before my eyes."

"Scale of one to ten, how well did you live your best self?" I said.

"Pickle, please," he said, slipping off his shoes. "It was an eleven."

"Did you find anything?" Miles said.

"Not yet," I said. "There's still the bathroom, two

9

bedrooms, and what I presume is an office, though it's locked."

The three of us exchanged smirks—as if that would be a problem.

Miles pulled out latex gloves and paper hats befitting a food services worker for himself and Arkady. It was kind of overkill for Miles, given his blond hair was buzz cut, but his attention to detail served him well as Head of Security.

Arkady shuddered as he slipped the paper hat over his black, chin-length hair.

"It doesn't have cooties," I said.

"It's a fashion blight." He brightened. "At least it won't detract from my stellar good looks." He wasn't wrong. Dude had cheekbones for days, pouty lips, and overall supermodel hotness.

I clapped him on the shoulder. "That's the spirit. Think positively."

We entered the kitchen and I led them to the victim, motioning to the body with a flourish. "Meet Tatiana Petrov."

"How can you be certain that's her?" Arkady circled the body. "We can't see her face. If she even still has a face."

I pointed to a thick white streak in her dark hair. "She's registered in the House Pacifica database and there's a photo. Her brother has a purple birthmark under his eye. That streak of white is her birthmark."

"I've met her before," Miles said softly. "She was there when Levi first took over House Pacifica and keyed the new wards to his blood. I didn't suspect her at all." He clenched his jaw.

Arkady reached out to pat his back, then jammed his hand in his pocket instead.

"Don't beat yourself up over it," I said. "We had no idea how far-reaching Chariot was."

We still didn't. Sure, we had a general understanding of

how they operated, but we didn't know the players or the precise scope of their range. To all appearances, Tatiana had been a leader in her field with a trustworthy reputation. Literally anyone could be one of them. How did I protect myself and watch my friends' backs when I didn't even know where to look?

"Tell me about the brother," Miles said.

"Yevgeny Petrov." I filled them in on my first meeting with Birthmark Man, up to and including my visit with Sergeant Tremblay. When I finished, I frowned at the body.

"What?" Miles said.

"I can't get past the fact that there weren't any wards on this place," I said. "Whoever shot her just waltzed in and judging from the angle of the body, caught her coming out of either one of the bedrooms or the office. She's a Weaver. Her brother worked for Chariot and she likely did too. Did she really trust them so unconditionally?"

"Not everyone has honed your levels of suspicion," Arkady said.

"It's common sense when you work for the bad guys," I said. "Villains aren't known for their undying loyalty."

"You work for the bad guys, too," Miles said. "From her perspective. Hell, you are the bad guy. Yet, you've taken on a team. How do you know one of them won't stab you in the back?"

"As if I need a knife," Arkady sniffed.

"Could you not make a joke, just once?" Miles said.

Arkady rolled his eyes. "Ooh, right. The commandment according to Berenbaum. Thou shalt not make light of anything lest anyone mistake it for thee not taking thine job seriously enough."

Their bickering had been an interesting glimpse into their current dynamic for the first minute. Now I was over it. "Back to Chariot."

"Chariot believes in the rightness of their actions every

bit as much as you do," Miles said. "Forget that for a second and it'll be your body we find."

"Please. Mansplain the dangers to me. My point that Tatiana should have kept her guard up stands. Her brother Yevgeny was murdered. She should have been on high alert."

"So let's find out why she wasn't," Arkady said.

After a half-hearted search of the small bathroom, Miles and Arkady opted for the guest bedroom where Yevgeny had been staying, while I searched Tatiana's room.

"It's a bust in here," I said.

A deafening clang rang out.

I sprinted into the guest room. Arkady stood half in the closet, bashing in a safe door with heavy swings of his now-stone fists. I stayed behind Miles who was a very handy shield until the door crumpled entirely, allowing Arkady access.

"And you were worried about me contaminating the scene?" I shoved Miles.

He started as the safe's metal keypad fell onto the ground. "The homicide cops will either think robbery was the motive or that this was a red herring."

"Not the point, dude. I'm a trained professional and this is just… not. At least concede I was right to search."

"Depends on what we find." Man, this guy wouldn't give me an inch.

Arkady's magic fists returned to normal. He reached into the safe and pulled out a camera. "Yevgeny, you perv," he said, scrolling through frames.

Miles and I crowded around him and I gasped. They were photos of my Jezebel predecessor, Gavriella Behar, and her former workplace, the Star Lounge, including the placement of security cameras and the back door from various angles of the parking lot.

"Gavriella was kidnapped at work," I said. I'd suspected as much, but confirmations were always valuable. "Yevgeny stalked her and cased the joint to figure out how best to snatch her without being seen."

Arkady handed the camera to Miles and leaned into the safe. "There are a couple more things in here."

The Android phone he removed was password protected so I said I'd take it to Priya Khatri, my best friend, part-time employee, and hacker extraordinaire. The other item was a thin metal lockbox. The lid had been busted open and there was dust in the crevice of the hinges.

I ran a fingertip over a hinge and rubbed the dust between my fingers. "Wood. An under-the-floor safe?"

I pulled out a handful of photos, but it took me a moment to recognize the girl. "It's Gavriella again." Her childhood through to early adulthood was captured in dozens and dozens of photos. "Given the lid was broken open, the contents, and the fact that Gavriella liked her hiding spots, this lockbox could have been taken from her apartment."

"Did Gavriella have a ward on her apartment door?" Miles said.

"Yes, and it was active when Levi and I went there," I said. "Oh, fuck. Level five Weaver. If anyone could disable it and then rearm it, it would have been Tatiana. They must have searched Gavriella's home after she'd been kidnapped. I wonder what they were hoping to find?"

"You think the cell is hers?" Arkady said.

"Possibly," I said. "Levi and I couldn't find it when we searched her place." I quickly sifted through the rest of the photos, hitting something hard at the bottom of the lockbox. A book with a reddish brown spine, it was Sir Arthur Conan Doyle's *A Study in Scarlet*, his first novel featuring my beloved Sherlock Holmes.

"Props to her fine taste in literature, but why lock this puppy up?" I flipped the front cover open and frowned. "What's this?"

Under the title on the first page was a message printed in block letters—perfect for someone who didn't want their handwriting recognized.

On the first line was a "3."

On the second was a "1."

And on the third line was another "1" paired with a question mark.

Underneath that said, "Thursday. Steam clock. 8PM."

"The steam clock could be the one here in Gastown." I rifled through the pages but there was no way to determine how old the message was and there was nothing else of interest.

Well, not until I got to the back page.

The men peered over my shoulder at the shaky drawing of a giant sunflower.

Miles made a disgusted noise. "Kids defacing books. Little brats."

"Dandelion," I said.

"Wrong. It's a sunflower," he said.

I stroked a finger over the flower as if I could draw warmth from it. "The Crayola color on the petals. Dandelion yellow. My favorite."

It was a happy color, like my home. Talia had joked about me going through my "monochromatic phase" which was much preferred to "the sassy sixes" of my peers. Dad had praised my prodigious artistic output, and my finished drawings crowded the front of our fridge.

"I don't understand," Arkady said.

"This was my dad's copy." Buzzing filled my ears. I felt like I was spinning in place, a hollow shell in a reality comprised of a thousand shards of glass, flaying me alive.

"Are you sure?" Miles said. "Lots of kids draw flowers."

I tapped the happy face in the middle of the flower with a small "A" for a nose. "I'm sure."

I dragged in a breath. I wasn't that child anymore, helplessly riding out the shockwaves of other people's actions on my life.

"Pickle," Arkady said, concern in his eyes, "there's blood crawling over your skin."

Fire laced my veins and snaked up my spine. I stoked that bonfire with a dark rage that blazed behind my eyes, threatening to ignite everything.

Sherlock Holmes famously said, "…when you have excluded the impossible whatever remains, however improbable, must be the truth."

This was mine: My father had taken away my magic. He'd then reached out to a Jezebel with some kind of coded message, making him more deeply entwined with this mystery than I'd ever imagined. Had he somehow always known what I was? Was this book part of some long con?

Was *I*?

"Hey, breathe." Miles kept his breathing slow and measured until I had matched it. "What do you want to do?"

I bundled up all my complicated emotions around my dad and shut them down along with my sputtering blood armor. I'd spent the past fifteen years in a state of uncertainty around him and I'd had enough of the past hanging over me. It was time for answers—and for closure. "Find out Adam Cohen's game once and for all."

And hope it didn't cost me everything.

Chapter 2

I tossed the cell into the lockbox and carried everything to the kitchen to bring home with me when we left. "Let's finish up already."

After a round of rock, paper, scissors to see who'd pick the lock, which I was too distracted to play and Miles flat-out refused, Arkady broke in.

It wasn't an office, but a darkened stairwell leading into a basement. Arkady flicked the light switch but when nothing happened, he pushed Miles in front. "Get going."

"Scared?" Miles smirked.

"Hardly, but exploring creepy basements is a stupid white-person move. People of color are infinitely smarter than that." He waved us goodbye. "Call me if you survive."

Miles pulled a coin out of his pocket and tossed it into the darkness. "No motion-activated traps."

"Ooh, brains and a pretty face." Arkady prodded Miles. "Move along, Mr. Badass."

Miles called up a ball of flame and he and I peered into the gloom. The way seemed clear. My patience was frayed and I wanted to go home and brood, so I manifested my full-body blood armor and shoved past Miles. The top step creaked ominously but nothing happened.

"Stick close," I said.

We crept down the stairs.

I stepped into the large unfinished room. "There's nothing—"

A length of orange yarn about the thickness of my thigh shot down from the ceiling and knotted around my ankle, yanking me upside down and into the air. Red-hot stabbing pain flared through the old injury on my right thigh. I did an ab curl to grab for the knot, but more yarn—purple this time—wrapped around my wrist, flinging me sideways toward the wall. My curses turned to shrieks.

Was my armor impact-proof or was I about to hit like a crash test dummy, my skull splatting like a cantaloupe? I tried to protect my head with my free hand, only to have another knot wrap around it and jerk my arm straight. I flailed my left leg and, in response, a blue strand snagged and bound it, flipping me.

Could this get more undignified? I was splayed spread eagle on my back in mid-air, my limbs tightly imprisoned, but at least I'd come to a dead stop without colliding into the wall. And people accused me of being a pessimist.

Miles hadn't fared any better except he lay on his side. "A fucking spiderweb. Are you kidding me?"

I wrenched on the yarn but it defied my low-level enhanced strength. "It's kind of poetic if you think about it. A Weaver, knotting her prey."

"That armor of yours fireproof?" Miles said. "I could burn us out."

"Go for it."

Fire burst forth from his forearms and the yarn knotted against his flesh glowed red. Yeah, show that string who was boss.

The fire crackled higher; the room grew hotter.

Sweat ran down the side of my face inside my armor, both dank and ticklish. I was boiling in my own protective suit. "Fought bravely. Died sous-vide." was not going to be my epitaph.

"Hurry up," I growled.

His magic flared so bright and high that it almost licked the ceiling. The yarn crackled.

"Gotcha," he said.

Uh-huh.

The yarn sizzled, the room filling with a noxious black smoke that sent us into paroxysms of coughing. His magic abruptly shut down, with no real harm done to the yarn.

Never send a man to do a woman's job.

"My turn." A sharp blood dagger, my weapon of choice, did zip against the heavy fibers. Huh.

"Much better," Miles bitched.

"That was just step one." Dropping my magic armor only bought me the slightest wiggle room, but it allowed me to send a silky red ribbon into the green yarn manacling my left arm. My powers hooked into it and I flinched. "Fuck. Fuck. Fuck."

My magic snapped back into me.

"What?" Miles said.

"I swear something just reached out and tried to touch my mind." Defense-system yarn was one thing, sentience was quite a different and unwelcome ballgame. A creepy crawly sensation scuttled over my skin. Only an idiot would go in for round two, but being trussed up like a turkey didn't leave a lot of options. "Okay, I know what to expect. Trying again." I shot my magic into the yarn once more and pulled as hard as I could.

The magic tasted like silk. I closed my eyes with a smile, a sharp buzz zipping through me. The most expensive whiskey was a cheap burn of moonshine in comparison to this honeyed smoothness. I drank deep, then pulled it out in a smudgy shadow, trapping it in my red forked branches.

The ropes quivered. One edge rose up in a funnel, the thick strands forming a multi-colored face with an open gaping maw.

I yelped. The section where I was shackled tore free of my magic branches, spinning to wrap me in coils. Blinded and barely able to breathe, I fought to catch hold of the yarn's magic again, but it kept slipping away. I couldn't tell which way was up, plunged into a relentless chaos that I couldn't harness, despite how hard I fought.

A loud grinding noise vibrated along the yarn. No, a muted gnashing. Exactly how a mouth full of teeth made of giant knots would sound.

I thrashed pointlessly against my prison. There were a lot of things that might kill me, including the truth about my father, so some dead woman with a string fetish and Weaver magic did not get that honor.

Even if I wanted my armor back to protect me from those teeth, I was too tightly wrapped. Adding it would crush me faster. In one jerky motion after another, I was drawn closer to the mouth. Or so I assumed, since I was completely encased in yarn that abraded the skin on my face and my eyes were screwed tight.

The more I tried to hook into the yarn's magic, the more it neatly evaded me. I had to catch it off guard.

"Miles!" I hoped he could hear my muffled words. "Burn it again!"

Knotted teeth clamped down on my right ankle and pain blazed up my leg. A change from the pain that generally shot *downward* from the poor femur held together by rods, courtesy of a car accident in my wild youth. The teeth ground down harder, trying to tear through the protection of my motorcycle boots' leather.

Limp with exhaustion, I braced myself for my ankle bone to snap, but the grinding stopped.

I sniffed. Smoke. I slammed my magic into the yarn's. Miles had provided enough of a distraction for me to once more hook into it. I could have kissed him. I ripped the magic free, snagged it into my red forked branches, and let those gorgeous white clusters bloom.

The rope disappeared, dumping Miles and me onto the ground. I swore as my ankle jostled against the concrete.

A thunderous crash boomed from the top of the stairs and I flinched, but it was just Arkady, who'd smashed the door open.

I blinked against the brightness of the lights switching on, and then Arkady jumped the stairs two at a time, his face wild. "I was kidding," he babbled. "I wouldn't have sent you down alone—I couldn't break the door down."

Miles lay on his back, winded, with a sooty streak on one cheek, but at Arkady's agitated manner, he sat up. "Nothing we couldn't handle. Right?"

"Right." I flexed my ankle, getting a sharp twinge, and hissed. "Badly bruised, but not broken."

Arkady nodded tightly, but he placed both hands on Miles' shoulder as if to assure himself of his well-being. Miles leaned into his touch, which apparently triggered their recollection that they were pissed off at each other, because they jerked apart.

Miles laughed, a deep belly guffaw.

"Don't snap on us now, Berenbaum," I said.

"You still worried about a lack of a ward?" he said.

I laughed, then winced because somehow even that hurt my ankle. "Yes, because Knotface only was rigged for down here."

"That sounds interesting." Arkady slid an arm underneath mine to help me up.

"It was something, all right." I leaned on him, shaking

20

my head when he tried to steer us upstairs. "There's one more door down here and after a welcome like that, I want to know what's behind it."

Miles pushed to his feet and carefully opened the door, only to be hit with a chorus of howls and the stench of urine.

"What the—" His hand flew up to cover his nose and mouth.

A quick glance to the walls revealed the room was covered in soundproofing. The sole object in it was a crate intended to house a large dog, but instead of one animal, five puppies of various breeds were crammed inside, crying piteously.

To be clear: I don't like dogs. However, one sliver of my cold, dead heart was apparently susceptible to puppies in distress. I'd been too late to save Tatiana from the murderer and too young to save my thirteen-year-old self's magic from my father's schemes, but dammit, I could do something now.

Arkady helped me kneel down beside the crate. This close to the small ocean of pee, I prayed I'd go nose-blind. The cage was padlocked, but I made short work of it.

The dogs had been locked inside away from their empty bowls, so I opened the crate door as wide as it would go. "Okay, little guys, come on out."

The animals crowded farther back.

"Miles? Could you?" I gestured to the dry dog food in the corner.

He filled them and three of us stood in the doorway, giving the animals a chance to leave the crate. The first one to do so was a tiny, sandy-colored pug. The puppies were so jammed up close that it kind of flopped forward in a half-somersault.

"Mazel tov," I said. "It's a girl."

She cautiously waddled over to a bowl, glancing at us every few seconds to make sure we didn't move. Once she'd ascertained that it was safe to eat and drink, she took her share and then coaxed the others out with a combination of nips and encouraging licks.

I sent Arkady for three warm wet towels. Each of us crept —or hobbled—toward one of the puppies to try and clean it off. No go. As soon as we got close, they yipped and bolted. It was like herding cats.

"What did that bitch do to them?" Arkady said.

I crouched down, cooing softly at the pug. For every step she took toward me, she took two back, but eventually she got close. I held out the towel for her to sniff, and when she didn't run, gently wiped off her ears.

The pug gave a satisfied huff and some of the tension left her body.

"Why lock dogs up in a soundproofed room?" I said.

The pug sniffled, as if wondering that herself, then she got this constipated expression on her face and her skin rippled.

Even as a non-dog person, I knew that wasn't standard behavior.

I scrambled back, wincing, as fleshy, wet tentacles exploded from her head, inset with teeth. So many teeth.

"That's why," Arkady said.

"Make it go away," Miles said.

"I refuse to Cruella de Vil this puppy." I skittered out of the way of a tentacle, flicking out at me like a wet towel.

"Did I say to skin and wear them?" Miles sidestepped a freaked-out poodle with a balletic elegance someone that massive should not have possessed. "The dog's been infused with magic somehow."

"You think?"

The poodle ran around in manic circles before breaking out in red eyes all over its body. This set off a Frankenstein chain reaction with one puppy bursting into flame, a black-and-white mutt sprouting a hammer head, and a black lab

22

with electric magic exploding out of it, bumping on its ass around the room.

Favoring my good ankle, I lunged for one of the pug's tentacles. It snapped back and hit my hand with a wet, meaty splat, the teeth almost breaking skin. I shuddered, lost my grip, and had to try again.

Arkady dove for the hammer-headed mutt before its flailing broke someone's foot. With both of his fists once more stone, he pinned the thrashing animal in place. "That is not behavior agreed on by the Geneva Accords, Colonel Puppy."

Miles had cornered the one that was flaming like a tiki torch. Cupping two large balls of flame in his palms, he stared it down until the dog acknowledged his alpha and rolled over, presenting his fiery belly.

Arkady nudged the pug away from the hammer-headed mutt before it could smash one of her tentacles. "Aw. The pug looks like my great-aunt Hyun-Mi. She had dental issues, too."

"Not funny." I glared at him.

"Gallows humor, pickle. You got this."

With a silent wish that I didn't hurt the poor thing, I hooked into the magic swimming through her tiny, panting body, shuddering at the sensation of pointy enamel embedded in wet flesh.

The magic in the pug didn't feel like third-party smudges, which smelled like feces and felt like maggots. First of all, it was nowhere near as strong, and second of all, there were too many scents and tastes mixed up here. I tasted four: mint, fish, salt, and chalk. But I couldn't discern the type of magic they represented.

I probed deeper, my brow furrowing. When the smudges had jumped into new hosts or someone was attacked with magic, like when a Medusa had turned my right side to stone, that invasive magic floated free inside a person.

"How is this even possible?" I said.

"What?" Arkady caught the hammer head mutt as he slipped loose, readjusting his grip on the puppy.

"The magic is knotted to them."

"Like with a magic artifact?" Miles said. "Tell me you're kidding."

"I'm not. Tatiana got multiple Nefesh to infuse their magic into this pug and then knotted the powers together to bake them in. Like with an inanimate object." I raised stricken eyes to the men. "Except these are living creatures with organs and hearts."

Tiki torch puppy gave a heart-wrenching little wail. Miles stroked its tiny body, murmuring soothing words, before nailing me with a scowl. "Fix this, Cohen."

"You think I don't want to? This is uncharted territory," I said, grabbing hold of the pug on her least toothy side. "What if I pull it out and yank a kidney with it? I could kill them."

Tentacle pug whimpered. If Tatiana wasn't dead, I'd have rained hell on her ass. The magic was so unstable that it was ripping these poor dogs apart.

I used my scary "don't die" voice that I used on Moriarty and hoped the puppy responded better than the car did.

"Wait." Miles pulled out his phone and began recording. "We'll document it for Levi."

"Or in case we have to answer for our actions later," Arkady said.

"Oh good, if I mess up this gets to be puppy snuff theater." Holding the pug in place, I sent my magic along the snare of knots inside her, searching for a weak point. A loose end that wasn't fused to the puppy herself.

I found the end of the tangle, like a tied-off thread, near her left front paw. Closing my eyes, I visualized my magic as a needle piercing the center of that thread. Instead of pulling the invasive magic out to tangle in my branches, I fed a

24

single hair-thin red branch into the first knot and made my white clusters bloom on it, dissolving the knot.

I cracked one eye. The dog panted shallowly, but she wasn't fighting me, so I continued along the spiderweb to the next knot and the next set of white clusters. By the time I'd dissolved all the knots and pronounced her magic-free, I was crashed on my ass, with my throbbing injured leg stretched out, and my shirt clinging sweatily to my back.

"One down, four to go," Miles said, tapping the button on his camera app to end the video and start another. "Let's see it, Cohen."

I bit my lip, my stomach churning. Flawlessly perform high-stakes magic surgery four more times?

The pug weakly licked my hand before growling at the eye-laden poodle who'd snuck closer, while the lab shot past, bumping along the ground in a propulsion of electricity.

I exhaled sharply and shook out my hands. I was all these puppies had. "Can you hold the fireball down?"

"Yes." Miles passed his phone to Arkady.

"Bring it here."

One by one, I wrangled the puppies and removed their magic. The lab almost fried me and the mutt tried to take a chunk out of my arm with its hammer head, but all of us survived.

Arkady placed his hand on the back of my neck, then snatched it back with a grimace, making a big show of wiping it on his jeans. "Wow, sweat monster. You okay?"

"Peachy."

"What kind of magic was on the yarn?" Miles took his phone back and stuffed it in his pocket.

"Good job, Ash," I said. "Thank you so much for your valuable service and for being super careful not to kill any of these poor dogs with magic you yourself barely understand."

"The yarn?"

"You are literally the worst. If I had to guess, it was level five Animator magic." I held out a hand and Arkady helped me up once more, supporting my weight.

The puppies had gotten their second wind, running around the space and tumbling on top of each other.

"Yevgeny was killed at a dogfighting ring, right?" Arkady said.

"Right."

"Having animals with magic opens up gambling opportunities," he said, "since it's no longer down to mass and muscle. But to do this to animals is totally unethical and cruel. They do not and should not have magic."

"Was this something that Tatiana and her brother did on their own or was it part of a bigger Chariot plot?" Miles said.

"I'm going to pay a visit to the men we apprehended from Chariot's lab," Arkady said. "Get some answers out of them."

"By way of…?" I mimed throwing punches.

"Miles doesn't let me beat people up. He's a stickler for doing things by the book." Arkady pouted.

"We don't want any reason for the courts to toss the case. It's bad enough that the only charge we could get them on was kidnapping," Miles said. "Most of the evidence was in the lab that they'd set up in Hedon. The facility here was barely more than a holding cell for those kids. Nor do we want to pour fuel on the fire with allegations of Nefesh brutality." Miles' brown eyes turned flinty. "Though I doubt you'll get far. Some high-powered lawyers got involved and transferred the suspects to a maximum security facility."

"So?" I said.

"The men are Mundane. They're out of our jurisdiction now."

"There are still legal ways to gain access to question them," Arkady said, disengaging the black-and-white mutt's teeth from the hem of his jeans. The puppy took it as a cue

26

that this was their new game and dug into the cloth with renewed vigor.

I raised my voice to be heard over all the barking. "I think I have my answer to the lack of a ward on this house. You saw how the dogs reacted when the magic burst out of them. They were a danger to themselves and anyone around them."

Wards worked differently than artifacts. The magic was overlaid onto an object instead of directly injected into it and then permanently fused together.

"Right. Wards sense hostile intent," Miles said. "Tatiana had to disable the ward whenever she worked on the puppies because they'd attack and subsequently be frozen with their magic neutralized, which would make it impossible for Tatiana to carry out these freakish experiments."

"Chances are she usually did have a ward in place," Arkady said, "she just hadn't reactivated it."

Miles eyed the crate with distaste. "I'm not putting them back in there. The cops can speculate about what went on in this room. Ark, help me gather up the puppies. We have to get them to the animal rescue shelter. We can phone the murder in on the way."

"*Ark*? Whatever could have earned him name-shortening privileges?" I said.

"Absolutely nothing." Arkady tossed the crate into the corner, where it hit the wall with a jarring clang.

"Arkady," Miles warned.

Arkady snapped off a sarcastic salute, and picked up the mutt.

"Jesus." Miles bent down to grab the pug, but she dashed between his large hands and beelined for me.

"Oh no, dog." I backed up, favoring my left leg. "I have a fifteen-year-old mystery involving my father to solve. I don't have time for you."

She thumped her tail imperiously twice.

27

"I'm allergic?"

She growled at me.

"Fine." I crossed my arms. "I'll come to the animal rescue, but that's it. We will not play with slobbery toys."

The tentacles and teeth had vanished, only to be replaced with something much worse: big, chocolatey puppy-dog eyes.

I tsked. This was basic, level-one con techniques: don't let yourself get suckered. "Nice try, dog. Save it for someone who likes your kind."

Chapter 3

Three hours later, the pug had been given a clean bill of health, a bunch of shots, and a ride to my house.

Arkady lugged all the dog supplies I'd hobbled around a pet store to buy up the stairs, along with Gavriella's lockbox. Meanwhile, I guarded with my life the bottle of wine I'd also picked up.

The dog pranced ahead of us, her new leash trailing on the ground.

"Are you freaking serious?" Priya pulled the front door open, her hands on her hips. "You stuck around some dead woman's home?" she fumed. "Were you hoping the murderer came back and upped their body count?"

"Arkady, you rat." I bent down for the leash. "When did you have time to even phone her?"

"Ash got a dog," he said, and dumped all the purchases into Priya's arms. Then he fled for the safety of his apartment.

Priya's eyebrows shot into her hairline at the sight of the pug.

"Arkady slept with Miles," I called out.

"Reeaaallly?" Priya stepped forward, "interrogation" written all over her face.

Arkady got his door unlocked and practically flung himself into his apartment. "Girl questions are strictly verboten," he said, his left eyebrow spasming, and slammed the door.

Ooh. Arkady had a tell. I'd seen him pull off undercover work, cool as a cucumber, but lean on him about his personal life and he got twitchy. No. That wasn't exactly it either. He was very comfortable deflecting with over-the-top sexual innuendo, but he was really upset about whatever had gone wrong between them. Vulnerable. That's where he got twitchy. Interesting.

Priya wrinkled her nose at the shut door, set the pet store purchases in the foyer, then crouched down and held out her hand. "Is this supposed to be a guard dog?"

"She's a temporary visitor. I wouldn't get a pet without speaking to you first."

The pug sniffed the outstretched hand, then warily nuzzled her nose into Priya's palm. "Does she have a name?" Priya said.

"Mrs. Hudson." I waved my hands, hoping to avoid further questions. "Look, it was the only thing I could think of on the spot and the vet needed something quick."

Priya's donkey-like braying laugh filled the foyer. "You Sherlock-named her?" She scratched the puppy's head, making kissing noises. "Who's a pretty girl who's living here forever? You are."

"Okay, no." I smacked her hand away. "This weird baby shit is exactly why I am not a puppy person and will not be keeping her. I just wasn't about to call her 'dog' all the time like a preschooler. The rescue shelter was full, and I was too tired to drive to the one on the other side of town, but as soon as I can find her a good home, she goes away."

My work wasn't conducive to having a dog. Mrs. Hudson deserved stability and a loving family.

"Uh-huh." Pri's green eyes narrowed doubtfully at me. "Come eat. There's Chinese take-out if you want some."

I was running low and scraped raw and I needed solitude to recharge, but Priya had never counted as company. She was just my Pri, and I could de-stress around her as easily as by myself in my bedroom. But something niggled at me. I squinted, calling up my mental calendar. "Hold on, isn't it Arianna's birthday dinner tonight?"

"Wasn't feeling it." She grabbed the leash from me. "More fun to hang out with you and Mrs. Hudson."

"Obviously." Because staying in with your injured friend and a dog you'd never met trumped dinner at the Thai restaurant you'd looked forward to eating at for the past month. Worse, tonight she wore a cream cashmere sweater with jeans.

After Priya's engagement had spectacularly blown up a few years ago, she had embraced pink the way a chocoholic embraced anything to satisfy their sweet tooth, even if it was stale chocolate chips in the back of a cupboard, poured directly into their mouth until the momentary bliss turned to shame and the detritus of an empty bag.

Anyhow, she'd worn a lot of pink. Sure, it was some kind of ruthless happy shield, but it also fit her warm and outgoing personality. Since her abduction last week, her clothing had become as muted as her life.

"Tamarind prawns and planning that spa getaway with your book club," I said. "You know you'd have fun."

"Some other time," she said. Her smiles used to light up her entire face with joy; now the ones I received were tinged with warning. "You need help walking?"

"I can hobble. But if you'd help with my boots and an ice pack, I'd be forever grateful."

Priya led the pug into the living room, which was where we ate most of our meals.

Our two-bedroom apartment wasn't a dump, since it had original fir floors and moldings around the windows and doors, but it only got light on one side, and there was a dark water mark from our leaky roof in the corner of the living room that we'd christened Fred, the Demon God of Moisture.

That said, it was a vaguely affordable rental unit in Vancouver which made it more precious than any water view or snazzy penthouse.

The sleek modern furniture in our living room was well beyond our pay grade, as we'd inherited it in my mother's last remodel, but we'd stamped our personality on it. Between all our books spilling off the large bookcase, the photographic prints of foreign locales we intended to travel to, and the pops of color from pillows made from sari fabric that Priya had picked up on one of her visits to her grandparents in India, it was cozy.

It was also completely tidy.

Priya didn't tidy. Laundry and dishes, no problem, but light cleaning? My darling friend was a little tornado of chaos, scattering her belongings around her like seeds in need of planting. I wracked my brain as to how this could have happened. There were no guests to impress and I didn't smell cumin or garam masala, so her mother hadn't stopped by. That left a frenetic cleaning outburst because she was worried about something.

I squeezed her hand. "I love you, too."

She stuck her nose in the air, flinging back her jet black bobbed hair. "Don't make me hear these things from other people next time."

I flopped onto the couch. "I literally just got home and would have told you if Arkady hadn't been in such a rush to spread the news."

"Yeah, he's worse than all my aunties." She carefully tugged off my boots and I sighed in relief. While the ankle was slightly swollen, thankfully, it wasn't sprained.

Pri had gone vegetarian for tonight's order, which was fine by me, since our favorite Chinese place had a deep-fried salty spicy tofu that was to die for. Though you had to eat it when ordered, because it got soggy if reheated. In the interests of combatting food waste, I made sure there was never any left. She'd also gotten Szechuan green beans, veggie chow mein, and a couple orders of fried green onion pancakes.

After she'd set out kibble and water for the dog, she elevated my ankle, draped an ice pack over it, and heaped my plate high.

"You make an excellent nursemaid," I said.

"Don't get used to it," she said, filling my glass very full of Merlot. "So, what happened?"

I filled my bestie in, starting with being summoned to the police station, the fact that Yevgeny had likely kidnapped Gavriella, and the magic inflicted on the dogs.

When Priya heard that, she cuddled Mrs. Hudson close. The puppy lapped up the affection. Great. I was going to have to pry the dog out of Priya's cold dead hands when it was time for her to go. Oh well, that would be an easy and almost eagerly anticipated problem, given what was on my plate right now.

Licking my fingers clean of grease from the savory onion pancakes, I pulled *A Study in Scarlet* out of the lockbox. "Then I found this."

"That's cool that Gavriella was into Sherlock," Priya said, snagging the last of the chow mein with her chopsticks, "but beyond the nice edition of the book, I'm not really sure why we care."

"Coded message. Look inside."

"Ah." She opened it. "Any idea what it means?"

"Not even a little bit. That's not the fun part. Flip to the last page."

She did and frowned. "A sunflower?"

I took a rather large gulp of wine. Then another one. "I drew that in my dad's book when I was six. This is Adam's copy."

"Holy shit," she breathed.

I held my glass up in cheers. "Here's to my father, still fucking up my life fifteen years after he abandoned me. L'chaim!" I drained the rest of the wine.

"What if Chariot wanted you to think Adam had given the book to Gavriella and it's their way of drawing you in? They know death triggers the next Jezebel."

"Yeah, but to all outward appearances, the first time Gavriella flatlined, there was no new Jezebel, and they may believe she ended the line. If they did manage to discover my identity in record time and bait that particular hook?" I ate a piece of tofu. "It's even more imperative that I confront Adam."

Priya topped my glass up. "Where do you even begin on a trail that cold?"

"Rafael."

"Your stuffy British Jezebel Attendant. He sounds like a delight." Priya wasn't overly fond of the man who'd snatched me away to a grove in an alternate reality and thrown magic tests at me to prove my Jezebel worthiness. To think most best friends only had to disapprove of exes.

The fact that I'd nicknamed him Evil Wanker probably did little to endear him to her either. Still, Rafael had an impressive ability to acquire information and despite his prickly exterior, he was really useful. It was going to be interesting when she met him for the first time.

"Attendants are the keepers of all Jezebel knowledge," I said. "They've documented us down to the tiniest details.

Hopefully, he knows whether Gavriella and Dad actually made contact or if this is a trap."

If it was the former, how did Dad find her? *Why* did he find her? And how was it connected to him warding up my magic? Even if he'd done all of it with the best of intentions to protect me, he'd denied me my magic heritage, making all these choices about my life without my consent. He'd also taken a Jezebel out of the fight. I would have had years of training and been better equipped to take on Chariot at full speed instead of playing catch-up. Had giving Chariot the edge been part of his intentions? Had he outed me now for the same reason?

I ran a finger around the rim of my glass, eyes downcast. What a mess.

The buzzer to the building's front door sounded.

"You expecting anyone?" Priya said.

I shook my head at her. "I have to pee anyway. I'll get it." My ankle had numbed out some, bringing down the ache to a tolerable level, but I still half-shuffled into the foyer. I pushed the intercom button. "Yes?"

"It's Levi."

How had he even—I dropped my head against the wall. Miles. Of course. My body just wanted to sleep and I couldn't handle an angry Levi reaming me out tonight. I pushed the button again. "It's been a really long day, and—"

"Miles told me about the book. I wanted to check if you were all right."

I briefly closed my eyes. Not that sex was on offer, but the two of us ended up there more often than not, and I wasn't up to it tonight. I was up to a non-sexual form of comfort from Levi even less. The more our relationship developed, the more complicated it became.

But he had come all this way. And as weird and new as it felt, we were friends now. You didn't just send a friend away like that. "Come on up."

"You want me to leave?" Priya called from the kitchen, once I got out of the bathroom. She was washing dinner plates.

I limped to the freezer and got a fresh ice pack. "No. I want you to crack into Gavriella's phone. It's in the lockbox."

"Ooh." She rinsed off a plate and placed it in the drying rack.

I grabbed another wineglass as Levi knocked on the door. "It's open," I called out, making my way into the living room and resettling myself on the sofa with the ice pack.

"Hey." Levi smiled as he entered the room. The Head of House Pacifica may have been smart and kind—not to mention ruthless when it came to protecting his magic community—but he was also irritatingly attractive, with olive skin over the long lines of a soccer player's physique and a sharp jawline softened by lush lips that one gossip columnist had deemed "the eighth wonder of the world."

Reluctantly, I conceded they weren't wrong. Memories of those lips still made me squirm.

He lay his hand on my cheek. "How are you holding up?"

Leaning into his palm for a precious second, I tamped down on the burst of warmth that rolled through me at the sound of that low, smoky voice. "You know me. Queen of Dealing with Shit. Which falls short of my goal of Queen of the Universe, but at least I have some form of royal status."

Levi didn't match my patently false grin. "Do you want to talk about it?"

"Not really. I've hit my quota on brain space for my father's possible motives tonight and have progressed to the much more pleasurable, wine drinking portion of the evening. You're welcome to join me."

"Sounds good." Levi dropped into the armchair next to me, his legs extended carelessly, and a lock of inky black hair falling into his face.

It was outside office hours so he was no longer in locked-down mode. His hair was cut slightly longer on the top than the sides, and usually slicked back from his face in a classic side part that emphasized the slash of his cheekbones. Now, it loosely framed his face. I curled my hands into my palms so I didn't wrap a lock around my finger and pull him close.

Levi sighed happily and settled himself against the cushions. He sported a bulky green sweater and dark jeans instead of his customary exquisitely tailored suit. I appreciated a man in a good suit but this unbuttoned version of Levi, the one who wasn't hiding himself, made my pulse kick up.

"How was your day?" I blurted out. "Um, drink wine." I hurriedly poured him a glass and thrust it into his hand so fast that it almost splashed over the rim.

"Filled with tedious zoning meetings." He gave me a quiet smile. A simple acknowledgment of two people enjoying each other's company. "Thanks for asking," he added.

Oh my God, was Levi blushing? He covered it by taking a sip of wine.

Priya entered. "Hiya, boss."

"Hiya yourself."

Priya pulled the Android out of the lockbox on the coffee table, getting comfortable in one of the other chairs. "Did you hear they found Gavriella's phone?" She pressed a sequence of buttons on the Android. "I'm bypassing the password."

"Yeah, Miles updated me on that and a few other things," Levi said. "Look at that. You did get a dog." He held out his hand for Mrs. Hudson to sniff, but she eyed him warily from the other side of the room.

I smirked. Meet the only female other than myself who's resistant to your charms. Then I remembered how fast he'd stripped me naked a few nights ago and amended that sentence.

"The dog is just visiting," I said.

Levi made a kissing noise at her and Mrs. Hudson waddled slowly but surely closer. Seriously?

He let the pug *boop* his finger, his glass of wine balanced on the arm rest.

Pulling the lockbox close, I scooped out the top layer of photos. After Gavriella had taken on her new identity, she'd had to shove all traces of her old life as Gracie Green into a lockbox hidden under a floor. "She never got to share her true past with friends or a lover. If she'd even had those. What an incredibly lonely life. You think all Jezebels keep themselves apart?"

"No," Priya said firmly. "I'm looking at one with a lot of people in her life and that isn't going to change."

But relationships changed all the time. Look at ours. Yes, Priya's kidnapping had just happened, but what if my naturally extroverted friend locked herself into this place of fear? It was my fault it had happened. What if we couldn't find our way through this? What if we continued on in this place of being held at arm's length until one of us broke, blew up at the other, and moved out?

I smiled absently as if in agreement, studying a picture of a young Gavriella laughing on a swing, being pushed by an older woman who must have been the grandmother who'd raised her. "Do you think her grandmother knew?"

Levi leaned over to study the photo. "You could ask your Attendant."

"Yeah," I said, not sure I wanted the answer. I was already hiding this side of me from my mother. Would I have to do the same if I fell in love? I'd always prided myself on living truthfully. How could I have a long-term relationship if I had to lie to my partner every day? What if I decided to have kids in the very, very far future? Being pregnant as a Jezebel felt reckless.

I wistfully sorted through photos of Gavriella's awkward teen years.

"Maybe tonight isn't the best night to go through those," Priya said.

"What's the dog's name?" Levi said. Mrs. Hudson had allowed him to scratch her ears.

"Mrs. Hudson," Priya said in a tone of unholy glee.

Levi threw back his head and laughed, his blue eyes dancing. The husky sound shivered down my spine. He was the devil. "Hope you like your new roommate, Pri. I believed Miles when he said that Ash didn't intend to keep the puppy, but Mrs. Hudson? You're not going anywhere, are you, girl?"

I picked her up and put her in my lap.

"Ash can't keep a cactus alive. Mrs. Hudson is going to be mine." Priya burst into evil cackles.

Then she and Levi fist-bumped. Fabulous. This day could not get worse. Or so I thought.

Chapter 4

I stacked the dirty dishes with a loud clatter. "If you are both finished disparaging my very capable nurturing skills—"

"Nurturing? Nice spin doctoring," Levi said.

I gasped. "It's empirical truth and we must all get onboard."

"Ta da." Priya held up the unlocked screen. "I'll poke around, see what I find."

"Good job, Adler." I applauded her. "You, on the other hand," I said to Levi, "can go find another minion to annoy."

"Before I go," Levi said. "You need to hear this." Setting down his drink, he stretched out his neck, rolled his shoulders, and cracked his knuckles.

"Any time now," I said.

"It's important to do this right." He exhaled quickly a couple of times like a boxer psyching himself up for his bout, then chanted loudly and far too enthusiastically. "We've got ruach, yes we do. We've got ruach, how about you?" Levi pointed at me.

My mouth was open. What strange reality had I tumbled into where the Head of House Pacific was repeating our teenage camp cheer in my living room? "Did you sustain a head injury recently?"

"Finish the chant," he said.

"We've got ruach, spirit through and through," I said in a monotone. "We're Camp Ruach, there for me, I'm there for you." I threw the lamest jazz hands ever. "Put that online, Pri, and I'll kill you."

"Too late," she said cheerfully, waggling her own phone. "Levi's part already scored me 100 likes. Besides, I didn't film you to protect your anonymity."

I sighed. "What a waste of my spectacular Broadway moves."

Priya tossed her phone onto the coffee table, resuming her search through Gavriella's Android.

"Okay, now that we've gone through that call and response exercise, do you want to tell me why we're doing our old camp cheer?" I said.

Levi leaned forward and the scent of his oaky amber scotch and chocolate magic that I was unfairly attuned to overpowered the lingering smell of Chinese food.

"It's not just a cheer. It's a sacred bond.' There for me, I'm there for you.' This new complication with your father is awful, but you're not alone. Just like Sherlock wasn't."

I made a raspberry at his earnest BS. Wow, these painkillers with the third glass of wine really made me floaty. "Levi, I appreciate it. I really do. But I also know where I stand. And if you were a true Sherlock fan you'd know that the only person going over the Reichenbach Falls to rid the world of evil will be me."

"God you're stubborn." Levi took a fortifying drink. "I didn't want to do this, but you're making me pull out the big guns."

Priya's eyes widened. "You brought Talia?"

Levi shuddered. "God no. Ash's mother wants to legislate

me out of existence. I try not to get within ten feet of that woman. No offense."

I shrugged. "None taken. What's the big guns?"

Levi pulled off his sweater and my eyes practically bugged out. Under it, he wore our old blue camp T-shirt with the words "Camp Ruach" emblazoned in silver. This shirt had fit a much shorter, skinnier Levi. Now it was stretched tight across his torso and the discrepancy between the exquisiteness of his ripped body and the innocent camp shirt brought on a dull pounding in my temples.

"You're ruining my childhood," I groused.

Priya leaned forward to ogle a strip of olive skin between his hem and his jeans. "Feel free to ruin mine."

I tossed a pillow at her, but my drugged-up aim was way off. It landed with a dull splat far short of its intended target.

"There are situations that as a Jezebel, only you can deal with," Levi said, "but the fallout from Adam's schemes doesn't have to be one of them, okay?"

He'd come by my house wearing a ridiculously too-small shirt in order to boost my spirits because he'd heard about my dad being involved. Because he knew I'd be mad and sad or just having a lot of feelings to sort out.

Because he wanted to make me laugh.

Other than Priya, how many people would go to those lengths for me?

I nodded slowly in response to him, trying to keep gravity mostly non-floaty, and said the words in my heart. "I can't believe you kept that shirt all these years."

"It was part of some stuff that Mom had me come pick up the other week." Levi shifted his weight like he couldn't get comfortable, then forced himself to relax back against the chair cushions. That was totally unlike his usual self, but maybe that shirt was really too tight to move comfortably in after all.

Mrs. Hudson jumped off my lap and ran to him like she wanted to comfort him.

He absently patted her head. "So. Good job with the Weaver. I didn't thank you yet, but I'm glad we learned who was behind the security breach. Each piece of intel is that much more illuminating. Who knows, maybe the magic on the dogs will even tie back to Chariot and not just have been a venture the Petrovs were engaged in."

I'd known Levi for fifteen years. Most of them as nemeses, about a month as hook-ups, and maybe a week as friends. None of those versions of him involved the verbal diarrhea he now spewed.

Having examined all the photos, I flipped them over one by one to see if any had writing on the back. "Mrs. Hudson, do not cavort with him. He's clearly stalling because he has something unpleasant he intends to dump on me."

He tugged on his shirt. "Speaking of camp, I, uh—"

"Levi." I motioned for him to get to the point.

"Mayan came to see me a couple weeks ago," he said.

I cut him off with an exaggerated groan.

Priya made a face at the screen. "Gavriella spent way too much time playing Solitaire." That was depressing. "Who's Mayan?"

"My ex," Levi said.

"An embodiment of evil." I made a stabbing motion. "Quite the talent really, since she doesn't even have magic."

"She's not that bad," Levi said.

"No, she's worse." Even though he hadn't dated her until they were both in their twenties, Mayan had gone to the same Jewish summer camp as Levi, Miles, and myself, all through our teen years. She'd elevated belittling me into an art form. Every summer had brought a new crop of rumors about my freak status—usually involving some form of Satan worshipping, because that never got old—cruel pranks, and on one memorable occasion, an accusation of theft, that only dumb luck and a witness willing to confirm my whereabouts had gotten me acquitted of.

"Admittedly, she wasn't the nicest back then, but her mother's death a few years ago changed her," Levi said. "She needs help."

"That's why you came over, wasn't it?" I said churlishly. "The camp stuff was bullshit to butter me up for this."

"I was worried about you. It isn't an either/or situation."

"Save your breath. If Mayan came to you with some damsel in distress routine, find someone else to handle it. I can't play nice with her."

"Let me remind you that you now work for me," Levi said, coolly. "Exclusively. You can't turn this case down."

"Oh boy," Priya muttered.

I shot him the finger. "Challenge accepted."

Priya grabbed the leash. "Want to go for a walksie?"

Mrs. Hudson toddled over to her, her paws clicking against the wood floor. Priya clipped the leash to her collar and the two of them left, the front door closing with a snick behind them a moment later.

Levi dropped all facades of humor in favor of a strained expression that Mayan, did not, in my opinion, deserve. He sank into a chair. "You're the only one with the investigative skills who also knows Mayan enough to determine if her behavior recently is…" He paused. "Uncharacteristic."

I'd trusted Levi with my entire career, and after everything we'd gone through, everything that I believed we'd come to mean to each other, my skills not only weren't valued, they were reluctantly engaged.

"Delighted you feel you have literally no other option," I said. "Besides, this can't be all that urgent if Mayan came to see you two weeks ago and you're just dealing with it now." A thought hit me like a linebacker rushing the winning team's quarterback at the five-yard line with six seconds left in the Super Bowl. "When specifically?"

Levi's brilliant blue eyes met mine. "The night of Omar's attack."

I laughed bitterly, dumping the rest of the bottle into my glass. "Your alibi."

"I didn't sleep with Mayan," he said. "We ended up talking late into the night and she'd had wine so she slept in the guest room."

Levi and I weren't exclusive. I could have slept with a dozen people since we'd first hooked up and Levi was certainly free to do as he chose. We had an understanding: we were friends who enjoyed each other's bodies. That was all I had time for, not small talk and visions of how comfortably he fit into my living room.

"Why do you feel the need to enlighten me about who is and is not in your bed?" I said.

"It's relevant to this case," he said.

I took a large slug of wine, choking it down past my tight throat.

"I'm not asking because Mayan and I are involved," Levi said. "She called me, very upset and insisting that we meet because she required help. But when she came over, the entire visit played out like two people catching up. No urgency, just reminiscing and her telling me about her life these days. The visit was pointless. I asked her what she'd been so upset about, but she acted like she didn't have the faintest idea what I was referring to."

"You think someone got to her?" Intrigued despite myself, I sat up so fast that my ice pack slid to the ground. "If she's really in danger, like in an abusive relationship, you should go to the Mundane police."

"I did," he said in a tight voice. "Even though she said she was currently single, I reached out discreetly to someone I trust on that force to look into it. The officer came back with nothing. According to friends, Mayan hadn't mentioned seeing anyone in some time now. She hasn't distanced

45

herself; there haven't been any odd bruises. Nor have there been strange withdrawals from her bank account. The officer conclusively ruled out domestic abuse or blackmail." He rubbed a hand over the dark scruff on his jaw. "I thought Mayan reached out to me because I was her ex, but what if she needed me as House Head to protect her from something?"

It was a fair assumption. A lot of people came to Levi. He'd recently told me about a Nefesh woman whom he'd helped get a refugee visa for, in order to get her mother out of a country known for its persecution of people with magic. Levi was the Godfather of his community, minus leaving horse heads in beds. As far as I knew.

"What could you, as House Head, protect her from?" I said. "She's a socialite Mundane. I'd be surprised if she knows anyone shadier than some dude with a line to designer purses that fell off the back of a truck."

"This morning I'd have bet that Tatiana wasn't mixed up with Chariot either."

I set my glass down. This conversation was killing my buzz. "Mayan isn't Tatiana and unless Chariot is in serious need of fundraising, she has nothing to offer them. She's never struck me as caring about magic one way or the other, so what would she get out of teaming up with them? She's not part of that organization."

"I don't think she is," he said with exaggerated patience. "But she was scared and she came to me over something. Now she may be missing."

"Why didn't you lead with that?"

"Because I don't know for sure," he snapped. He exhaled slowly. "Sorry. I haven't been able to get hold of her for a couple days and she hasn't been in to work. She did leave her boss a voicemail saying she was taking some time off, but it was very last-minute and she didn't give a reason. That's not like her, but on the other hand, she didn't simply disappear without any notice so is there actually cause for alarm? Who knows? But that initial call of hers is bothering me."

"Did you think I'd refuse? I don't like her, but I don't wish her active harm." From anyone who wasn't me.

"Fuck, Ash, would I rather that the woman I'm currently sleeping with not investigate my ex? Funny, that." He pulled his sweater on, but I got the impression it was more so he didn't have to meet my eyes as he spoke than because he was cold. "I felt weird about how concerned I am when it might be nothing."

If Levi's feelings for Mayan had resurfaced then we wouldn't be anything for much longer. I folded the cuffs of my sleeves over my hand. I missed being the Ash who thought Levi had only come over to cheer me on, not the one ensnared into unfinished business with his ex.

"I'm a professional," I said. "I'm not going to swoon hysterically because you have a past. That's not what we are."

"Then you have more of a handle of what we are than I do," he said. "Tell me things aren't insanely blurred between us."

"We're friends."

"Mmm. Do most of your friends know how you sound when you moan their name because they're inside you? Have you shared your scars with them? Or—"

"Fine," I said through a clenched jaw. "Things are somewhat blurred."

"I'm not here because you're my only option. I'm here because you're the only one I trust," he said softly.

All I'd ever wanted was to fulfill my dreams of being a private investigator with a lifetime of fascinating cases, but even getting a toehold in this industry had been a struggle. I'd been the only female P.I. in Vancouver, and the boys' club of the other agencies wasn't exactly welcoming. But even though I'd started my firm as a Mundane, and thus not as employable as the Nefesh P.I.s, I'd scraped my way up to an office with a small clientele and good word of mouth.

About a month ago, my world was blown open when it turned out I had magic. Not just any magic either: undocumented blood magic, bestowed on descendants of the actual Jezebel from the Old Testament by the goddess Asherah to stop Chariot. Its original members had been the men representing each of the Ten Lost Tribes of Israel who'd first released magic into the world.

Jezebels and our blood magic were the only ones who could undermine their plans for immortality and to become gods on Earth. The same way that Jezebel in the Old Testament undermined the Jewish patriarchy with her continued insistence on the worship of the goddess Asherah—Yahweh's bride and the person I'd been named after.

Shocking as this magic acquisition was, there was a definite upside. I'd gone from dealing with unfaithful spouses and minor insurance fraud to rogue smudges, kidnappings, and murders. This Mayan case might be equally as challenging.

I had two choices. Refuse Levi and deal with the fallout, or get over feeling like he was picking Mayan over me, just like he'd done every time he'd laughed along with her taunts back at camp. I hadn't cared then, because Levi was still a dick in my estimation at the time, but he was right. Things between us were blurred now.

Levi sat there stiffly, his eyes imploring as he waited for my answer. Note to self: no more looking directly at puppies or Levi. Both resulted in complications.

Even though I meant what I said about not refusing if Mayan was in trouble, I really didn't want to be the bigger person. I was a Jezebel, not a saint, and to put aside my revenge fantasies and help Mayan—at Levi's behest? I swear, demon horns sprouted from my forehead.

I pressed my fingertips to my temples. No horns, just the

remnant of a headache. "Like you said, I work exclusively for you, *boss*. I'll find Mayan and determine why she contacted you."

"Ash—"

The fight drained out of me, leaving me sagged against the cushions. "If you really care, Levi, then go home. I've hit my limit for tonight."

He nodded. There was a second where he hesitated on his way out, like he was going to kiss the top of my head, but he didn't, and the front door closed softly behind him.

Chapter 5

I wasn't up to diving in to Mayan's case tonight, but I was too restless to go to sleep. My thoughts kept circling back to my dad. Every attempt I'd made to locate him in the past had failed. Did *A Study in Scarlet* finally give me a lead?

"He took off a couple months before my magic showed up, and we know he paid me a visit in the hospital. So Adam was still in town at that point." My hands tightened on the book. I pressed it to my chest and not to my nose like I foolishly wanted to, checking if any trace of Old Spice and lemon candies still clung to the pages.

"If this isn't some ploy by Chariot, then it makes a difference if Adam gave Gavriella the book before or after he had the Van Gogh ward up your magic," Priya said. She'd returned from her walk shortly after Levi had left. "If it happened afterward, the manifestation of your magic might be what prompted him to make contact. He might have been protecting you."

"Maybe. I can't indulge in wishful thinking." Cold hard facts with their irrefutable logic and sharp clean edges would be my guides.

I checked on Mrs. Hudson, exhausted from her

marathon around the block and now snoring softly on a blanket.

"Rafael is my best bet." He was due to return to Vancouver in a couple of days and meet with our newly assembled team, but this couldn't wait. I pulled a chain out from under my shirt with a wooden ring threaded on it, which had belonged to Rafael's father, Gavriella's Attendant. "I'm going to the library. Can you watch Mrs. Hudson? It shouldn't take too long."

"Possession is nine-tenths of the law."

"If you make me keep repeating myself on the dog's temporary status, I'll tell your mom that you're single again."

Priya shuddered. "And subject me to her matchmaking? Some friend you are. Just remember, it takes a village to raise a puppy."

"One-track mind, much? We can have our custody battle over a dog I'm not keeping when I return."

"Uh-huh." Priya held up the Android. "What do you want me to do with this? It's a dead end."

"Not surprising, given how under-the-radar Gavriella lived. I'll put it in the office safe with the photos tomorrow." I grabbed *A Study in Scarlet*. "Wish me luck."

Putting the ring on my finger, I vanished, reappearing seconds later in a large, round windowless room. This was only the second time I'd been here—wherever in the world this was—but nothing had changed. The center section was taken up by five square smooth pillars, each about waist-height. Three of them glowed softly, one was actively dark, and the final column had no particular lighting effect.

One section of the curved walls was covered with custom-built shelving. The top shelves held a jumble of scrolls, the center section was lined with chunky leather volumes, and the lower ones contained more modern Moleskines and journals. The furnishings were a mishmash of periods: an antique desk with a hole for an ink pot, a modern rectangular cherrywood table with two chairs pushed up against it, and two vintage high-back chairs with tufted sage green upholstery.

Rafael appeared less than a minute after I did, alerted to my presence somehow. Pale and always wearing an article of argyle, tweed, and/or a bowtie, Rafael gave off a very mild-mannered librarian impression on first glance. Deliberately so. There was nothing soft or beta about him.

"Greetings and salutations," I said. "Love the bowtie. Who knew they came in plaid?"

"I had so hoped to be free of you before our scheduled joyous reunion." His posh British accent grated.

I slammed the book down on the table. "Why didn't you mention this?"

Rafael blinked owlishly behind his round glasses. "Sir Conan Doyle? I assumed he was known throughout the Commonwealth. There was a popular television adaptation of his works for those of you who you are illiterate."

Stuff like this was exactly why I'd nicknamed him Evil Wanker.

I flipped the book open to the interior title page and tapped the printing. "This."

Rafael elbowed me out of the way, frowning as he read it. "Did you take this from Gavriella's apartment?"

"No. Some of her possessions were found at the home of a Weaver who was shot dead. As was her brother at a different location. He worked for Chariot and was likely the one who kidnapped Gavriella. I found this book in a stolen lockbox at the Weaver's house, along with photos of a younger Gavriella, and her phone. No laptop though."

"Her last one died about six months ago and she never got around to buying a new one. I think she recycled the old one," he murmured, examining the book.

"What does the message mean?" I said, impatiently.

"You have no inkling what this means, and yet you're so agitated about it." He handed the book back to me. "Why?"

"This copy was my dad's."

Rafael did a double take. "You're positive?"

I gave a bitter laugh and showed him the sunflower drawing. "Seeing as I drew this? Yeah."

"Do you recall me mentioning a longer conversation about the Jezebel history in your future? I believe it's time for us to have it." He grasped my elbow and tugged me into the space in the middle of the five pillars.

"Ouch. Watch it," I said, limping.

"Sorry. Do I want to know how you injured yourself?"

"Probably not."

The way he positioned me so precisely felt like I was being prepared for a sacrifice, perhaps by death rays that would shoot out of the columns.

Rafael pushed his glasses up his nose and walked clockwise around the pillars, touching his palm to the top of the three that were illuminated. The pillars lowered into the ground in a twisting motion, leaving three brittle scrolls on yellowed papyrus hovering where the columns had been. Each one was small but thick and bathed in golden light.

I sucked in a breath at the scent of a hot sandstorm from an ancient magic that flooded my senses. My mouth watered and I reached for the closest one, stopping short and pressing my fist into my stomach. Raw flayed pain twisted through my muscles at the strain of denying myself a taste.

"It's the same magic as the angel feather." I knocked Rafael to the ground.

"What in good heavens are you doing?"

We tussled, but I was stronger and I pinned him down. The magic that rolled off these items was weaker than that on the feather had been, but my body still throbbed in yearning, the pain in my ankle relegated to a very distant second.

"Saving you, asshole," I said. "So you don't become compelled." The angel feather's magic was so powerful that one person had died because of it and others had been brought close to ruin.

Comprehension dawned on Rafael's face. "Ah. You refer to the feather. No, Ashira, while these scrolls are angel-made, they are not of an angel themselves. I'm unable to sense their magic. Their pieces hold no allure, though their contents are the reason you Jezebels exist."

He was wrong. I was affected. The siren song urging me to dive into that magic was a rushing in my ears that almost drowned out his words.

I got up, drawn to the scrolls like a moth to the flame.

But my will won out and I hobbled away from the pillars, straddling a chair backwards. I gripped the top like a shield. A crack appeared in the wood and I loosened my hold a fraction. "What are they?"

"Three-fifths of the *Sefer Raziel HaMalakh*. A mystic text written by the archangel Raziel with all kinds of secret wisdom." He paused. "Including how to bring angel magic into our world."

Hysterical laughter got stuck in my throat. My organs were being knotted in spasmic longing over a how-to guide? "That's how the original ten men of Chariot did it? They followed some instruction manual?"

"Essentially. Merkavah, the Hebrew name for Chariot as you know them, determined the *Sefer* was their ticket to holiness."

I blotted the sweat beading on the back of my neck with my sleeve. "We've been taught that they were trying to achieve Yechida, the fifth and highest level of the soul in Kabbalah. The one that allowed them to commune with the divine, but that wasn't it. They wanted angel magic to achieve immortality. Become gods on Earth, right? How'd they fuck it up?"

Rafael shot me a concerned look because I was holding myself upright solely by the death grip I had on the chair. "Are you ill?"

I waved at him to continue while I still had the presence of mind to focus. The taste of the hot gritty sandstorm clogged my throat and dusted my lips. I sucked my bottom lip into my mouth but it brought no relief.

"We don't know how the *Sefer* came to earth," he said, "but once it did, it cracked into five scrolls, and luckily, Chariot only got hold of one. It was enough to allow them to release magic into our world, though they didn't count on others ending up with it." He wiped some dust off of one of the pieces. "Unless they have all five, the formula for immortality is denied to them."

Lucky Rafael that he could stand there unaffected when every molecule in my body cried out.

I swallowed to get some moisture into my mouth. "So, Asherah showed up and created the first Jezebel to engage in some back-and-forth game of who's got the pieces?"

"She created your kind to destroy the book."

"But the joke was on her, wasn't it?" I said. "The magic of each individual piece defeated the Jezebels' abilities and so we hide them away in hopes Chariot doesn't find them."

Lots of perfectly nice people followed Kabbalah with no evil intentions, but of course, as with any ideology, there were those wanting to twist it to their own ends.

"You were created specifically to destroy them." He removed his glasses, blew on the lenses, and then wiped them clean with the hem of his vest. "Why ever would you be unable to complete that task?"

"I couldn't destroy the feather." My vision was getting blurry. I stood up abruptly, breathing heavily.

"Obviously," he scoffed. "That was part of an angel."

"But Nefesh magic is diluted angel magic, and I can destroy Nefesh magic."

"Exactly. Very heavily diluted. Even the tiniest part of an actual angel is beyond your capabilities. Should an angel ever deign to show itself on Earth?" Rafael shuddered. "Regardless, the scrolls we have here are merely pieces and we need the *Sefer* in its entirety before a Jezebel can destroy it."

I dragged my feet towards the scrolls, as if pulled by an invisible string. "Close the pillars," I grated out, harshly. "I passed your damned tests. I proved myself a Jezebel. To exploit my weakness like this is just cruel."

"What weakness?"

I stilled, my fingertips a scant half inch from one of the scrolls, the soft glow turning my skin gold. "The cravings, damn you."

"What on earth are you talking about?"

"The cravings!" My anguished cry bounced off the walls. "The constant longing to take magic that Jezebels have. How do you not know this?" My hand closed around the papyrus, its rough edges scraping against my skin. One taste.

I brought forth a silky red ribbon of magic and sent it into the scroll. A zen-like high infused my soul as I fell through that cosmic dust, bathing in it. It sang to me in a chorus of celestial voices, cradling me tenderly as I drank.

The library fell away and I was back in the grove where Rafael had tested my magic, pink almond blossoms falling gently on my skin. I reached out to touch one, laughing in wonder.

But it didn't last. The magic on the scroll hollowed me out and soon I was in the familiar, black, all-consuming void outside the grove. I wanted to leave, struggled to hold onto any sense of myself but the magic ate me up from the inside. Darkness pressed in, threatening to devour me.

There was no way out. I was overwhelmed and beaten and the only thing I could do was surrender.

Into that nothingness came a trickle tasting of the

freshest river stream. The trickle became a flood, rich and clear and life-affirming.

I came to on the library floor, straddling Rafael, his magic a smudgy pull from a bleeding gash on his forearm. I'd wound it like taffy around the finger that I sucked into my mouth. Bile rose in my throat and I tried to shut the connection down but Rafael clamped on to my wrist, thrusting his arm closer.

His magic ran down the back of my throat, washing away the taste of sandstorm and easing my cravings. There were no red forked branches, no clusters, simply a slowing of his magic back down and then a quiet pop of release as I instinctively unhooked from the scroll's magic, unharmed and sated.

I should have been consumed with horror but my body hummed, the siren song quiet, and the sandstorm already a hazy memory. My ankle didn't even hurt any longer.

Under me, Rafael's pupils were dilated, his cheeks flushed, and a very prominent erection pressed against my thigh.

"Um." I scrambled off him.

"Quite," he said, sitting up and hugging his knees to his chest.

A long silence ticked out between us. I thought I knew the meaning of the word "awkward." Nope. All those other times had merely been practice for this World Series of embarrassment.

"Had I known we were going in this direction, I'd have bought you dinner." I bit my lip. Rafael didn't respond and just continued to look pained. I racked my brain for something to say to diffuse the situation, something, anything. "Is it gone?"

Rafael glanced down at his lap and blushed further. He cleared his throat. "This wasn't about you."

I frowned. Really? Because right now I was finding that a

little hard to believe, what with his flagpole dick straining against his trousers. "Well... good?"

"I mean, you're an attractive enough person, but that connection..." His fingers flexed, his eyes gleaming fervently.

My heart sank. In quieting my siren song, Rafael had gained one of his own. He'd just been trying to help me and now his chest was panting and he looked so desperate to get another taste.

"You're not thinking clearly. Your magic. I took it." My heart hammered in my chest. What I'd done was monstrous by itself. The fact that I'd made him enjoy being stripped of his magic was even worse. He was going to hate me when this wore off.

Rafael frowned, then brightened as though some brilliant idea had just occurred to him. I wasn't sure what exactly could be so wonderful about losing your magic, but he still wore a dazed expression so his thinking probably wasn't totally rational right now. "You're applying Nefesh logic to my magic. My powers were bestowed upon me by Asherah, as yours were. You can't destroy my magic. You simply used it as a remedy. At my instigation. There was no lasting damage. I feel it already replenishing itself." He stretched languidly, a content smile playing at his lips.

Fuck. Was this part of the bond between Attendants and Jezebels? A way to create intimacy between two people otherwise stuck in a relatively isolated bubble? Because that was messed up.

"Is this how Jezebels control their urges? We feed off our Attendant's magic?" Start my day with a healthy breakfast and thirty seconds of Rafael. I dropped my head into my hands with a strangled groan.

"Not up to this point, but it appears there's a first time for everything." He escorted me to one of the high-backed chairs. "Wait here," he said, and disappeared.

I sat there with my hands clasped between my knees, taking in the quiet of the room. The pillars were once more intact, hiding the *Sefer*, but I didn't desire its magic. I gently circled my right ankle in one direction, then the other. I'd been in such a rush that I'd come to the library in sock feet.

With no swelling and no more sharp twinges, I was free to dwell on my upset stomach, the thickness in my throat, and the all-over nausea that I'd somehow betrayed Levi. Which was ridiculous.

If no other Jezebel used their Attendant in that fashion, there was another way to silence the urges and strengthen myself against the *Sefer*. Good. Not that I'd known any better when I sucked—*medicinally ingested*—Rafael's magic. Really, it was no different than say, getting an IV bag of drugs for any other condition. Even if IV bags tended to go limp as you drained them, not—

Rafael appeared with a delicate china teacup on a saucer, steam curling off the top, and I jumped halfway out of my seat. My eyes bounced all over the room desperately looking for somewhere innocuous to land.

Brows furrowed, he pressed the cup into my hands, his fingers folding over mine. "A spot of Darjeeling. I hope you like milk and sugar."

"What? No scones?" I said. He bit his lip and I shook my head. "A joke, Rafael."

"Tea is a serious business. I wouldn't wish to offend."

I took a sip, the sweet milky liquid scalding my throat but also incredibly soothing. "You're not going to be impossibly British and avoid this conversation, are you? Because you and I just went further than I did with my first boyfriend."

Rafael dragged a chair up to mine and dropped into it. He gave me a crooked smile and a knot formed in my gut. "I fear that you are something of a conundrum, Ashira Cohen."

"Tell me about it. I'm thinking of having buttons made to that effect. But what specifically are you referring to?"

"These cravings of yours." He toyed with his dark wooden ring, burnished to a high-gleam, that was identical to mine.

"Yeah, what's up with that?" My smile was easy, but my ribcage constricted. "You Attendants really need to warn us about how bad those get, because man, I have had it up to here with unexpected surprises."

Rafael jutted his chin towards the myriad of books lining the shelves. "No other Jezebel in our vast and storied history has had them."

"Gavriella had them. That's why she took Blank." Though anything that cost me my magic wasn't an option.

"Gavriella used the drug to escape many things in her life," he said, "but this wasn't one of them. You hold the exciting and somewhat dubious distinction of being the only one addicted to magic."

I set the teacup down on its saucer with a rattle, tea sloshing over the rim. Each of his matter-of-fact words battered and unmoored me, as if the universe had considered my determination to succeed as a Jezebel no matter the obstacle, smiled maliciously, and said, "good luck."

Rafael pulled a linen handkerchief out of his vest pocket and mopped up the spilled tea. "While you can sense magic on the *Sefer Raziel HaMalakh*," he said, "it shouldn't have any effect on you. In fact, you shouldn't even sense it from a distance. Only if you send your magic directly into a scroll should you be able to verify its presence. The ward that suppressed your powers all those years must have interfered with the natural order of things in terms of how you interact with the *Sefer's* magic."

I choked on the sip I'd taken to calm my nerves. I'd been so focused on the "what," that I hadn't considered the "how."

Rafael thumped my back, his hand lingering a moment too long.

I jerked away. That damned tattoo. Another reason to never forgive my father for what he'd done. His actions had hampered my abilities and forced me into a twisted relationship with my Attendant that I saw no way out of.

I exhaled slowly. Find Adam. Get answers. Move forward. That was the plan and I was sticking to it.

"How bad are the cravings?" Rafael said.

Was he worried or hopeful? "Usually, about a two or three out of ten. If I'm midway through destroying someone's inherent magic and that gets aborted for some reason, it gets worse. A taste of angel-affiliated magic? I'd take crashing a car into a concrete wall again over its awful beauty. Though they're gone now. Thanks to you."

"I feared those scrolls were killing you and did the first thing that popped into my mind."

Pip. Pip. You have cravings. I can calm them. So very reasonable, when I wanted to hurl my cup against the wall. Rafael had made it clear that I was his reckless and barely-capable player in the fight against Chariot. If he wasn't railing against this massive shortcoming, then he was still brainwashed by my magic on his.

"You weren't wrong," I said, "but that was quite the gamble."

"It was. However, my magic is rooted in serving and protecting my Jezebel. I send out the magic that tests potentials, I am keyed to this library to safeguard it, and I have healing magic specific to my Jezebel, should she require it."

I leaned forward. "If you'd found me years ago, would both you and your father have been my Attendants?" My daddy issues didn't run anywhere deep enough to have wanted this dynamic with Rafael's father.

"No. As there is supposed to only be one Jezebel at a time, there is only one Attendant at a time. I took over my father's duties when he died. It would seem that my protective qualities extend to quieting your cravings. It was a risk I had to take." His eyes went soft and dreamy as he spoke, his finger tracing the gauze now taped over the gash in his arm.

Fuck. On top of everything, I'd wounded him.

How long was this enchantment going to last? I snapped my fingers under his nose. "Cut it out."

"Should those cravings continue to plague you, and when it comes to the *Sefer*, I almost guarantee that they will, then you'll be in need of my particular assistance, and only mine." His smile was smug, his pupils still glassy.

"There has to be another way," I said.

He actually pouted for a second, before a crafty gleam entered his eyes. "We have a solution and we will avail ourselves of it because I'll not let anything stand in the way of you doing your job. Those scrolls must be found and destroyed and you are susceptible to their magic." He shrugged, artfully careless. "Without my aid, I'm not sure how many more episodes like that one you can be brought back from."

Rafael's commitment to the cause was absolute, but addicts elevated con artistry to a survival skill. Rafael's words were true, but given his current condition, they were also a justification. Thing is, considering his magic remedy was the only thing that currently worked, what choice did I have either way?

I pulled on my collar, as if that could help me drag air into my seized-up lungs. Reason. Intelligence. Deduction. Those were the qualities I prized, not feeding like the undead off the hot guy I'd enthralled. I preferred my men willing. Like—no.

I searched for something in the room starting with the letter A for the self-soothing technique I'd learned in counseling after my dad left. *Armchair, bowtie...*

"Then it's settled," Rafael said. "We may proceed to the actual reason for your visit."

Nothing was settled. This was a disaster and we couldn't have a rational conversation. Chances were exceedingly high that when Rafael snapped out of this, he wasn't going to be thrilled that he'd felt this way about me. In fact, he'd probably be quite distraught and not want to be around me for a while. I couldn't walk into danger with him in that condition and expect him to have my back.

Glasses, hand…

"How is Adam's book connected?" I said.

"When Gavriella flatlined back when she was still Gracie," Rafael said, "it was during a mission. She'd stolen a piece of the *Sefer* away from Chariot, giving us the three we currently have. Luckily, my father got to her in time and saved her life, ensuring that piece stayed ours. But as you know, with her death, your magic activated." Rafael caught himself tracing the gauze and stilled his hand. "Gavriella insisted on moving here to try and find you. She had no connection to this city and her death certificate was public record. She and my father hoped they'd have an edge in finding the next piece."

Nails, oxygen… My breathing was shallow.

"Did Dad give the book to Gavriella or was this intended for me?"

"The book was in Gavriella's possession," Rafael said. "Though that doesn't negate it being placed at that Weaver's house and used to draw you out now."

"Regardless, Dad got her that coded message, so he must have known about Jezebels and wanted to help." Signs pointed to him being a good guy.

"Or it was a trap even then," Rafael said. "Chariot had pulled this stunt before. We have no way of knowing which it was, because the contact never showed up."

"The contact has a name," I said in a sharp voice. "Adam Cohen. My father."

Rafael inclined his head at the correction and clasped my hands between his. "It may be best for you to prepare yourself for the worst-case scenario. Adam didn't make the meeting. There are many potential reasons for that, some more upsetting than others."

All this needy touching was making my skin crawl.

I stood up abruptly, pacing the room. "He's not dead. My father is a level four Charmer. He can talk his way out of anything. If he was working for Chariot and planned to betray them, they could catch him in the act and he'd still be able to assure them of his loyalty. Also, I'm not convinced he didn't show up. Adam's self-preservation instincts are finely honed. If he suspected that Gavriella had the upper hand going into this, he'd have aborted it. I assume she had some plan to bring this unknown contact in for questioning?"

"Of course."

I folded my hands together, staring down at the long fingers that I'd inherited from my dad. We used to press our palms together when I was little to see how much more mine had to grow to catch up to his. If I did it now, would they finally match? Or had his hands, like everything larger than life that I remembered about my father, diminished?

"There are a lot of unanswered questions," I said, "but Adam is out there and I will find him. What else can you tell me?"

"Gavriella was unsettled by the fact that someone, friend or foe, had learned of her new identity so quickly," Rafael said. "It irked her that she was never able to solve who had reached out to her or for what purpose. Plus, there was the matter of the sunflower drawing. She was convinced that it, too, was part of the coded message and it drove her barmy trying to figure out what it meant."

I smiled. It would have driven me crazy as well.

"Though why use a Sherlock Holmes novel to send the message and not a simple letter?" Rafael said.

"Dad liked to get personal with his marks," I said bitterly. "To disarm and build trust."

"He sounds like quite the character."

"He has his moments. So, there's still one unclaimed piece of the *Sefer* out there and it's all tied to Adam."

"It would seem so."

This was bigger than my need for closure. Finding my father was a vital step in stopping Chariot—provided they didn't find me first.

But then all my tiredness pressed in on me like a blanket. I yawned, hastily covering my mouth. "Sorry."

Rafael's condition showed no sign of diminishing. A good night's sleep would do us both good. Then we could discuss our problem clear-headed.

I scraped the chair back. "I'll see you when you get to Vancouver."

"I shall wait with bated breath."

Aw, shit. He wasn't being snarky. I fiddled with the wooden ring on my finger. Was it irresponsible of me to run out on him? But at the same time, how much of this was my responsibility? It *would* wear off, wouldn't it?

Rafael brushed a lock of hair out of my face. "Get some rest. Until we next meet, my Jezebel."

Chapter 6

Wednesday morning, I woke up on my back, the blankets barely wrinkled. Usually, I slept sprawled out, playing a constant game of sticking my feet in and out of the covers to regulate my body temperature until the blankets twisted ninety degrees. I'd slept as motionless as the undead, and that only reinforced how vampiric I'd felt sucking on Rafael's magic. I kicked the covers into a messy ball out of spite.

Mrs. Hudson whined at me from her dog bed on the floor. The pet store owner had tried to convince me to buy a crate for her but she'd shied away from the display so violently that I hadn't had the heart to force her into one. I'd sprung for an uber-plush bed that was designed to calm anxiety, and she did look pretty calm, if I said so myself.

It turned out that puppies did not have any respect for the sacred first morning cup of coffee and would pee on the floor if not walked upon waking, whether a person was decently caffeinated or not.

"Do this with your new family," I said, squatting on the balls of my feet to wipe up the puddle. I threw the sodden mess in the trash and washed my hands before jumping in the shower.

After donning a pair of jeans and a red sweater to show this day who was boss, I dished out puppy food and clean water. "Where'd you get to?"

Mrs. Hudson sneezed and I followed the noise to the living room. A sound of horror squeaked out of me.

Priya grinned, running her hand along the pink sweater that Mrs. H now wore, as if my former bestie was some kind of showroom model. "She loves it."

Priya was in a taupe dress that dulled her brown skin. I considered the odds of getting away with a break-in that only stole the clothes in her current color palette.

"You know what she'd really love? Matching with you," I said. "Your bright pink cowl neck sweater would be just the thing."

Priya gathered up the packaging that the doggie outfit had come in. "Nah."

"If you're not wearing pink, then it's not going to be inflicted on the pug, either."

"She's not going to wear black," Priya said.

"She's not going to wear anything. It's the best thing about dogs. They're clothing optional." I tried to tug the ridiculous article off, but Mrs. Hudson nipped at my finger.

Priya smirked and flounced out of the room, just as the buzzer to the building's front door went off. We went weeks with no visitors, so why had we suddenly turned into Grand Central Station?

"Yes?" I said testily into the intercom.

"It's me."

Awesome. Nothing capped the glow of morning-after magic devourment like a visit from one's mother. Why was Talia here? We hadn't spoken since our tacit understanding to pretend that I didn't have magic and would continue to live as a Mundane putting my detective skills to work for an insurance company.

Reluctantly I buzzed her in, meeting her on the landing. "This is a surprise."

She kissed my cheek, immaculately turned out as always, with pearl buttons on her smart pantsuit and her hair in a sleek bob. Talia was every inch the high-powered woman-on-the-go, as befitted her position as the Senior Policy Advisor for the provincial Untainted Party. We had the same dark hair, but she had gray eyes where I'd inherited my dad's brown ones. "Darling. Let me take you for breakfast and hear how your first few days on the new job are going. Any interesting fraud cases?"

Yeah, my father. "It's early days still. I'm not sure I should be—"

"I'm off." Priya slid out the front door in a beige coat, her custom-built pink laptop sticking out of her open computer bag, and Mrs. Hudson on a leash. "Oh. Hi, Talia."

They hugged. My mother was genuinely fond of Priya and I suspected that in the event of a friend divorce, she'd keep the non-biological female.

"You got a puppy?" Talia did not attempt to pet the dog.

I waited for Pri to stake her claim on Mrs. Hudson, but she decided to buck tradition and throw me under the bus.

"Oh, not me. Mrs. Hudson is Ash's dog."

"Mrs. Hudson?" Talia said faintly. She mustered up a smile. "I'm happy to see you so settled."

Wow. We were really digging into the fantasy version of my life. I didn't have the energy to tell her the dog was temporary. "Yup. Settled. That's me. About breakfast—"

"Just a quick bite." She smiled politely at the dog. "We can go somewhere with a patio so the puppy can come."

Shoot me. She was being inclusive of the dog. Priya raised her eyebrows at me, like "You have to go," and I rolled my eyes back in a "No kidding."

"Great," I said. "Let me get my stuff."

Priya and Mrs. Hudson stayed with Talia, chatting, while

I shoved doggy supplies into a backpack and grabbed my purse and leather jacket.

Breakfast happened on a heated patio at an upscale restaurant where Talia breezed us past the line-up. A server was instantly at our table to take our order: an egg-white veggie omelet for my mother and waffles with extra whipped cream for me. Then the two of us engaged in stilted conversation like minor skirmishes: me spinning lies about how fascinating insurance fraud was and my mother giving updates on the bill she'd written to dissolve House Pacifica here in British Columbia and put Nefesh governance back into Mundane hands.

That policy had worked brilliantly before Houses were created—so long as you didn't mind pesky things like witch hunts.

It was already April and the provincial Parliament would end in late May. There wasn't enough time to get the proposal into shape for this spring session, so the Untainted Party was gearing up for when Parliament returned in the fall. The bill would have its first reading in the legislature, with printed copies distributed to all parties. At that point, it would go to a second reading, where the proposal would be debated and a vote taken. Based on those results, it would proceed to the committee stage or die. If it continued, successful, it would go through more debates and a third reading. The last step was to achieve Royal Assent from our Lieutenant Governor, who represented the Queen's official approval since we were a Commonwealth country. From there, the bill would pass into law.

Meantime, my mother and her cronies were getting the legislation word-perfect and feverishly making backroom deals to secure support across party lines. Support on an oppositional front would be Levi's main priority right now as well.

It was hard to tell if Talia was honestly trying to connect

with me or offering a warning to keep up my charade. I kept a bland smile on my face, but inside I seethed. How could she still be going ahead with this when she knew I had magic too?

"Our momentum on this issue is very exciting," Talia said. And she did sound excited, like she used to get when she was helping me put jigsaw pieces together as a kid and she could see the whole thing coming together. Not like it was for something that would actively harm me.

The waffles turned to cardboard in my mouth and I dropped my fork. "Could we not discuss this anymore?"

She flinched, almost imperceptibly, but I caught it. I'd spent a lot of time in my teens deconstructing her every minute reaction. "The Party has always wanted this." Her look was almost beseeching. "It just happened at an... unfortunate time."

Unfortunate, as in her daughter went and landed herself with magic, but so long as I kept it hidden all would be well? Did Talia assume I'd value my own self-preservation over loyalty to fellow Nefesh, seeing as how recently I'd become one of them? I pushed my last piece of waffle around in the puddle of syrup. To be fair, I'd never been much of a joiner.

I wiped my mouth. "I need to get to work. My Mundane job. So Mundane."

Her eyes flashed, but before she could answer, a cheerful voice boomed out, "Good morning, ladies."

It was Isaac Montefiore, Levi's father. The man who'd physically abused his son as a child and now was publicly backing the Untainted Party's bill, despite the fact that this legislation threatened to destroy everything his son fought to protect.

Levi had inherited his father's black hair, though Isaac's was shot through with gray, and those blue eyes. On Levi, they were as dazzling as the ocean when he smiled. On Isaac they were flat and calculating.

Mrs. Hudson growled at him. I scratched her ears, reinforcing that behavior.

Isaac and Talia greeted each other warmly and then he turned to me with a hearty handshake. "Ashira." He rolled the "r" in my name with his Italian accent.

Levi had the same accent since he'd been born in Rome, but it only ever came out when he lost control. I thought fondly of all the ways I'd ever made him lose said control and allowed Isaac's small talk BS to wash over me.

Until he said, "I understand you've been visiting my son a lot at work."

You Nefesh-hating fucker. I wouldn't put it past him to have a mole at Levi's office feeding information to Isaac that would at best discredit the House, and at worst help this horrible bill become law.

My mother shot me a sharp look. "It's nice that those two have grown close."

I almost snorted, because her tone made it clear that a boric acid enema would also be nice. To Talia, Levi was the enemy, so to have me fraternizing with him was a potential minefield. "My best friend started working for them on an IT project. I go to visit her."

Talia gave a shaky laugh. "Priya. Of course."

Isaac smirked. "My son's loss."

My father had worked for Isaac when I was younger and I'd bet he knew where all of Isaac's skeletons were buried. Sadly, Adam wasn't around, and Isaac would be no help in learning what had happened to Dad, since any business dealings they'd had had ended a couple years before my father left.

"I doubt Levi is too upset. We were never really close." Making my excuses, I whisked Mrs. Hudson away with a sigh of relief and drove to my office.

Back on home territory, I strode through the reception area of the shared workspace that housed Cohen Investigations. The pug danced underfoot on her new collar and leash, examining the exposed brick, original oak floors, and steel cross bracings. With a soft huff, she deemed the place acceptable.

Coming to my office had always been a bright spot in my day, and it had been with a heavy heart that I'd shut down my website. The Mundane private investigation firm that I'd worked so hard to establish was no longer open to the public. I didn't have the heart to take down the stenciling on my door and I couldn't declare myself Nefesh and change my detective license either, since I had to keep my Jezebel magic secret.

Bryan, the dog-crazy insurance agent who shared the space along with Eleanor, a graphic designer, murmured hello from the leather sofa, not taking his eyes off his laptop. When he'd asked about my new contract in his industry, I'd given the name of a global insurance firm, and he'd merely nodded. If my cover story passed the Bryan test, I figured it'd hold up to the casual observer.

Mrs. Hudson barked, and Bryan perked up, practically long-jumping the couch to get a better look. "You got a puppy!"

At his approach, the dog shivered closer to my leg, whining softly.

"She's just a temporary visitor." I scooped Mrs. Hudson up and she snuggled into my chest. "Nothing personal if she's skittish around you, she's a rescue pup."

"That's okay," Bryan said. "It looks like she's very happy with you. What's her name?"

"Mrs. Hudson," I said.

"Cute." He obviously had no idea where the name came from and thus no opinions on it one way or the other. I liked him more for it.

"Hey," Priya said, opening my office door and stepping out.

Priya only worked for Team Jezebel one day a week. The rest of her time was now devoted to overhauling House cybersecurity. As the person who had hacked them the most often, she was uniquely qualified for the job.

"Today is not your allotted day. Did something happen?" I sniffed the air. "Do I smell pakoras?"

Priya rocked back on her heels, her eyes crinkling in amusement. "Yup. The meeting got pushed and then Mummy asked me to make a special delivery."

I groaned. "Make it go away."

"I warned you the first time this happened to say no. You've only yourself to blame. I'll get Mrs. Hudson some water." Priya headed into the kitchen.

Bryan lit up. "I have some doggie treats. Be right back."

Mrs. Hudson cocked her head at me, her little black nose glistening. Why were pug's faces so consistently damp?

"Feel free to bite the person inside." I took a deep breath and entered my office.

Five minutes later, even Mayan didn't seem so awful. I leaned back in my new, non-deadly chair with its added cushioning. Lumbar support was a beautiful thing. "To clarify," I said, "a seven-foot-tall she-devil pinned you against the wall on Saturday night, stuck her tongue down your throat and, I quote, 'sucked out your soul, your free will, and your Fortnite know-how'?"

Arnav, the scrawny fifteen-year-old sitting in one of the client chairs on the other side of my desk, bounced his leg at tweaker-level speeds, an energy drink clutched in his hands. "Yeah. Her name's Ellie. You gotta get it back."

"Your soul?" I raised my eyebrows at Priya.

"Told you not to talk to my cousin." She blew compressed air into her keyboard.

"I told Geeta I was now only working for the insurance firm." I gestured at Arnav. "She doesn't seem to care."

"Our family drama is your family drama," Priya said.

"Hey," Arnav protested.

"You're here because a 'she-devil sucked out your soul.' Your protest is noted and summarily ignored," Priya said.

I nudged Mrs. Hudson away from the tin foil package and slipped her another dog treat, before helping myself to one of the crispy vegetable balls. "Your mother made me pakoras. How was I supposed to refuse?"

The pug toddled off to play with some chew toys that I'd bought.

"Mom's evil that way," Priya said.

"Harsh, Pri. I'm telling Auntie." Arnav shook his head, then frowned at me. "What do I need my soul for?"

"Nothing that I can think of in the foreseeable future."

Mrs. Hudson nosed half-heartedly at a ball, then turned her attention to a colorful twist of rope.

"My Fortnite skills, though. Those are important," Arnav said. "There's a tournament tomorrow."

After my office had been trashed by a suspect in a previous case, Levi had completely restored it with all new upscale ergonomic furniture, reframed a university graduation photo of Priya and myself, and replaced my dart board and mounted holder. That was generous enough, but he'd gone one more step and hung up a set of framed Sherlock Holmes book covers, transforming this room from a nice office to a space that was uniquely mine.

I now gazed upon those prints, seeking strength. Sherlock would never have put up with this shit. Arnav had been a drama queen since birth and I resented being tagged to deal with his "latest crisis" as Geeta had put it the first time she'd delivered me the fried deliciousness that guaranteed my compliance.

"Here's what we're gonna do," I said. "What's your Fortnite character called?"

"Psycho Bandito." Arnav leaned forward with the manic enthusiasm of someone about to launch into a very detailed description of a topic only slightly less painful to the listener than stepping on a Lego.

I quickly cut him off. "Ellie's last name is what?"

"Ramirez."

"And the guy she decided to date instead of you is who?"

"Logan." Arnav froze, then hurriedly backpedaled. "That has nothing to do with it. She stole my skills, dude."

Priya snorted and Mrs. Hudson barked, pawing at a squeaky toy that was shaped like a deranged cow.

I plucked the energy drink out of Arnav's hand. "You want your skills back? Drink water and get some sleep. This hyped-up sugar shit is messing with your concentration and reaction times."

"You sound like my mom," he huffed.

I pulled my mini Taser out of my desk drawer and thunked it down. "Unlike your mother, I have weapons and am licensed to use them. Were you a willing participant in the kiss?"

"Yeah," he mumbled.

"Then that's the end of it. If Ellie wants to kiss you at a party and then date someone else, that's her right. Enjoy the memory and do not disparage that girl again. Understood?"

"Yes. Geez." He pointed to the two lone pakoras that neither Priya nor I had eaten yet. "Can I have one?"

I held up the Taser. "Go away. Now."

Arnav slunk off.

A jackhammer started up outside in the latest round of constant construction tearing up Gastown's streets. Its pounding matched the headache taking root in my temples.

Mrs. Hudson had dismissed the other toys and was now slobbering contentedly on the cow's head.

"I'm impressed you figured it out about the other boy," Priya said.

"My powers of deduction are unparalleled."

We clunked the two last pakoras in cheers. There was no

point keeping food from Priya. Especially anything made by Geeta. Priya'd just change all my passwords in retribution, and I'd been locked out of my accounts too many times during our university days when Geeta first started feeding me to want to go through Password Hell again.

"Well," Priya said brightly, stuffing her laptop into a computer bag, "Arnav lived to see another day, so my work here is done."

"I hate you." I let Mrs. Hudson lick my fingers clean.

"Kiss your dog for me." Priya grabbed her coat, and left.

Mrs. Hudson settled down to snooze with one paw on her new bovine friend.

Before diving in to Mayan's case, I slid the wooden ring on for a quick library jaunt. Hopefully a good night's sleep had cleared Rafael's head and we could discuss what had happened like two non-ensorcelled human beings.

It was the first time I'd come to the library and no one else immediately showed up. I puttered around, searched the bottom shelf for any notations on yours truly (no success), and sent six text messages to Rafael over the span of twenty minutes. There was no sign or word from him.

He'd still show up to the team meeting, right? His embarrassment wouldn't overpower his duties, would it?

Returning to the office, I opened the new shiny laptop that Priya had bought me. I'd protested such a generous gift, but Priya had declared my old laptop an affront to technology and insisted she was doing this as much for herself as me.

It was a very Priya statement, and especially in light of her post-kidnapping struggles, not a gift to be refused.

Checking that Mrs. Hudson was still asleep, I googled Mayan Shapiro. Her various profiles for the past year were filled with images of a fashionable woman with sleek burgundy tresses. Always dressed in black, the photos were mostly of Mayan at various hot spots, interspersed with her work on behalf of the Lung Cancer Foundation, her fitness regimen, and the occasional photo of her in a bikini on some tropical beach with a drink.

Mayan came across as poised, confident, and sought-after socially.

I examined the photos and posts from two weeks ago, flipping back and forth between those and the previous entries for any differences.

It was such a subtle thing that I almost missed it. Every photo prior to that time showed her wearing a necklace with a diamond heart pendant. None of the photos since then had it.

Me: *What's the deal with Mayan's heart pendant?*

Imperious 1: *Good morning, Ash. I did sleep well, thank you for asking.*

Me: *You need to get over this small talk fetish of yours. The pendant?*

Imperious 1: *It was her mom's. Mayan's worn it since Dani passed away from lung cancer when Mayan was twenty-three. Why?*

Me: *She stopped wearing it right around the time that she came to see you.*

Imperious 1: *She wouldn't take it off. Not willingly.*

Levi's anxiety punched through the cell signal. Time to distract him.

Me: *FYI, I spoke with your charming father this morning. I think he has a mole in your office.*

Imperious 1: *Old news, Sherlock. We've been feeding him information for months.*

Me: *How devious of you. I'm impressed.*

Imperious 1: *That's a euphemism for turned on, right?*

Me: **middle finger emoji**

Smiling, I returned to my search, stopping on a photo taken last weekend of Mayan at some club. Not somewhere trendy, more a cocktail bar from the 1960's, a grand dame painted in heavy reds with velvets and brocades where you could still see her regal beauty, even if it was faded. That was unlike Mayan's usual hangouts, but it had a retro charm that appealed to me. The bartender probably knew how to make a proper drink and served it in a heavy, cut highball glass.

The extent of my thoughts would have been "cool," were it not for one thing: the image carved into the bar of a heart with a crown and scepter. I zoomed in on the photo.

What was a Mundane like Mayan doing in Hedon?

Chapter 7

Nowadays, there were three ways into Hedon, a place stitched together from pockets of our reality but existing outside of it. The first was via a gold coin that took the user anywhere in that world that they wished to go, free of charge. The second was by using bronze tokens, which also took a person directly to their desired location, but with a cost, usually in the form of a memory. That added to the Queen of Hearts' insights about a person, because knowledge was power. I'd recently tangled with those tokens, and while handy, I wasn't sure they were worth the price of admission.

The final way in was with a plain coin stamped with an "H," which was used at one of the fixed entrances located in our world. These only required a cost the first time you entered.

Traveling to Hedon: painful, dangerous, and for me, unfortunately essential. Too bad any easier, backdoor entrances into the world had recently been sealed up for good. Coin travel it was.

Distance-wise, the drive to House Pacifica HQ was a short one, but our offices existed in entirely different worlds. Mine was in Gastown, a gentrified cobblestoned neighborhood with trendy cafés, pricey lofts, and hipster boutiques on the edge of one of Canada's poorest areas.

House Pacifica sat on a prime piece of real estate in downtown Vancouver, surrounded by office towers branded with corporate logos. Shaped like a seven-story "S" on its side, it changed color depending on the light, the time of day, and possibly Levi's moods. On this early evening in April, it was bathed in a rosy glow, but I'd also seen it in an inscrutable jet black and a hard bluish-silver. Had I been in charge, its color palette would have been far more limited.

From past conversations with Arkady, I'd learned that Miles' office wasn't on the seventh floor along with the other executives, but the sixth, where all security was housed.

Compared to the banks of monitors and the hum of activity in the security hub, his office at the back was a cool oasis of calm, painted in soothing blues with a lot of greenery in hanging pots, and a small water feature burbling away in one corner. The only way I'd have been more surprised by it was if I'd caught Miles in yoga pants doing sun salutations.

"Considering the amount of travel you do to Hedon is nil, you can spare some coins," I said.

Mrs. Hudson tugged on her leash so I unclipped it from her collar.

"I made an exception last time because of the urgency of those smudges and the missing kids," Miles said. "But if you want coins to get you in and out, follow protocol and buddy up."

"That's not a good idea." I tossed the deranged cow squeaky toy into the corner and Mrs. Hudson ran for it as fast as her chubby little legs allowed. "None of your security people have ever been there before, which means they'll be subjected to the Queen looking deep into their heart. Then she'll head trip them with it, and who knows what condition they'll be in at that point?"

"They're trained professionals. They'll handle it." He raised a hand to cut off my protest. "You wanted to work exclusively for the House with a team and our resources at your disposal. Well, you got them, so you don't get to race off on your own when security protocol dictates otherwise."

"This is ridiculous. It's a simple visit to question some people in a bar." Miles wasn't officially part of Team Jezebel, so if he didn't know about Mayan, then the case fell under client/P.I. confidentiality and wasn't mine to spill. "I've traveled to Hedon by myself multiple times."

The puppy dropped the slobbery toy on my shoe. Turning my grimace into a smile so her feelings didn't get hurt, I petted her for her cleverness.

"Yeah, and the last time you almost ended up as a living statue in the Queen's garden. This is non-negotiable, Cohen." He crossed his arms.

"Fine. Where's Arkady?" I flung the cow away again and wiped my fingers on my jeans.

"How would I know? I'm not his babysitter," Miles snapped.

"You're his boss and it's work hours." Gasping theatrically, I covered my mouth with my hand. "Did you two do something unprofessional?"

"Choi has a big mouth."

"Arkady didn't say anything. The two of you weren't exactly subtle at Tatiana's."

Miles flushed. "He's not here. He's following up on whether anyone tried to infuse magic into the abducted teens."

"Wow. Good to know you have enough self-awareness *not* to be a giant hypocrite and tell me your personal life is none of my business. Given how invested you are in mine."

"Don't push me."

"Is that a dare?"

Miles leaned back in his chair, his legs crossed, and his

hands steepled together. "It's a reminder that your way in to Hedon is through me. So, settle the fuck down."

Our gazes clashed.

I had a war to win. Miles was a minor skirmish at best. "Well, I can't take Priya and I won't bring a stranger, regardless of how well you think they'll handle it. That leaves you."

"There's another option. I'll go with Ash."

Miles and I swiveled towards the door. Levi lounged there, one hip propped against the now-closed door.

His navy suit was sharp looking and well-tailored. He'd complemented it with a matching tie with whimsical tiny white polka dots. Levi's work style was generally more conservative. That tie looked like something a girlfriend would pick out for him, humming cheerfully as she helped knot it around his neck. She'd straighten it, and Levi would bend down with that small delighted smile that was as surprising and brilliant as a solar flare, pressing a kiss to my—

"No way." I shook my head emphatically. "I mean, to going. To Hedon."

"Second that," Miles said.

Levi gave us a wolfish smile. "Isn't it great that I outrank you both?"

Mrs. Hudson squeaked her toy at him, earning a quick scratch. I whistled and snapped my fingers, but she ignored me, enthusiastically dry humping the cow. Huh. Mrs. Hudson preferred cowgirl. Or was it always doggie in her case?

Miles stood up and stalked toward Levi. "You're not going there for your first time with only this one as back-up."

"Much as you don't need to be such a dick about it," I said, "I concur. Why would you possibly want to go there? It's not Vegas. Trust me, what happens in Hedon does not stay there. Also, you're too close to this case and I don't want you getting in the way."

The puppy lost interest in the toy and took a drink from Miles' water feature.

Miles snapped his fingers. "Dog. Down."

I muttered sorry and grabbed the pug, setting her in my lap.

Without the buzz of chatter from outside, the room was left in a charged silence.

Levi dropped into an empty chair, his legs crossed. How he managed to do that without wrinkling the line of his bespoke suit was beyond me.

"When Chariot held the auction to sell smudges," he said, "they implied that either the Queen or I were the ones behind it, effectively turning us into scapegoats for when it inevitably went wrong." Levi's blue eyes glittered dangerously. "The enemy of my enemy is my friend. Facilitate an introduction, Ash. It's time I met the Queen of Hearts."

"You can't ally yourself with the ruler of the black market." Miles grabbed a stress ball off his desk, practically grinding the thing. "If the Untainted Party find out, they'll crucify you."

I pointed at Miles, nodding. "That."

"They're out to crucify me regardless."

He wasn't wrong. We'd learned at an auction a couple weeks ago that someone had fed the Party misinformation, implicating Levi behind the rampaging smudges with a view to securing dictatorial power. That was compounded by a rumor that a magic virus was on the loose, all to propagate how dangerous Nefesh are, and the Party had run with all of it.

"When Chariot was snatching kids out of *my* territory," Levi said, "they used the Queen's name to do it. Their actions have allowed the Party to weaponize. I want the key to disarm them and kill this proposed legislation."

"Then take a team," Miles said. "Or I'll come."

"That's a great idea," I said. "Make it an official parlay. I'll drop a word in the Queen's ear to arrange it when I go there, *by myself*, without the two most powerful people in the House that she could potentially take hostage. You can't just drop in on her like you're storming the castle. Would you go unannounced to another House Head?"

"Depends if I wanted to catch them off guard," Levi said. "Which I won't be doing anyway, given the alarm system around anyone entering her domain for the first time."

"No, you'll be handing her your weakness."

Levi arched an eyebrow, as if him being weak was laughable.

I put Mrs. Hudson gently on the floor so I didn't accidentally strangle the wrong neck.

The pug trotted back to her cow and pounced on it. Oh, brother. When she only attempted to rip into its belly instead of getting amorous, I relaxed.

Levi watched me with a tiny grin, which he smoothed out into a serious expression under Miles' thunderous glower.

"You're not invincible, asshole," Miles said. "I'd be happy to prove it right now to keep you from going."

"Invite the Queen here," I said.

"She won't come." Levi loosened his silk tie, pulling the fabric from around his neck with a soft swish and stuffing it in his pocket. I'd have cheered the loss of the tie, except Levi was prepping himself for the trip, deliberately softening the arrogant alpha-ness he normally wore like a second skin. "I already tried. We're going."

"Whoa, there, Magic Mike," I said. "Knot that back up and march upstairs to your office. I'm not taking you."

Levi pointedly met my eyes and undid the top button of his shirt.

"Look, I'm not the best person for this delicate mission,"

I said. "The Queen and I concluded our previous business on a rather tentative note."

I'd professed that I wasn't her enemy, she'd countered with a "not yet" and that whether I stayed that way remained to be seen. It seemed prudent to steer clear of her for a while, not force a meeting with someone who could complicate things for her. The Queen didn't appreciate complications.

Miles pinched the bridge of his nose. "Were you going to tell me about this invitation of yours?"

Levi's phone buzzed. He glanced at the screen and typed a quick response as he spoke. "No point, since it didn't happen. This isn't some rash decision. I've given it a lot of thought and I'm willing to pay the price if it establishes a tentative rapport."

"Don't pull her into this fight with Chariot," I said. "I don't trust her yet."

"She's already in it, whether she likes it or not." Levi dropped the phone into his pocket and rubbed his temples. "I just came from a meeting with our allies in the government."

When Houses were formed in Canada, they were established at a provincial level. House Heads fought for them to be written into the federal constitution, but that never happened, which gave the Untainted Party a lot of leverage now.

"How bleak is the situation?" Miles said.

"There's more support for this bill than I'd realized," Levi said. "If it went to a final reading tomorrow, it would pass into law. I want to kill it before it gets to the First Reading. Chariot's antics with the smudges emboldened the Party to move forward with this audacious idea they'd never dared to propose before. I need leverage about how and why this all came to pass. The Queen is well placed to gather information and it affects her, too." He levelled a flat stare at me. "Knowledge is power. The Queen knows that better than anyone."

Yeah, it was practically her motto. I chided myself for mentioning that to him.

"I'm fighting for this House's existence, for the safety of my people, and the gloves are off," Levi said.

I buried my face in my hands. Levi was putting the Untainted Party—and my mother—in the crosshairs. Yes, they'd started it, and of course he had to protect his Nefesh community, but where was I supposed to stand in this fight?

"First Mayan, now this. You're putting Ash in a hell of a position."

I jerked my head up, gaping at Miles. His brown eyes were clouded with concern. For me. That was... okay.

"You think I don't know that?" Levi's expression was grimmer than I'd ever seen it. "If our House is legally dissolved, it'll plunge Nefesh in this province into a dark age of persecution." He reached his hand out to me, then dropped it into his lap at the last moment. "You're my best shot at getting her to meet. Will you please take me to the Queen?"

Cursing Levi out in my head, I ran the wooden ring over my lip, the chain pulled taut. What did Levi mean by leverage? Information? Buried skeletons? Physical violence?

Both he and the Queen were ruthless when it came to the well-being of those under their protection. If I set an alliance in motion, there was no going back, and there'd be no halfway measures.

I was Nefesh now. More than that, I was a Jezebel. I'd accepted a responsibility to keep people safe from Chariot's global designs to gain unmeasurable power, so how could I turn my back on a fight involving a similar problem in my own backyard?

Talia had chosen her political beliefs over me, tolerating my magic only as long as I kept it hidden and pretended to be Mundane, but she was still my mother. Our relationship was completely different from Levi's with his father. Not so easy to jettison.

"I'll take you," I said icily, "but if any harm comes to my mother as a result of this, I'll never forgive you."

Levi's eyes were troubled and distant, almost lost. "I know."

He shook off his stupor, his air of invulnerability wrapped once more around him like armor. A very brittle armor. He caught me staring and steeled his jaw, his spine straightening.

"Give us the coins, Miles," Levi said. "We leave in twenty minutes. Ash, I'll meet you in the lobby." He strode out without a backward look.

Miles gave me four tokens. "Keep him safe."

"From the Queen? I'll do my best."

He shook his head. "From himself."

Chapter 8

I left Mrs. Hudson with a delighted Priya, who'd gotten far too attached. As soon as I had a spare minute, I'd take the puppy to the rescue shelter. I'd have to let them know that synthetic blankets made her itchy and not to separate her from her squeaky cow paramour and that her favorite flavor of doggie treat was bacon. But take her I would, because she deserved to have a settled family life.

Levi and I walked over to Harbour Center, a tower that housed both the downtown campus of Simon Fraser University and a revolving restaurant on the top with 360° views of the city. The door to the restaurant also happened to be the entrance into Hedon from Vancouver.

He'd illusioned himself as a blond man so we wouldn't be spotted together, or his destination tracked.

"Slow down," I said, practically jogging to keep up with his long strides. "You're not going out for a night on the town. Best case scenario is trauma and danger in a reality that shouldn't exist."

He did this goofy little dance. "Exactly."

I fell out of step with him, pretending I didn't know the giant weirdo.

Levi laughed and caught my hand, pulling me along. Most people would be shitting themselves at meeting someone like the Queen. Or at least, they'd be super cautious instead of leaping into the situation like it was the most fun they'd had in a long time.

"You do remember this isn't a social call," I said.

Levi sighed, all humor gone and a weight seeming to settle around his shoulders. I wished I could take my words back. "I'm House Head. I never forget what's at stake," he said.

"Okay, Leviticus." I squeezed his hand. "Let's have ourselves an adventure. You're welcome."

"No, *you're* welcome for my genius idea of hiring you in the first place." He winked and pulled the skyscraper door open.

After convincing the woman manning the cash register to take the coins, a basic weeding-out ploy, we were directed to one of the glass elevators that crawled up the outside of the forty-plus story building.

Levi dropped the illusion once we were inside the car.

Unlike my first time, when I'd been wedged in with a boisterous Greek family, Levi and I were alone. This was good, as the menace rolling off him would have scared the bejeezus out of any poor schmuck stuck in here with us.

I crossed my arms and leaned back against the wall, watching Levi instead of the magnificent view of the skyline, water, and North Shore Mountains. "Are you scared?"

"No," he said. "But it suddenly got a lot more real."

"My first time involved my father." Levi coughed a laugh and I winced. "Very bad phrasing. The first time I took this route, the Queen saw into my heart and discovered that what I wanted more than anything was to be reunited with Adam." I snapped my fingers. "And there he was. It wasn't enough that he appeared exactly as I imagined he would, or that he smelled of Old Spice and lemon candies.

If I wanted to get in to Hedon, we had to play a trust game."

"Shit." Levi leaned against the railing with a hard exhale. "Of all the people."

"Right? I'm telling you this so you'll be ready for whatever's coming. As much as you can be."

"Well, you obviously kept it together and won the game," he said.

"No. Trusting Adam was beyond me. I threw a knife into his solar plexus and shattered the illusion. Whatever secret desire you're harboring? Be prepared to destroy it."

Levi gave me a long measured look. "I'll remember that."

"At least your dad won't make an appearance," I said.

Levi didn't answer.

"After everything he did to you? You can't wish he was in your life."

"I don't. But…" He fiddled with his cuff links. "He wasn't this horrible abuser twenty-four hours a day. He played soccer with me. A lot. Taught me how to handle the ball and told me stories about how growing up he dreamed of playing for Italy in the World Cup. My father is smart. He saw the potential of cryptosecurity and the importance of data when they were still kind of a frontier to conquer. He worked hard and he built up his business. I admired that about him."

"Is that why you developed that virtual reality tech? To impress him?"

Levi put his hands in his pockets, watching the floor numbers change. "I challenged my predecessor for House Head as a fuck-you to him, that's for sure."

"Right. That was the only reason. Not to protect Nefesh."

"Fine. The fuck-you was a secondary reason. But I love taking care of my community and I wouldn't have that if it weren't for Isaac."

"It's not that easy to write him off," I said.

"Much as I've tried." He suddenly looked a lot more tired and older, like he hadn't gotten enough sleep in a while. He turned a weary smile on me. "Does that make me a fool?"

"It makes you human."

The elevator slid to a stop and the doors silently opened.

I manifested a blood dagger, my blood armor covering me from head to toe. I wasn't sure what demon of Levi's we'd face, but better to be safe than sorry. I exited the elevator first, inching forward, and braced for whatever illusion to appear.

Nothing did.

I spun in a slow circle. "Maybe as a House Head, you're off the hook?"

"You really think the Queen makes exceptions?"

"Only painful ones."

"I feel so much better now." He followed me onto the white tiles in the welcome area outside the restaurant.

The revolving door spun lazily, alternating a flickering view of tables covered by crisp linens in full sunshine with a foreign night, its crescent moon an eerie shade of yellow.

Levi stared, rapt. "I had no idea."

"Wait until you get inside. Hedon seems all exotic but it's dangerous. Don't forget that."

"Grazie," he said sarcastically. "I didn't become House Head without one or two survival skills. Or brain cells."

"Even when I hated you, I didn't think you were stupid. But you've got to admit, there's a part of you that loves risky ventures. First you went into the virtual reality biz, which no one would consider a sure bet, then after you invented whatever thing it was you did there and made a gazillion dollars selling the company, you went for your next crazy challenge. House Head. Except that hasn't been as thrilling as you'd hoped, has it? That's why you've been so eager to be part of my Jezebel investigations." I spread my hands wide.

"Keep telling yourself that," he said bitterly.

I frowned. What I'd said was maybe a little snarky, but it wasn't a lie. "I feel like this is becoming a fight. Why—"

"I know exactly what I'm getting into and I *will* keep them safe," he snarled. His eyes blazed and his breaths came in harsh rasps.

Huh? He wasn't making sense and he'd gone from zero to Hulk-rage, which was totally unwarranted. I stepped forward, hands up, but he didn't react. In fact, on closer examination, he wasn't looking at me, but rather slightly over my right shoulder.

Cold fingers of dread trickled down the back of my neck. I turned around.

A second Levi stood there. Physically he was identical to my Levi, except he wasn't. There was an impregnable air about him. A flawlessness. I had the feeling that if he removed his shirt, there wouldn't be any scars.

I couldn't hear anything the pretender was saying, but the real Levi's face was red and the veins in his neck throbbed. I was scared he was going to stroke out from rage. My blood dagger held aloft, I rushed the pretender and bounced off some kind of shield.

"Whatever impetuous action you were about to under-take. Don't." Moran, the Queen's henchman stepped out of the revolving door, holding his motherfucker of a sword. He wore his normal white disco-inspired suit and boots, his white hair cut shorter than the last time I'd seen it.

I pressed against the forcefield I was stuck in. Now I couldn't even hear my Levi's side of the argument. All I could see was the anguish on his face. I gripped the blood dagger so hard that my palms burned, but my vicious slashes failed to penetrate the shield.

Dropping my blood armor, I slammed my magic into the forcefield, tearing it down.

Another one immediately sprung up.

Three more times Moran and I played this game until I snarled, "Enough."

"That's not for you to determine." Moran watched the proceedings dispassionately. "Nor is it your place to intervene."

"How is this Levi's heart's desire?"

Moran laughed. "Wherever did you get that idea?"

"Isn't that the price when entering Hedon for the first time? The Queen looked into my heart, saw my deepest desire, and gave it to me."

Results not as expected.

"Did she?" Moran's sword disappeared. "Or did she look into your heart and see your deepest fear?"

That visit with my fake father had brought up my worst nightmare. I'd been forced to trust him—and failed. Then I'd killed him. Was that my deepest fear? That the release of my magic had started me down a path where I'd have to kill Adam?

Impossible. I would never… But what if I had to in order to get the scroll? Not literally kill him, but take his magic? Break him. For all intents and purposes destroy him as definitively as if I had murdered him. Images of the gibbering mess that I'd reduced Mr. Sharp to rose up hot and thick, making me gag.

I swayed backwards on my feet like I'd been punched.

"You're not entirely wrong," Moran said. "Often our deepest desires are tightly bound up with our worst fears. You faced yours, and now Mr. Montefiore must confront his."

I tore the magic out of the force field one final time. There was a slight pull on the air around me, and it dissolved. But it was too late.

93

The fake Levi was gone.

So was mine.

My blood armor snapped back into place and I stared Moran down with a cold smile. "Technically we're not in Hedon yet, so you're not protected by the Black Heart Rule."

"Correct. Bluster and threaten all you wish, Ashira, but that won't bring him back."

"What did you do to him?"

Moran plucked a thread off his sleeve. "Did you know that Mr. Montefiore is the first House Head to ever visit the Queen? Willingly," he amended.

"That's no reason to hurt him."

"The Queen is not going to hurt him."

"She's already hurt him." I'd had to face my father, Levi had to face himself. How many new scars would he bear in places I'd never see?

"If he can't take care of himself, what use would the Queen have for him?" Moran gave me a low sweeping bow, stepped backward into the revolving door, and was lost to sight.

Levi had to prove himself.

There was nothing I could do to help Levi with his immediate situation. Losing the armor and the dagger, I stepped through the revolving door, bracing myself to be overwhelmed by a deafening, nauseating magic.

But I wasn't.

Still eternal night, the sticky quality of the air was gone. The magic was a cool mist. I started, double checking I was in the correct place, but as always with this entrance, I'd come through to the tiny plaza with the weed-choked fountain. I'd always found Hedon's magic repulsive, yet the foundational magic that had been a blaring dissonance making my skin crawl had changed into a vanilla bean–scented kiss.

Hedon had been broken, but its last remaining Architect

had fixed it beautifully. It could no longer be expanded, but it was also no longer in danger of blowing apart at the seams.

Following one of the crooked cobblestone streets into the business district, I stopped at the kiosk with the electric blue ramen bowl floating above it. A bald man whistling a jaunty tune rolled out handmade noodles on a large board. I asked for directions to the cocktail bar with the Queen of Hearts' logo and he sent me to a street three blocks over where the Green Olive was located.

This area was a trippy cross between *Blade Runner* and a renaissance fair, all bathed in the glow of dozens of magic signs that hung in the sky brighter than any neon. Women in velvet gowns sung choral harmonies to entice buyers to their stall, which sold deadly-looking wind-up toys made of metal and spite.

Another stall was shrouded in smoke, with only a steampunk cat mask visible through the swirl of fog. A paw extended wearing an intricate ring made up of dozens of tiny gold and silver gears.

"Poison to settle your debts?" a voice purred. "It's thought-activated."

The gears lifted off the band and flew together, transforming into a black pointed barb.

"Handy, but not what I'm in the market for," I said.

"Another time." The barb fell back into the gold and silver gears adorning the ring and the paw retreated into the mist.

I hurried around a corner into an outdoor covered market. There were no walls, but fluted columns soared up to a glass ceiling. One stall showcased pyramids of spices in jewel tones that promised both enhanced flavor and useful benefits like paralysis and death. Another featured rows and rows of eyeballs. The proprietor lifted her eye patch to pop an eyeball in. With each blink, she enthusiastically described all the various modes: night vision, X-ray vision, and—she glared at a rat scurrying by, which dropped dead on the spot —looks that killed.

I declined her promotional offer of twenty percent off my first eyeball.

The rows grew narrower as I made my way to the back. This area was mostly given over to restaurants, a cacophony of smells from garlic, seafood, and baked goods to something acrid that made my eyes water. Clanging cookware assaulted my senses.

There was only one non-food stall here. Liquids in a rainbow of colors were housed in glass bottles, some delicately wrought, others heavy enough to bash someone's skull in without any damage to the glass. Alongside them were unguents in cracked clay pots and shining tins, their lids open to display the goods.

For a perfume stall, there should have been a riot of scents but I could smell nothing over the food.

A woman with pale gold eyes stepped out of the stall, offering to sell me a rose-red perfume that she promised would induce love. Refusing, I tried to zigzag sideways to the exit, but I was blocked by a kiosk rolled directly into my path.

"How about this?" She followed me, holding up a gorgeous bottle with art deco flourishes and a fat, tasseled perfume pump. Inside, a midnight-blue liquid swirled.

"No, thanks." To avoid her, I jogged diagonally to my left, accidentally knocking aside a plump man whose arms overflowed with prickly scarlet plants that looked otherworldly.

"It's an experience like no other." The woman with the bottle followed me.

I tried to speed up but my passage through the press of shoppers and chaos of deliveries was impossibly slow and I stopped in frustration.

There was a furtive waving from my right. Adam, or the

fake Hedon version I kept encountering, stood wedged between a raw foods bar—the food in question being eerily unidentifiable—and a place with rows of chicken feet hanging by the entrance. Wearing the battered black trench coat he'd been so fond of, Fake Adam motioned me over, but I shook my head.

The Green Olive and its answers about Mayan awaited. I had no time for gameplaying with Reasonable Facsimile Dad.

Unfortunately, my hesitation allowed the woman to catch up to me. She sprayed a plume of perfume in my face. "Very good, yes?"

It smelled cold and sharp, like being outside at 2AM and hearing a creak from behind. You know it's nothing. It's nothing. But it's not nothing.

I plucked at my clothing, my eyes darting around the market. "What scent was that?"

She was gone.

Everyone was staring at me. Cold sweat beaded the back of my neck. I sought out Adam, because even the illusion of my father was better than the sneers of derision and voices pitched low.

I couldn't find him. Sound and color spun distortedly. I clapped my hands over my ears, paralyzed. There was no way out.

A phalanx of the Queen's Guard, in black tactical gear with mesh obscuring their faces, marched into the market. The Queen's logo of a heart with a crown and scepter was stitched on their upper arms. They stopped, their gazes homing in on me.

The Queen had sent them. Bringing Levi had forced her decision into whether I was her enemy or not.

My heart kicked against my ribcage twice and I bolted, fleeing up the narrow rows. The vibration of thudding boots shivered up through my feet. How would I escape them?

There. Just ahead, peeking out from behind the side wall of a storefront. Adam watched me with a forlorn look.

I sprinted over to him. "Help me."

"You had your chance to escape, little jewel." Adam held out his hand. "Now you have to hide."

The guards marched closer.

"Show me." Clasping hands, we ran blindly through the market until the covered area fell away into a dense thorny thicket. Was his grip too tight? Was he leading me only to betray me?

I tore free and, crouching low, eased into the bushes, twisting through them until I'd lost him. My leather jacket took the brunt of the damage, my arms up to protect my face. I stopped, listening for footsteps, the branches comforting in their confinement.

I could stay here forever.

No, they'd find me here too. I had to go deeper. Hide so thoroughly that no one would find me.

"Good girl." Adam appeared, squeezed in next to me in this tight space. "I taught you well."

He hadn't taught me, though. He hadn't been there at all.

And he wasn't here now.

Sorrow, heavy and dense, welled up inside me. I manifested a blood dagger, feeling the weight of it so irrevocable in my palm. Then I lifted the blade and slashed myself.

Chapter 9

The pain in my forearm was accompanied by a clarity that cut through the fog of this induced paranoia.

"You," I said to False Adam, "begone."

"Little jewel—"

No, I knew better now. There was one person in Hedon who knew enough about me to conjure that image of my father up in the first place. One person who would want me incapacitated and unable to fight back.

The Queen.

My blood pounded in my ears but I kept my anger in check. Levi was with her, unaware he might be a pawn in this game.

"You don't know me," I said. "Not really. You can extrapolate some general hopes and fears, but if you really wanted me to give up, then you should have given me amnesia because I won't quit."

"Interesting," he said, so like the Queen, that I shivered. "But are you prepared for how deep the shadows go?"

He disappeared, as did the thicket. I was in the perfume market once more, hiding under a table, and still being stared at, but this time in alarm by a couple of shopkeepers.

The dagger. Right. I made it disappear and crawled out. "I come in peace."

I ran back to the perfume stall where a man in colorful Middle Eastern robes and a bushy beard asked if he could help me.

"Where's the woman with the pale gold eyes?"

"I'm the only one here. This is my stall."

"Impossible. She was here." Everything else about the stall was the same. "What types of perfumes are these?"

"Not perfumes," he said. "Emotions."

Silly me. "And you just go around spraying sample feelings on unwitting patrons?"

The shopkeeper looked horrified. "That is forbidden. To do so is to risk the Black Heart Rule."

Was it now? "Did the sirens go off a few moments ago?"

He shook his head. Some rando had happened to defy the edict and just gotten away with it? Not likely. The Queen had masterminded this.

I couldn't and wouldn't hide from her. She'd made her move, now it was mine. I sought out the guards, demanding to be taken to her.

They ignored me so thoroughly, I may as well have been a ghost.

"Fine," I snapped. "I'll go to the palace myself."

The guards surrounded me. "You will not," one said, with absolute authority. "If you do, you face the dungeons."

With that, they swept past me. Standing here seething wouldn't help Levi and it wouldn't advance my search for answers with Mayan.

I got fresh instructions to the Green Olive from the market, but when I arrived, the bar was in smoking ruins. The entire blackened structure had collapsed in on itself, heat still shimmering off the wreckage. It was only identifiable by the martini glass sign with the words "Green Olive" that sputtered magically in and out.

The taste of ash coated my lips.

Guards cordoned the area off, one of them arguing with a short, pudgy man in a pinstripe suit with red suspenders and spats, those weird white shoe coverings with black buttons up one side.

"Don't tell me you can't do anything!" the man cried, spittle flying from his mouth. "He torched my bar."

The guard pushed the man back a few steps. "Obviously not, Alfie," she said, in an Irish accent. "Since he died two months ago. Now get out of our way so we can find out who did." She pointed and he moved to the other side of the street, his shoulders slumped.

I approached him, my boots crunching over random sooty debris that had rolled onto the street. "Sorry about your bar."

Alfie clenched his fists. "This is just the beginning, but they won't listen."

"The beginning of what?"

He made a show of looking around and then he leaned in. "Gunter's revenge," he whispered.

"What's that?" I pulled out my phone and called up a photo of Mayan.

"Gunter said I stole his business and his woman. Swore to come after me and take it all away, including my life." He blotted his sweaty forehead with the red handkerchief.

"I guess you're not under the Queen's personal protection."

He scoffed. "Hardly. Very few are."

The Black Heart Rule didn't apply as a deterrent to keep Gunter from coming after Alfie, though Gunter's deceased status should have been a pretty effective obstacle. "Did you do what he accused you of?

Alfie snapped his suspenders, making his belly jiggle. "It was a good business and she was a fine-looking woman. But now look at it." He gestured to the smoking beams.

"The bastard destroyed the business that he, himself, started."

"Isn't Gunter dead?"

Alfie fixed me with a look of scathing incredulity. "He swore revenge. Like death would stop him."

Okay, crazy man. Enough indulging you. "Listen, a friend of mine told me about your place and now she's missing. Do you remember seeing her?"

He studied the photo of Mayan. "Oh sure. She's been here almost every night the past couple weeks."

"She has? Was she with anyone?"

"Nah, came in alone."

"Did you ever see her leave with anyone?"

"Not that I remember." He gave a start and his eyes grew wide. "I ain't done nothing."

"I doubt that's the case, Alfie. Why else would you leach of all color in that manner?" Moran said, sauntering up to us.

Even without any sign of Moran's sword, Alfie's eyes bugged out of his head. He spun and ran off.

"Aren't you going to chase him?" I said.

"No. Alfie's an irritant, but he's harmless. Come. Her Highness is ready for you."

I planted my hands on my hips. "Is she now? You don't want to dose me up with a little Eau De Meekness to ensure my obedience?"

"So dramatic." Moran took my arm and we shifted— from one step to the next coming out onto the Queen's flagstone terrace.

She sat on a loveseat wearing a formal red gown. Levi was across from her on a rickety chair, his expression tight, almost like he was caged in.

Moran positioned himself to the Queen's left.

"Ah, blanquita," she purred in her Spanish-accented English. "Mr. Montefiore has been most passionate about his circumstances, but I am unable to help and, as you brought him, I would like you to take him home."

"I've done everything you asked," I said. "Moreover, anything you've agreed to, whether you liked it or not, was of your own free will. If you have a problem with me, then talk to me. I'm done with these games."

"What games?" Levi said, the calm he was going for undercut by the strain in his voice.

"You forget your place," the Queen said.

"Or I finally understand it," I said. "I'm not simply a pawn on this gameboard anymore. Even queens can be toppled."

Moran's sword appeared in his hand. "Very bold of you to assume I'd allow you to threaten Her Highness and live."

"Not a threat," I said. "If I can't take care of myself, what use would the Queen have for me? Right, Your Majesty? Ally or enemy. What's it to be?"

I had enough enemies, and besides, I admired her.

"Impatience is a folly of youth." The Queen crossed her leg, her red stiletto dangling from her foot. "Surprise me with something of value."

Like jewels? No, that wouldn't work. What would? The Queen always said knowledge was power. There were a number of things about Chariot that I could enlighten her on that would be a surprise, but I was loath to give her too much on that front. Not until she was firmly in my corner. I'd find something else relevant to her interests that could cement the deal.

"I do that and we have an alliance? No more games. No more giving up memories when I come here. And I want a gold token for passage."

A sly smile curled over her lips. "Chica, if you can surprise me, I'll agree to whatever you'd like."

"Deal."

"You're willing to make a deal with Ash," Levi said, "but

won't concede the value of allying with House Pacifica when we're both being targeted?"

"It is not the first time, nor will it be the last," the Queen said. "You are a figurehead, Mr. Montefiore. A powerful one, but a figurehead nonetheless. I don't think you have the cojones to bring anything of worth to myself or Hedon. See yourself out."

Levi gave a one-shouldered shrug and stood up. "I'll go, Your Highness," he said, "but remember this. Hedon needs us more than we need you."

The Queen arched an eyebrow. Uh-oh.

I ran over and tugged on Levi's sleeve, but he was immovable. Jeez, Levi, you were undoing all my fine work of five minutes ago. "Thank you and have a pleasant day," I said.

"Are you threatening me in my own home?" She tilted her head with a curious expression, much like a cat. Or a tiger looking at prey who hasn't behaved properly—before they slashed their throat with a lazy claw.

"Not at all," he said. "I'm simply reminding you that Hedon is safe and whole, and cannot be expanded anymore. Abraham was most forthcoming, including where all the entrances and exits are around the world."

"You told Levi about Abraham?" the Queen said to me.

"No. I swear." I was so discombobulated under her glower that I'd forgotten all about the existence of my armor and was half-hidden behind Levi, using him as a shield.

"She didn't need to." Levi tugged me out to stand beside him. "Abraham was registered in my territory. Did you really think I'd overlook the presence of one of the original architects of Hedon? Oh, and he's under my protection now. Help me or I'll make life very difficult for you."

I don't know what Levi's problem was that he'd conjured up that more formidable version of himself back at Harbour Center, because right now he was pretty damn impressive.

Even the Queen reappraised him with a cool glance. "I could seal us off."

"You could, but you won't," Levi said. "This place has very few natural resources. You need the stream of goods that traffic in and out of here. Now, someone is targeting us both. If you persist in your isolationist position, I'll persuade every last House Head to make sure you're cut off. Your population would riot, and we all know what happens to monarchs who fail to provide bread. The Queen of Hearts could share the same fate as Marie Antionette."

Moran stepped closer to Levi and me.

I didn't even have a bronze token to get us out of here. My economy class coin required us leaving the palace and getting back to that weed-choked fountain. Really, Levi? Did you have to bust out your cojones in quite this fashion? Miles would kill me if Levi got turned into a statue.

Hostility bubbled between the three of them while I tried to shove Levi, who stubbornly planted his feet, refusing to back down.

"Who's the German you were so interested in when you were helping Omar, chica?"

I blinked, carefully forming a response. "He was involved with a person of interest."

"Is he Chariot?" she said. "Mr. Montefiore would like me to be forthcoming. It seems fair to get something up front. A little quid pro quo of good faith."

"He is."

"And what is his importance to you? Specifically. You were very agitated at the prospect of his return."

"That's Ashira's business," Levi said, with a dismissive wave.

"Funny. She said it was House business and as she's confirmed he works for Chariot, that makes it my business." The Queen crossed her legs and leaned back against the cushions. "Should you wish to proceed."

Levi shot me a contrite look.

Damn it, Levi. This was exactly why I didn't want the Queen involved. She already knew too much about my father. I didn't want to add the fact that he'd coerced a Van Gogh into warding up my magic and the means by which it could be warded up once again.

We were working toward ally status, not besties at camp sharing everything over friendship bracelets.

My self-preservation skills were unparalleled—with everyone except the Queen. Now I'd been neatly maneuvered into a position of having to expose yet another vulnerability. So, I'd turn it into a strength. Was this information enough to get me the alliance? "He killed a Van Gogh who the House had in custody. The same Van Gogh who originally suppressed my magic."

I waited for her follow-up question demanding details, but it didn't come. She and Moran exchanged a long and complicated look.

"I will agree to an equal and open exchange of information only as it pertains to why we were both set up to take the fall at the auction," the Queen said.

Levi got his alliance but I didn't get mine. I was positive that she hadn't known about the Van Gogh and my ward; however, that information wasn't surprising enough. Whatever I presented had to be truly noteworthy to secure her agreement. It wouldn't be easy, but I'd find something.

"Not good enough, Highness," Levi said. "I want everything you discover that even tangentially relates to that. I'll provide the same in return."

The Queen studied him for an uncomfortably long time.

To Levi's credit he didn't fidget. "Don't underestimate my worth or my power. Now, have I demonstrated my usefulness enough for you?"

"You have," she said. "I'll grant your complete exchange of information."

I raised my hand. "One more thing?"

The Queen gave an incredulous laugh. "You have chutz-pah, I'll give you that. Go ahead."

I showed her the photo of Mayan. "She's a Mundane who I believe first entered Hedon a couple of weeks ago."

Beside me, Levi tensed, but he didn't say anything.

"Should she mean something to me?" the Queen said.

"You know everyone who comes through for the first time."

"Not by their face," she said. "Only Mr. Montefiore has visited for the first time during that period. If this Mundane was indeed here, she'd been here before."

Oh, what a tangled web we weave. If Mayan had angered the wrong people in Hedon, we might never learn what happened to her.

Judging from Levi's clenched jaw, he'd reached the same conclusion. Don't shoot the messenger, dude.

Chapter 10

The Queen returned us to House HQ. Once in the elevator, Levi ordered me to come up to his office after I'd picked up Mrs. Hudson.

"Is it wise for me to continue being seen here with the mole and all?" I said.

"He doesn't work on my floor. But when we're in public together, we'll keep up appearances of hating each other."

"Not a problem." The elevator doors opened on the sixth floor in full view of the security area. I shot Levi the finger and stepped off the elevator.

I wound my way to Miles' office. "Knock. Knock."

"Levi's back? He's all right?"

I hesitated and Miles went as still as the bonsai delicately growing on his desk. "That first visit isn't easy," I said. "But he's unharmed and he got his desired results."

"Good enough."

"Where's Priya?" I just wanted to go home.

"She's off-site at a meeting."

"Did she leave Mrs. Hudson with you?" Miles shook his head. Fuck. "If she checks in, tell her I want the dog back."

I hadn't realized how much I'd been hoping to distract

myself with the puppy until I stood there alone and adrift by the elevators. The thought of returning to my office felt desolate. I attempted to contact Rafael, because even that conversation would be better than being by myself, but once again got no response.

Well, I wasn't going anywhere before Levi and I debriefed. I headed for the top floor to play "get past the House dragon and into Levi's office."

The Executive level was filled with the hum of Very Important Activity set amidst stunning views of the city, while Levi's personal art collection featuring works from Escher to Dali graced pale gold walls.

I stopped at the long reception desk outside his office doors. "Hello, Veronica."

Levi's Executive Assistant was actually a sleek blonde woman, not a flying lizard, though she had a tendency to flare her nostrils and possibly belch invisible bursts of smoke whenever I approached. She protected Levi like a dragon-in-designer-clothing guarded treasure, but despite her many faults, she was irritatingly organized and well informed.

I steeled myself for the inevitable comment on my appearance.

"You got a puppy?!" She held up a squirming Mrs. Hudson, who barked and wagged her tail. "Huh. Look at that. She missed you?"

"Obviously. I'm a delight." A hot possessive fury coursed through me and I snatched the pug out of Veronica's French-manicured clutches, along with the bag of puppy supplies leaning against the desk.

"No need to be rude," she said, snippily.

Mrs. Hudson licked my jaw. That's right, puppy. Show the dragon lady who you love.

"Levi wanted to see me," I said.

As if summoned, the door to Levi's inner sanctum swung open.

"Going home with the dog that is most emphatically not yours?" Levi had removed his suit jacket, his shirt rolled up to expose his corded forearms.

This version of Levi provoked an even deeper longing in me than his naked body did. And a deeper irritation. Most of the world never got past the embodiment of House Head or the charming social version. They never saw behind the title, but I did, and this vulnerable Levi, with dark scruff shadowing his jaw and a softness to the line of his shoulders, had mattered to me. So why wasn't the reverse true? Why hadn't he listened when I said that involving the Queen wasn't smart? Aside from his token protest, he'd had no problem using me to get what he wanted.

To be fair to Veronica, she barely paid Levi any attention, other than to hand him a couple of colored files. Whatever protective urges she felt for him, they weren't sexual.

"Are we debriefing or not?" I said.

Levi motioned me into his office. "Hold my calls," he tossed off over his shoulder. "Sit," he said. "You look like you need a drink."

"Always." I nodded at the half-empty tumbler on his desk. "I see I have some catching up to do." I sank onto the sofa next to the wood burning fireplace, stretching out my legs to give a drowsy Mrs. Hudson more lap real estate.

Give Levi his due: he didn't stint on the booze. Out came the premium bottle of Jack Daniel's Limited Edition Number 27 Gold. He poured a splash into a second tumbler and handed it to me.

The alcohol slid down my throat like ambrosia, much like Rafael's magic had. I coughed, suddenly choking on the whiskey. "Went down the wrong way," I sputtered. Composing myself, I found my happy self-righteous place. "You must be pleased with yourself."

"You never mentioned that the Queen knew about the German." He sat in his desk chair.

"That's not the point. I asked you not to bring her into this."

"I'm sorry it made you uncomfortable but we're in a 'greater good' situation. You of all people, as a Jezebel, should know that."

"For fuck's sake, I agreed to help you, didn't I?"

Levi took a sip of his drink. "Then why are you so angry?"

Because you didn't put me first. Because after all we've become to each other and all we've been through, I thought that meant more to you than it did. I'm your present and Mayan is your past. But somehow all I am is just another weapon in your arsenal.

"The Queen now knows that a Van Gogh can ward me up," I said. "I'd rather she didn't."

"She could have found that out a number of ways," he replied.

For a smart man, he was incredibly obtuse.

"You're right. Let me give you the rundown on what I learned about Mayan." I updated him as succinctly as possible, though truthfully, there wasn't much to tell.

"Have you had a chance to learn anything more about your dad's book?"

"Not really. Is that it?"

Levi tapped his finger against his glass. "Do you know why I held off threatening the Queen for as long as I did?"

"Because you didn't think of it sooner?"

"Because you weren't there yet. I wasn't going to play that card until I had you next to me and we could both flee if necessary."

"No person left behind, huh? Smart team protocol."

"Fuck team protocol. I wasn't leaving *you*."

"Oh," I said faintly.

Over the mantel hung a large photograph of a road running through a green landscape. The ground rose up in the center of the photo to split in two, effectively turning the road into a half-open zipper. The photographer had taken an item rendered almost invisible through familiarity and shown that through his lens, it contained wonder and surprise, not just utility.

I looked back at Levi and pressed my hands to my cheeks.

"You weren't the only one who got life lessons from their father," Levi said. "I learned never to reveal anything that mattered."

My heart lodged in my chest, beating erratically. I wished I could run my fingers around the edges of our relationship and understand its true shape. There were too many facets to us, and just as with a diamond, more facets didn't mean more brilliance or more sparkle. As my father had said, "If you want to spend the extra money, spend it on clarity."

"I met him once, you know?" Levi said. "Your dad. Back when he still worked for Isaac. I was about ten and Adam had come over for a meeting. He showed me this magic trick with a coin he put in my hand except when I opened it, the coin was gone."

"I remember that one. It was on the table in front of him and you never noticed. Two basic tenets of a con. Misdirect and hide the con in plain sight." A wistful ache throbbed behind my ribs.

"He gave me the coin to practice with. I said that my dad didn't like magic, and he laughed saying that Isaac had no problem with it when it suited him. Then he pressed the coin into my hand and told me I could practice in secret."

"Did you?" I said.

Levi smiled. "No. I had a very short attention span back then. But I didn't want to hurt his feelings so I promised to hide it in my special hiding place and practice every day."

"That's cute."

Levi tilted his head, pensive. "Your dad gave me a magic trick to dazzle and entertain. Mine…"

I wanted to wrap my arms around his waist and lay my head on his chest, feeling his heart beat under my cheek. I settled for cuddling the puppy. Mrs. Hudson resettled herself without waking up. "Isaac played soccer with you and he's the reason you're here, guiding all of us. When it feels too dark, sometimes the only thing you can do is hold tight to those happy times because they still count." I paused. "Unless your mom has a car you can steal and crash. Then you've got options."

He sighed. "She doesn't drive."

"Sorry, dude. You're shit out of luck. Good memories it is. So, what's another one that you have of Isaac?"

Levi perked up. "He has this antique mantel clock in his office. His most cherished possession. Takes meticulous care of it, has this whole ritual with a key to wind it properly."

"Did he have you help him?"

"Never once. The clock creeped me out as a kid anyway. It had this quote from the Old Testament engraved on it. 'You must not make idols for yourselves or set up a carved image or sacred pillar, or place a sculpted stone in your land to bow down to it. For I am the Lord your God.' Magic fell into that same category for Isaac. An abomination."

"How is this a good memory?"

Levi wheeled his desk chair close to me and leaned in conspiratorially. "One day I'm going to smash that thing into smithereens. That'll be a great memory."

"Wow." I lifted an imaginary crown off my head and held it out to him. "King of Dysfunction."

Levi took it. "No need to rest on formalities. You may call me 'My Liege.'"

"I could, but we both know that will never happen." I paused. "Why didn't your mother leave him?"

"She was scared of what Isaac would do to her if she did.

113

His own father had left him and my Nonna when he was little and he had massive abandonment issues." Levi gave me a pointed look.

"Imply that I have anything in common with your father and I'll stab you."

Levi mimed taking the crown off his head and putting it on mine.

My smile faded. "I did learn one thing. Not about the book. No other Jezebel has ever experienced magic cravings, and if I suffer a few more episodes involving angel magic, I may be beyond help. I may be anyways." My feeble attempt at humor didn't land.

Levi's gaze raked over me, leaving me hot and cold and strangely uncomfortable in my own skin. "The feather is locked up. You're safe."

"If only it was that simple." I told him about the *Sefer Raziel HaMalakh*, stopping short of Rafael's role in bringing me back from the brink of insanity.

"I miss living in ignorance."

I patted his thigh. "I know."

He threaded his fingers through mine. "While you're beyond help in many, many areas, this isn't going to be one of them."

"Some things are beyond even your indomitable will." I softened my words with a squeeze of our fingers. "Not that I plan on shuffling off this mortal coil any time soon. Just that these urgings are a bit more of a wrinkle than I'd anticipated."

"To put it mildly."

"Yeah, well. A gift for understatement. That's me."

"What are you going to do when you assemble the book and then have to destroy it, if you risk being lost to that magic?"

"Um." I disengaged our hands. "There's kind of a way

114

that keeps me safe. Like magic medicine? It also takes away the cravings."

Levi's eyes narrowed. "That should be a good thing."

"When Asherah created Attendants, the magic she gave them was all about serving and protecting Jezebels. Cool, huh?"

"You're saying that so optimistically that I'm already worried."

"It turns out that I can ingest Rafael's magic, and it doesn't destroy it, and all my cravings go away. Magic healing, bitches," I finished weakly, with my fist raised.

Levi rose and crossed over to his desk, apparently filled with the sudden need to straighten the three folders laying there. "Rafael is fine with that arrangement?" he said in an inscrutable tone.

"He's my Attendant. My fellow team member."

"I'm your team member." He gave the files a final sharp tap.

"You're my boss. The Charlie to our Angels." I shifted the pug because my left leg was falling asleep.

"The Mycroft to your Sherlock and company?" Levi said.

"Quit making erroneous analogies to Sherlock. You pain me and embarrass yourself. We've established you're Watson."

"Who was Sherlock's partner." He set the pendulum toy on his desk in motion, the balls clicking together.

"I mean, technically… Stop changing the subject. I require answers. Assistance. Right now Rafael and his extensive knowledge of all things Jezebel is best positioned to offer it."

"And his magic," Levi said.

"That too."

Levi was quiet for a moment, then he stopped the pendulum toy mid-swing. "You're right. I realize I can get a little—"

"Highhanded? Overbearing?"

"Protective. But don't mince words or anything."

"I never do."

"However, you still didn't actually answer the question. Even if you're not taking his magic, there has to be a toll."

My Attendant losing control, my inability to understand what he needs. Him hating me.

"We haven't discovered it yet, but Rafael is fine with the arrangement." Did that sound too forced? Too cheerful? I didn't want Levi getting the wrong impression. Which was actually the right impression. But really, what good would it do telling him about the whole arousal thing? Not that Rafael and I were doing anything wrong. I'd never suck off another man, getting him hot and bothered, if that were the case. Not unless I didn't have a choice. Shit, Ash, stop thinking.

I dropped my eyes, petting Mrs. Hudson like the fate of the universe depended on it.

"I'm glad he was there for you."

Startled, I met Levi's gaze but there was no censure there. Just concern. "That's not what I expected you to say."

His lips twisted wryly. "Me neither."

"If it makes you feel better, there's still only one other member of my monster support group."

"You're just saying that because I make biscotti."

"It doesn't hurt."

The last of the indigo and tangerine streaked twilight faded away, and lights in surrounding office buildings dimmed into maintenance mode. It was my cue to leave, but there was one last thing I had to say.

"I saw you. Both of you, at the entrance to Hedon."

Levi tore his gaze away from the view. "Ash, I may not look it, but I'm tired. I don't want to be psychoanalyzed again."

"You're wrong."

"About what?" he said, defeated and exhausted.

"Your heart's desire," I said. "Your worst fear. You're already so damn capable. You aren't going to let your people down."

He swirled the amber liquid in his glass. "I appreciate the vote of confidence, but—"

"No 'buts.' You took on the Queen. This capricious ruler who never wants to get involved has agreed to share information with you."

He slashed his hand through the air like "enough." "She was concerned about my threat to cut the place off."

"Please. The simplest response would have been to behead you or stick you in her Garden of People. She could have done away with both of us with no one the wiser. She agreed because in her eyes you're a worthy player on the gameboard. If the Queen believes that, the Untainted Party doesn't stand a chance."

"You aren't onboard with my beheading?"

"Only forty-five percent of me. You still have your uses." I blinked innocently at him. "In that you now sign my paycheck. All joking aside? Don't let your father win. You were a little kid and Isaac physically abused you. That didn't make you weak or helpless. You survived and instead of repeating the cycle, you're so incredibly compassionate." I placed my hand on my loudly growling stomach. "Whoops. Sorry."

"Do you want to eat something?" Was he asking me out or was he planning on ordering take-out and feeding his employee after their debrief? "Why don't you and Mrs. Hudson come over and I'll feed both of you?"

It might have been a perfectly innocent offer, but Levi's house was tangled up in memories of incredible sex. That was great. I could handle sex, I just wasn't certain about blurring it with dinner before I'd figured shit out about us.

"I'm beat and the pug needs a walk. I'll grab something on the way home."

"You're sure?"

No. I'm not. Which is why I'm going home while I have the willpower to do so. I averted my gaze from his mesmerizing blue eyes, busying myself standing up without waking the puppy.

"Rain check." I did a double take at the book sitting on his desk. *The Hound of the Baskervilles.* "You're reading Sherlock? I knew your knowledge was only Wiki deep."

"Wow. I'm trying and all I get is grief."

"That might be kind of very sweet."

"I've got your back." Levi brushed his lips over mine.

That wasn't in question. But he also had my trust, my respect, and my friendship. Now he was reading Sherlock because it was important to me. Levi Montefiore, who had no free time to speak of and who had been the bane of my existence during our youth, was reading a book simply because I liked it. So many things were different between us and I was constantly wondering where I stood. Life had been so much easier when we couldn't stand each other.

Chapter 11

Let it never be said that it took Ashira Cohen more than one pee-fest on her floor to learn her lesson. I bolted awake on Thursday morning as soon as the puppy did, hustling to shove my feet into boots, clip a leash onto her collar, and get her outside to do her business.

At least it wasn't raining. I hopped from foot to foot to stay warm, my breath misting the cool April air, and the jolt of adrenaline from my rude awakening amping the curl of anxiety tingling through me.

Today was the first official meeting of Team Jezebel. I wasn't worried about Rafael meeting Priya or Arkady, but Levi had insisted on being present, and the ways those two could dislike each other were legion. Who had more authority, who had more of a claim on me, whose reaction was the most valid should I suddenly give in to my cravings and fall upon Rafael's magic like an eight ball of cocaine?

There was also a part of me that worried Rafael had washed his hands of me altogether.

My stomach was almost too knotted up to guzzle down the coffee that Priya shoved into my hand when the pug and I got inside. It turned out the gesture wasn't all that altruistic.

She decided it gave her leave to lounge on my bed as I tore through my closet deciding what to wear.

I scowled at her ivory tunic and matching leggings. She looked like a soccer mom.

"Who exactly are you trying to impress?" Priya said, scratching Mrs. Hudson's tummy. "Because your window with me shut a long time ago, Levi's already onboard, Arkady barely tolerates your authority so the effort is wasted on him, and your Attendant seems more resigned than excited about this gig."

I sniffed a blue sweater, grimaced, and pitched it into the corner. "As the Jezebel on the team, I feel it's up to me to set the correct tone."

"Which is what?"

"I. Don't. Know." I tossed my leather pants on the bed and paired it with a long sleeved T-shirt. Black and blacker.

"Maybe I should lend you some pink," Priya said. "Infuse some optimism into the cynical disdain currently projected."

"This is why I've done shit on my own and not in a group."

"Because of the color-coordinated outfits? Isn't it your general dislike of all mankind?"

"That too." I pushed her off my bed. "Let me get dressed."

My nerves hadn't abated by the time we reached the office. I juggled the dog's leash and three take-out boxes from Muffin Top containing a variety of baked goods and grabbed the door handle. Priya had the box of coffee that I'd purchased at Starbucks, along with a bag of creamers and a box of sugar cubes.

Eleanor poked her head out when we entered the reception area. "Is this Mrs. Hudson?" She crouched down and tentatively extended one hand to the pug, a large latte cup with the dregs of foam around the edges, and Muffin Top's new logo on it, in the other.

I dropped the leash and the puppy trundled over to her.

"I'm more of a cat person," Eleanor said, giving the pug a half-hearted pat. Shocker.

"I'm more of a cactus person," I said.

Eleanor frowned. "But you got a dog?"

"She's not—"

Priya cut off the rest of my sentence with a sharp boff across my head. "Ash is expanding her horizons."

That's right. I was. "You're a fan of Muffin Top, huh?" I said.

Priya and Eleanor both blinked at me in surprise. I glared at Pri. How quickly she'd forgotten I'd evolved into social Ash.

"I only recently started going there." Eleanor tapped the logo on the latte cup. "That's my design."

I'd misjudged her. No, I'd dismissed her skillset entirely. It was a timely reminder that people had facets and clarity was key. Would I be able to see Adam clearly? I was still furious at him for leaving us and suppressing my magic—and desperate to see him again. Why couldn't I pick one emotion and commit? Would I be able to reconcile all his facets when I finally found him? And what would happen if I couldn't?

"The logo is super cool," I said, flipping open the lid on the top bakery box and proffering its goods.

Eleanor smiled and helped herself to a muffin. "Thanks."

"You're welcome." I wrangled my keys out of my pocket and unlocked the door to Cohen Investigations, spending the next ten minutes arranging and re-arranging the muffins, donuts, and scones on random platters scrounged from our shared kitchen. I'd grabbed mismatched mugs and some spoons as well.

When my attempts to exquisitely plate the goods still

looked like I was hiding evidence of food theft, I gave up channeling Martha Stewart and dragged an extra chair into the office so all five of us could sit.

Ten more minutes until anyone was expected. I flipped through *A Study in Scarlet*, but it didn't yield any more clues than the other forty-two times I'd perused it. With a long-suffering sigh, I dropped into my chair, my hands folded primly in front of me and my leg jiggling.

Priya winged a stress ball at me. "Quit it. You're rocking my fancy desk." Her cell rang. "It's my House cyber crew." Answering the phone, she walked out of our office.

Rafael was the first one to arrive, at five minutes before the 10AM start time. Today's ensemble consisted of another bowtie, this one blue to match his shirt, over which he wore a light brown vest and matching plaid tweed jacket.

Under other circumstances, his early arrival would have been a good omen of where we stood, but though he smelled like tea and first edition novels, he looked like this was the last place in the world he wanted to be.

I waved him to a seat. "About the other night—"

"Unless your other team members are tardy," Rafael said in his poshest and most clipped voice, "they will be arriving at any moment. There is no reason to hash out your shortcomings when it is imperative that you conduct yourself as befitting a Jezebel."

"*My* shortcomings?"

Priya strolled in. "Well, hello, professor. Welcome to the colonies. I'm Priya."

Rafael got this befuddled look as he shook her hand. "You're not what I was expecting."

"I hope that's a good thing," she said, with a toss of her hair.

Jesus. Kill me now. Wasn't there some sister code about chicks before Dickensian-looking extras who your best friend had snacked off of? I might have made a mistake in not getting her up to speed on what had gone down between the two of us. Not down. There had been no going down on anyone. It was a business transaction. I mentally winced. Hostile takeover?

"Pri," I said, "could you give us a moment?"

"No need." Rafael studied the copious amounts of food laid out on the desks. "Are you expecting rather more of us than you said?"

"Muffin Top is an exceptionally good bakery and I'm very hungry," I said. "I don't fault them for having such *enthralling* products, but if I did get too *attached*, I'd hoped I be honest about how badly I *craved* it. Admitting the problem is the first step."

A muscle in Rafael's jaw tensed. "Good thing my willpower and self-control is top notch. I doubt I'll fall prey to the same temptations you do."

I gasped. How dare he pin this all on me? Priya shot me a weird look.

Levi showed before I could respond, right on the dot of ten. He was in his most suited-up House Head self, complete with cuff links, tie, and leather briefcase.

"Levi Montefiore, this is Rafael Behar," I said.

"The man who's contracted our services," Rafael said. "I must say, I was surprised you agreed to take on this fight. Most wouldn't."

"Most don't have a stake in it." Levi set his briefcase on my desk and tossed his suit jacket over a chair. Any other territory he wanted to mark? "Chariot is undermining my House. I don't take that lightly."

"So long as you realize that your House is only one concern in a global problem," Rafael said. "If it comes to gaining an edge on Chariot or actively protecting your House, I trust you know exactly what decision my Jezebel and I will have to make."

"I wouldn't dream of impeding our quest to annihilate

Chariot," Levi said, formality cutting off him in sharp edges. "And she's not your Jezebel."

"Right. We're a team, so I guess technically I'm everyone's Jezebel." I rolled my eyes. "Can we please pretend like we're listening to me?"

"Then it's a pleasure to be working with you," Rafael said to Levi.

Their handshake was a touch longer and more forceful than necessary.

Person most likely to upend harmonious vibes of new team = X.

Do not solve for X.

Priya jumped in and hit Rafael with her infallible charm, asking him all kinds of questions about England and his move here. His expression remained vaguely suspicious, like he wasn't used to talking about himself.

"Any reason you're channeling a Jewish grandmother with all the food?" Levi dragged the chair with his jacket draped over it up next to mine and opened his briefcase. "There's nothing to be nervous about."

I closed my eyes briefly, inhaling the comforting smell of his oaky amber scotch and chocolate magic scent. Calm rolled over me. Then the unbidden taste of Rafael's cool, clear magic rose on my lips, and I rolled my chair farther away.

"Evil won't be defeated on an empty stomach." I waved a hand like this explained everything, really just trying to clear away Rafael's magic. "Anyway, it'll give us something to snack on while we're waiting for Arkady."

Levi extracted a slim case, which he unzipped and set on my desk with the excited pride of a parent who's nailed their kid's birthday present.

I frowned. "Why do you have a set of lock picks?"

Levi heaved a disappointed sigh and removed a basic brass cylinder lock common to most front doors with the bolt slid out. He set it next to the case. "I trained you. You train me."

"You did exactly one training session before abandoning me to seek help elsewhere."

"Semantics. Now, how do I pick a lock? I've wanted to know ever since that time the camp staff took away our candy stashes and locked them up. Miles would never teach me."

I primly clicked the bolt shut. "Because it's not something a House Head should go around doing."

"Come on, Ash." He unlocked it again and gave me a cajoling grin. "Miles is the grumpy one, you're the fun one. Which pick do I use?"

Even if he mastered this skill, when could he really use it? Plus, it would piss Miles off.

Levi's eyes shone brightly and I caved.

I snatched the ridged pick rake out of his hand, replacing it with another tool. "Tension wrench. We'll go with the fast and dirty method. Scrubbing. Essentially, you use the wrench to apply tension on the plug inside the lock, while with the pick lock, you lift the pins inside, clearing the shear line."

Levi's mouth silently repeated the words as I said them, like they were a spell he was committing to memory or he was afraid he'd lose them if he didn't practice. His eyes never left my hands. Like all this was a magic trick, and if he blinked, he'd miss it.

I demonstrated how to insert the wrench into the bottom of the keyhole. "Apply the tiniest bit of pressure and turn it like you would a key. But don't bend the wrench too much."

Levi took the wrench from me and started practicing, following my instructions with a dogged thoroughness, a tiny smile playing on his lips.

Arkady arrived with a muted wave of apology. "Sorry. I

was on the North Shore and there was an accident on the bridge that tied up traffic for two hours."

"Arkady Choi," I said, "Rafael Behar."

"Good to meet you," Arkady said.

"Likewise," Rafael replied. No bruises were incurred in their handshake.

"Mrs. Pugson, we meet again," Arkady said, helping himself to coffee with a liberal splash of milk. "Don't let me disturb your rutting."

The dog had whined until I'd brought along the damn squeaky cow toy, which she now used to conduct an experiment in friction and her nether regions.

"They're courting," I said. "Avert your eyes."

Arkady took the seat next to me.

I dug in to a jelly donut. Getting through this meeting was going to require sugar. "Rafael, help yourself. I've got a ton of food here."

"No, thank you," he said. "I don't eat sugary treats in the morning. I had yogurt and granola."

"Surely, one little scone couldn't hurt." Priya wagged a flaky triangle pastry at him like the snake in the garden of Eden. "We could split one."

Pri's flirting generally had more subtlety than a missile guidance system. This wasn't merely interest, it was a new and more exotic coping mechanism, with an Ash-shaped complication.

Why did it have to be Rafael of all people who'd cracked her shell?

However, the ever-present flutter of anxiety when I was around Priya lately eased at the sparkle in her eyes and the mirth in her smile, and Rafael wasn't engaging beyond polite friendliness, so what harm could it do?

Not to mention, that polite friendliness was a heck of a lot better than what he'd thrown at Levi and me. Maybe

Priya was my ticket to lowering Rafael's guard enough for him and me to have a serious talk.

"The straights are at it again," Arkady said quietly to me, nibbling on a muffin. "How many couples are we going to have on this mission?"

I sarcastically took a huge chomp of my jelly donut in his general direction as a response. Yeah, it was going to be weird if this kept up, but she wasn't the Priya I could talk to about everything anymore. And I wasn't the Ash who felt comfortable barging into her life all the time.

"You'd do well to improve your eating habits," Rafael was saying. To me. "A Jezebel needs to be in tip-top condition, and a proper diet is the first step in mental and physical clarity."

Levi barked a laugh. "This is Ash we're talking about."

I elbowed him and in return he stole a piece of my donut. "I'll take that under advisement," I said.

"No, you won't," Levi said.

"No, I won't," I agreed cheerfully.

Rafael took my plate with the donut away from me. "Without you operating at your best, you put us all at a serious disadvantage."

I snatched the plate back. "We *all* need to bring our A-game," I said, trotting out my best "playing nicely" smile. "Let's just get this meeting going. Pri, could you please shut the door?" I selected the lock pick with three ridges and slapped it into Levi's hand. "Insert this at the top of the lock. Keep the pressure up with the wrench and scrub the pick back and forth." I mimed the motion. "Rafael, why don't you give us a short history of Jezebels?"

"Wait. I have an update before we get started," Arkady said. "Remember the two men we captured when we rescued those teens Chariot was stealing magic from? They committed suicide."

My bite of donut stuck in my throat. "In a maximum security prison?"

Arkady ripped off a piece of banana chocolate chip muffin. "Handy, huh? Apparently, they didn't want to do time and were pressing for immunity in exchange for a deal to expose some higher-ups."

"If they didn't realize the nature of the people they were dealing with," Rafael said, "they were too stupid to live and best removed from the gene pool."

Levi nodded approvingly, his head bent over the lock.

Arkady had spoken to some of the kids we'd rescued as well, who'd assured him that Tatiana's experiments had not been conducted on them.

"That's a relief," I said. "Okay, Rafael. You're up."

To Rafael's credit, slim though it was, he delivered a clear and precise summation of Jezebels' history, worthy of the finest university professor.

"All Jezebels are descendants of their namesake, with the potentials' bloodlines traveling through the mother, like in Judaism," Rafael said, in conclusion to this portion of the lecture.

Levi nudged me. "I'll pay you one hundred bucks to tell that to Talia."

"Get real. That's worth at least a cool five hundred. Besides, I'm saving it for a special occasion," I said.

Arkady raised his hand. "Is anyone else having trouble with the fact that we're talking about a goddess like she was some random historical figure? Goddess, people. Original divas who are only supposed to exist in myth and legend?"

Priya raised her hand. After a second, Levi joined her. I shrugged and threw in with the rest of them.

Rafael gave a tiny smirk. "I shudder to think how you'll all handle it when I bring up angels."

Arkady thunked his head on the desk.

"Angels?" Priya said weakly. "First there are goddesses walking around, and now we have angels, too?"

"Get ready for your minds to be blown," I said, and cracked my knuckles, "because the real fun part? Nefesh magic is diluted angel magic."

Arkady patted down his chest and arms. "I've been touched by an angel? Where?"

Priya brayed like a donkey, and Levi made some joke about how they'd all been touched by angels at some point, and Rafael looked extremely uncomfortable again.

Ladies and gentlemen, my team. "Never a dull moment in Jezebel investigations."

Chapter 12

Rafael moved on to the *Sefer Raziel HaMalakh* and the scroll breaking apart when it fell to Earth.

I stifled a yawn as he explained in unnecessary detail about how difficult the second piece had been to obtain.

Levi pulled out the lock pick, turning to me with a forlorn look. "Help," he whispered.

Blinking away my stupor, I covered each of his hands with mine, adjusting his hold. They were warm and strong, but he yielded completely to me.

"While Jezebels are given strength to aid them in the fight," Rafael said, frowning at me, "that isn't their prime talent."

I snapped my attention back to him, hands folded on my desk.

"You don't have to be the strongest," Arkady said. "It's like how Frodo, a seemingly unremarkable little hobbit, was the best ring bearer because he could resist its lure."

Rafael nodded smugly. "Quite."

"Nerds," I muttered, my eyes darting back to Levi. There was the cutest littlest dip between his brows, drawn together in intense concentration, while he bit his bottom lip with even white teeth.

"How many pieces do we still need to find?" Priya said.

Rafael smoothed down the front of his vest. "We have three of the five pieces that make up the *Sefer* and Chariot has one."

"How can you be certain?" Levi said.

"The pillars that house the pieces were also a gift from Asherah. Each pillar with a scroll in our possession is lit up. When Chariot gets a scroll, a pillar goes actively dark, and for any scrolls unclaimed by either side, the corresponding number of pillars remain neutral in appearance. When Gavriella flat-lined, she'd just stolen one of the scrolls away from Chariot."

"Right before my powers activated," I said. "About fifteen years ago. The message." I flipped open *A Study in Scarlet*. "The '3' stands for our pieces of the scroll and the first '1' is for theirs. But there's a question mark after the second '1.' My father didn't actually claim to have the scroll, he just dangled the possibility." I licked a smear of sugar off my finger. "What's the criteria for a pillar going dark, thereby confirming Chariot has one of the pieces?"

"As far as we can ascertain, one of the Ten must take possession of it," Rafael said.

"If Adam had the scroll," Arkady said, "he'd have handed it over and the pillar would darken."

I shook my head. "You're not thinking of this like a con. Chariot has had over four hundred years to amass information on the Jezebels, and I guarantee that my father combed through all of it. If there was even the slightest possibility they knew about the pillars…?" I glanced at Rafael.

"They might," he said.

"Then my father would have made sure our side couldn't know for certain one way or the other whether he was telling the truth. That would have been part of the lure with the coded message. All the Ten had to do was not technically take possession of the scroll for Adam's con to work. Leave it with Adam to hide. As for Adam not making contact in the end?" I filled them in on my theory.

"If you're right," Priya said, "then we don't know whether that one scroll is still in play or not."

"What are the chances of you turning your dad to our side?" Arkady said. "Because we could use someone like him."

"And yet we have someone like me," I said waspishly. "The actual Jezebel."

"Pickle, don't be jealous. It's unseemly."

"What do we know about the missing piece?" I said.

"It has an interesting history," Rafael said. "I assume you all know of Hitler's obsession with the occult?" Off our murmured assent, he continued. "The Nazis forced Jews to register their possessions. At first it was the more valuable items like artwork, stocks, books. That was extended to dishes, toys, even family photos. This was part of Hitler's campaign to stamp out all Jewish identity, but it was also a way for him to root out precious occult items. He coveted the *Sefer*." Rafael was completely in his element. "There was even more historical precedence for Jews being tied to super-natural objects. In 1713, Rabbi Hirsch Frankel was sentenced to imprisonment in Germany on the basis of having a library of books said to contain examples of sorcery, such as how to use oaths and amulets to overcome demons, see the future, and speak to the dead."

"Jews were responsible for bringing magic into the world, which gave Hitler a focal point for his hatred," Levi said. "They had it. Hitler didn't."

"Smarter than you look," I murmured.

"Not on everything." Levi scowled at the lock.

When my dad had taught me how to pick locks, I was eight and it seemed like the hardest thing in the world. I'd felt clumsy and confused, but he'd never let me keep on feeling that way. He knew that it took time. And when I'd finally gotten it, he took me out for a towering sundae with all the toppings that made us both sick, but we agreed had been totally worth it.

"You've lifted three of the five key pins," I said. "It just takes practice. You got this."

Levi rolled out his shoulders one at a time. "Hell yeah, I do."

"Ironic that this obsession with supernatural power was something that Chariot and Hitler shared," Arkady said.

"What's ironic," Rafael said, "was that during WWII our side formed a sort of truce with Chariot, acknowledging Nazis as the greater threat. We both wanted to keep the missing scroll out of their hands. While we weren't going to help each other, there was a tacit agreement not to hinder each other, either. A Jezebel in 1943 tracked the piece to a Jewish family in Germany, but by the time she got into the war-torn area, the family had been deported to Dachau and all their possessions seized."

"You said it yourself," Priya said. "Jews had to register their belongings. That meant there were records and those records were used by various governments, initially the French and German ones, to reunite objects with their owners."

Rafael's eyes gleamed with approval and interest. "Yes, exactly. Not many people know that. How did you?"

No, no. Go back to the cool professionalism. Didn't these people know the saying, "Don't shit where you live"?

I glanced at Levi, who winked. Hypocrite, thy name is Ash.

"Records are databases," Priya said, with a hair flip. "And I excel at getting data that people like keeping hidden."

"That would be an incredibly useful skill," Rafael murmured.

Priya smiled like the cat that swallowed the canary and daintily popped a piece of carrot muffin into her mouth.

Rafael blinked as if to compose himself.

Arkady avidly watched all of us, his coffee mug cradled in his hands. I was tempted to give him a bowl of popcorn.

"Yo, Attendant," I said. "I'm guessing your people also searched these records."

"Of course." Rafael said. Priya got approval, I got frostiness. "My predecessors failed to find anything that matched the description. For all intents and purposes, the scroll was lost."

"Too bad you didn't have more bodies on this before," I said. "Why didn't Asherah create an army of us if this was such a threat?"

"She never expected the fight would be dragged on this long," Rafael said. "Not only did the pieces prove more challenging to find, other factors came into play that she could never have anticipated, such as war, politics, and other interested parties."

"I don't buy it. She's a goddess and this was pretty damn important." I'd heard enough half-truths to recognize one now. "What aren't you telling us?"

Rafael glanced down at his sleeve that concealed the gash he'd gotten from our encounter and his lip curled for a fleeting second. "I've told you the salient facts. A smart strategist understands when to illuminate a truth to aid a cause and when revealing it merely weakens the foundation."

I picked up one of my many non-working pens and tapped it against my thigh. "If that's the normal M.O. of Attendants, no wonder we're still searching for pieces."

"Ash," Priya admonished.

"How fortunate that your brief time as a Jezebel has given you such a grasp of what's best for the cause," Rafael said.

Priya and Arkady exchanged glances and even Levi looked over at us.

I snapped the pen in half, a drop of ink splashing onto my thumb. Our dynamic around my cravings wasn't ideal, but Rafael was the one who'd chosen to serve up himself up on a magical healing platter, so how about he took some damn responsibility for his actions, instead of nursing his wounds and his pride?

"Being a Jezebel has given me perspective you don't have," I said. "This is our first team meeting, and while I appreciate you wanting to present our side in the best possible light, if we're to succeed, we need all the facts, no matter how unpleasant. I'm sorry if I pushed you out of your comfort zone, but maybe I was the shock this system needed."

"Beg to differ," he said coldly.

A loaded silence choked the room.

I jumped up, grabbed a handful of darts and began firing them into the dartboard.

"Was Asherah not strong enough to make more Jezebels?" Priya said to Rafael. "You mentioned that she only had a few faithful left and a lot of myths involving gods speak of how their power is tied to people's belief in them."

Rafael bestowed a smile upon her, like a teacher with a clever student.

Imagining the dartboard was his stupid mug, I shot those suckers into where his eyes would be.

"You're quite correct," Rafael said. "Asherah wasn't strong enough. The goddess only possessed a fraction of her power by this point, since so few believed in her. As you can imagine, this isn't a fact we like bandied about publicly, should Chariot find a way to use it against us."

Arkady leaned back in his chair until it was tilted up on two legs. "How much damage could they do with the info?

It's not like she's made an appearance since and could be captured."

"Chariot are masters at manipulation and exploitation," Rafael said. "All information can be weaponized. You mustn't show weakness on any front."

I sank the last dart into the dartboard and Levi patted my chair. When I sat down next to him once more, he squeezed my thigh before continuing to work on the lock while I leaned in toward him, like a flower gaining warmth from the sun.

"What else can you tell us about them?" Arkady said. "Other than they're steeped in a Kabbalistic ideology and operate in the shadows."

"The group is always ruled by ten people," Rafael said. "Originally it was the ten men who represented each of the Lost Tribes of Israel, but in modern times, both women and non-Jews have been among the leaders. Though the last time one was unmasked was in the mid-twentieth century and we have no idea who is in command now. Think of them as a global consortium with money and manpower we simply cannot match. They are powerful people with their fingers in a lot of pies."

Priya nodded somberly, discreetly texting under her desk.

Adler: *He could stick his finger in my pie.*

Me: *Please get laid tonight and not by him.*

Adler: *Don't be greedy. You've got one of your own.*

Me: *You've got the wrong idea.*

She rolled her eyes.

"I should let the Queen know this about Chariot." Levi tossed the unopened lock and tools on my desk with an exasperated sigh.

"I beg your pardon," Rafael said. "The Queen?"

"Of Hedon," Levi said. "I've formed an alliance with her to root out information about Chariot."

Rafael slammed his hand down on Priya's desk. "Are you out of your bloody mind?!"

Levi's mask of pure haughtiness slid into place. "I'm doing what's necessary to protect my House."

"By giving classified information to a criminal?"

"Levi is only sharing what's relevant to learning more about Chariot. The Queen is also investigating from her end," I said. "She won't break her word, once given, and she won't sell us out."

"You knew about this?" Rafael's jaw got tight.

"I thought we were only exchanging salient facts." I fiddled with the wooden ring on the chain. Rafael had been raised to treat all of this with the utmost secrecy and I'd pushed that need-to-know circle wider and wider. This was Rafael's life and Levi and I hadn't even done him the courtesy of including him in the conversation. "Yeah. I did."

I bit into my second donut to help me get the fortitude to solve this problem.

"Slow down there, sugar rush," Levi said.

I bit back a stupid grin because that's what I'd called Levi when we were in our Lillian and Santino personas. I nodded at the lock. "Quitters don't get to throw shade."

He made a snarky face and picked up the tools again.

"We don't know for sure that Adam actually had the scroll or if he was bluffing Gavriella," Arkady said.

I nodded. "Legitimate databases may not have yielded results, but the dark web might. Pri?"

Priya rubbed her hands together. "I'm on it."

"If you can find whomever ended up with that piece after the war," Arkady said, "I'll pay them a visit and try to establish a trail from that point to Adam. Verify whether or not he actually had it."

"I'll provide you both with a detailed description of the scrolls," Rafael said.

"Why can't we see them ourselves?" Levi said.

"That wouldn't be wise," he said.

Levi's eyes narrowed. "Why not? You don't trust me?"

Rafael hesitated a beat too long. "The only people who can use magic to appear in the library are Ashira and myself and I refuse to remove the scrolls from where they are safest."

Levi pressed his lips into a thin line, but he didn't argue the point.

I pushed away my donut, feeling slightly queasy. "Priya will search the dark web. Arkady will follow up with her findings. Rafael, help me build a timeline. We'll start with the night Dad left and go through to when this meeting with Gavriella was supposed to occur. Since you Attendants document everything so thoroughly."

"Is there anyone else you can reach out to about your father?" Rafael said. "Family perhaps, who might have seen him after he left you and your mother?"

"They're in Montreal," I said. "He was estranged from his parents and didn't have any siblings."

"It still might be worth following up," Priya said. "Arkady, since you're waiting on me, why not check out the Maison de Champlain database and follow up discreetly? If that's okay with Ash."

"I wouldn't," Arkady said, with a dismissive shake of his head.

"Why not?" she said.

Arkady spread his hands wide. "Ash said they were estranged. Adam wouldn't have reached out to them and if they haven't bothered to contact their own granddaughter in all this time, why open old wounds?"

"He's right," I said. "Dad wouldn't have contacted them. I don't know what happened, but there was no love lost there. His parents made their choice not to have me in their life. They're not family and I don't want to go down that road."

"That's wise," Arkady said.

Why did he sound so definitive on the matter? The man was an enigma. Just when I thought he was trustworthy, some tiny detail aroused my suspicions anew. My gut told me he wasn't Chariot—but he was hiding something.

There was a click and Levi's eyes grew wide as the lock tumbled open, a boyish grin splitting his face. "I did it."

"Told you," I said.

"Miles is not going to be happy with you," Arkady said in a discouraging tone.

"What else is new?" Levi said.

"I meant Ash," Arkady said.

"So did I," Levi said.

I elbowed him. "Show some gratitude for your new criminal skill set."

"If you two are finished dragging Levi down the path of villainy," Priya said, "could we maybe figure out if there's anyone else to investigate in terms of getting a lead on your dad?"

I nodded. "There might be someone I could try."

The one lead out of all of them that I'd never followed up with. It was time to go see the person my father had dubbed "the Midnight Madman."

Chapter 13

"Rafael. Could I speak to you please?" I said.

Rafael was chatting with Arkady about our next move, Levi was proudly putting his lock-picking equipment back in his briefcase, and Priya had taken the leftover pastry to share with Eleanor and Bryan.

Mrs. Hudson pawed at me, so I tossed her cow toy for her to fetch or dry hump. She was a healthy modern female with needs. No judgment.

"Now," I said, when Rafael didn't answer fast enough, and dragged him into the empty reception area for privacy.

"Was securing House Pacifica resources for our cause merely a ploy for you to develop an intimate relationship with Levi?" Rafael said, his eyes flashing.

"Huh? Busted. Having nothing else to recommend me, I appealed to his big strong protector self, because there's nothing I love more than playing helpless to get a guy interested."

"Ah. You were already sleeping with him, weren't you?"

"We'll make a Seeker of you yet." I wiped some dust off the rubber tree plant next to the sofa. "Do you have a problem with that?"

"If it compromises our mission in any way, your arrangement with him ends. Personally and professionally."

"So you don't think going to the Queen compromised us?" I said slowly.

He scratched his jaw. "How certain are you that she won't use this information against us?"

"Chariot tried to make her a scapegoat when they were stealing magic from those kids. She won't forgive that and she certainly won't get into bed with them."

"Your methods are unorthodox, but I concede that there is merit to them. Chariot expects us to act like lone wolves. They won't anticipate these tactics."

"Thank you for being understanding, and I'm sorry. We should have discussed going to her with you first. I promise to be better at looping you in."

"I appreciate that." He turned to leave, but I held up a hand to stop him.

"I'm not done. This whole 'first rule of Magic Snacking: there is no Magic Snacking' business isn't going to work. It happened and it likely will again. If we don't find a way to deal with it, it could destroy our working relationship. I can't fulfill my Jezebel duties without you." I paused, looking for a delicate way to frame this next part. "Is it possible that your response in regards to assisting me with my problem went farther than merely the effects of that connection?"

He stared at me blankly, then shuddered. "I assure you I'm not sexually attracted to you."

"It's not a fate worse than death," I snapped.

"Says you. That type of relationship does not bode well for Attendants and Jezebels."

"Then what are you so uptight about? Admittedly, our situation isn't great for either of us—"

"How, precisely, is it a problem for you?"

I glanced around to make sure we were alone, and still lowered my voice. "How about the part where the only thing

141

that quiets my cravings and brings me back from the brink is sucking you off?"

Rafael grimaced.

"Ingesting your magic." I slapped my hand against my thigh. "You know what I mean."

"Your actions were taken out of necessity."

"As were yours. I craved that connection, too."

Rafael crossed his arms, his flush deepening. "Not as much as I did," he muttered.

I threw up my hands. "You win the suffering Olympics. Mazel tov. Big deal. You had an involuntary physical reaction. Wait. Do you feel taken advantage of? Because I'm really sorry about—"

"Upon further, more clear-headed reflection," he said, "what transpired was not the best approach to your dilemma regarding your cravings."

Say "your" one more time and I'm going to punch you. "How should we deal with it?"

"If there is a scenario where the scroll's presence is at all a possibility," he said, "I'll accompany you and be the one to physically handle it. However, I will not be thrust back into that position."

The finality in his voice was absolute. The siren's song lurked at the back of my skull, waiting for the chance to once more take center stage, and if there was no other cure? I'd be on my own. However, it was a workable enough solution for now. Reasonable even.

So why did I feel like a door had closed between us?

There was still one situation I couldn't handle on my own. "When the time comes to destroy all the pieces of the *Sefer*?" I said. "I'll need you then."

"That one time, I'll assist you." He dropped his gaze to his feet, tension in every line of his body. "The entire episode was a… challenge to overcome." The last part was spoken softly.

I seized on the opening. "Rafael—"

"Meantime," he said briskly, "I'll endeavor to find a viable alternate fix to your magic difficulties." He couldn't have retreated further into his stiff upper lip self if he'd tattooed the British flag on his face. Before I could reach out to him, he pivoted sharply and returned to the office.

I exhaled, leaning my head back against the wall.

"What the hell is going on with the two of you?" Levi drew closer, sipping on a steaming mug of coffee.

"We're still working out the kinks in our relationship." Shit. No. Not kinks. Annnnd new topic. I smiled benignly.

Levi stilled, his coffee cup halfway to his mouth. "That smile is frankly worrying."

"It's a perfectly normal smile." I patted my lips. Not too many teeth. Not too wide. "You're imagining things. Now, how do I get a plane ticket to Antigua authorized? Or the House jet?"

"What's in Antigua?" he said in a voice laced with deep suspicion.

"My dad's best friend. Uncle Paulie."

"Wouldn't your mother have checked in with him when Adam first disappeared?"

"She did, but Uncle Paulie denied knowing anything."

Priya exited Eleanor's office with a now-empty tray, leaving the door slightly ajar.

Levi glanced at it, then grasped me by the elbow.

"Need help?" she said, shoving the tray at me. "Here. Wash this."

"We're good," Levi said, hauling me down a short hallway.

"Okay," Priya said, sunnily.

"You're useless," I called out, hoisting the tray in one hand.

Levi stuffed me into the small kitchen. "What if your Uncle Paulie is a member of Chariot?"

"He's not," I said with a scoffed laugh.

"You seem awfully sure of that."

"Oh, I am. That's not Paulie's thing."

"What's Paulie's full name? Is he registered with the House?"

"Paulie Peterson."

"Doesn't sound familiar."

"He's Mundane, so you wouldn't have come across his name in your database." I disengaged from his hold. "Honestly, Levi. You said you'd fund my Jezebel activities. This is a very promising lead."

"A lead which you never checked out before now."

I turned on the tap and squirted dish soap on the tray. "You're really stuck on that point."

"He lives in Antigua?"

"Nearby." I scrubbed at some hardened pastry before giving the tray a good rinse. "On a tiny island called Cariva Cay."

Levi pulled out his phone and began scrolling.

I lunged for his phone with a wet hand, but he held it out of reach. "What are you doing?"

"Checking for airstrips." Levi frowned at the phone. "The island's nickname is Inferno? Why have I heard that before?"

I scooted past him to the drawer with the clean tea towels that was also helpfully near the door for a quick escape if necessary. "Beats me."

He clamped his hand down on my shoulder. I could have easily shaken him off, but taunting the beast was unwise. Levi's eyebrows shot up, having found his answer online.

Here we go.

"Those months-long, drug-fueled parties going on about five years ago," he said. "Where people died. Your uncle was behind them?"

Grabbing a tea towel, I vigorously dried off the tray.

"Paulie owns Cariva Cay, but those deaths were ruled an accident. He wasn't even charged."

"At best, he's a slippery fuck with good lawyers. At worst, he's—" Levi threw up his hands. "Is this guy some cult leader? A criminal overlord?"

"Petty criminal. He came from old money in the States, steeped in a stringent evangelical Christianity. Only kid, black sheep of his family, but he inherited everything when his parents died." I tried to push Levi out of the way to reach the high cupboard that the tray belonged in, but he didn't budge.

He gripped the counter behind me, trapping me in place. "Well, his moral upbringing really led him astray. How did he end up doing that shit?"

Heat poured off his body and his eyes bore into mine like blue crystals. Pressing the tray to my chest, I bit my lip against the urge to commit an HR violation and kiss the hell out of him.

His gaze dropped to my mouth and he snatched the tray away, shoving it in the cupboard.

"I don't know because it happened long after Dad was gone," I said to his back, "but I remember my parents talking about how Paulie was prone to a dark, self-destructive streak."

His hand tightened on the cupboard handle, but he closed the door gently. "You can't be serious about going there."

"Look, he came to see me when I was in the hospital after the car crash and told me that if I ever needed him, that his door was always open. I never took him up on it because at first I was too angry and he was too close to Dad and then after that, well, he moved far away, and there was the Inferno business and it didn't feel appropriate."

"Appropriate," Levi said in a strangled voice. He

scrubbed a hand over his face. "You're banking on him being the same person as when you were a kid. People change."

I was about to protest that Paulie would never hurt me, but I didn't, because the truth was I wasn't sure. If I was being honest with myself, that was part of the reason I'd never gone to see him before, but finding Dad's book had set a clock ticking and my options were limited. Paulie was a viable lead; I felt it in my gut.

It didn't mean I was going to be stupid about this.

"What if I took Arkady?" I said.

Levi relaxed a fraction of an inch. "Keep talking."

"He has military training and stone fists to keep me safe. Nothing has ever produced even the weakest lead about Adam's whereabouts. Not cops, credit card statements, phone records, social media, or all the databases I have access to." I ticked off the items on my fingers. "I think Paulie is worth a second try."

"Why?"

"Time. Seeing me, his little Ash, might make him more amenable to spilling any secrets that Dad entrusted him with. Adam and him were tight. Check in with Miles. If the two of you don't believe that Arkady and I will be safe, then I'll respect that," I said.

My heart hammered in my chest. I'd relied on myself for so long, been the final arbiter of my actions. To open myself up and consider other people's instincts and experiences was wise now that I had a team, but that didn't make it easy.

Levi turned the phone over a couple of times, then put it away. "I'm not giving you the jet."

I threw my arms around him. "Commercial airlines, here I come."

He returned the hug with a sigh. "You're going to be the death of me."

"Only if it's from a heart attack or stroke. But if it makes you feel better, you could get hit by a car tomorrow."

"Only marginally," he said wryly. "I'll have my travel agent call you when the ticket is ready."

He headed back to my office and I followed close on his heels.

"Thank you, Leviticus. Meantime, I'll be safely engaged interviewing the support staff at the Lung Cancer Foundation. Receptionists and assistants are a fount of information." Especially when a tiny bit of sleuthing had turned up some useful dirt on one that could be used to apply pressure to an otherwise closed-mouthed friend.

Rafael was placing the last of the empty coffee cups on a tray. Ooh. Maybe I'd get him doing laundry yet.

Levi retrieved his suit jacket from the chair. "Hey, Arkady? Grab your sunscreen. You're going with Ash to see her uncle in the Caribbean."

"Sweet." He punched the air.

"The Midnight Madman?" Priya shot up out of her chair so fast it flew backward and bounced off the wall.

I made a frantic shushing motion at her.

Three sets of male eyes fell upon me. Even Mrs. Hudson regarded me with doggie disdain.

"That was my dad's nickname for him, not a legal description." I sighed. "I meant what I said, Levi. I'll stand by your decision."

"Go," Levi said, resignedly. "Just come back in one piece."

"I will."

Once Levi left, Arkady and I hashed out the best approach, while Rafael and Priya worked on their respective tasks. We threw out Arkady posing as my bodyguard, because it was too overtly aggressive, and also, we didn't want to tip our hand of his abilities if things went south.

None of the other suggestions were viable until Arkady snapped his fingers. "You need a reason to go see him out of the blue and ask him about Adam. What if I go as your

147

fiancé? If you were getting married, you'd want to know what happened to your father and if there was any way of contacting him to be there."

"That's smart," I said.

Priya's laptop binged. "Holy cow," she said. "We got a hit."

I came around her desk. "On what?"

"Moran's real identity."

I'd asked Pri to look into it, but had given up on finding anything. "Seriously?"

"It's not his actual name, but it's a start." She showed me an old photo of a group of guys in their mid-teens posed in front of a bumper car ride. "One of them posted about the summer he worked for a traveling fair about thirty years ago. This guy?" She pointed out one with white-blond hair. "The poster mentioned his Russian accent."

"That's pretty slim," I said.

"Ah. But I haven't gotten to the best part. The fair was located just outside a ghost town in Northern California. Wonderland, California to be precise."

I sat down heavily on her desk. "Get me his contact information."

"Already on it."

After confirming that everyone had their to-do lists, I announced I was off to work another case. "Pri, can you lock up if I'm not back?"

Priya waved me off. "I'm working from home for the rest of the day. Mrs. Hudson can stay with me." She rarely worked at home. She had a few cafés she rotated, enjoying the social interaction with the employees and other regulars.

I threw on my leather jacket. "Don't change your routine on my account. I should run her over to the animal shelter."

"Don't worry about it." Priya slipped Mrs. Hudson a doggie treat.

"Pri—" She raised her eyebrows at me, her jaw tilting up

at a stubborn angle, and I stepped back from that line. "It's not fair to keep pawning her off on you."

"Why not?" she said. "She's family. My aunties watched me when Mom had to work. How is this different?"

"My family had the same deal when we moved back to Canada," Arkady said, texting Levi for the travel agent's contact info.

The way everyone was rallying around the dog, around me, felt less like a team, with nice enforceable office hours, limited socializing, and okay, a professional dependence that I was only just getting used to, and more like a village. Sure, Priya and I were all up in each other's lives, but she was one person. Talia and I maintained a carefully cultivated space at the best of times, and my life becoming this messy, rowdy, people-filled entity made my mouth go dry. Especially given Pri's guardedness, Arkady's secrets, this shitshow with Rafael, and my complicated status with Levi. My life was a house of cards.

"We'll discuss her status later." I dangled my fingers, but the dog only spared me the most indifferent glance.

"Her heart belongs to the cow," Priya said.

"Fickle dog."

Chapter 14

Any plan to ask Olivia, the front desk receptionist at the Lung Cancer Foundation, if she'd heard from Mayan was rendered moot when I showed up to find Mayan herself in the lobby, leaning against the large reception desk and signing off on some file.

It was a large, airy space. On one side hung lung cancer prevention posters, while the other was taken up with framed photos of the Black and White Ball that the Foundation put on every year as its big fundraiser.

I studied Mayan as I approached—before she saw me and tensed up. Her body language was relaxed. She was comfortable in her element, laughing with the receptionist as she handed the folder back.

"Mayan Shapiro," I said, my boot heels thudding against the floor.

"Yes?" Her polite smile faltered and she stepped back. "Ash? What brings you here?" She lowered her voice. "Oh my God. Does your mother have cancer?"

"It's a business matter." I pulled out my P.I. license. "Can we speak privately?"

Mayan swallowed, one hand playing with the thin gold

chain still minus the diamond heart pendant around her threat.

What prompted that reaction?

Olivia's eyes gleamed behind her red-framed glasses before she busied herself with a stack of phone messages.

Fun as it was to make Mayan uncomfortable, I had no desire to blow her professional reputation. "I'm looking for an old camp alum and was hoping you might know what had happened to her."

Olivia visibly lost interest.

"Certainly," Mayan said. "Should we go up to my office?"

"Nah. Let's just step outside. This'll just take a moment." I wasn't giving her home court advantage. I wanted her off-balance. Levi had handled her with kid gloves and gotten nowhere.

The gloves were off.

I led her outside to a bench out in the front plaza.

She sat down and smoothed out her skirt. "I'm sorry."

"For what?"

"How horrible I was to you. It, well, it doesn't matter why. My teen years weren't great, but that doesn't excuse how I behaved and I apologize." She folded her hands in her lap.

I'd never actually imagined this exact scenario. Revenge fantasies by the dozens, sure, but not a freely offered up apology. Especially not one delivered so perfunctorily. It was as if she'd followed some kind of script. Had I been a betting woman, I'd have laid odds on Mayan never acknowledging our past.

Rule one of a con: create rapport with your mark.

And always get the jump on them. What did she feel the need to stay a step ahead of me on? I leaned back, my arms outstretched along the top of the bench. This was becoming almost fun.

"You want to really make it up to me? Tell me what you

were doing in Hedon."

"Hedon?" She didn't break eye contact but her still-folded hands twisted. "What's that?"

"Cut the crap. I saw you in the Green Olive. Made you a lot more interesting than I ever would have given you credit for."

"Excuse me?" she said, frostily.

"Oh." I wrinkled my brow. "Have you not replaced spinning class with frequenting criminal dives? My bad."

"At least I have two working legs. Whereas you've added crime to all your other pathetic affectations in hopes of being 'interesting.'"

Ah, there was the Mayan I knew and dreamed of inflicting torturous humiliation upon. If Levi thought she'd changed, he was easily snowed. Except he wasn't. He was as suspicious as I was. Was Mayan his weak spot, because if not, how'd she convince him she was nice now? I'd seen her in camp plays and she wasn't that good an actress. Porn stars trod the boards as Shakespearean thespians in comparison.

Unless being around me brought out her best teen bitch. Also an option.

Mayan reached into the pocket of her blazer and pulled out a package of Gitanes. She flicked it open, and put one of the short, stubby cigarettes to her lips.

My brows rose for a second before I smoothed out my expression. Why would a woman whose mother died of lung cancer and who worked for a foundation dedicated to research and prevention of the disease take up smoking?

"Why were you in Hedon?" I said. "Maybe there's a way we can mutually benefit. It's smart having someone watch your back over there and at least with the two of us, we know who'd be wielding the knife that stabbed us."

That got a laugh. She patted her pockets, and I moved in with a lighter. I let my fingers brush against her skin, carefully sending my magic inside her.

Nothing. She was totally Mundane with no invasive magic, though in my limited experience, if she was compelled in some way, there wouldn't be evidence of that.

Mayan coughed a bit when she inhaled. The cigarettes had a distinctive aroma. "I didn't have business there," she said.

I flicked the lighter on and off. "Of all the gin joints in all the world, you didn't just stumble into that one."

Mayan watched the glowing tip turn to a funnel of ash, before she shook her head sharply and tapped it off. "There was a guy who I hooked up with. He brought me."

My gut said she told the truth, but the Queen of Hearts said that Mayan hadn't come through for her first time recently. "Damn. There goes your interesting factor."

She shot me the finger.

"Maybe he's the one I should be speaking to. Got a name?"

"Is there actually an alum you're trying to find?" She fanned the smoke in front of her face, with a moue of distaste.

"What do you think?"

"In that case, my personal life is none of your business. Whatever you're up to? I want no part of it, and I pray I never go back there." Her voice shook with conviction. Taking one last drag, she stood up and ground the cigarette out under her boot heel. "I have work to do."

She strode off, jerked the front doors to the building open, and was lost to view.

I flicked the lighter on, running my finger through the bottom of the flame as I eliminated the impossible. Clone? While a showdown with multiple Mayans where I had to guess who the real one was by systematically destroying them would be a hell of a Saturday night, science had not yet advanced that far.

When I was about fourteen, I'd gone to the wedding of a

distant cousin with my grandparents. Bubbe hated the bride and couldn't understand how these two were a couple. Her working theory was that the bride was a demonic double. This was a bit of Jewish lore that said everyone at birth has a demon created in their exact image. Forty days before a person's birth, a voice from the heavens proclaims who that person is destined to marry. This voice, heard by angels and devils alike allows the devils to marry off the demonic double instead of the real thing. Doom ensues. Of course, Bubbe also said I was a demonic double, so there was that.

Who was I kidding? Mayan was already the demonic double version and she certainly hadn't been replaced with the nice version.

Was she compelled? She didn't behave like she was. Compulsions resulted in a one-track mind. Mayan didn't have that.

Drugs?

I grabbed a napkin from the grilled cheese sandwich food truck parked at the curb and, picking her cigarette butt up by the tip, wrapped it up and carefully put it in my pocket. Cigarettes were a phenomenal source of latent evidence. Our skin was constantly regenerating with newer layers. Skin cells around the hands, face, and feet, especially, had high levels of cell removal. It was likely that cells were left on the cigarette, while each puff left traces of saliva. It was a goldmine of DNA, with both saliva and epithelial cells to test.

I didn't have anyone at a forensic crime lab who owed me a favor, but I did have a direct line to the Head of House Security. Since Miles was already looped in on this case, I wasn't breaking client confidentiality. I fired off a text asking for help.

There was one other possibility: Mayan's mystery man. "Hooked up with" sounded very past tense and casual, but words meant nothing. Experience had taught me that people believing themselves in love did stupid things. If that was the case here, Mayan might have taken up smoking to impress the dude or bond, but she'd have to be massively head-over-heels for it to override the tragedy that smoking had wrought in her life.

Depending on his agenda, he might provide the surprise value to cement my alliance with the Queen.

My gut said he wasn't out of her life; therefore, my next order of business was to learn his identity. The officer that Levi had reached out to had canvassed friends on that front, and there hadn't been any mention of a boyfriend.

If he was the reason Mayan had taken off that heart pendant, started smoking, and hanging out in Hedon, then he might not be the kind of man she told her friends about. Or knowing he was a bad-boy fling, but not a physical threat to Mayan, they may have kept mum about him.

Something had happened when Mayan was over there. She wasn't so easily shocked that just going to a bar would upset her enough to never want to go back. Her friends might not recognize him as a threat—that was my job. I'd promised Levi I'd find out what happened to her, and if I had to engage in some morally gray activities to keep Mayan safe, like low-key blackmail, then I could live with that.

Jumping off the bench, I strode back inside and up to the reception desk. "Your fundraiser is coming up, isn't it?"

"Oh, do you mean the Black and White Ball?" Olivia said. "Would you like tickets?"

Mayan would be there. From her social media profile, she hadn't missed a year since she'd started working for the Foundation.

"Give me two." I grinned. "It's my excuse to ask this guy out. Can't say no to a good cause, right?"

She smiled back. "He'd be a jerk if he did. That'll be four hundred even. Could I get your email for our mailing list please?"

I tried not to choke as I handed over my credit card and

155

spelled out the junk email I kept for anyone selling me something. "I hope he has a tux. Why I always go for musicians is beyond me."

Laughing, Olivia gave me the keypad to enter my pin number. "You like the bad boys."

"The one thing Mayan and I have in common."

"I wouldn't know about that."

"I think you would." I leaned on the top of the desk. "Here's the thing, Olivia." She started at my use of her name. "I've seen photos of you and Mayan and I know you're chummy. I'm trying to track this guy down who Mayan was seeing and I'd appreciate your help."

"Sorry."

"He's not good news. Help me help her."

"I'd like you to leave."

"And I'd like an answer."

She reached for the receiver. "I'm calling Mayan."

"You do that. Then I'll mention how when you were still going by your married name back in Toronto, you were fired from the non-profit you worked at with accusations of theft."

She dropped the receiver back in its cradle. "How did you know about that?"

"Short answer? I'm a very thorough private investigator. Now, I'm sure you've turned your life around and I'm happy for your past to remain there. If you give me a name."

She worried at her bottom lip with her teeth. "I never met him. She only went out with him a few times."

"A name."

"Jonah Samuels."

"Did he ever come around here?"

"No. Their meetings were very much on the down-low. Except…"

I made a "get on with it" motion.

"A man came to buy a ticket to the fundraiser a couple of weeks ago. Mayan was coming back from lunch and even though they didn't speak, she looked flustered for a second at his presence."

"Did you get his email?" She had. I typed it into my phone along with a description of him. "Does she have a date for the ball? If this guy is going to be there, she should have someone with her, making sure he doesn't get close."

"Yes. She's going with Levi Montefiore." She gave me the receipt and the tickets.

"Is she now?" I waited for my outrage and betrayal to emerge, but honestly, I was worn out from the constant game playing. I'm sure he'd have a perfectly acceptable reason for not mentioning it, and it's not like he could have been my plus-one, but I was over him keeping me in the loop only when it suited him. Especially on this case, where he'd come to me for assistance. Levi, you ass.

I received a text with the good news that Miles did indeed have an in at a lab and they were going to do a rush toxicology workup on the cigarette. I dropped the sample off, now free to track down Jonah Samuels.

It didn't take long. In his early forties, Jonah was older than I'd expected, with a nerdy red-headed cuteness about him. His profession was listed as Medical Researcher. His lone social media profile wasn't sparse enough to set off any bells, more that it had the air of someone who was a half-hearted poster. There were no photos of him and Mayan together anywhere public. That would fit if he'd truly been a casual hook-up.

He wasn't registered in any of the Canadian House data-bases. Neither was I, so that didn't rule him out being Nefesh.

Levi's travel agent phoned. Not only had Levi come through with two tickets to the island of Antigua on a red-eye flight tonight, he'd splurged for business class. Though not for first class, so maybe this was the equivalent of economy in Levi's world.

I made arrangements to get the tickets from the agent so I was spared dealing directly with Levi. I wasn't sure what, if anything, I wanted to say to him yet.

After racing home to pack, Priya tried to make me do a video for the dog in case she missed me. I refused; Priya filmed me anyway. It consisted of sixteen seconds of me scowling at the screen in dead silence. As a reward, she gave me the contact info of the man with the Wonderland recollection. That call would have to wait until morning.

Arkady and I cabbed it to the airport that evening.

"Here." He shoved a ring box at me.

I stifled a yawn. "Am I about to become the luckiest girl in the world?"

"Yes. For the remainder of this trip you are my one true love. Savor what no other woman will ever be."

I popped the box open and, confronted by the large pear-cut jewel, whistled. "Not too shabby."

"It's the finest in cubic zirconia. Daddy loves you, baby."

"Considering why we're going, let's leave off the creepy father references, shall we?" I slid the ring onto my finger. "This'll do nicely."

To give Arkady his due, you'd have never known I didn't possess his genitalia of choice. He was so solicitous, carrying my bag, my hand clasped in his. When he told the ticket agent all about our fake engagement and how he was nervous that I wouldn't say yes, even I was on the edge of my seat, hoping I'd accepted.

The woman was putty. He even smoothed over the weirdness of flying to Antigua for one night with just carry-on luggage by saying we were going to get my uncle's blessing in person, since he'd helped raise me, but work obligations prevented us from staying longer.

The lies fell from his lips like honey and everyone in his wake lapped them up.

We got our spacious seats for the first leg of the journey

to New York. After one last charm offensive for our female flight attendant, Arkady stuffed his ear buds in and ignored me to watch the latest Marvel movie.

Fine by me. Best he not see—and report back to Levi—how many of those stupid baby bottles of booze I put away. Or the two extra desserts our flight attendant brought that I stress-ate. No tiny pretzel packages for this business-class flyer.

I laughed softly. Arkady could be asleep and he still wouldn't miss those details. I ordered another Jack Daniels.

I wanted Uncle Paulie to have all the answers and for him to have none in equal measure. My last crash had shattered my femur. Would I get off as lightly in this aftermath? I finished the drink with trembling hands.

The plane hit turbulence and dropped with a sickening lurch. I spilled my booze, swearing viciously as I blotted my clothes with a linen napkin. Balling up the napkin, I poked Arkady.

"Friends don't interrupt friends at the good part," he said.

"Distract me."

"Aliens are about to annihilate us."

"Never mind." I rested my head against my darkened entertainment screen in defeat.

Arkady made a disparaging noise. "Miles and I slept together."

"No kidding." I sat up. "Was the sex bad?"

"Pickle, I can make sex with anyone good. It was…" He frowned. "*More* than I expected."

"But?"

"He overthinks everything." Arkady held out his left ear bud. "As do you. Now shut up."

I slid the ear bud in, lay my head on his shoulder, and let myself be soothed by the world blowing up.

Chapter 15

Antigua in April was hot to my Canadian blood and annoyingly humid. Arkady and I dropped our bags off at the resort we'd been booked into. I peeled down to a tank top and a pair of long shorts, slapped on some sunscreen, and called the poster.

It was a fairly brief chat. He didn't remember the blond guy's name. When pressed on how he could be certain of the Russian accent after all these years, he replied that it had stuck out because the kid was traveling with a Hispanic carny family.

I hurriedly grabbed a pen. "Do you remember their last name?"

Sadly, he didn't. He'd worked the rides, not the midway, and hadn't had much interaction with them.

"What about the company that ran the fair?" If they were around, they might have employment records from that time.

That he provided. Thanking him, I hung up. A Russian kid and a Hispanic carny family in Wonderland—was this the genesis of the Queen of Hearts? I tapped the pen against the table I sat at. Knowledge was power, but knowledge could also be deadly. I still intended to know exactly who I was dealing with, but I'd asked Priya to look into this before learning about living statues, and how dangerous the Queen actually was.

I left a message for the company. I'd decide what to do with this information once I heard from them.

A text came in from my mother.

Talia, Destroyer of Egos: *Breakfast the other day was lovely and I'm happy you're settling into this new chapter of your life so well.*

I deleted three responses before settling on "okay."

Talia, Destroyer of Egos: *Priya may be working for the House, but you shouldn't go there too often to visit her. The optics aren't good. Are you available to help out at a Town Hall meeting this afternoon? Various family members of my staff are volunteering.*

Talia had always negotiated my presence at her events, never asked. Apparently, our little work fiction had gained me some freedoms. Was that what my breakfast invitation had been about? She knew I'd say no to all events from here on in and that was her way of keeping up appearances? Making sure the optics looked good?

Damn my lack of clarity.

Not that our previous relationship had been all that fulfilling, but there'd been a brutally honest transactional logic to it that I almost missed. At least we'd both gotten something out of it. Now that we were locked into "all lies, all games," dealing with her was exhausting and sad.

This so easily could spin out into fewer and fewer engagements until we were family in name only. The fiction about me being Mundane was imperative to the cover story hiding my Jezebel status, but I wanted—no, I needed—something genuine to connect with her over.

Was I going to get my father back, only to lose my mother?

Me: *Away on business. Sorry.*

She didn't respond.

Arkady knocked on my door. With one glance at the text chain, I slid my phone into my pocket and we went out hunting for a way to Inferno.

Our first stop was a helicopter charter company located in a tiny storefront, jammed with travel posters showcasing the beauty of Antigua and hand-lettered signs advertising all their various tours.

The owner, a woman with a close-cropped graying afro and a colorful sundress, lost her wide smile when she heard our request. "What do you want to be messing around with that fool Caligula Jones for?"

A younger man came out of the back office at her loud words. "No one is going to fly you over there. Heard the airstrip is part jungle again."

"Who's Caligula Jones?" Arkady said.

I shrugged. "Beats me."

"That crazy man who lives there," the owner said.

"That's your uncle?" Arkady blew out his cheeks.

The younger man whistled. "You've got one messed up family."

"Honorary uncle," I said. "And Caligula Jones sounds like a ridiculous constructed persona." I tsked. "He always did have a tendency to self-aggrandization."

The younger man shook his head. "He hunts people for sport."

"He's a slightly shady old dude on an island," I said. "This isn't *Running Man*. He'd be locked up if that were the case."

The owner wagged a finger at her employee. "She's right. That wasn't proven. But those parties of his did enough damage. Brought in all the wrong people and engaged in who knows what kind of depraved activities. And that's when he was still receiving visitors. You'd best stay away."

Disheartened, I thanked them and we left the office, the cheery jangle of the bell over the door a discordant note.

"That certainly spices this adventure up," Arkady said.

"Should we still go through with this?" I said. Arkady had army and black ops training. I'd defer to him.

"The name, the people hunting, it sounds like a lot of hot air to keep unwanted visitors away. Let's see if we can hire a boat."

Arkady took charge, judging rightly that the men down at the docks would deal better with another man. Unfortunately, finding a boat for the hour-long trip led us to increasingly higher prices and more unseaworthy crafts.

The last possibility in the marina was a black sailor called Jacques whose surliness made my personality seem like it was spun from cotton candy. Though he was hot in a buff bald guy way. After seeing our documents marking me as Mundane and Arkady as Nefesh, Jacques agreed to take us over for an exorbitant sum of cash.

"Yo, Jacques," another boat owner called out. "You got duct tape and tarps? I hear Caligula pays extra for body removal. Doesn't like the hassle."

"Your uncle has a hell of a PR machine," Arkady said. "I'm impressed."

"Only the finest of depraved psychopath rumors for Paulie," I said.

We stepped aboard Jacques' banged-up speedboat named "Blow Me."

I pushed aside a coil of rope to sit on the cushion-less bench. "Is the boat named for a general hatred of mankind or…" I mimed snorting cocaine.

Jacques regarded me with a flinty-eyed stare. "When we get to the island, I don't dock. You jump out and wade to shore."

"But you'll wait for us?" I said.

He grinned unpleasantly. "Depends on how much you annoy me."

Arkady threw up his hands. "We're fucked."

Jacques raked a slow gaze over him. "You, I might stick around for."

"Well, of course you would, darling." Arkady preened.

I shoved my engagement ring in his face. "Sitting right here. Darling."

Arkady groaned. "Women."

Jacques flashed him a smile and started the outboard motor.

The sound rattled through the boat, up my poor ass, and into my teeth, where it knocked my jaw around like a heavyweight champ. Then the speedboat roared off. I clung to the bench for dear life, each bump sending me flying into the air, while salty water drenched me.

"This was the best you could find?" I yelled at my useless fiancé.

"It's perfect," he whooped.

"No. It's not. I am a Jew. We wandered in the desert for forty years. We like land." My voice rose in a screech as I almost flew out of the boat. Did I mention that lifejackets were not included on this fine vessel?

"I haven't had this much fun since the golems." He stretched his arms out along the boat's railing. "We should have gotten engaged sooner."

My life flashed before my eyes. Well, I think it did. It was hard to tell for the tangle of locks permanently plastered to my face, given we were driving into the wind.

"Make yourself useful," I said. "Tell me how to get your overthinker to be nice to your fiancée."

Arkady tilted his face into the sun. "Good luck with that. Miles takes his job as Levi's personal security very seriously."

"He sees me as a threat."

"Not in the way you're thinking. Look at it from his

point of view. Miles ensuring Levi's safety means Levi is free to govern the Nefesh to the best of his ability. Miles is thorough and thoughtful when he assesses a risk. The combination of your history with Levi and you being what you are makes you a volatile and unpredictable element that he can't simply assess and neutralize. It's not your fault, but he can't predict from moment to moment how your mission is going to compromise his. That's a lot of added pressure."

I gazed out over the choppy waves. "Did he say all that to you?"

"Miles? Are you kidding? The man is hardly forthcoming. It's a winning combination. Overthinking and not sharing." Arkady booped me on the nose. "You're not the only one who can read a situation, pickle. Try to see where he's coming from."

"Fine." It's not like it would be reciprocated.

By the time Jacques pointed out the island in the distance, I was soaking wet, had swallowed half a pound of my own hair, and my butt was a screaming, bruised mess.

Desperate for some posterior relief, I wobbled my way to the prow, gripping the railing for dear life. White foam frothed on the churning waves and the closer we got, the more the cloudless sky became streaked with blue and pink. The sun turned to a sinking ball of brilliant red, casting everything in a hellish glow.

It would have been a photo-worthy sunset were it not the middle of the afternoon.

A giant tentacle rose from the water and snapped around my arm, yanking me partway overboard. My sunglasses sailed into the sea with a splash.

Acting on pure adrenaline, I manifested a perfect replica of Moran's big-ass sword and hacked through the tentacle.

Blood spattered on me as a black eye appeared under the surface.

The kraken whacked the boat with its massive head.

Lurching sideways, I ran back to Arkady, but he was gone. I pressed my hand to my heart. Oh, my friend. I'd avenge your death.

"Jacques!" I spun around to order him to go faster, but there'd been a shift change.

A hooded and robed figure in billowing red robes now captained the boat. "You must pay the ferryman," the figure boomed.

I ran at the figure and nailed him with a roundhouse kick. "Paid."

The ferryman stumbled to one knee.

I grabbed his head and smashed it into the railing. "And a tip."

His went crossed-eyed, his pupils glassy, but he recovered enough to grab me and wrestle me to the ground. In the blink of an eye, the rope slithered off the bench and lashed my limbs to the steering wheel column.

The fibers chafed my skin, binding me tight. I called forth a red blood dagger and cut myself free.

The ferryman rose up to a terrifying height. "You're Mundane."

"I've been Mundane in my past." I flipped the blade to my dominant right hand. "But this is a beautiful new world."

"Even if you're Nefesh," he boomed, "you can't have two kinds of magic."

My spiky blood armor snapped into place. "I'm a well of surprises. You can find out how deep and dark I run, or you can return me to safety."

The air crackled with tension, the boat bobbing like mad in the waves that churned angrily. I stood there, feet planted, jaw firm, not giving an inch.

For one blinding moment, the sun blazed blood red above the horizon.

Then all was normal: a cloudless sky, a kraken-less sea, blood-free clothing.

Arkady sat in the same spot, midway through some story about another sailing trip.

I held up my hand to interrupt him. "Did nothing out of the ordinary just happen?" I squinted against the sunlight, mourning the loss of my sunglasses.

"Other than I deigned to dazzle you with a fascinating tale that you apparently failed to listen to? Nada."

Jacques, you fucking Houdini. "Take us in to shore and no tricks," I said to him.

He leveled a steady gaze at me, taking my measure, then he nodded reluctantly.

Once he'd complied, I sat down beside Arkady. Failing to find an elastic in my pockets, I twisted my hair up and shoved the blood dagger through it to hold it in place.

"Well, that's a look," Arkady said.

"It's all the rage in Paris."

The craft slowed to a stop, bobbing gently about fifteen feet from shore. Jacques cut the engine, watching me warily.

"Are we supposed—?" I yelled, my ears still ringing from the roar of the motor. "To jump?" I finished at a normal volume.

"Yes." Jacques engaged the anchor.

"From where? Show me."

Jacques walked to the back of the boat. "Here."

"Fine." I held out a hand to Arkady. "My love? Some help?"

Arkady pulled me up and escorted me to where Jacques stood. In a beautiful move that didn't telegraph a thing, he twisted and swung his fist, knocking Jacques' lights out.

The captain swayed and crashed to the deck.

"Why the code word?" Arkady said. We'd arranged that if either of us called the other "my love," to assume we were under attack.

"There was a whole thing with a kraken and a ferryman. Very Greek myth."

Arkady shook his head. "Illusionists."

"Right? Remember that where your hero is concerned."

"Nah, Levi's different."

"Whatever, fanboy. Stay here and keep an eye on Jacques."

"No way. I'd be skinned alive if I let you go onto Inferno by yourself."

"Tough. I'm pulling rank. You have to keep him unconscious because we can't have a Houdini running loose and messing with us."

Arkady conceded the wisdom of keeping Jacques out of an already volatile situation, but it was the best of all the suck-ass scenarios, since we had no way of gauging how long my reunion would take and the illusionist could not be allowed to wake up.

"Keep yourself safe." Arkady sat down on the top step of the metal ladder leading into the sea, his jeans rolled up, and his feet dangling.

Flip flops in hand, I jumped into the warm water, which was only thigh-high, and waded to shore. This was much more pleasant than the glacial lake that Camp Ruach had been situated on. I stepped onto the white sand beach.

My hair had tumbled down onto my shoulders. I looked around for the dagger but it had vanished and I couldn't call up another one.

My magic was gone.

I waded back out into the water.

"What's wrong?" Arkady leaned out of the back of the boat, his hands cupped around his mouth.

I made it knee-deep before another dagger appeared in my palm. "Inferno is a magic-free zone."

Chapter 16

"Get on the boat, Ash."

"But we've come all this way for our blessing." I couldn't turn around now. Chariot could not be allowed to get their hands on another piece of the scroll, and I couldn't walk away from the best lead on finding my dad that I'd ever had. I threw him a thumbs-up. "Back soon, babycakes."

The dagger disappeared again as soon as I hit the beach. I was magicless, but I wasn't weaponless. I had my brain. Jezebels were chosen because we were the best Seekers. Magic and strength were handy tools in our toolbox, but deprived of that, it came down to our wits.

I could do this.

Behind the beach, about fifty feet from shore, was a dense press of palm trees jutting out crookedly from the ground and blocking any view of the rest of the island.

Shading my eyes with one hand, I scanned the island for any tell-tale elevation where a house might be located. There was a rise off to my right.

I headed into the jungle. The thick canopy kept it dim and cool under the trees.

Other than birds and some creepy crawlies, the dirt path

up the hill appeared deserted, but the back of my neck prickled. I was being watched but, for some reason, not apprehended. Yet.

I'd been walking briskly for a few minutes, when there was a loud snuffling and crashing of dry branches to my left. I pressed back behind a tree in time to witness three wild pigs barrel past. One of them stumbled, close to where I'd been walking.

A volley of arrows shot out of a hidden hole to embed in the tree across from me. I pressed a hand to my racing heart. Another couple of steps and I would have been the one to set off that tripwire.

To badly misquote Shakespeare, "Whether 'tis nobler to suffer the slings and arrows of a boobytrapped jungle, or wave my arms and call out the guards?"

I put two fingers in my mouth and whistled. "I demand an audience with Caligula Jones." When nothing happened, I called out again. "Tell Paulie Peterson that he's got a visitor."

Three square-jawed men built like tanks melted out of the trees. Each man was armed with a sub-machine gun slung across his chest.

"How do you know that name?" The one whose forehead was more of a twelve-head stepped forward.

"Take me to him and find out." I tried not to stare but he also had this vast swath of unibrow and I couldn't help mentally fitting him for a Flintstone loincloth.

"Mr. Jones doesn't like tourists." He unslung his gun.

"Wait! Kill me and Paul—Caligula will be very displeased. We all know what happens when he's displeased, right, gentlemen?"

They exchanged an uneasy glance and I felt a stirring of unease. Geez, Uncle Paulie. How far off the deep end had you gone? If I'd believed his behavior was as extreme as their reactions suggested, I'd never have left Arkady on the boat.

"On second thought," I said, "I could just leave, never to return."

Unibrow grabbed my arm and dragged me in an entirely different direction than I'd been headed. I tried dragging my feet to slow his progress but without my enhanced strength he hauled me along like I weighed nothing.

Eventually the trees thinned out to a large clearing in front of a run-down plantation-style house featuring a dilapidated veranda, weather-beaten eaves, and missing siding.

"This is where the illustrious Caligula Jones lives?" I said, hoping to shake the visions of serial killers dancing through my head. "What kind of lame-ass hedonist is he? Sheesh. Where's the miniature replica of Versailles?"

"He burned that one down," Unibrow said.

I'd been kidding. Yikes. I struggled in Unibrow's hold, but he dragged me up the stairs.

Unibrow banged on the door, which was rotted through in places. "Mr. Jones?" Receiving no answer, he opened it and pushed me in ahead of him.

I gagged at the overpowering stench of stale booze and unwashed body.

The ratty curtains were drawn in the front room, but through the holes I could just make out a tanned man in a leopard print bathrobe seated on a shabby brown recliner. He was face down on a mirrored tray.

"Mr. Jones?" Unibrow gently prodded his shoulder.

Uncle Paulie started, jerking up with traces of white under his red nose. He stared at me through bleary eyes. "Who's this? Never mind. Don't care. Kill her."

Unibrow smirked in triumph, still gripping me in an iron-clad hold.

No. I was not about to die on this godforsaken island at the whim of this narcissist. I planted my free hand on my hip. "Too busy with your pity party, Uncle Paulie?"

Paulie's bathrobe fell open to reveal a pair of leopard print Speedos. "What did you call me?"

"You heard me, old man." I averted my eyes. "Gawd. Cover up. Circumcisions shouldn't be visible through swimwear."

"Leave us," he snapped at the guard, belting his robe tight.

"Told you." I smirked twice as hard at Unibrow as he released me.

"You still have to make it off the island," he murmured. He snapped out a salute to his boss and left.

"Ash. I…" Paulie looked around at the shambles of the room and sprung into motion, gathering up empty bottles, while I pretended to be fascinated by the clutter of vinyl albums spilling off a threadbare sofa.

I picked up one of the covers. It was a greatest hits of polka music.

"Even as a kid, I knew your taste in music was shit." I crouched down by the record player on the ground. The album on the player was David Hasselhoff singing "Do the Limbo Dance." That appalled me more than the coke.

"You never came to see me," he said.

I risked a glance over my shoulder. Paulie sat in the recliner once more, the bottles shoved unceremoniously in a corner. I moved aside some of the records and took a seat, the sofa creaking. "I was busy being angry and then you were busy being whatever the hell this is."

"A legend."

Uncle Paulie had been at the top of his chosen profession, illegal though it was. But he'd fled to this island, throwing parties that pushed every known definition of self-indulgence. I glanced at the coke on the mirror. He'd had to fill the void in his life with constant numbing—where were his real relationships? He'd had my dad. Had that been his sole social lifeline? Could I have ended up this way if Priya hadn't pushed me out of my comfort zone?

I twirled a finger around the room. "You're more like a cautionary tale."

Paulie laughed, a rusty unused sound, and my heart clenched. "Why are you here?"

"What happened to my dad? And don't give me the same BS you told Talia. You knew his secrets."

"And I've damned him every day for it."

"Then tell me." My words came out thick and pleading. "Did he mean to leave us or was there an accident?"

Paulie scrubbed a hand over his face. "Don't make me do this."

My stomach dropped into my toes. "He meant to…"

"…Yeah."

I gave a strangled laugh. "Don't hold out now, Uncle Paulie."

He closed his eyes briefly and swore.

At some point, when I was twelve, Adam got hired for a job. The ultimate score. Paulie didn't know what the gig was, just that over a few months, Adam became withdrawn. One night shortly before my thirteenth birthday, my dad came to Paulie, scared. Whatever he was involved in, it was deep and deadly. In order to protect us, my father decided to leave. Pretend we didn't matter.

Paulie's words washed over me, reducing me to a ghost wandering through my youth, searching in the blackness for a spark of hope and finding none. If Dad had cared about a get-rich con to set him up for life, he could have charmed some wealthy asshole into handing everything over. He was ironically unmaterialistic. He liked the con more than the gains. This wasn't about money, which meant that Dad's ultimate score was the promise of immortality.

"Did he ever mention Chariot to you?"

Paulie shook his head. "Like some name for the con? Nah, nothing like that. He called it the Holy Grail payout."

The *Sefer* would seem like a Holy Grail to those obsessed with it.

Chariot. Chariot. Chariot. The word thudded dully in my ears with each heartbeat. Should I mourn my father for being a fool? Hate him for that same reason?

"Who was he working for?" I said.

"There were some secrets he wouldn't even share with me. Adam called him 26L1."

"Real helpful. Where did Dad go?" My voice sounded tinny. Or maybe my body was just too far away.

"Nowhere at first. He had to stick around and see this job through."

A vein pulsed in my forehead. "Was he in town for my birthday?"

Paulie nodded.

Mom had planned to throw a party, because thirteen was a milestone, but to me it was simply one more day in my tally since he'd left. Talia had tried to make the day normal. She'd bought me a sugary supermarket cake and queued up my favorite films, like the three of us had always done.

It was so normal, it hurt.

"When did he leave? As far as you know?" I glanced longingly at the bottles of booze in the corner but they were empty and there wasn't a fresh stockpile.

"Not until after your accident."

"Which was a Friday," I said.

"I know, kid. Talia phoned me. The sight of you laying there…" He pulled a silver flask out from the side of his chair, uncapped it and took a swig. "Here."

I took it and drank deep.

"Adam phoned me late Monday night, early Tuesday morning," he said.

I sat up straight. That was the night he'd visited me in

the hospital. The night my magic had first manifested. "How can you be sure?"

"I've gone over those last days a million times, trying to see what I missed. If I could have done something different. They're etched in my mind." Paulie fiddled with his belt, his gaze distant for a moment. "You know, I was quite the forger back in the day. It's how I bought Inferno."

"Yeah. Paintings mostly."

Paulie rubbed his thumb and index finger together. "Good money in that. But I could forge anything. Adam called with a special request. Two items. A fake passport issued out of Montreal in the name of Avi Chomsky."

Same initials, of course, because it was easier to remember a fake name that way, and Adam had grown up in Montreal and was bilingual if his French was ever tested.

"And the other forgery?"

"To reproduce a scroll. Rush job."

The flask slipped from my hand, boozy fumes wafting up as the liquid pooled onto the floor. "Was the scroll old? Yellow, kind of brittle?"

"That's it. Written in Hebrew and... some other language." Paulie was starting to slur. I was losing him.

Dad hadn't bluffed Gavriella about possessing the scroll. But which version had he planned on giving her?

"What happened to the scroll?" I said.

Paulie's head nodded forward. "Took it. With the fakes. Thursday. Last time I saw him." The pauses between words got longer.

I reached for him, and his eyes shot open.

"Never rush a con," he said in a bleak voice, before nodding off.

If my father had lived by a rule, it was that one. Rushing a con was a surefire route to disaster. He'd spend hours in his cramped study with the door locked. I'd crept in once, when he'd gone for a coffee refill. Even with his Charmer magic, he'd compile detailed profiles on his targets, writing cramped notes in some code I couldn't decipher. In retrospect, it wasn't all that different from the legwork I put into a case. Except with more fleecing and a deluded self-righteousness about the fact that he only hit those who deserved it.

Amazing what my mother had turned a blind eye to in the name of love. Guess she'd found a strategy that worked for her—and kept it up to this day.

"Did you ever hear from Dad again?" I shook Paulie, but he was out too deeply to rouse.

Unibrow returned. "You need to leave."

"What's wrong with him?" I said.

"Too much."

"Of what?"

"Everything. Let's go."

"Wait—"

Unibrow grabbed me around the waist, carrying me off like I was a football.

I struggled, but without my enhanced strength couldn't budge his grip. "I just need to know what happened to my—"

Unibrow carried me through the house, dumped me outside, and slammed the door.

Dad had witnessed my magic and then commissioned the fake scroll. Why?

I sat on the stairs, my head pressed to my bent knees. If he'd initially left to protect us, could that desire have gotten stronger after seeing my magic?

What if Dad had made a deal to give them not just the scroll, but Gavriella as well? In return, Chariot would help him leave town, and set him up somewhere, maybe even to continue doing their bidding. But they'd leave us alone and my secret would be safe.

Adam would have required something irresistible to bring Gavriella close enough to use his Charmer magic on her and capture her for Chariot. If I were Chariot? I wouldn't risk any real piece of the *Sefer* getting near a Jezebel. Thus, the fake.

Anger flared in my belly, scorching and bitter. Every replayed word of Paulie's dripped like gasoline. Adam's protection was a hollow shield, a shell game. Of all the sins Adam had to answer for, the worst was that a real father wouldn't have been stupid enough to love the rush of the game over his own family in the first place.

Chapter 17

The rest of the trip was uneventful. I begged off enjoying the island nightlife, staying in with room service and some P.I. databases to track down Avi Chomsky, while Arkady went out on the town. I searched until the words swam on screen. The trouble was that Avi—Adam—could be anywhere in the world, using any date of birth, and that was if he hadn't gone off-grid entirely.

He might have chosen a getaway that he had no connection to. But what if he hadn't? According to Paulie, my father had initially left to keep us safe. What if he'd ended up somewhere that had, if not an actual connection to our family, then an emotional one?

My parents had gone to New York for their honeymoon. That was a possibility. Then there was Zihuatanejo, a beach town on Mexico's Pacific Coast. We'd gone there when I was a kid, and while I didn't remember a lot about it, I had flashes of jumping in the water, going to a crowded market every day to buy fresh papaya, and both of my parents laughing a lot. They reminisced about that trip a ton over the years.

By the time Arkady stumbled back to his room next door

just before dawn, I had a plan. Since we had to stop in New York anyway for his return flight, Arkady would check out the three Avi Chomskys I found in the different boroughs, sending me current photos. If that was a no go, from there he'd fly to Mexico and see if anyone fit that name. I'd have done it, but I had a fundraiser to attend.

Arkady grumbled a bit about not packing for an extended vacation, but agreed.

Since Paulie had confirmed that Adam had the scroll, we didn't need Priya to track down the previous owner, so I'd fired off a text taking her off that.

I'd barely gotten any sleep from my allotted cat nap when I was woken by a call from an unfamiliar number. It was the fair company. I pushed past the grogginess to present my credentials and ask about employee records from thirty years ago.

Unfortunately, about twenty years back, they'd all burned up in a fire. I tried not to let my excitement over their misfortune show, but the lack of documentation wasn't a coincidence. A Hispanic family, a white-blond Russian kid, Wonderland—this was the genesis of the Queen of Hearts and Moran.

"Were you working for the company back then?" I said.

"You bet," the man said. "We're a family business. I've been here more than forty years."

I asked him about Moran, but he had no memory of him.

"Did the family who worked the midway have a daughter?" I did the math, guessing at her current age. "Probably her early twenties? Striking violet eyes?"

"Serafina." He infused that name with a heavy dose of wistful nostalgia.

"What did she do there?"

"Told fortunes. Mostly love affair stuff." He chuckled.

"She claimed to see into people's hearts. It was catchy. Got her a lot of business."

"Holy. Shit." I clutched the phone, leaning forward as if I could physically pull more information out of him. "What was her last name?"

"Sorry. Don't remember. Serafina wasn't her real name either. Just a stage name."

I grabbed the complimentary pen provided by the hotel. "Is there anything else you remember about her? She may be in line for a healthy inheritance if I can track her down." I pulled out a tried-and-true excuse that generally had people happy to share their knowledge.

"I don't remember that, but her favorite lipstick was Lovestruck Red."

"Uh, okay. That's random."

"She gave me a napkin with a lip print on it at the end of that summer. And, well, I may have stolen her lipstick. I was young, dumb, and had a terrible crush on her."

"Do you still have them?!" I shrieked into the poor man's ear.

"Maybe? Could have ended up packed away with my yearbooks and such."

"Would you check? Please. This is very important." After a few more minutes, I think I managed to convince him that my request was perfectly reasonable and professional. He promised to take a look today and if he found them, he'd FedEx them over to me.

I asked him to use a blood seal on the package. Offered by post offices and courier services, blood seals looked like the wax seals of old. They were affixed to a letter or package to prove they hadn't been tampered with or opened yet, because once a blood seal was broken, the packaging was destroyed. Law firms used them.

I hung up and did a happy dance around the room. Lip prints were unique to individuals and used these days in

DNA analysis much like fingerprints. Even identical twins had different lip prints. It was less certain how much DNA a lipstick from thirty years ago could yield, but stranger things had happened in cold cases. This might not get me the Queen's identity, but it could provide a very solid genetic profile that would prove a substantial breakthrough in learning her real name and potentially tracking down other members of her family.

Thoroughly elated with the morning's events, I traveled to the airport with Arkady. We made our flight to New York with no issues and then parted ways: me back to Vancouver and Arkady remaining in Manhattan. He was a happy camper since he'd scored a fancy hotel stay and clothing allowance from Levi.

By the time I made it home on Saturday, I was running on fumes and the scent of lemon lamb from the Greek restaurant on the ground floor of my apartment building made my stomach growl.

Shortly after my arrival, I received a call from the lab. There were no drugs in Mayan's system.

After scarfing down some food, I took Mrs. Hudson for a walk and a quick game of "fetch your cow girlfriend," then I jumped in the shower to scrub off my travel grime.

Beyond the obvious color scheme for the dress code of the Black and White Ball that night, it was also formal attire, so my options were limited. None of my black dresses were fancy enough and even if I had the time or money, I had no inclination to buy a gown that I'd never wear again. With a shudder, I rummaged on the side of my closet containing clothes that Talia had sent over for one event or another until I hit scratchy fabric.

Gritting my teeth, I pulled out a white confectionary of a dress. My mother, in a moment of either wild optimism or temporary amnesia about who her kid actually was, had purchased it for a university graduation party she'd wanted to throw me. We'd compromised: I didn't burn the damn thing and she'd moved the event to a nice Italian restaurant, where I didn't have to dress like a swan.

The top was a fitted bodice covered in white sequins with a ruffled ballgown skirt made of poufy layers of crinoline. Even Disney Princesses tossed their heads in disdain at how hard this dress was trying.

Mrs. Hudson took one look at it and raised her leg. I whisked the dress out of the way and she gave a little whine and lowered her leg again.

"Right sentiment, wrong night, dog."

I wriggled into the outfit with zero enthusiasm, then, holding the abomination against my chest so it didn't fall off, stomped into the kitchen. "Help."

Priya choked on her mouthful of cereal. "That is beyond my skill set."

"Shut up." I sucked in a breath as she zipped me up.

"I can't believe you still have that dress."

"It was an out-of-sight-out-of-mind kind of thing."

She tugged gently on one of my locks. "What are you doing with your hair?"

"Nothing? I'm wearing sparkly eyeshadow and foundation. My face is already suffocating. Can't that be enough?"

Priya rolled her eyes. "Come on, Cinderella."

I dragged my feet as she pulled me into the bathroom. "Do I haaaaave to? It's a work night."

Priya shoved me down on the closed toilet seat lid, while Mrs. Hudson seated herself on the bathmat, watching the proceedings with doggy enthusiasm.

"Levi is going to be there," Priya said. "Levi's ex is going to be there. And she isn't going to look like an escapee from an Off-Off-Broadway production of *Frozen*."

"That second 'off' was unnecessary," I said.

"If you're gonna do this, then own it."

The next ten minutes were torture. Priya curled,

pinned, and twisted my hair into a frothy updo. It was also kind of great because Priya filled me in on the latest love saga of one of the regulars at Higher Ground, which meant she'd gone out to work while I was away. I gave my usual non-committal grunts and tried not to let my grin slip free.

"You really should have a date for this," she said.

"I do. Rafael. Ouch." She'd stabbed me with a bobby pin.

"I didn't realize you two had that kind of a relationship."

"My fake fiancé, who incidentally would have reported my every move back to his hero, is out of the country. The man I'm sleeping with, who I can't be seen in public with, is going with his ex. That didn't leave a lot of last-minute options."

"Hmph."

"You want to ask him out," I said.

She pinned my last curl in place. "I'm thinking about it. He was such a shit to you that initially I planned to simply have some fun and throw him off-guard, but I actually enjoyed talking to him. Is that a problem?"

"Maybe wait until he's settled in and we've got a working rhythm with Team Jezebel."

And I'd found some other solution to calm my cravings.

"All right." Priya stepped back and studied me critically. "There's just one thing missing."

I followed her into her bedroom. She opened her underwear drawer and pulled out a square jewelry box, opening it to reveal a tiara of tiny flower-shaped crystals nestled on blue velvet that had been for her big princess wedding.

"And here you gave me crap about this dress when you hung onto that thing?" Priya scowled at me. "Sorry," I said. "I don't understand. That time in your life was so painful. Why would you keep a memento of it?"

She ran a finger lightly over the crystals. "Part of me

believed that as long as I kept it, my happily-ever-after was still possible. I know better now."

I winced. "You're dealing with trauma. Don't give up."

She smiled gently. "I'm not. I know you've been worried about me, but as scary as that kidnapping was, it's not the reason I've been pulling back. I've needed—I still need—time to figure out how I want to live moving forward. Ravi and I had a lot of passion, and a lot of problems that we never addressed. When that ended, I decided my romantic happiness was best served if I was in control of the relationship." She half-laughed. "That didn't work either. When I do decide to date again, it'll be from a place of looking for my equal. More importantly, I'll know that whatever happens, I'm my own happily-ever-after."

"That's a pretty good realization." I eyed the tiara dubiously. "Are you still going to keep it?"

"Damn straight. I look amazing in bling. I'm going to wear it to the supermarket, to work, for my massage therapy appointments… It's my reminder that I'm not a princess. I'm a queen. And tonight?" She placed the tiara on my head. "You need to remember that, too. Just bring it back."

I tilted my head from side-to-side and smiled. Mayan could suck it. "I'll return it safe and sound. I promise. Am I ready?"

"As you'll ever be. Kick ass, Holmes."

THE THEME of the ball was "A Night in Fairyland" and the decorating committee had outdone themselves. The ballroom at the historic Hotel Vancouver, painted in tones of cream and gold with crown moldings, gold-framed mirrors, and Edwardian frescoes, glowed with an otherworldly beauty under the hundreds of tiny white twinkling lights strung up.

I checked my wrap and stepped into the animated swirl

of partygoers. Men strutted about in tuxes, while one fabulous guy outshone everyone in a black bejeweled ballgown that made even mine seem a little plain.

Not to be outdone by their elegant counterparts, the women dazzled in outlandish gowns and gems that they wore with the giddy air of young girls attending their first formal party. My dress fit in just fine, and the tiara was the perfect crowning touch.

I made a slow circuit of the room, looking for Jonah Samuels, but I found Mayan first, conversing with a group of people. She was stunning in a sleek black dress with a 1920s vibe to it and a slight train in the back. Her hair was pinned in some complicated braid and held in place with a large black rose ornament.

One of the people in her crowd shifted, revealing Levi.

His stark beauty took my breath away. He was one of the taller men in the room, and under the lights, his black hair shone like a raven's wing. His tux was impeccably fitted to him, the white dress shirt pressed crisp, but his bowtie was the tiniest fraction askew. My fingers twitched with the urge to fix it, to tease him about it and get some snarky retort from those lush lips that would inevitably make me laugh.

Our gazes snagged. I glanced between him and Mayan, and widened my eyes in an exaggerated expression of surprise. He stood there, deadpan until I was done, at which point, after a brief—and pointed—perusal of my outfit, his lips curled up in the briefest smirk.

I clutched my beaded handbag, calculating the best trajectory should I need to wing it at him. No, that was a princess reaction. I straightened up to my full height, my confidence more dazzling than any of the crystals.

Levi's eyes narrowed. Mayan had to touch his arm twice to get his attention and he looked away before I did. Heh.

"There you are." Rafael was at my elbow. "Sorry for being late."

"No worries. I'm glad there were no problems with the ticket I'd left for you," I said.

His tux was equally as bespoke as Levi's and while it didn't send my heart into the same annoying palpitations, he was worthy arm candy.

"Help me do a sweep for Samuels and keep an eye on Mayan." I subtly indicated who she was. Since Rafael and I worked together, he fell under client confidentiality. I straightened his bowtie and he flinched.

I dropped my hand. "On second thought, let's split up." I melted into the crowd, my jaw set, and bumped into someone's back. "Sorry," I muttered as the person turned around.

"Ladylike as usual," Levi sneered, holding two wine-glasses. He flicked his eyes to the left, where a couple of Untainted Party cronies of my mother's and a group I recognized as House employees avidly watched our interaction.

Awesome.

"Careful with the angle of your chin there, Montefiore. You might topple over backwards from all the weight in your fat head." I helped myself to one of the glasses of white wine and tossed half the shitty drink back. For make-believe antagonism, our encounter pinched my heart—as if our deepening relationship had all been a dream and I'd just woken up to the cold reality again.

"You have the manners of a goat," Levi said.

"Better a goat than a pompous ass throwing his weight around." I stilled.

It wasn't just Jezebels who suffered under the weight of overwhelming expectations. We had a choice in accepting the Mantle, but Attendants were born to it. Serve and protect made for a narrow, lonely life, especially when that was the sum total of it. Was there any room for failure in Rafael's mind, and was that how he saw his reaction to helping me with the cravings? Not as a healing win, but as a disaster on an inherently personal level? I'd been prepared for his resentment once the effects had worn off, but I hadn't taken into consideration his shame.

The quartet in the corner launched into a soft song. Light and lively. An answering fizziness began in my stomach, bubbling outward into my throat and down to my toes, but mine was sour.

"Ash?" Levi murmured. "Are you okay?"

I shoved the glass back in his hand. "Go bore your date. I've got more important things to attend to."

Chapter 18

I found Rafael in the far corner of the ballroom leaning against the ornate wainscoting by the window, watching Mayan. "Listen." I looped my arm through his, falling into a slow circuit of the room. "This fight needs you. I need you. If you're beating yourself up over what happened, stop now. You did it because you had my back, just like I have yours. We'll find a way through this together, okay?"

He tensed, struggling with some decision, and I braced myself for him to walk away.

"What happened between us was... disquieting." His silence after that had less to do with the large, boisterous group we had to veer around than the thoughtful expression on his face. "While Attendants historically have remained in the background, we pride ourselves on being the bedrock that allows you to operate and succeed. But during that episode, I wasn't a rock, I was out of control. I had become the weak link in this fight." He gazed off into the distance.

"I'm far from perfect, but that doesn't mean you have to pick up the slack on that front. You're not infallible, nor do you have to be."

"If I fail, people die." Rafael's grip tightened on the wineglass he held. "There is no room for failure for any of us."

"Who died, Rafael? Gavriella?"

He stared into the Pinot Noir, which had the flat dark color of blood.

"Your dad?" I said.

"Suffice it to say, we can't afford to be weak, because Chariot will exploit that. We can't expose ourselves."

That had always been my thinking, as well. Except that a continual show of strength was exhausting and, ultimately, brittle.

"You aren't weak and what happened wasn't proof of some character deficiency." I gently pried the poor wineglass from his death grip and set it on a table, a crystal chandelier bouncing prismic dots off of it. "The opposite, in fact. In making yourself vulnerable like that, you made us both stronger. That's what you need to focus on."

His brow furrowed. "I didn't expect this level of understanding from you."

"Yeah, well, don't get used to it. And don't shut me out anymore. My magic issues, this missing scroll, we're scrambling now because my father chose to run away with some very dangerous secrets. Communication is essential." We stopped in front of the musicians as they launched into a waltz, and I swept Rafael a playful curtsy. "Meantime, can we start this evening again? Greetings, Rafael."

He gave me a wan smile. "Hello, Ashira."

"You clean up well, Attendant mine."

"And you…" He wrinkled his face.

"Yeah. Yeah. Don't strain for a compliment with this dress. You'll hurt yourself."

"Thank heavens." He grinned. "You look lovely, if somewhat unlike your regular self."

Mayan stopped to speak with some servers, so Rafael and I positioned ourselves at the long table covered with charcuterie, the cheeses, cut meats, and crackers presented on carved wooden boards accompanied by glass bowls of pickles and preserves.

"What happened with your uncle?" Rafael said.

I looked longingly at the delights on offer, then down at my white dress, and picked up a plain cracker, nibbling on it while I summed up the events at Inferno in a low voice.

Rafael procured me another glass of white wine from a passing server's tray. "You confirmed he had the scroll. Good work. You'll find him."

I gave him a tired smile and raised the glass in cheers. "You bet I will."

"I can put this new information against the other time-line data. We should meet tomorrow. Every slight advantage is one we must act upon immediately. Your office?"

"Sounds good."

We spent the next couple of hours doing endless tours of the room. Jonah didn't show, Levi and I kept our distance, and Mayan spent all her time talking up the benefits of the Lung Cancer Foundation.

I'd nursed my glass into the dregs, I couldn't eat in case I dropped anything on this stupid dress, and I'd given up on anything interesting happening. I was ready to call it a night and go for french fries when Mayan glanced at her phone. She touched Levi's arm, said a few words, then slipped from the room. I trailed her out to the lobby, planting myself by the rack of tourist brochures on offer.

Jonah Samuels waltzed into the hotel. In his pressed formal wear, he blended in with the rest of the crowd milling about here. The two of them had a brief but intense exchange. There was nothing alarming about their body language. Mayan wasn't tense or scared of Jonah, nor was he crowding her space or intimidating her in any way. Jonah said something that had Mayan glare at him, before yielding with a resigned head nod.

He settled a large blue heart-shaped stone on a gold chain around her neck. Mayan gave him a tolerant smile.

Whatever was up between them, Mayan was a free and willing participant.

Jonah continued into the ballroom, while Mayan headed for the restrooms.

I followed him over to the tables containing items for the silent auction. Catching Rafael's eye, I nodded at our quarry. I didn't expect any trouble, but I'd brought Rafael here to watch my back.

Jonah studied the bids on a wine tasting tour.

I stopped at a glossy card detailing another item that was up for auction. "Five hundred dollars for high tea? I better get to eat my body weight in tiny sandwiches for that."

Jonah gave me a smooth smile. "The tea is for two people so unless you're planning on showing up stag, I think you'd be disappointed."

"Maybe I could bring a stuffed animal, like I used to when I had tea parties as a kid." I wrinkled my nose—hopefully adorably and not like a cocaine addict jonesing for a fix. "Girl thing. I'm sure you didn't have tea parties."

"No," he said, amused. "Nor did I have stuffed animals. I had imaginary friends. Fierce ones who I built forts and stormed castles with."

"Such a boy. And do you still storm castles, Mr…?"

"Call me Jonah."

I readied myself for him to extend a hand to shake so I could check if he was Mundane or Nefesh, but he clasped his hands behind his back.

"Ashira," I said. "So those castles?"

"Sadly, they remain unstormed," he said. "I'm involved in medical research."

Yeah, yeah. Give me something else to work with. "That sounds interesting. What kind?"

"I advanced a bonding technique. It's actually very boring."

"I'm sure it's not."

"You're very kind, but I recognize that glazed look. How about you?"

"I'm in politics." I tilted my head. "I don't suppose I could interest you in a drink? Perhaps somewhere quieter, like the rooftop bar?" I intended to steer the conversation to Hedon and work in my acquaintance with Mayan, but those weren't topics one just dropped in to casual conversation with a stranger.

"I'm flattered, but I'm afraid I can't stay. I just came to support this important cause."

Bollocks. "My loss. Lovely meeting you, Jonah."

"You as well, Ashira."

I sailed into the crowd, giving Rafael the signal to keep an eye on Jonah, since I couldn't very well turn around and stalk him. Mayan was safely ensconced in a conversation with an elderly couple, so, frustrated at being rebuffed, I stepped out of the crowded ballroom to get some air. I wound through the hallways, the noise growing distant behind me. A door to one of the smaller event rooms was cracked open, and I slipped inside. It was partially set up for some dinner function.

"Who were you talking to?"

Startled, I spun around.

Levi stood in the doorway.

"Jonah Samuels. My top suspect behind Mayan's erratic behavior."

"I wasn't imagining things, then."

"No."

He nodded, satisfied. "You'll keep me updated?"

"Obviously. Now, if you'll excuse me." I brushed past him, but he grabbed my wrist and jerked me flush up against him.

Levi claimed my mouth in a hard, brief kiss.

"What was that for?" I pushed against his chest, my fingers only flexing against his pecs for a second before I stepped back.

"A placeholder until I can get you out of that ridiculous dress."

"Keep sweet talking, Montefiore. I'll be putty in your hands. Also, you have a date. Remember?"

"It's a public relations stunt. Mayan's an upstanding Mundane citizen." He pulled a handkerchief out of his pocket and wiped all traces of my red lipstick from his mouth.

I gripped my handbag. Better to clutch that, than Levi's shoulders and mark him again. "Not so upstanding if she's hanging out in Hedon."

"Being seen with her reinforces the idea that I have friends and relationships with all kinds of people, both magic and non-magic."

"There it is. My perfectly reasonable explanation." I tapped my bag against my thigh, accidentally hitting the clasp and spilling all the items inside to the ground. I dropped to my knees, gathering everything up. "Fuck."

Levi crouched down to help, but I pushed him away.

"I don't need your help." I shoved my driver's license back in the bag.

"There's nothing to be jealous of." He gathered up my credit card and keys.

I lunged for the lipstick, making a break for it. "Of course not. The explanation so reasonable that one wonders why you didn't just tell me instead of letting me show up and find you here. Would a quick 'Hey, Ash, I'm going to the ball with my ex who was a total bitch to you for most of your life, but it's a PR stunt' have killed you?"

Levi stood up, still holding on to my credit card and keys. "Yeah, that would have made everything better."

I held my hand out for my belongings, which he relinquished. "We'll never know because you didn't man up and have the conversation. You didn't just disrespect me on a personal level, you did it on a professional one as well. What if your presence had thrown a wrench in my plans? A little heads-up would have been appreciated."

"Back at you, sweetheart. At least my surprise seeing you here was genuine."

I did a final check to make sure my possessions were all back in my bag. "Yet you keep assuming you can keep things from me and I won't find out."

"Then you could have asked. Unlike you, who didn't tell me you'd be bringing a plus-one."

"Aw, baby." I snapped my clutch shut. "There's nothing to be jealous of."

"We'll never know because you didn't man up and have the conversation," Levi said.

Our glaring contest did little to quell the anger swirling around the room.

I blew an errant curl out of my eyes. "Rafael is my backup, okay? Not my date."

"He's not doing a very good job." Levi trailed a finger along the bare skin from my shoulder to the inside of my elbow.

That's it? He was okay with all of this now? How could he emotionally turn so quickly? Did this not mean as much to him as it did to me?

I jerked my arm away. "I only need him for actual threats, not annoying unwanted attention."

Levi stepped back, his face closed-down. "Let me know what you learn about Samuels."

He headed for the hallway.

Great. Sayonara, asshole.

My comfort zone urged me to let him go. Levi, with his talented lips, his reasonable explanations, his wry humor, and his way of understanding me like no one else did, was anything but comfortable.

There were ten feet to go before he reached the door, and a finality in the set of his shoulders to him crossing that threshold.

He'd changed the shape of me, but I'd changed him, too. He was the one man I'd relished standing toe-to-toe with, but could the very thing I liked most about us turn into a crushing weight that we wouldn't survive?

Five feet.

What if he hadn't let go of his emotions around me being here with Rafael that easily and I was letting him walk out without verifying it?

I bit my lip.

Three feet.

Fuck it. My comfort zone was getting kind of stifling.

I sprinted over and blocked his path to the door. "Were you jealous?"

"Yes." He rubbed the back of his neck. "Even though coming here with Mayan was the right move politically, it was the wrong one for us. I knew it would hurt you and I fucking took the coward's way out. I'm sorry. Am I forgiven?"

"Depends." My stern voice was at odds with the smile that threatened to break free because this mattered to him. I mattered. "Are you still jealous, even knowing that I'm not on a date? Because I'm openly on the arm of someone else, when you and I have to pretend that we hate each other?"

"Yes," he said softly. "That's not what you wanted to hear."

"No. That was the right answer." I reached up on tiptoe, because even in heels I was still shorter, and kissed him.

He resisted for a second, and then his lips moved against mine. The faintest rasp of stubble scratched my chin.

I curled my hand around his hip, his thigh muscle

tensing under my palm, and sank into him, earning a low groan.

Levi placed a hand on the small of my back, sucking on my lower lip. His tongue found mine, and we pressed together so tightly that I was dizzy.

My fingers snaked into his hair, sifting through the silky locks, while Levi framed my face, almost reverential in his touch. I savored his taste and the quickening of his breath that matched my own.

This kiss was a beginning, a promise of more to come. It was a maelstrom, churning up emotions I wasn't yet ready to name.

Reluctantly, I stepped back, opening my eyes as I sucked in cool air.

Levi stared back at me, his expression calm. "Will you come over tonight?"

I swallowed to get moisture into my suddenly dry mouth. "Yes."

"Will you stay all night?"

"Yes?"

His lips quirked up in a half-grin. "This isn't Jeopardy. Frame your answer as a statement."

I'd slept over at men's houses before, guys I'd been casually dating, but they'd been in that box from the get-go. Levi had started out as something much different, and every time our relationship shifted, hell, every time I saw a new side of him, I had to reframe my view of this man. Spending the night curled up against him, asleep and vulnerable, was a huge shift.

Was that a bad thing? Boxes allowed me to distill people, but did that limit my understanding of them? Limit my thinking? I swallowed the knot in my throat. Could I do away with boxes on a case-by-case basis? One person at a time, the same way I solved an investigation one piece at a time? Hadn't I already, with Eleanor and even Rafael?

I rolled the idea around of taking Levi out of the box I'd comfortably slotted him into and it wasn't the dark hole of terror I'd expected. If I could save the world, I could have a talk about what exactly we wanted from the other person and then rock the follow-through.

"Well?" he said.

"I'll take 'all the ways Levi will entertain Ashira when she stays all night' for a thousand, Alex."

He ducked his head, allowing a sweet smile to break free. "Promise?" I nodded and he caught my hand, turning my palm upright and pressing a single kiss into it before leaving.

My fingers traced my swollen lips. If I didn't run screaming in the night, we'd get to the good stuff. I exhaled sharply. Fuck balls. I didn't mean sex.

Back in the ballroom, I helped myself to a couple of the tuna tartare on thin spicy crisps.

"Jonah just left," Rafael said.

"Here." I handed him one of the appetizers. "Eat. Drink and be merry. Might as well enjoy this fancy-schmancy ball."

I was licking tuna juice off my finger, which was actually zestier than one would imagine, when Mayan made some excuse to Levi and left the ballroom again.

This time, she left the hotel entirely. All right. Now we were getting somewhere.

Chapter 19

Mayan hailed a taxi from the stand out front of the hotel. Our under-the-speed-limit grand chase landed us at Harbour Center and the entrance to Hedon.

I allowed her a brief head start inside. The Queen hadn't refused me entry until she'd made her decision regarding our alliance, so I should be allowed in. Would she try to head trip me again? Potentially. Was it worth the risk of solving this case? That remained to be seen, but I'd been hired to find out what Mayan was up to and this was my big break.

Rafael, used to a support position, bless him, didn't kick up a fuss about me going on my own, though he was impressed that I'd had the foresight to bring the two tokens left over from Miles with me tonight.

"It was kind of a no-brainer," I said. "Mayan was going there on a regular basis and with Jonah having bought a ticket to the ball, it was a reasonable assumption she'd end up in Hedon again and I'd be traveling."

My Attendant volunteered to wait for me at Harbour Center. "If you're not out in two hours, I'll sound the alarm. Call the rest of the team."

"That's an excellent idea."

Mayan was already in the elevator up to the top floor by the time I'd convinced the security guard on duty to accept my token and let me through. The second my car opened on the restaurant level, I dashed through the slowly revolving doors into Hedon.

I peered down the narrow roads leading away from the small plaza, rewarded with a glimpse of Mayan turning a corner. Silently, I hurried after her.

Since it was always night here, there wasn't some set sleeping schedule. The world was buzzing with activity, which helped mask my pursuit.

She stopped on a residential street, either side lined with low narrow apartment buildings painted in garish colors. I tailed her into one on the corner that was a violent shade of chartreuse and smelled of cheap incense. The buildings were so skinny that there was only one apartment on each of the four stories.

I pressed into the shadows in the stairwell.

Mayan crouched down by the door knob on the second floor and picked the lock with the ease of a seasoned burglar. Slipping off her shoes, she crept inside.

I removed my own, then flew up the rest of the stairs, racing through the long apartment to the lit bedroom at the back, but when I was only halfway through the living room, Mayan pulled her black rose barrette from her braid and tossed it in the air.

The rose transformed into a black barb, exactly like the poison one in the ring that the steampunk cat had tried to sell me. It zoomed toward Alfie, who sat up in bed, gaping at the barb now embedded in his arm that was already melting into his flesh. Black lines snaked out from the point of impact.

"Gunter," Alfie croaked. "You still reek of Gitanes."

"I swore to take everything from you." Mayan patted his head. "Now I have."

Alfie tried to raise a hand, but it fell limply back onto the covers.

"Bye, Alfie." Mayan saw me in the doorway, swore, and bolted for the window.

Alfie was dying and his murderess was getting away in the opposite direction. I couldn't let either happen.

Alfie rasped in a breath. His complexion was ashen and the left side of his face drooped like a stroke victim.

Trusting I could find Mayan or Gunter or whatever the fuck was going on, I dropped my handbag, jumped on the bed and slammed my magic into Alfie, but the poison was just that. Poison. Not magic.

I sprinted across the room and leaned out the window.

Mayan jumped the final few feet from the fire escape to the ground.

"Mayan!" I clambered out onto the fire escape. "You're a bitch, but you aren't a killer. Give me the antidote."

Her features twisted in an ugly sneer, illuminated in the moonlight. "There isn't one."

A curtain in a neighboring apartment twitched. A face briefly appeared and then quickly moved out of sight.

"There has to be a way to stop this," I said. "You went to Levi. He sent me here. Let me help."

Mayan's expression softened; she looked lost. "You can't."

No. I wasn't losing her. Or Alfie. This wasn't ending in tragedy.

I hefted a blood rock in my hand and whipped it at Mayan's retreating figure, blessing all those hours of darts.

It hit her square in the back, knocking her to the ground. Her knee cracked against the cobblestones and she cried out, tumbling onto her back. Not gonna lie, that was eminently satisfying. Really, I was to be commended on my considerable restraint in not throwing a dagger instead.

"You cunt!" She cradled her injured knee in her hands.

Even if I could have discounted every other aberration

about Mayan, this demanded my attention. Mayan despised the "C" word. She'd torn a strip off kids numerous times at camp for using it. She had to be compelled somehow by this Gunter or someone acting on his behalf. Like Jonah.

Behind me, Alfie wheezed, spasming. The black lines had invaded every inch of exposed skin.

It was a minor miracle that the Queen's guard hadn't arrived to check out the commotion and cause problems, because saving Alfie was my utmost concern. But how? He was barely breathing. There was no time to find him a healer and if there was no antidote, then he'd die.

Unless...

"Hold on, Alfie." Running like the hounds of Hell were nipping at my heels, I sprinted down the fire escape, and ripped Mayan's necklace off.

She clawed at me, biting my arm, so I decked her. Her head lolled back against the dusty street. Unconscious was safer than dead. It may not have been the most optimal over-all, but if we broadened the definition of "unharmed" from "not a scratch on her" to "still breathing, thanks to yours truly" then I hadn't broken my promise to Levi.

I hauled ass back to Alfie and pressed the pendant against his skin. His eyes fluttered shut.

I forced his mouth open and made him lick it.

His heart stopped beating.

With a strangled roar, I shattered the stone in my fist.

Blue powder erupted in a puff, coating Alfie's face.

There was a sizzling noise and the smell of bitter licorice, then the black lines on his face disappeared.

"Come on." Tossing back the covers, I ripped his pajamas open, rubbing the powder into, well, not every inch of him, but all the PG inches. I left his underwear intact.

His ribcage jerked once before falling into a steady, if slow breathing. The black lines were gone, and when I sent my magic inside, I confirmed that he was poison-free.

One murder charge down. One problematic woman to bring home so I could solve what, exactly, was going on.

Alfie opened his eyes. "Gunter?"

"You're safe. Do you need a healer?"

He wiggled his fingers and toes and took a couple of deep breaths. "No. You saved me."

"No more stealing people's shit, okay?"

He gave a shaky laugh. "No promises."

Grabbing my clutch, I climbed out onto the fire escape to find Mayan's prone body surrounded by two of the Queen's Guard, both with mesh covering their faces. They were determining whether or not to lift her. I jogged down to them.

"I've got this, thanks," I said.

One of the guards, a woman from her build, crossed her arms. "Who are you?"

"Her sister. Idiot had too much to drink and fell."

"You want help?" she said.

"Enhanced strength. I'm good." I'd gotten Mayan on her feet, my arm around her waist, supporting her, when she woke up and started screaming that I'd tried to kill her.

She moved with a flailing panic.

"She's lying," I said. I tried to grab Mayan, accidentally elbowing the second guard who was attempting to help her.

The first guard blasted me back against a streetlamp with some kind of psionic wave. The metal post clipped me hard in my shoulder blade and I swore loudly.

Priya's beloved tiara snapped into two pieces, clattering to the ground, and bouncing along in a half-roll until they came to a stop.

I gasped, but it was a clean break. I could fix it.

"Don't move." Producing a pair of magic suppressing cuffs, the first guard advanced on me.

Did the Black Heart Rule apply to the Queen's Guard? If Mayan escaped, I might never have the chance to question her and stop this once and for all. However, if I saved myself by attacking the guards, I might well end up a living statue in the Queen's garden.

Alfie! He'd corroborate my story.

"I can prove—" I began.

The guard with the cuffs deliberately stepped on one half of the tiara, grinding the crystals to dust.

An inhuman cry tore from my throat. Locking my blood armor into place, I rushed the guard, tossing her across the alley.

No alarm went off. I hadn't triggered the Black Heart Rule, but I was beyond caring. Priya's tiara was ruined and Mayan was laughing like a hyena, about to get away with attempted murder.

The second guard ran at me. Grabbing him in a head-lock, I patted him down for another set of cuffs, and suppressed his magic, dumping him onto the ground.

Mayan was limping away.

I caught up to her and spun her around.

Her eyes gleamed maliciously. "You can't watch me all the time. I will finish what I started."

That's when a very familiar voice said, "Rumors of a disturbance and who do I find? Hello, Ashira."

Moran was flanked by a half dozen more guards who'd cut off our escape route.

Mayan whirled on me, her eyes wild. "You've ruined everything."

A black smudge flew from her body, whizzing toward me.

Moran's sword appeared in his hand. "Wh-what—"

Normally, I'd have enjoyed rendering him speechless, but there wasn't time to gloat.

I dropped my blood armor. "It's a Repha'im. A soul of—"

The Repha'im wound around me like a python, squeezing the life out of me.

If this was a Mundane, I was dead. Jezebels could only destroy Nefesh souls. I fired a red ribbon of blood magic into the Repha'im, tasting dust, but when I impaled it with my red forked branches, it tore free. Shit. Was it Mundane?

One of Moran's contingent hurled a fireball at it.

The Repha'im released me and blanketed the guard in a giant shadow. The guard gasped and his lifeless, deflated corpse slithered to the ground.

Two more rushed the Repha'im. I knocked them out of its path with brute force, and they turned on me, but Moran yelled, "Hold!"

The guards fell back, but their desire for retribution shimmered in the air. If I didn't kill this, they'd direct it at me, a convenient scapegoat.

I squared my shoulders and sent more branches into the Repha'im. For a dead spirit, it fought like a man with nothing to lose.

My heartbeat slowed and my vision tunneled in and out. I couldn't breathe under its frenzied onslaught, my branches sputtering in and out of existence, overpowered.

Moran yelled something but his words blew away on the breeze. Color leached from the world and I fell to my knees. Scowling, he stomped over and stabbed me in the arm.

I screamed, but that rush of pain gave me enough of a boost that time and color snapped back into place. Branches exploded around me, impaling the Repha'im. The clusters bloomed; the shade was destroyed.

I pushed a sweat-soaked lock of hair out of my face, holding my arm. Blood gooped through my fingers. "You asshole."

Moran gave one more long, hard look at the spot where the Repha'im had been before he shook himself out of his stupor. "Merely a flesh wound. Now, if you will, what is a Repha'im?"

"A dead person's shade from Sheol, the underworld. The land of death, silence, and forgetting." I helpfully sprinkled in a few interesting trivia facts that I'd learned, including the fact that I'd only been able to kill this one because it was Nefesh. "Surprise!"

For a brief second, Moran was engulfed in electricity— his actual magic ability—but he quickly shut it down.

"Well, that can't be good for your blood pressure," I said. "Feel free to convey my surprising information to the Queen."

"How did it get into Hedon?" Moran demanded.

"Still unclear on that part."

"I suggest you find out and get back to me then."

Well, at least the alliance wasn't totally off the table after that little debacle. I had the Queen's stage name and the lip print and lipstick might give me a genetic profile, but she'd gone to great lengths to hide her identity and not every surprise was well-received. I'd wanted the knowledge for myself, not to put myself into a more dangerous situation with her. Would I play that card as a last resort? Probably, but it would have been nice if the Repha'im had been enough to seal the deal.

"You killed Gunter?" In the melee, I'd lost track of Mayan. She sat on the ground, sobbing softly, her eyes trained on me.

"I did."

The charge of murder galvanized the guards and they advanced on me.

I tried to manifest my armor but I was out of juice. "Calm your tits. I killed Gunter's spirit. Corporeal Gunter was already dead. Ask Alfie, owner of the Green Olive." I gestured at Mayan. "Let me take her back and all this becomes Levi's headache."

Moran looked between me and guards, fingers tapping against his sword hilt.

My stomach flipped over in dread. The Queen didn't like complications and I'd brought this massive one to her door. One visit to the Queen's dungeon was enough for a lifetime.

Moran clenched his jaw. "Escort them to the exit. And Ashira? Should you have an ounce of self-preservation, stay out of Hedon for a good, long while."

"You of all people should know I'm terrible at following orders."

He tapped the flat edge of his sword.

"But I'm happy to try." I scooped up my purse, depositing in it the wreckage of the tiara and my promise to Priya. I'd sworn to the person I loved most to keep this one thing safe and I'd failed. It was her talisman. Her way to move on with confidence. How much of a setback would its loss be?

I bowed to Moran. "Your Henchmanness. Until we meet again."

Chapter 20

Dawn had broken on Sunday morning by the time I staggered out of the elevator at Harbour Center, carrying Mayan. One of the guards was a healer and he'd fixed her injuries up, but she was still in shock. He'd also treated the sword cut on my arm.

"You're all right?" Rafael saw us and quit pacing. I nodded. "What took so long?"

"I didn't want the good times to end." I deposited Mayan gently on a bench.

She'd stopped crying, but she was pale and unnaturally quiet. The only thing she'd asked on our trip back was whether Alfie was alive. When I assured her that he was fine, she'd nodded, relieved. She hadn't spoken since.

I called Miles, briefly explaining the situation. He instructed us to wait there, which gave me time to get the story out of Mayan.

"Mayan."

She sunk further into herself.

"Tell me what happened. Why did you first call Levi?"

Mayan remained silent, her chin cast at a stubborn angle.

I leaned in, determined to get answers out of her, but Rafael put a hand on my shoulder.

"Allow me," he murmured. "Mayan. We require your assistance. It's vital that we understand what led us to the events of this evening."

It was the British accent, I swear. She gave him this melty look and nodded.

It was the age-old story of girl meets boy, girl discovers boy is a necromancer, girl asks ex for help only to have dead person bent on vengeance stuffed inside her by said necromancer. Jonah hadn't lied about his advancements in bonding techniques.

"Do you remember everything that happened once Gunter was inside you?" I said.

"Yes. I wish I didn't. I was still me, but there were certain things I couldn't control." She rubbed her hand vigorously over her mouth. "It made me smoke and—" Her hand flew to her neck. "I said I'd never take that pendant off. I swore in Mom's memory."

Mayan could once again uphold her promise. Unlike me. "I'm sure she'll forgive you the gap."

"You don't have to be a bitch about this. It wasn't my fault."

My hands curled into fists. "How about when you found out your fuck buddy was a necromancer, you went and actually applied for asylum or something at House Pacifica instead of just phoning Levi and continuing to wander around like everything was fine and Jonah wasn't a potentially dangerous asshole who'd come after you? I don't care that it wasn't your fault. A guard died, Alfie almost did, and the two of us came way too close to ending up on the wrong side of the law in Hedon." I brushed a hand over my purse. "I broke a promise to someone tonight as well, and mine isn't fixable, so forgive me if I fail to give a shit about the specific degree of your complicity."

"Quite a speech," Levi said lightly. He'd entered along with Miles.

"Jesus. Stop creeping up on people." I stood up. "She's all yours." I walked out without a look back.

It was raining and I didn't have a jacket. Gritting my teeth, running on adrenaline and fury, I rubbed my goose-fleshed arms, my ruined filthy dress dragging through puddles. I was still barefoot, having left my shoes in Hedon, and my feet were freezing.

Levi fell into step beside me and draped his trench coat over my shoulders.

"How does it help for you to get wet?" I said, tugging it close.

His limo glided around the corner and pulled up to the curb next to us.

"Fucking hell, Levi. Do you have a tracking device implanted on you?"

"What was the promise you broke tonight?" His voice held only a mild curiosity but the corners of his eyes were pinched tight.

"Priya's tiara. From her almost-wedding. I'd promised to keep it safe and it got broken in all this bullshit." I stopped suddenly, forcing Levi to turn back for me. "You thought I wasn't going to come."

He shrugged. "It's been hours. You didn't call."

"I was investigating the case you hired me for and a little busy. But thanks for your show of faith." I stalked off again. Levi and I were impossible. No, he was impossible. I was fan-fucking-tastic except he kept doubting that fact. Because he'd sorted me into a box.

I shoved his trench coat back at him.

"Get in the limo." He opened the car door. Levi and his driver had an agreement. Simon only pretended to be the typical limo guy and wait on Levi when it was important to keep up appearances, but beyond that they were friends.

Sometimes when Levi called me from on the road, I'd hear him make an offhand joke to Simon, or Simon ribbing Levi about his tight schedule and not leaving enough time for his lady friend.

For, you know, me.

All my protests died on my lips. The weather was shit. My feet were bare. I wasn't about to walk home like this. Was I really so hellbent on being right that I'd hurt myself to prove a point? The old Ash, maybe, would have done it. But what about the current one?

"Fine. Take me home. My home." I clarified, since Levi tended to take those kinds of commands literally.

The limo was as warm as the inside of a dryer, but I still shivered.

Levi raised the tinted privacy glass between us and Simon, who shot me a smile in the rearview mirror right before he was blocked from view. "If you get pneumonia because you're stupid enough to walk off in the rain in April without shoes or a jacket, don't expect paid sick days," he said, and wrapped his arms around me.

I burrowed into his heat. "I'm taking all the sick days and billing you time and half because you have shit taste in exes. Next time get one with half a brain."

His chuckle vibrated against my cheek. "You really laid into her. Did you enjoy it?"

"Not as much as the rock I hit her with," I said into his chest. Some of the cold and stiffness seeped away, replaced by an exquisite tiredness. More than that, this felt nice. I didn't have to be a queen or a Seeker, and no one expected me to be unassailable. This was just me as I was right now, wet, and still covered a little in blood, seen for who I was and feeling like everything was possibly going to be okay.

"You can't give me even a smidgeon of plausible deniability, can you?"

I glanced up at him through my lashes. "It was the most

prudent course of action at the time. I expect you want details now."

"Nope. That's the last thing I want. We'll debrief with Miles later today." Levi sat back, regarding me with a serious expression and I clenched the folds of my dress. Had Levi sorted through the many layers of us and come to the conclusion that this was more hassle than it was worth? "What did you think was going to happen?"

Oh. He meant Hedon? "Not the gong show that did, that's for sure."

"With us. When you promised to come over."

I squirmed on the seat, dropping my gaze to my dirty feet. Grr. Short of flinging myself out of a moving vehicle, it seemed we were having our talk, even though I didn't have a carefully planned speech ready. I crossed my arms. "Everything between us is messy and crosses all kinds of lines, and that's not working. For me."

"Same."

He didn't have to agree so fast. I wiped a smear of blue powder off from the crook of my elbow, my arms covered in goosebumps and missing his warmth. "Okay, well, we either declutter down to boss and employee, or…"

I left a generous pause in case he felt like jumping in, but Mr. Bossy had become Mr. All-the-Patience-in-the-World.

I wasn't relationship-averse, but this was Levi and me. We'd been nemeses for so many years. Sex was one thing, but what if he laughed at me for suggesting more? Part of me didn't think he would, but the part that still heard his mocking laughter and years of taunts pulled up the drawbridge and got the boiling pitch ready.

It was very fine metaphoric boiling pitch, but empty fortresses were lonely places. And I missed having a home like this, somewhere I felt I could be my full self. I hadn't felt like that in a long time.

I took a deep breath and steeled myself. "Or we try having a relationship."

"Huh. I owe Miles twenty bucks," he said.

My eyes narrowed. "You bet on this? Against us? Wow."

"Not so much against us as against you," he said, with a shrug. I gaped at him and he gave me a bright smile. "You've hated me most of your life and stone obelisks warm up to people more easily than you do."

"I'm a giant rock in this scenario now?"

"Yup." He brushed his nose against mine. "But I've cracked you."

"I don't know if this is a good thing."

"Are you my girlfriend?" he said.

"Ugh. How about your lovah?"

"Not how I will ever introduce you. Partner?"

"You know this is all hypothetical since there are only like four people who can know we're together," I said.

"I don't care. I'll know."

His conviction sent champagne bubbles sweeping through me. However, I wanted to hire a plane and skywrite the fact for the world to behold, followed by watching all the haters I'd accrued over my lifetime choke on their disbelief and envy.

"We're the only ones that matter," I agreed.

The limo idled at Levi's wrought-iron gate.

I sighed. "This is your home. We're going to have to discuss your inability to follow orders."

"I took it as more of a suggestion." Levi folded his trench coat over one arm.

"Uh-huh."

Turning up the driveway, Simon deposited us at the front door. Levi made me wait until he'd unlocked it before having me step out into the rain.

I got inside and pressed my back against the door, my handbag in a death grip. I looked like a grubby drowned swan and I was Levi Montefiore's girlfriend. Fine, yes, I used the dumb word. Was there some formal ritual that happy, well-socialized people normally engaged in at this point? I dragged in a nervous breath, and caught wind of the most tantalizing scent.

"Did you make biscotti?" I dashed past him into the kitchen, a cozy space with red appliances and glass tile that mirrored the sunny blue of his eyes when he was amused. Round spice tins were stuck to a long magnetic board and braids of garlic were pinned to the window frame.

Three trays of chocolate cookies sat cooling on the quartz counter top of the center island. Did his anxiety levels come in flavors? If so, was chocolate a mild twinge of concern or the dark recesses of icy panic?

My smile broke free, my toes curling under like I was in a dippy romcom, despite the dirt I'd tracked in on his floor.

"Why is my baking funny?" He stood stiffly in the doorway.

"You only bake when you're stressed." I poked him in the chest. "You were actively scared I'd changed my mind."

He opened his mouth like he was going to argue the point then a crafty look stole over his face. "The not knowing was the worst. You should probably make it up to me."

I worried at my tattered ruffles.

Levi lifted my chin with a finger. "I was kidding. We don't have to do anything tonight. You can just shower and relax."

"What if we're not compatible… that way?"

"Sex?" His eyebrows shot into his hairline. "Did I imagine all the other mindblowing times?"

"Well, no, and obviously, I'm exceptional, but there was no pressure before. We're a thing now. We're exclusive."

"Oh shit, we are?" He jogged to the door. "Jeeves, release the harem."

I grabbed him by the belt and hauled him backward,

wrapping my arms around his waist and burying my face against his spine.

"Bella." He placed his hands over mine and squeezed. "It'll be amazing because it's us."

I nuzzled my face closer to him. "You're very good at this."

His laughter rumbled against my cheek. "Baby, I'm the best."

I snorted, and laughing, he turned in my hold. Going up on tiptoe, I pressed a butterfly kiss to his lips. My pulse seemed to be everywhere at once: the tips of my fingers, behind my knees, and in my stomach.

Sunlight spilled into the room, painting us in golds and yellows. Wrapped up in Levi, something restless in me settled, home at last. I never wanted it to end.

I pressed my hand to his jaw and closed my eyes for a breath, savoring him nuzzling my palm.

"Give me five minutes to wash off this grime," I said.

"Then what?"

I grinned and skipped off to his en suite bathroom.

The large glass shower with a rainforest spout and pebbled tiled floor was fit for a queen. It would do. I cranked the jets to hot, but before I could try and extricate myself from this dress, Levi was there, unzipping me.

"I told you earlier, I was the one getting this off you."

"I'll allow it as an example of my graciousness." The fabric didn't pool silkily to the ground. It plopped off, still half-formed.

"It looks like it's going to walk off." Levi helped me step out of it.

"We should be so lucky." I stepped into the shower and crooked a finger at him.

Levi stripped naked and stepped inside, swinging the door closed in record time. "So. Here we are." Water streamed over his sculpted body, steam swirling around us, cutting us off from the world. His eyes took on a hooded, lazy look and he reached up, brushing the backs of his fingers against my cheek.

I unconsciously licked my lips and Levi moved in. The kiss whispered to the parts of me that I'd kept hidden. Dr. Zhang had reinforced my femur with metal rods after my car crash, but I'd been the one to fortify my heart in the aftermath. Except this was Levi and he saw me—all of me. I melted against him, wet and pliant in his arms. My racing heartbeat slowed to meet his steady one, anchoring me.

He picked up a lemongrass-scented bar of soap and lathered me up. I closed my eyes, my hands splayed on his chest, enjoying the play of hard muscle as he soaped my body up in long smooth strokes and the wondrous experience of being cared for and cherished. Of knowing that I wasn't alone.

My stress swirled down the drain along with the dirt and all my doubts. The warmth of water on my back barely registered against the scalding heat from each pass of his fingertips.

There was a squirting noise and I giggled.

"Down, smutty. It's shampoo." He massaged it into my scalp then tilted my head back to rinse it off with care. "There. You're all clean."

I wrinkled my nose. "Not that clean." Sliding a hand to wrap around his dick, I stroked him experimentally, marveling at how something so hard could still feel so silky.

"This can be about you," he said in a tight voice. His muscles were tense from strain, but his eyes were filled with sincerity.

"No, baby, this is about both of us."

The smile he unfurled was almost blinding in its joy.

I raked my gaze over every impressive inch of him before biting his left nipple, the light sprinkle of damp hair on his chest scratching my chin. Beneath my lips, his heartbeat spiked.

Hot water continued to sluice over me, falling in rivulets off my curves. I closed my eyes, letting my mouth and hands guide me.

Raking my nails along his abs, I sank to my knees, one hand snaking around his calf, the other stroking his cock. My belly clenched at the slow thrust of his hips and I swirled my tongue around the head of his dick. Marking him. Drowning in him.

Levi growled, his hand tightening in my hair.

I shot him a wide, filthy smile, batted my lashes, and deep throated him, my cheeks hollowing out.

Levi bucked off the wall, muttering a low stream of Italian. He braced a hand against the sandstone tile, jerking into even harder lengths in my mouth. Both God and my name were invoked.

I throbbed for him, a fine edge of pain adding a darkness and a wildness to my desire.

Suddenly he tugged me up and hopped out of the shower.

"Problem?" My ragged breathing almost drowned out the sound of rushing water hitting the pebbled tiles.

"Yes." Levi slipped on a condom and jumped back under the spray. He swung me around so my back slapped against the glass, wrapped my legs around his waist, and thrust inside me. "Luckily, I'm a genius at problem-solving." His lips claimed mine as he rocked against me, raking his nails along my side.

I gasped against his mouth.

Heat pulsed off our skin, the air practically shimmering with our electric connection. Our gazes snagged in a shared moment of tenderness, before he seized my mouth in a deep, sensual kiss. His hands roamed my body and the hard glide of his skin against mine wound me higher and hotter.

The room was drenched in the musky scent of our sex, overpowering the smell of the shampoo and the traces of dirt around the drain, the headiness of the two of us, now so much more together than we'd ever been apart, overwhelming me.

I came so hard, white spots danced in front of my eyes, Levi following with a shudder.

We both blushed as our eyes met, the water still streaming over us.

Levi reached over and twisted off the tap but we didn't move.

I was glad of the time to let my racing heart slow. I inhaled deeply, letting my lungs fill with moist air before slowly exhaling, and sliding my feet to the ground with a small wobble.

Levi brushed a wet strand of hair off my cheek, making me very aware that I was standing naked in a shower with him and everything had changed.

Droplets plopped off my breasts into tiny splashes at my feet. I cleared my throat. "Towel?"

He looked at me a long moment before turning away to open the door and deposit the condom in the trash. I shivered as the cold air hit me, but it was only for a second because Levi soon had me bundled in a thick cocoon of terrycloth. As I toweled off, I snuck a few looks at Levi drying himself, rivulets of water trickling over his muscles.

Once he was dry, he padded into the bedroom and crawled between the covers, with a look in my direction like he didn't believe I'd stay.

Ye of little faith. I curled into his side, pulling the blankets snug up to my neck.

Levi glanced off to the side and quietly laughed.

I poked him. "What's funny?"

"I'm happy," he said simply.

"Me too. But we have to…" I shook away the rest of the sentence, wanting this bubble of us to last.

Levi rolled over to face me and laced his fingers through

mine, looking utterly spent. "Just a nap. Keep the world out a little longer," he murmured drowsily.

"I'd like that." I watched him fall asleep, smoothing down a cowlick. His dark lashes lay against cheeks still flushed from the heat of the shower and I smiled at the soft snort he let out, pressing my hand against his shoulder until he shifted against me and settled back into a deep slumber.

A ray of sunshine swept in from the window and bathed the room in a dream-like glow as Levi's soft breaths evened out. Careful not to wake him, I pressed a kiss to his knuckles. And there it was: I was happy.

This kind of joy, pure and unfettered, had always seemed so unreachable, like it only happened to those with incredibly good luck who sought it out and worked hard for it. And granted, I wasn't the kind of person who let many others past my guard. But this was worth it, worth all the scariness and fear of judgment, this beautiful surprise that didn't require me to do anything other than to enjoy it. I closed my eyes, knowing that no dream would be as good as this new reality.

Chapter 21

I woke up before Levi did, the two of us entwined like puzzle pieces. He'd thrown a leg over me, one palm resting on my thigh over my scar. I'd always been a light sleeper with other people, waking up at the slightest movement, forgoing cuddling. Immediately, my thigh tensed under his touch and I placed my hand over his to move it. Nowhere to run to. Nowhere to hide.

Except I was okay with that. I didn't want to run or hide. I just wanted to be seen for who I was.

I left his hand on my leg and relaxed back against him.

Tucked under his glasses on the bedside table was a copy of *The Memoirs of Sherlock Holmes*, a collection of short stories, including *The Final Problem* where Holmes went over the Reichenbach Falls. I ran a finger along the spine, imagining lying next to him, reading to unwind after a hard day.

I basked in the realness of this moment. This wasn't going to vanish. It just felt stable. Constant. A goodness without doubt to it.

Levi scrunched up his face as his eyes fluttered open and gave me a sleepy smile. "You're still here."

"Yeah. I need to borrow some clothes."

"Ah."

I cuddled closer to him. "Plus, I wanted to be."

He kissed me. "Better."

His phone buzzed with a text as mine rang from somewhere out in the living room. Naked, I ran for it, catching the caller just before it went to voicemail.

"Good morning, Attendant," I said sunnily. "Did you get any rest?"

"Where are you?" Rafael said.

"At Levi's. Why?"

He made a despairing noise. "I should have known. When I agreed to this team of yours, I assumed it was implicitly understood that all personal dealings came a very distant second to your Jezebel responsibilities."

"How exactly have I been remiss?" I went into the kitchen.

"I've been sitting here at your office for an hour. Luckily Bryan was here or I'd have been waiting in the street."

"We never set a time to meet. Normal people would do that first before showing up." I rooted around in the cupboards until I found an espresso cup and stuck it under the spout of the De'Longhi espresso maker on the counter. I hit the button for the beans to grind.

"It's 11AM," Rafael said. "Normal people have been at work for hours, not playing hooky."

"It's Sunday," I said.

The espresso maker clicked twice and a thin stream of aromatic coffee ran into the cup.

"Evil doesn't sleep," he said. "This was never an issue with Gavriella. If you aren't going to take this seriously because of your personal life, then perhaps we need to revisit the entire team idea, given that you're allowing your relationships with these people to impinge on our work."

I smacked my hand on the counter. "My family was destroyed because of Chariot and these scrolls and being a

Jezebel. So yes, Rafael, I take this all very seriously. However, I was a mite tired from saving a man's life, killing a Repha'im, and generally not getting beheaded in Hedon, and I took a fucking nap."

Levi, now dressed in jeans, handed me a pair of sweats. Cashmere ones, because of course cotton was too peasant to clothe him during leisure time.

"I'll be there in half an hour." I hung up first and threw my phone on the counter. "That little—" I yanked on the pants.

"Wanker?" Levi said, dryly. "He's not worth popping a blood vessel."

I exhaled, tugging the sweatshirt over my head and replaying my conversation with Rafael. Actually hearing it instead of just reacting to it. Rafael had asserted an ownership over my Jezebel position and our mission from day one. Unsurprising, given he was next in a long line of men who'd been mentors, healers, and allies to the women their life's work revolved around. If Rafael was no longer the person his Jezebel needed most, no longer critical to a cause that he'd devoted his life to, but just some bookish dude who dug up information in his secret library while others were out in the field, then why did he matter?

"He's jealous," I said.

Levi paused, coffee pot in hand. "Of us?"

"Yeah, but not like that." I had to roll all the cuffs up to fit my limbs. "I didn't know I was a Jezebel, but Rafael was born and raised to take on his position. It defined him. Now I've reduced him from half of a duo to simply part of a team that I put in place. He feels threatened." The side effects of helping me overcome the cravings and Rafael's subsequent view of himself must have made everything worse. "I need to talk to him."

"Here. It's medicinal." Levi handed me a biscotti.

Shooting back the espresso, black and bitter, I bit into

221

the cookie. A dense, rich chocolate zinged my taste buds. "Where have you been hiding these?"

"These are not biscotti for all and sundry," he said.

"I support you in that. Give them all to me. And to Priya, because if she finds out you're holding out on her, she'll tie you up in Password Hell. Also, you understand that your sweats cost more than my best work outfit, right? Do you put them on after your milk bath, Your Lordship?"

"We're in a relationship. You can't bust my balls anymore."

I laughed and patted his cheek. "You're adorable."

Levi shook his head in resignation. "Miles texted. Mayan gave him Jonah's address. It turns out it was a fake. He'd rented it from a couple while they were on vacation and there's only one Jonah Samuels registered with any House in North America. Eighty-three years old with invisibility magic."

"Fake address, fake name." I ate another biscotti. "I'm not sufficiently caffeinated for this."

"Come back after you meet with Rafael. Miles wants to debrief."

"Later. I've got an idea worth following up about Jonah."

"Okay. I've arranged for the limo to drive you."

"Words never uttered by ninety-five percent of the world's population. Well, relationships are all about compromise." I snagged three more biscotti for the road. "If I kill Rafael, will you help me bury the body?"

Levi stole a biscotti back with a shrug. "Why not? I've got nothing better to do today."

I pressed a sweet quick kiss to his mouth. "This arrangement is going to work out fine."

〜

SIMON DROPPED me off at my apartment to pick up Mrs. Hudson and so I could change. Levi had graciously agreed to burn the dress, and I wasn't giving Rafael more ammunition by showing up in Levi's clothes. A padded envelope had arrived for me from the man at the fair company, sealed with a blood ward, ensuring that the envelope had not been tampered with.

I gently probed it with one finger to determine the contents. I couldn't tell if the napkin was inside, but the lipstick tube was there. If I intended to take it to the lab, it would have to wait until Monday morning. I slid the envelope into my purse, unopened.

Fortified in all-black and with a wriggling puppy accompanying me, I drove over in Moriarty to my office to confront Rafael.

I'd purchased him a delicate jasmine brew from the fancy tea house on the corner as an olive branch. The helpful tea server said that jasmine promoted peace. Healing. A deep and quiet inner joy. Everything that Rafael needed more of, I figured. I'd almost gotten an entire pound bag of the tea leaves for him, but from Rafael's grimace when I handed him the offering, you'd have thought I'd brought him a head on a platter.

"It's in a take-out cup," he huffed, all fussy and pissy in tweed.

I smiled tightly and drank out of the cup, keeping it for myself. "There. Problem solved."

"Are you well rested now? May we proceed?" Rafael said bitingly.

I took another sip, needing all the peace and inner joy at this moment. "Yes. But before we do, let me just say that I'm grateful to have you in my corner. You're irreplaceable and this fight is impossible to win without you. Nothing about our journey together has been as you expected and that can't have been easy."

I was shit at this kind of thing, which was why I'd prac-
ticed my speech on the way over. The heartfelt words were
somewhat undermined by Mrs. Hudson under Priya's desk,
making disturbing squeaky noises with the cow, but I think I
got my point across.

"Why don't you tell me what you've discovered?" I said.

That took some of the wind out of his sails. He circled
the desk, somewhat warily, and picked up the journal. "These
are my father's records. Adam took possession of the fake
scroll and passport on the Thursday morning after your accident. The meeting with Gavriella was set for that same
Thursday night."

"We're missing the critical hours of the afternoon and
early evening. That's where we'll find our answers. When did
Gavriella get the book with the message proposing the meeting?" I said.

"The day before. Wednesday. It was left on her café table
while she'd gone to pick up her order. She never saw who
left it."

"So we'll never know how he found her."

"Through Chariot, I expect. Gavriella had to move a
number of times as they closed in."

Obviously, I'd suspected as much, especially after my visit
with Uncle Paulie, but the matter-of-fact way that Rafael
said it, reducing my dad to this sole identity, hurt. I wanted
to tell Rafael about the man who could never get the lumps
of raw batter out of his pancakes, or how he used to dance
with my mom in the kitchen while I did pirouettes around
them, but I didn't, because to Rafael, only one aspect of my
dad mattered.

Was the same true for himself? That the Attendant identity he'd been raised to live up to was the only relevant part
of him? Rafael was wrestling with his ghosts.

"Ashira?"

"Sorry. I was just thinking about my father."

Rafael paused. "Don't get attached."

"To who?"

"Whom." Off my eye roll, he added. "Anyone."

I tossed Mrs. Hudson a treat. "Too late. I'm not being ousted from my life."

"Can you live with the consequences should you endanger your loved ones?"

I'd been through this with Priya on my last case. She'd been kidnapped because of me. I'd tried to remove myself from her life but she wasn't having any of it.

"That's their decision, not mine."

Rafael tsked. "That's a very cavalier attitude."

"Don't you get lonely?"

He pushed his round, black frames up his nose. "This cause—"

"Is not human companionship, dude. It's solitary and lonesome as hell. Let's just be honest about it: it sucks bigtime."

"This from a confirmed misanthrope."

I brushed a biscotti crumb off my sweater. "A former confirmed misanthrope. Despite all my previous inclinations otherwise, we need this team. Sure, there's always the chance that someone could prove to be a liability or be used against me, but the usefulness of our combined skills will help in the end. Our friendships will make a difference. I know it."

"Personal connections in a situation like this are a double-edged sword," he said.

"Very rarely is anything totally good or totally bad. Even if you knew we were going to fail, do you really want to live in a bubble so you never experience hurt?"

I had, and even with Priya all those years, my life had been poorer for my lack of other relationships. Now other people were slotting into my life: Arkady, even Miles. And especially Levi. I took another sip of tea to hide my smile. Who had Rafael had by his side besides his dad? And had the relationship gone beyond the duties of teaching Rafael his responsibilities?

Rafael stared down at the journal, his mind obviously far away. He didn't share his thoughts, shaking himself out of his stupor a moment later. "I ascertained that the codename your father used for his boss—26L1—fit the same pattern as the only other recorded codename we have. A number followed by a letter and another number. Though no Attendant or Jezebel ever cracked it."

"Do you mind if we share the codename with the Queen?" I said. "It falls under the parameters of the agreement with Levi."

He frowned. "This will take some getting used to, but very well."

A text came in. "It's from Arkady," I said. "He emailed me photos of the New York Avi Chomskys and wants my opinion if any of them are Adam." I opened my laptop to see the photos on a larger screen, but couldn't bring myself to log on. "Sorry." I scrubbed a hand over my face. "I'm being horribly unprofessional. Just give me a minute."

Rafael pulled out his phone, hit a few buttons and set it on the table between us. He'd literally set a one-minute timer.

I opened my mouth to lay into him and he nudged me playfully.

"Fucker," I muttered.

"Rethinking your stance on personal connections, perchance?"

I scowled at him, his levity giving me the push to keep going. "If Dad's been in hiding then it's plausible that his hair color, eye color, and weight are going to be different than I remember." I pulled up a photo on my phone of my father that I'd scanned a few years ago.

It was the summer before he left. Dad and I were sitting on the grass in our backyard, laughing about something I no longer remembered. It was a perfectly ordinary moment, one of thousands I'd taken for granted. At least, that was what I'd told myself when I'd snuck the photo out of the albums that Talia had in storage and made a copy. I'd had all these opportunities to make memories with my father and I'd wasted them because I didn't realize how finite they were. Then I'd gotten angry at him for not giving me more chances. No one wanted to grow up without a parent—how could he do this to me?

But now I could appreciate that the big moments in my life—my high school and college graduations, me getting Moriarty and Talia finally trusting me behind the wheel again, my first job—all of these were things Dad had denied himself so that I could live a perfectly ordinary life free from harm. His leaving me wasn't the biggest asshole move: it was the greatest gift of love.

Clarity. Dad still had a lot of explaining to do, but it was time to acknowledge that there was a lot more to him than just the parts that made me angry. Time to take him out of the box of the man who'd abandoned and betrayed me and remember all of him.

"So, this is a picture of Adam." I blinked quickly, hoping Rafael wouldn't see how damp my eyes were. "His basic face shape would be the same. I can start by comparing the bone structure and—"

Rafael took my phone away. "You're a mess. Allow me."

"How can I refuse such a compassionate offer?"

"You can't." He motioned at my laptop. "Come along, log in. I'm desperate to go out for some real tea after this."

I pushed my unlocked computer over to him. "I'm literally crying over my dad here and all you can do is complain about the tea. You're terrible."

"Not terrible," Rafael said, clicking over to my mail program, "only British." He took forever to sort through the possible men, carefully comparing each one to the old picture of Adam, all while I bit my fingernails down to the quick.

Mrs. Hudson wore herself out and fell asleep.

"This is the only potential candidate." He turned the screen around.

My breath caught. The man could have been Dad's brother. But close only counted in horseshoes and hand grenades.

"It's not him." I fired a text to Arkady to continue on to Mexico.

Rafael moved over to the framed book covers on the wall, examining them. "I went with Miles when he drove Mayan home. She was quite distraught."

I groaned. "Shit. I didn't mean to dump that on you. I couldn't deal with her and had to get out of there. Hey, is there anything in all your Attendant journals about necromancy? One of the journals did mention Repha'im."

"Our knowledge of Repha'im is quite superficial and there's unlikely to be anything on necromancy. That's not why I brought up Mayan, however." He stopped, cleared his threat, then looked at the ceiling. "You did well. Often Jezebels tend to only be able to promise revenge for those who have been wronged, not actually be able to prevent the wrongs before they are undoable. Your methods may be unorthodox, but you saved Mayan from being imprisoned and from blemishing her conscience. And you saved Alfie as well."

I almost fell out of my spectacularly comfortable chair. Rafael, praising me? Admitting that even though he didn't agree with how I got there, my solution was sound? Quick, someone check my pulse. But the glow soon wore off as I remembered the rest of what had happened last night. What I still had to deal with.

"Thanks, that means a lot." I said. "But it wasn't all sunshine and rainbows. I broke a tiara that Priya let me borrow. I'm sure that seems silly in the grand scheme of chasing Chariot and saving lives and everything, but well, without betraying any confidences, it was quite precious to her."

How many more casualties could our friendship take? Priya had been with me through so many bad things, but everyone broke somewhere. And as much as I hated admitting it, Rafael had a point. The war with Chariot was going to cost me a lot more than I wanted to pay.

But Rafael didn't twist the knife. He sat on Priya's desk and regarded the ceiling as though some secret of the universe was written there. "You value that friendship. It's nothing to apologize for."

"Now who's the reformed misanthrope?"

Rafael rubbed his thumb over the spine of his dad's journal. "I appreciate what you said earlier about me being irreplaceable. Ever since that meeting, I've felt like the odd man out when this fight is my birthright and the others are all just recent arrivals to it. Then when I found out about you and Levi going to the Queen? It felt like this end-run because I wasn't necessary anymore."

"I'm sorry if we made you feel you didn't matter. If *I* made you feel that way," I said. "Because only you've got the magic touch." I gave an exaggerated frown. "Too soon?"

"You're incorrigible." Rafael may have sounded unimpressed, but the corners of his lips quirked up. He tucked the journal under his arm. "If there is nothing more pressing to work on, I'd like to continue cracking the codename."

"Go nuts." I tossed the take-out cup. "And if you want a nice brew while you do so, go to Moon Café two blocks over in the red brick building on the corner. You'll appreciate the selection."

"I might at that. What will you be working on?"

I logged out of my email. "If Arkady doesn't find Adam in Mexico, we'll be back to the entire world as a possibility

229

for finding the missing scroll. None of the Ten have it or the pillar would be dark, so it's reasonable to assume it's either still in Dad's possession, or he was the one who hid it somewhere."

"Sounds plausible."

"I've checked in the past and was never able to find a safe deposit box if Dad had one. He wouldn't have hidden the scroll in our old house because by the time I had the accident, Talia had already listed it for sale." The loss of my home had been one more factor in taking that life-changing joyride. "I'm totally stymied as to how else to search for it."

Confronted with a problem, I generated a dozen ideas to deal with it. Granted, half of them were shit, but they gave me a place to start. With this scroll, I felt like I was wandering around in a labyrinth, and every time I turned around I hit a dead end. Forget finding the exit, I couldn't even get to the center to take a breath.

Rafael stood up. "This isn't all on you, Ashira. You have a team to help you." He paused and smiled. "You have friends."

I CHICKENED out of going home in case Priya was back from her yoga class, instead driving over to the west side of town.

I rapped on the familiar front door, pasting on a bright smile when it opened. "Hiya, Rebbe. Got any leftover wedding cake?"

Ivan "Rebbe" Dershowitz had been part of a recent case of attempted murder that I'd solved, involving a fake Angel of Death and the dungeons of Hedon. Good times. A fleshy man in his fifties, he took a bite of the shrimp sandwich in his hand, mayo dripping on to his sweater. "You'd think those people had been living off war rations the way they fell on the food. Not a crumb left."

He turned around and shuffled into the house. I took the open door as an invitation to follow.

"Can I bring the dog?" I called out.

He grunted affirmatively. "Come to the kitchen."

I hurried through the house, eyes downcast so I wouldn't have a PTSD flashback from all the creepy bird decorations in this place. Luckily, the kitchen was a bird-free zone.

"You like shrimp?" he said.

"What bad Jew doesn't like shrimp?" I sat down at one of the barstools pushed up to the island while the pug nosed around the room, sniffing at corners.

Ivan laughed and pulled sandwich fixings out of the fridge. "Rachel won't touch them. Bottom feeders. She pretends not to know what I'm eating when she's not around."

"Is she away?" I didn't see any extra dishes or a sweater of hers draped over a chair, and the house seemed quieter. Lonelier than I remembered.

He used an ice cream scoop to get the shrimp salad out of the Tupperware. "Rehab."

"Really?"

Ivan spread it on one slice, topping it with a dash of salt and pepper. "There was an incident at the wedding. The Queen requested that Rachel seek treatment."

"Her requests are hard to refuse. I take it Rachel agreed."

"She was mortified." He sighed, eyes closed for a long moment, his wedding band winking in the afternoon sun. He cut up some avocado into delicate strips, laying them on the sandwich. "You didn't meet her at her best, but she's a good person."

"Then I'm glad she's getting help."

"Me too. Straight across or diagonal?" He indicated with the knife that he meant how did I want my sandwich cut?

"Diagonal," I said.

"Because you get a wider soft part to bite into."

"Exactly."

He presented the plate. "Ta da."

I took a bite. "Dayum. This is good."

"It's the avocado."

"How's the happy couple?" I licked a gloop of mayonnaise off my lip.

Ivan rinsed off the ice cream scoop and placed it in the sink. "Beats me. You think when a person pays for a honeymoon they could get one phone call. Apparently they don't have reception in the French Riviera." He clapped his hands together. "So, we have sandwiches, small talk, and a very cute puppy. What do you want from me?"

"Information."

"What would I get out of this deal?"

"Depends on how useful you are," I said around a mouthful of shrimp salad. "I'll compensate you financially for your time at the very least."

"How about a question for a question?"

The last question game I'd played had ended up with me narrowly avoiding being chopped up for parts in a cockamamie Dream Market in Hedon. While we were now in the real world, I was kind of gun-shy about doing that, because Ivan was still a criminal.

On the other hand, thanks to my association with the Queen, it was doubtful he'd risk hurting me, and I think I secretly amused him. Besides, if all else failed, my magic trumped his.

I picked up the other half of the sandwich. "All right, but I won't dish on the Queen or anything that falls under a confidentiality agreement."

"Ask away." He popped the lid on the Tupperware and put it in the fridge.

"Do you know any necromancers?"

Ivan scooped up avocado skins and pits and deposited them in a countertop composter. "Did you know that necromancy is highly forbidden in Judaism?"

"I did not and that counts as your question, whereas you have not answered mine."

"Neatly done." He was silent as he wiped down the island counter. "There was this one guy I heard rumors of during my incarceration." He winked. "If you want his name, you gotta ask."

"What was his name, Rebbe?" I polished off the first half of my sandwich and wiped my mouth with a paper napkin that he handed me.

"No clue. He was known as the Shidduch."

"A Jewish male matchmaker."

Ivan pointed the rag at me. "Now why would a young secular person such as yourself know that?"

I grinned. "That's your second question. You made this delicious sandwich so I'll let you rescind, if you like."

"Eh. I have a natural curiosity about people. Rachel says it'll get me into trouble one day. I stand by the question."

"My grandparents were very religious. That's how they met. Why do you think this Shidduch was a necromancer?"

"Supposedly, he was a Charmer. Say you were in the market for some military compound blueprints that only a certain general had access to. If you traveled in the right circles and had enough money, the Shidduch would charm that general and you'd have your plans."

"I'm familiar with how Charmers work."

"There you go, then. My turn," Ivan said. "What's your magic?"

"I'm Mundane." I swallowed my last bite of shrimp. That had been a mighty fine sandwich.

"Don't insult my intelligence."

I slid off the barstool. "I'm not going to hurt you," I said, waiting for his nod, before I picked him up. With one hand.

"Enhanced strength," he said, once I'd set him on his feet.

"Yeah. Low level."

"Why hide it? That's not worth being Rogue for."

"You checked me out?"

Off my look of surprise, he tapped his finger to his nose. "That attempted murder hit close to my daughter. You bet, I checked you out."

"It wasn't on purpose. I grew up Mundane. A recent accident kicked it in. Rare, but it happens. I registered with House Pacifica pretty much right afterward, but there's some kind of backlog processing it." Like indefinitely.

"Fascinating."

"Back to the Shidduch," I said. "Charm isn't necromancy."

"Is that a question?"

"In this context? Yes."

"I knew a guy, Moishe, who'd been charmed by this Shidduch. Moishe was still himself, except not. He'd always been kind of goofy but after the compulsion happened, he became sly. Cruel. A lifelong boozer who just up and quit. Never touched a drop again. There was something off about the whole situation."

"Yeah, that could be necromancy. The living take on qualities of the deceased spirits inside them," I said. Gunter had enough agency to carry out his revenge against Alfie. "The possessed remain cognizant, if not always in control." Like Mayan smoking Gunter's preferred brand of cigarettes, despite her abhorrence of smoking. At least whatever magic he'd possessed during his life hadn't transferred over. Last night might have ended very differently.

Mrs. Hudson scrabbled against my pant leg and I picked her up and put her in my lap, scratching her ears. "If the Shidduch is the same man that I'm looking for, it's quite the clever handle. A matchmaker introduces two people to be wed. This necromancer introduces a deceased spirit to a living person and weds it to them somehow. Any idea how to find him?"

"I can get you to someone who does. Provided you tell me what exactly was the deal with the feather that compelled Omar. How did the two men who originally stole it off the archeological site fit into this? Who was the German you were so worried about?"

"That's more than one question."

"That's my price."

Answering meant telling him about Chariot, but how else could I track down this Shidduch and learn if it was Jonah? Chances were it was, because necromancers were exceedingly rare, but either way, he had to be stopped as quickly as possible.

Ivan was the most expedient route to end this, but as genial as he came off, I'd never trust him with that kind of information.

"Thanks for the sandwich." I put Mrs. Hudson down, wrapping the leash firmly around my wrist.

Ivan stepped between me and the doorway. "It's like that, then?"

I stood up and met his eyes. "It's like that."

He shifted his weight and my magic danced under my skin. I watched him for any sign of his light magic, ready to lock my armor into place.

"You let my dad choose," he said. "You kept my daughter's magic safe."

"Huh? Oh. Yeah. I did." Ivan's father, Abraham, was one of the original architects of Hedon, and when the foundational magic needed to be fixed, the Queen had forcibly recruited me in gaining Abraham's assistance. My methods had gotten the job done, but put me on her shit list. "Did he enjoy the wedding?"

Ivan smiled fondly. "He danced with Shannon. I haven't

seen him dance since Mama—" He shook off the sorrow that flashed across his face. "You did a mitzvah for my family. Hedon. Go to the Green Olive and talk to the owner."

"Alfie?"

"Who's Alfie? Name's Gunter."

That was going to be tough… but not impossible.

Chapter 22

"I don't have an endless supply of tokens," Miles bitched. He tried to get comfortable on the stool pushed up to the counter island, before giving up and standing. "Rein her in, Levi."

Levi was so at ease in his kitchen, pouring me a cup of coffee, then stretching up to reach the sugar on the shelf above the sink.

I wanted lazy Sunday mornings in here doing a crossword puzzle together and cooking dinner with laughter, wine, and good music streaming from the speakers. There was no one else I'd ever envisioned that way, the picture of this domestic bliss settling over me like a fuzzy blanket.

"She wouldn't ask if she didn't have a good reason," Levi said.

"Thank you," I said. "Milk?"

"In the fridge."

I doctored my beverage, looking around hopefully for the biscotti.

"Treats after the meeting," Levi said.

"You don't even know what I needed," I said. "Maybe it was a teaspoon."

"Uh-huh." He smirked.

Miles crossed his arms, his eyes cold. "Fuck me. You two are together. This is going to get messy."

"Unlike you and Arkady?" I said.

"No, it won't," Levi said.

"Then tell me, *boss*, who's your Head of Security? Me or your new girlfriend? Because if it's me, then let me do my job."

All the points he gained for his deductive skills blew away at his massive assholery.

I stirred the sugar in with enough force to make tiny whirlpools in the mug. "You want to compare dicks? Because you'll lose. I answer directly to Levi."

"I bet you do," he said.

"Miles," Levi warned.

Mrs. Hudson barked at Miles, lolling on the puppy bed in the corner that had shown up this morning. First Priya, now Levi. There were going to be a lot of broken hearts over this pug.

"Any case that Levi puts me on, or anything to do with Chariot, counts as House business," I said. "Should I require House resources, you suck it up and provide them."

"I'm not your fucking lackey," Miles said.

"And I'm not some wild card out there wreaking havoc. I've looped you in every step of the way, on everything I'm working on. You've hated me since we were teens and if you don't get over that, you're going to be the one to fuck up big time and put House Pacifica in danger."

"I don't dislike you," Miles said. "I'd have to give a damn about you one way or the other for that. I just don't trust you to put the House first. Like I do. Every time."

"Enough," Levi snapped. He waved a teaspoon at us in monarchical fashion. "Both of you. Ash, if Miles determines your request undermines some aspect of House security, you need to respect that."

"Tokens don't fall into that category," I said.

Levi shot me a beseeching look. I rolled my eyes and took a sip of coffee, mostly so I wouldn't chuck the contents at Miles' fat muscly head.

"Miles," Levi said, "get Ash a supply of tokens so she doesn't have to keep asking."

"We're burning favors," Miles said, grimly. "You better be damn sure it's worth it."

"It's worth it," Levi said.

Miles was rubbing a hand back and forth over his sleeve. I'd seen him do that before, after I'd killed the smudge that had been inside him. A gesture born of stress.

Annoying as he was, I tried to see this from his perspective. We had to start somewhere.

My request was costing him favors, which didn't sound good. The least I could do was be appreciative of that fact and lessen any other potential stresses for Miles regarding this situation. Like him having to worry about his team.

"It might be for the best if I was exempt from House protocols in going to Hedon. That way—"

"You could royally mess up diplomatic relations with them." Miles spread his hands wide. "Though if you get yourself killed over there and out of my hair, then I won't have to worry about you anymore."

Well, I tried.

"I'm pretty hard to kill." I manifested a blood red dagger, holding it up to the light. "You, on the other hand, have no handy armor to protect you."

"I said enough!" Levi swiped the dagger away from me and threw it. It embedded into the drywall, vibrating. "You two are my most valuable resources and the two people I trust the most. I don't give a fuck if you like each other, but you will respect each other and have each other's backs. Do I make myself clear?"

We muttered our assent.

"Though I agree with Miles," I said. "Anyone I take is a potential liability. Keep them here as first line of defense for the House."

Miles stared at me, faintly puzzled, then he nodded. "You can handle yourself there. Okay. You're free to come and go as you please, but getting tokens is trickier. There's only ever a set number of them in play and the ones who control their dispersal are touchy."

"Touchy as in easily hurt feelings?" I said.

"Touchy as in shoot first and ask questions later. It's not easy finding people willing to play middleman for a House and buy them."

"Get me into Hedon this time and I shouldn't be asking for more," I said. "This necromancer business should get me the alliance with the Queen and my all-access pass."

"*I* don't agree to that," Levi said.

"I do," Miles said. "*My* people. *My* determination for the good of the House. Are you going to override me on this?"

The air roiled with an angrily coiled tension.

"Your call," Levi said tightly.

Miles' cell rang. "Update me," he said into it.

Mrs. Hudson jumped off her doggie bed to nose around in the rest of the house.

I shifted forward to track her and Levi squeezed my shoulder.

"She's fine," Levi said. The second Miles hung up, he said, "Well?"

"Ashford," Miles said.

Levi swore softly. "There's no way it doesn't go farther than him."

"That's it. He'd gotten in deep on some gambling debts and Chariot offered to wipe them clean."

"Who's Ashford?" I said.

"Our crooked cop." Miles stared into his coffee mug with the look of a man who wished it would transform into something a lot stronger. "The one who told the German assassin where to find Yitzak."

"It wasn't Novak? No way!" I said. "You sure?"

I'd have put good money on the fact that Staff Sergeant Novak of the Nefesh police department, asshole extraordinaire, especially where I was concerned, was the corrupt element.

"Positive. Novak's a dick, but he's honest." Miles rubbed at his blood-shot eyes. I'd snagged a nap today. How long had Miles been running around cleaning up all these messes? "I fucking hate dirty cops."

"Double and triple check your sources on this," Levi said. "Ash, run down everything that's happened, starting with your visit with Paulie. Arkady filled me in on some of it, but I want your version."

Levi's only comment about my time in Inferno was to ask if I had a problem with him giving the Queen the codename.

"If they can find 26L1 faster, have at it. Rafael is on board with it as well." I was wrapping up the salient points when the doorbell rang. "You expecting someone?"

Levi shook his head. "I'll get rid of whoever it is."

Mrs. Hudson raced back into the kitchen, chasing a fly.

While Levi went to answer the door, Miles sat there looking vaguely uncomfortable. A moment later I heard Mayan's enthusiastic greeting.

I laughed without any humor. "You invited her."

In the spirit of our new truce, I waited for Miles' apology for springing her on me. For a second, it seemed like I'd get it. That was until he nonchalantly topped up his coffee.

"You're not questioning my decision as Head of Security, are you?"

"Wouldn't dream of it." I clenched my jaw so hard I took off a layer of enamel.

"… This is a very nice bottle of wine, thank you." Levi

led Mayan into the room, holding some fancy-ass bottle with a bow stuck to it.

She wore her heart pendent again.

"I don't know what I would have done if you hadn't helped—" She saw me and stopped short. "I didn't realize you'd be here," she said curtly.

"Why not? Because the hired help isn't generally invited?" I said.

Levi shook his head, but a small smile played on his lips.

Miles extended an arm, inviting Mayan to sit down at the breakfast nook. "How are you feeling?"

She word-vomited feelings all over the room. And sure, I wasn't a feelings person even on a good day and I was working on that, but this was a lot even for someone who had listened to a strongly empathetic friend like Priya unload. No one should need this much hand-holding through their own emotions and still have a driver's license.

I cut my eyes sideways to the blood dagger stuck in the wall. Levi raised his eyebrows at me, and I heaved an aggrieved sigh and sat down at the table with the others.

The puppy caught and ate the fly, then settled at my feet.

"Mayan, coffee?" Levi said.

"No, thank you. I'm still jittery." She shivered.

"Right then." Levi joined us, taking an empty chair between Mayan and Miles. It happened to be the closest chair to where he'd been standing and I wasn't threatened by Mayan. I was, however, deathly curious to see how far she'd go putting the moves on Levi.

"I need you to take me through your time with Jonah from first meeting him to this morning. But if it gets too much, just say the word and we'll pause, okay?" Miles could be compassionate when he wanted to.

Mayan nodded bravely.

The gist of the story was that she'd met Jonah at a supermarket, of all places, here in Vancouver one night. They hit it off and started seeing each other. He was a very private person and didn't like to go out a ton, but that didn't set off any alarms. He was kind and funny and quite involved in his work as a medical researcher.

"When you said you'd gone to Hedon because you'd hooked up with a guy, you meant Gunter, not Jonah, didn't you?" I said.

Mayan blinked at me. "How'd you know?"

"I'm a private investigator. My job is literally to put the pieces of a case together." Mack on my boyfriend all you want, but do not diss my abilities.

"I know that, but…" Flustered, she fiddled with her heart pendant.

"You're doing great," Miles said, with a hard stare my way. "Keep going."

They'd been dating for about three weeks when Mayan showed up earlier than she was supposed to and overheard a phone call. Jonah was arranging with a client to charm the head of a pharmaceutical company into handing over some formula.

"It was the first I knew of his magic. Or what I thought was his magic. I couldn't have guessed Jonah was really a necromancer," she said to me. "That doesn't make me stupid."

"Of course not," Levi said.

I mentally eyed her moral high ground, wishing it would open up and swallow her. "I'm sorry for saying that to you when I didn't have all the facts."

She nodded stiffly. "I pretended that I hadn't heard the call, but that night I phoned Levi. I really meant to tell you when we met," she said, "but Jonah came over before our visit and that's when it happened." Her bottom lip trembled. "Could I get a glass of water?"

Levi squeezed her hand, his expression troubled. "Of course."

I hated this. Not that they had a past, but that her pain was his pain. He was beating himself up for her suffering, even though none of this was his fault.

Mayan took a half-hearted sip of the water and then ran a finger around the rim of glass.

"Did you remember what happened that night?" Miles said.

Her face twisted. "Oh yes. Jonah said if I was going to tattle on him, I should have all the facts, but once that thing was inside me, I couldn't rat Jonah out. It was physically impossible."

"How did Jonah get the Repha'im out of Sheol?" I said.

"He just pulled it out? One second it wasn't there and then there was a ghost thing hovering in front me." Mayan pushed the glass away, leaning into Levi.

He put his arm around her, glancing at me. I made a "don't worry about it" motion with my hand.

"Did Gunter ever speak to you?" I said.

"No." Mayan buried her head in Levi's shoulder.

"You're upsetting her," Miles said.

"Then the faster we get through all this unpleasantness, the better," I said. "Did Jonah speak to the Repha'im that first night?"

"He called it Gunter and made a weird joke about my suitability as a wife."

"Because he's the Shidduch." Grinning, I slammed my hand on the table. "Hot damn!"

Thinking this was some game, Mrs. Hudson rose onto her back legs, scrabbling at me with a paw. When I didn't engage, she trotted out of the room once more.

"What is wrong with you?" Mayan said.

"What do you mean by Shidduch?" Miles leaned forward, his head tilted to one side.

"I checked in with a contact of mine." I filled them in on everything Ivan had told me. "Everyone thinks he charms people, but that's not it at all. He's matchmaking. Spirits to flesh. Making deals to give the deceased another chance at life in exchange for whatever his client has hired him to do."

"Necromancy is rare but putting souls into live bodies is a new twist on the magic I hadn't heard of before," Miles said. "It's involved communing with the dead or for the couple of level fives in history, puppeteering the departed spirits for a very brief period of time to carry out simple actions."

"But I'm not powerful," Mayan said. "He didn't have to do this to me."

"No," I said gently. "He didn't. You were a threat. That's why he went after you and violated you in the worst way. Do you have access to a good counselor?"

Mayan looked at me as if she was seeing me for the first time. Maybe she was. "I can find one."

"That's part of why you want to go into Hedon, isn't it?" Levi said to me. "How would that help to find Jonah? Gunter's dead."

"And I have no idea how to find Jonah. I swear," Mayan said. "I don't have Gunter's memories. I'm not even sure why he hated Alfie so much. Just that he did and I was forced to carry out his revenge."

"I believe you," I said. "There could be another way."

"You think Alfie knows something?" Miles said.

"Wait," Mayan said. "You're not allowed to go back there. The man with the sword and appallingly retro suit said so."

"You forgot to mention that part in your debrief." Levi pushed his chair back. "May I speak with you a moment? Alone?"

"No," I said.

Levi did a double take. "No?"

"If you're planning on speaking to Alfie, then in light of

this new information, I'm reinstating House protocol on you," Miles said.

"Also no," I said. "After Moran's warning to stay away, the Queen'll take any House operatives accompanying me as a show of force. Besides, have any of them been there as often as me? Survived as much? Even met the Queen?"

Miles reluctantly shook his head.

"I've been useful enough to her that I should be given a little leeway in terms of being heard out, and she was the one who said to surprise her. I go alone."

"You're going to push your luck over there one day," Levi said, "and—"

I raised my palms. "And what? You were fine with it when I told you the Queen wasn't happy with me but you had an agenda to fulfill. You don't get to pick and choose. I'm going."

"No," Levi said. "You're not. You're off the case. Miles, assemble a team."

"You said this wouldn't get messy." I leaned forward, my hands folded on the table, and calmly met his gaze. "Think very carefully before you play that card, Levi."

"Are you blackmailing me?" Levi's voice had gone dangerously quiet.

"If you think so little of me that you believe I'd ever do that, then this is a mistake. I want you to make clear decisions that don't change when your emotions get engaged."

"He didn't mean it like—" Miles looked at Levi and sighed. "Messy."

"I'll hire you," Mayan said.

My mouth fell open. "What?"

"I don't know what's going on here, though I'm starting to get an idea." She moved her chair away from Levi. "Your misguided sense of responsibility is going to blow up in your face one day, Levi. You should have told me about you and Ash."

"You were upset," he stammered.

"It's okay," I said. "If I thought I had to worry about him and other women, I wouldn't be with him. I trust the big idiot. Completely."

"This isn't about trust," Levi said.

"I'm well aware." I drained my coffee.

"Still," Mayan said, frowning at Levi, "by worrying you'd hurt me, you put me in an embarrassing situation. I'm sorry, Ash."

"No apology necessary, but thank you."

"I meant what I said. I want to hire you. You're the best person to find Jonah and make sure he never does this to another person."

"I am, but I'm also under an exclusive contract with the House on this investigation," I said.

"You'd honor that, even with Levi threatening to remove you?" she said.

I nodded. "It's Levi's call. I won't go behind his back. If I start justifying certain behaviors just because something isn't going my way, I won't be able to live with myself."

Levi exhaled in disgust. At himself. "Your membership in the support group is revoked."

I pursued my lips, halfway to forgiving him. "Do I still get biscotti?"

"Whenever you want, bella."

"Am I off the case?"

Levi scowled at me. "Miles, give her the tokens. House protocol doesn't apply. I still get to worry," he said. "But I won't cross the line into preventing you from doing your job."

"I can live with that. Uh, one other thing? Don't worry about getting hold of the Queen to pass on the information about the codename. I'll probably end up doing it while I'm over there."

Levi's eyes flashed, and then he let go and thunked his head against the table. "Fuck balls."

Progress.

Confronting some of the Queen's guard in Hedon and demanding to speak to their boss worked surprisingly well. They brought me to Moran in no time flat, who was sitting at a marble table in a tiny café.

"Must I educate you on the definition of a 'good, long, time?'" He set his frothy cappuccino on a saucer.

"Where are you?" I waved my hands around like I couldn't see him.

Everything in here was white, other than the gleaming copper espresso maker. Even the pretentious barista concocting some hipster brew was an albino.

"Hilarious," Moran said drolly.

Mrs. Hudson, who'd accompanied me on this jaunt, ran around in circles, thinking once again that my hand movements were the beginning of some new game. I tied the leash around the arm of the chair and sat down at the table, calming her down.

Moran bent over, examining the puppy like it was a small explosive device. "Is your life not hectic enough that you seek to incorporate dog ownership into it?"

"The pug is temporary. I bring gifts."

"Of the Trojan Horse variety?" He dismissed his guards.

"Ye of little faith. 26L1."

"Should that mean something to me?"

"If not now, hopefully soon. It's a codename for a member of Chariot. We're working to decode it from our end."

"Ah. This is part of her deal with Mr. Montefiore. I'll pass it on to the Queen. Is that all?" He picked up his coffee, holding the cup with such precision that one snap of his wrist and my nose would be toast.

I adjusted the angle of my chair to avoid that possibility.

"That's not all," I said. "The Repha'im I took down? Gunter? He was the contact person for a necromancer who went by the handle of Shidduch. I'd like your help in finding him."

He laughed. "Ashira, this is the black market. I'm not about to curtail the activities of any of our citizens."

"The Shidduch wasn't a citizen. He operated in Vancouver."

"Then I fail to see how this concerns me."

"Remember how I asked the Queen about Mayan? She said that Mayan must have come through before, but she hadn't. She was able to get into Hedon for her first time through the fixed entrance—undetected—because she had a former resident inside her."

Moran abruptly set his cup down on the saucer.

"I'm assuming that's a security breach you'd rather not have," I said. "Surprised?"

"Not enough to offer you an alliance."

"Come on. The Queen needs someone to act on her behalf as this originates outside her territory. Just like she did with Omar. I took care of that for her. Let me deal with this. I'll ensure the breach is shut down. All I ask is any information she has to locate Jonah." I smiled and spread my hands wide. "Quid pro quo is a beautiful thing."

"Why not ask Alfie where this Shidduch is?" Moran said. "He took over the bar. Perhaps he took over other aspects of Gunter's business as well."

"That was my first stop here today. He didn't know anything about it, and considering how grateful he is that I saved his life, he wasn't lying to me."

Moran blotted his lips on a pristine white napkin. "The Queen does not wish to involve herself further with matters outside Hedon at this juncture."

My hands twisted on my purse. Before I could second guess what my gut was saying, I'd unzipped it and laid the envelope down on the table between us. "What if I had something the Queen never expected in a million years? Would you guarantee the alliance and help me then?"

Moran regarded the envelope with suspicion. "Such as?"

"Serafina's DNA." I took a breath, expecting ten more seconds to explain myself, but my words had barely left my mouth when the café disappeared and I was engulfed in darkness.

My breath was harsh in this confined space, the tip of my nose brushing... stone? I tried to batter at my prison but my hands were frozen at my sides. I was entombed as a statue. I began hyperventilating, then screaming.

But no one heard my cries.

Chapter 23

How long before I'd go mad locked away, able to hear people talking and laughing outside my tomb as though all was normal, when I was alone for eternity?

I'd never feel the sun warm my face, the grass tickle my bare feet. Never hear braying laughter or smell that oaky amber scotch and chocolate scent. Adrenaline flooded my system, my muscles locked tight with no release and my heart threatening to explode out of my chest. I bit my lip, the blood beading on my tongue, salty and hot, in counterpoint to the cold sweat rolling over my skin.

I'd yelled myself hoarse when a strip of light pierced my eyes, revealing the Queen.

Mrs. Hudson was barking. The Queen couldn't have hurt the puppy, could she?

"You showed your hand too soon, chica." She made a tsking noise that was devoid of all mercy and held up the napkin with the lip print and the lipstick tube. The envelope would have been destroyed when she opened it.

"You jumped to conclusions." Talking hurt. My voice was a growly rasp. The air inside the statue was dank and tasted of soil.

"I don't think so," she said. "You were rooting around in my past."

"You root around in mine on a regular basis." My voice was muffled inside the stone, but loud enough to be understood. "The letter was sealed with a blood ward. Not mine."

"You can undo wards, chica."

"Undo them. Not reseal them with that same person's blood."

Her eyes narrowed. Two slits of unimpressed violet. "And so?"

"Knowledge is power." I coughed. My muscles were knotted up, my limbs trembling. "But not all knowledge is worth having. You wanted to be surprised. Hence the contents. I wanted to prove I could be trusted. Hence the unbroken seal. I want you as my ally, Highness."

Something in her features shifted, like a predator moving through the tall grass and stilling, trying to assess prey or competitor. Her manicured hands tapped the tube. Two, three taps. A pause.

"You do surprise me," she said. "Perhaps that is your greatest strength."

The stone disappeared. Without the support, my legs buckled, and I collapsed on the vast expanse of lawn in her garden, staring up at an eerie yellow crescent moon and unfamiliar constellations, feeling very far from home. I averted my eyes from the other statues, fighting to get my pulse under control.

The Queen loosened Mrs. Hudson's leash enough for the pug, who was unharmed, to scamper over to me and lick my face. I scooped her up, her warm little body a welcome comfort.

Her Majesty was resplendent in red leather pants and a red sweater that hugged her curves. Her dark lustrous hair was pulled into a high ponytail. "Do you plan to continue to dig up my past?" she said.

"No."

"And what of your present, Ashira Cohen? Were I to ask you about Jezebels, how forthcoming would you be?"

A sense of calm settled over me. "If you were my ally? Entirely."

She quirked a brow.

With one final pat, I released Mrs. Hudson, who immediately attacked a stray dandelion.

"You've always kept your word. I can't—no, I don't want to undertake this fight on my own." I stood up. "For now, will you help me find Jonah?"

The Queen handed me the leash, along with my purse that she'd also been holding. "It's doubtful I'll find him faster than you."

I swallowed the knot in my throat. She didn't want the alliance. Nodding, I started off across the lawn with the puppy, bound for the tiny plaza and my way home, when the Queen called my name.

"That was a compliment, chica. Learn to recognize them."

A flash of gold flew at me. I caught the item one-handed. It was a token, the same as Moran had, heavy and permanent. The all-access pass.

My giddy grin was barely professional. "Is this the beginning of a beautiful friendship?"

She rolled her eyes, but there was a hint of a smile on her lips as she walked away.

I was practically skipping as Mrs. Hudson and I emerged at Moriarty, still parked in the parkade next to Harbour Center. I'd won over this mysterious, smart, conniving, and dangerous woman. Think she'd lend me her stylist?

I checked the time on my phone and winced. I hadn't been gone as long as I'd feared, maybe three hours, but parking fees around here were a bitch.

As I got the pug settled in the car, a photo came through

of a man with half of his face puckered in old burn scars, carrying groceries.

Arkady: *Avi Chomsky. Zihuatanejo edition. This him?*

I zoomed in on the photo, but while the general facial features matched my memory, I couldn't make a definitive call. He was definitely a contender. This was the most real that my reunion with Dad had ever been. I was excited for this new door, this new chapter in our relationship to open up.

Me: *I'll see you in Mexico.*

~

ARKADY WOULDN'T BE in Zihuatanejo to greet me because he had to dash back to Ottawa to deal with a family issue that had come up. Levi did not throw a shit fit when I phoned him upon hearing what had happened in Hedon, which I gave him all the credit for. But he was so relieved that I'd gotten out in one piece that he didn't seem capable of any other emotion. Even the alliance and my shiny new token only warranted a faint "way to go."

Shock and joy warred within me. I had the gold coin, I'd secured a valuable ally. But at the same time, all I wanted was to ask Levi to cancel all his meetings so that he could curl up under the covers with me. I wanted to forget about my dad and Mexico and Rafael and codenames, just stay in, eat biscotti, watch Netflix, and try to remember how to breathe fully without worrying that I'd run out of air.

"You can't just take off," I said to Levi's grumble that I was taking Rafael to Mexico. "You'll give Veronica a brain aneurysm." I pulled the emergency brake up, cutting the engine, but leaving the radio on. I patted the passenger seat and the pug scrambled forward with a happy bark.

"Isn't that your life goal?" Levi said.

"Obviously, but I have to be the one to make her head

explode. It's no fun if I only get an assist and not the actual score on goal. Besides, I'm not taking Rafael for his stellar company. He's a contingency plan. If the scroll is there, he has to handle it."

"All right. Hey, maybe we could get away for a weekend? I find myself thinking fond thoughts of a certain hot tub in Tofino."

God, yes. That would be my reward, after the Queen, and all the emotions surrounding finally seeing Dad. Alone time with Levi.

"It's a date." I eyed my apartment window. "I should go upstairs and pack. The flight's in three hours."

"Don't you just heave things into a suitcase? I don't see this as a stressful issue for you."

"Priya's home. I haven't spoken to her since last night." Today had proven that life could throw a deadly curveball at any moment. Relationship issues were not to be put off, not when you valued the person involved.

The traffic report ended and the radio announcer moved into the news. The first story was the passing of local philanthropist Richard Frieden, age seventy-nine. It cut to a sound bite from Jackson Wu.

"As you all know," Jackson said, "Richard was a lifelong friend, mentor, and business partner of mine. Not to mention a great supporter of the Untainted Party."

Levi snorted. "Try one of the original founders of the party. The guy was a weasel."

I snapped off the radio. "Okay Coach, I'm going in."

"You got a plan?" Levi said.

I glanced at Mrs. Hudson. "Even better."

Given the amount of kisses that Priya lavished on the pug, you'd think they'd been stranded on a desert island at some point with only each other for company, and after a tragic separation where Priya feared the dog lost at sea, were together at last.

She wore a teal sweater. I could have cheered. I never wanted to see her in some version of blah again, which made it all that more imperative for this to work.

I opened my handbag and pulled out the remnants of her tiara, setting it silently on the coffee table.

She swallowed audibly. "How...?"

"On a case. I'm so sorry. I should have taken it off, but everything happened so fast." I put Mrs. Hudson on the sofa and steeled myself. This was going to be the hard part. "How about you keep the pug?"

"Excuse me?"

I took a deep breath. "I know I can't replace the tiara, but the two of you have bonded. I'm happy to help you take care of her."

Priya let the puppy lick her fingers. It was working. I'd ruined her tiara and I felt awful, but I'd given her something else that was special to her. Animals were a great source of comfort and could help her move forward.

"I would have forgiven you, you know," she said. "If you'd allowed me the space to feel sad and angry for a couple of days, this would have blown over. It was an accident. But giving me the dog? God, Ash. How clueless are you?"

This was a great plan. Wasn't it? Hadn't I gotten better at seeing others more clearly, and in turn anticipating their emotional needs? "I was trying to make it up to you," I said softly.

"You can't. But instead of acknowledging that fact and letting me have my space, you treated me like a child, bribing me with a freaking puppy, and completely invalidating my feelings. I don't want your dog."

"She's not—" At Priya's hard stare, I shut my mouth.

Shaking her head, she walked into her room and closed the door.

I stayed there in the common area, Mrs. Hudson panting amicably at my feet. This was supposed to have gone so much differently. "I really blew that one, huh?" I said to the dog. "I pulled the same overprotective crap on her that Levi pulled on me. I can be pretty dense for a smart woman."

Mrs. Hudson put her head on my shoe consolingly and then scrambled into my lap. I sighed and checked the time. If I hurried, I could drop her off at the animal shelter and still make it to the airport since I was only taking a carry-on. Except I'd have to gather all her stuff and she needed a quick walk and a feed and the thought of her whimpering in a cage all alone instead of on her comfy bed in my room left a dull ache in my chest.

The puppy, however, wasn't an adult human who could fend for herself if I fucked up.

Tatiana had conducted these awful magic experiments on the dog and yet she'd still had hope. She still trusted humans enough to be the first to venture out of that cage. She never bit me or anyone else, no matter how much they deserved it, despite having experienced so much cruelty at the hands of others. She'd trusted me to get the magic out of her, and I had. She was the Pug Who Lived.

How could I not want her after all that?

I pressed a kiss to the top of her sandy-colored head. "For better or for worse, you're stuck with me."

She thumped her tail.

"I love you, too. Oh." Nope. She was just trying to get to the squeaky cow which had gotten stuck between two sofa cushions. "We'll work on that."

I left Pri a note saying I was going away for work and not to worry if I wasn't around.

Levi agreed to watch Mrs. Hudson while I was gone. I was in such a rush, I barely had time to dump the pug and all her stuff into his arms and give him a quick kiss before hopping back in my taxi.

Rafael and I met up in the lounge outside the gate. There wasn't much to do while we waited to be called for boarding, so we read the closed captioning on the news playing on mute on the mounted TV screens.

Jackson Wu's sound bite about his friend was being replayed along with news of a looming transit strike.

"I appreciate you sticking to the plan and letting me handle the scroll," Rafael said. "As promised, I'll help when it comes time to destroy the *Sefer*, but until then?" He fiddled with the straps of his leather carry-on bag. "I never want to experience that all-consuming loss of control again."

Focusing on Rafael's well-being was better than my shaky existence. "You won't have to."

Even for an overnight flight to Mexico, Rafael was nattily attired in another argyle vest and bowtie, his linen shirt sleeves precisely rolled up. "I've brought a special container for the scroll."

"Is it a Tupperware?"

"No. Though they're surprisingly useful, Ashira. If you stopped for a moment to read the journals, you'd know this as well. Now, we should get through this without anything going—"

I slapped a hand over his mouth. "Let's not tempt fate, shall we?"

A commercial came on the TV featuring some loving couple videochatting via laptop with their daughter who was away at university.

I pulled out my phone, calling up my contact list of favorites, my finger hovering over Talia's number. Should I have given her some warning about trying to find Adam? My mother didn't like surprises and I hadn't considered what her reaction to her Nefesh husband's reappearance might be. How could I expect a genuine connection when I hadn't, even for a second, thought what this could mean, both personally and professionally for her? Given her some warning to prepare?

I might not like Talia's way of reaching out to me in our

new normal, but at least she'd tried. All I kept doing was dropping bombshells on her.

Rafael nudged me. "Look."

The TV had cut to a story about arrests made in the murder of a brother and sister who'd been part of a dogfighting ring. One of the gang members, a Mundane, had confessed to the killings. The footage showed a man with his head down, being led away in handcuffs.

I made a sound of disgust and put my phone away. "Chariot found some patsy to take the fall."

"Not everything is tied to them."

"So it's a coincidence that Yevgeny and Tatiana, both of whom had ties to the organization, were taken out?"

"No," Rafael said. "It's a result of their greed. If their experiments with the dogs were intended to undermine the gang, then that's motive. One thing about Chariot that we've learned over all these years is that they are very pragmatic. If someone is of use, the organization keeps them around."

The gate agent called our row to begin boarding.

"It's betrayal that's one strike and you're out," Rafael said.

I grabbed my carry-on and swung it over my shoulder, hoping to hide my shiver. "Nothing like a clear company policy."

Chapter 24

Modern Zihuatanejo had retained all the charm that I vaguely remembered from the trip with my parents when I was little. Narrow cobblestones wound through downtown past bustling restaurants. The water was clear and fishermen spread their daily catches out on the sand by their boats at Paseo de Pescador. The air smelled of coffee, frying chilis, and a tinge of exhaust.

Arkady had provided me with the name of a pub where this Avi Chomsky hung out, along with the fairly regular hours that I'd find him there.

The Crushed Barnacle made my favorite drinking hole, Blondie's, look like the Four Seasons. The décor took its inspiration from Davy Jones' locker, emulating a shipwreck with splintered beams, half a ship's carcass hanging lopsidedly from chains on the ceiling, and bleached fish bones scattered on the sand floor.

"Charming," Rafael said, sidestepping a skeleton wearing a dusty pirate hat that was perched on one of the bar stools.

The bar was packed with men, all of them cheering the very loud soccer match on the big-screen TV.

I muscled my way to the bar, slapping off some

wandering hands, and, in the case of one particularly persistent creep, whose Hawaiian shirt was stretched tight over his beer belly, threatening to stab him with my dagger.

"I'll stab you with *my* dagger," he leered, showing me his missing teeth.

"Do it and I'll rip it off and shove it up your ass."

He belched and returned his attention to the game.

I ordered a couple of beers that both looked and tasted like piss, and Rafael and I wandered through the bar. We found Avi in the back room, playing a round of darts with a thin man who reeked of pot. Avi wore a faded black t-shirt, khaki shorts, and flip flops.

Rafael raised an eyebrow at me and I shook my head. Avi's features were a plausible match, especially given the burns, but he was too short to be my father.

I sagged against the doorframe, reaching a hand out to steady myself. Get it together, Ash. A dead end didn't mean the end of the trail. I almost turned around right there and then, airport-bound to go home and find a new path to pursue, but the coincidence bothered me. I could buy the existence of other Avi Chomskys in New York, but here in Zihuatanejo? The place had less than one hundred thousand people and wasn't exactly famed for its Jewish population.

Their game wrapped up and Avi pulled the darts out of the board. His opponent paid up and shambled back into the front room.

Avi sized Rafael up. "Want to play?"

Rafael smoothed a hand over his vest. "I was known as Double Trouble back at my local pub."

"Oh yeah?" Avi said. "Real sharpshooter."

I groaned. Double Trouble meant you couldn't quite hit the double necessary to win the game. "I'll play you."

Avi gave me an indulgent look, then shrugged. "I like to spice things up with a bet, but we can go easy." He slapped three hundred pesos down on the table next to him. Just over twenty bucks Canadian.

"Sure." I matched his bet and took my darts.

I got a couple of "lucky" throws in, but lost the game. I shook out my hands. "I can do better. Play again?"

"You going to lose again and then fleece me on the third game?"

I smiled grimly. "How about I just trounce you on this one?"

"You think you can?"

"Try me."

Avi pulled out his wallet. "How much?"

"An answer."

He stilled. "To what question?"

"Play and find out."

Avi moved his T-shirt to show the butt of a gun. "I'd prefer to know now."

"26L1," I said.

His gaze went distant, then he shook off his stupor and put away his wallet. "I got no issue with him."

I barely caught my flinch. This was it. The point of no return. "You know who 26L1 really is," I said.

"Is that why he sent you? I got no more clue now than when he hired me and arranged the wire transfer. Assure your boss I don't know what his name is and I'm happy to keep it that way."

"What was the wire transfer for?" My voice sounded tinny and very far away.

He laughed. Not even cruelly, just like he was genuinely amused by the question. "He had a horse he needed put down."

My heartbeat slowed like there was a lead weight tied to it. I'd gone from a childhood viewed through rose-colored glasses to an adolescence and early adulthood in a cold unforgiving gray, but I'd been secure in the knowledge that the bottom had already dropped out of my world and I'd survived. It couldn't get worse than this.

How wrong I'd been.

If you want to spend the extra money, little jewel, spend it on clarity.

My father was dead.

The world turned red. My blood armor locked into place and I slammed a fist into Avi's jaw, sending him crashing into the far wall.

One team scored and there was a roar of cheers from the front room. Rafael hurried to the doorway, standing guard.

"How did you resist his Charmer magic?" I advanced on Avi, but after three steps, my armor disappeared. I desperately tried to summon my magic but there was only empty space.

Avi pushed to his feet, his gun drawn.

Rafael shielded me, one arm thrown out to each side to keep me behind him. "Ash, he's a null."

The one possibility I hadn't considered because nulls were so rare. Then again, who was I to talk?

Avi waved Rafael over to the table, demanding we both keep our hands where he could see them. "I'm also a very good shot, so step back. Who are you?"

A sluggish fear swam up from deep in my core as I stared down the barrel of that gun, but it was flash frozen into a cold, hard ball of rage. "Ashira Cohen. Did you kill my father?"

"Possible. I killed a lot of people."

"Avi Chomsky was his alias."

"Aw, girlie. Did you come here looking for some kind of closure? He didn't suffer, if that helps. One clean shot."

"When?"

"Hmm. It was after Cuba, so maybe fifteen years ago? Look. I was hired to a job. I did it. It was business, nothing personal."

My father was dead, and with him every last shard of hope I'd so carefully nurtured all these years. And for what? Men playing power games? A bullshit dream of immortality? My fists clenched.

"I wouldn't." Avi cocked the trigger. "You have no magic and this isn't the kind of place where anyone is going to come running to help you."

"What were his last words?" I ground out.

Avi shrugged. "You think I'd remember that after all these years? Come on."

Right. A job. So inconsequential that Dad's dying words weren't worth remembering. I blinked hard to clear the wetness from my eyes.

"And the scroll?" This couldn't all be in vain. I couldn't have lost him for nothing. Something good had to come out of this.

"What scroll?" Avi scratched his chin with the gun.

Rafael grabbed the pint of beer and chucked it at Avi. It fell short, smashing on the ground, beer staining the sand, but the noise caught Avi off-guard.

I grabbed a dart and chucked it.

It hit him in the arm, causing his shot to go wild. The sound in this small room was deafening, but no one bothered to investigate. Tough crowd.

Rafael lunged at Avi, wrestling him for the gun. He slammed Avi with some kind of complicated forearm strike, smoothly yanking the gun from his grasp.

Avi stumbled back.

"Drop the nulling," Rafael said, the gun trained on Avi.

"Fuck you."

Rafael coldly fired a bullet into Avi's foot.

He screamed, and fell to the ground, writhing and bleeding.

Two misshapen swords appeared in my hands. I tossed them away, my magic flaring wildly.

264

"Now," Rafael said, "what happened to the scroll?"

"There wasn't one." Avi's hysteria-tinged words had the ring of truth.

The ball of ice in my core cracked and broke, releasing a slithering darkness. I jumped Avi and started wailing on him, smashing his jaw to pulp. "There has to be a point."

"Ashira," Rafael snapped.

Everything was red: my vision, my fists, Avi's face. But it still wasn't enough. It wasn't even beginning to be enough. I called up my magic and hooked it into his.

Rafael grabbed my shoulders, but I threw him off, dimly aware of my Attendant crashing into the table that still held my beer.

I wrenched Avi's magic out of him and stabbed my red forked branches into it.

He gasped and clutched at his heart.

So weak—and mine for the taking. My last sliver of rationality yelled at me to stop. I was killing him. This was a line I could never uncross, never make up for, but it wasn't too late.

I smiled, pouring more power into him. I was the instrument of a goddess. An eye for an eye.

Avi spasmed, his eyes rolling back to show the whites. His face disappeared, replaced with my father's, wearing an expression of deep sorrow and disappointment.

With a frustrated cry of rage, I pulled my hands away. Avi's magic snapped back into his body. He was unconscious, but alive.

"Get out of here," Rafael said, already calling for an ambulance. "I'll take care of it."

He didn't look at me as he spoke.

I stumbled outside, wracked from head-to-toe with violent spasms from stopping the process of taking Avi's magic. I made it as far as the beach out back, where I collapsed in the shade of a nearby palm tree, my heart skipping beats. Plagued by dizziness, I clawed at the sand.

A woman in a housekeeping uniform from one of the hotels crouched down to ask if I needed help. Water? A doctor?

She was so kind, slinging my arm over her shoulders to help me up. She didn't deserve to have me sneak my magic inside her, exhaling in the sweetest relief when I confirmed she was Nefesh.

I had never hated myself more for what I was about to do, but that siren song in my head was drowning out the very ocean itself.

"Ashira!" Rafael sprinted across the sand to us. He took me off the woman's hands, assuring her that he would get me help. Believing I was suffering from sunstroke, she told him where to find the nearest clinic, and hurried off to her shift. Safe.

"Help me," I whimpered.

His expression hardened. "You promised," he snarled.

My legs buckled; I was almost bent double, sweating while the world swam drunkenly around me. Every particle of light stabbed me in the eyeballs.

Rafael dragged me to behind a boat parked on the sand and tossed me on the ground. His shadow fell over me, blocking out all light. "You knew this could happen if you aborted the magic destruction. I should have trusted my instincts. You're a liability, but you won't make me one."

I reached a trembling hand out to him, flinching as he abruptly pivoted, leaving me convulsing in the brilliant sunlight.

The world dipped and swirled, a fever dream pulling me under. It was getting harder to resist, but I had to. I had too much to live for. Spasms rocked me in burning waves. I was on my knees, hyperventilating with my forehead pressed to the sand, and holding on to my loved ones' faces like talismans. My ears popped and blood dripped from my nose, but bit by bit I fought my way back until the pain receded. I took a full, slow breath. Rolling onto my back, I blinked up at the clouds through bleary eyes, my thumb and forefinger pressed against my nostrils to staunch the bleeding.

Motion flickered in the corner of my vision, and I turned my head to find Rafael squatting nearby, watching me, one hand over his mouth.

"At least this'll make for a juicy entry in my Jezebel file, right?" The bitter words scorched my throat.

He poured some water from a plastic bottle over his handkerchief and gave them both to me. "Yes." He said it like it was penance.

I scrubbed my face, washed off the dried blood, and drank deeply.

When I tried to stand up, Rafael was there to help, but I declined his outstretched hand and got myself on my feet. Standing was the extent of my abilities, however, so I allowed Rafael to get us to the airport and check us in without arousing too much suspicion.

Levi's travel agent had arranged for stand-by tickets on our return flight since we hadn't known how long it would take us to deal with Avi, and we managed seats on the last plane back that night.

Luckily, my condition had more or less worn off by the time we cleared security. Rafael led me to the gate and then hesitated, his eyes on departure boards and passengers dodging each other's luggage as they hurried to their destinations. He opened his mouth, looked at me, then closed it. With a sigh, he slipped off to join the crowds browsing the shops and getting overpriced food before catching their flights.

I didn't call him back. I couldn't blame him for wanting to get away from me.

I sat in numb silence on a plastic chair watching excited

passengers come and go, wondering how anyone could be happy when my father was this traveler who was never coming home, and waiting for the tears to come. Hoping they would because Dad was dead and I felt nothing beyond a grim anticipation for revenge on the person who'd orchestrated his murder.

We boarded in silence.

Dad had tried to con Chariot with the fake scroll. That was the only thing that made sense. He'd intended to give the true piece to Gavriella, and somehow this 26L1 had found out. One strike. Dad's betrayal had been his death warrant.

There was one piece of the puzzle that my brain kept worrying over, though: what had happened to the real scroll?

It was much easier to dwell on that. I eyed Rafael, who was pretending to be engrossed in an article about the hottest beachfront resorts in Thailand. I didn't require ice in my drink given the frostiness rolling off him.

"I'm sorry I broke my promise," I said, "but how about you have a modicum of empathy for the shock I was in? If I ever find myself in that situation again, I swear to never ask for your help. And hey, if I die, you'll get that nice liability-free Jezebel you want so badly."

He stared at the same page for another minute before closing the magazine. "That was said in the heat of the moment, and I apologize. I was wrong. You're not a liability. You've learned more in your short tenure than many in their entire time as a Jezebel." He finally looked at me and for the first time I realized how fragile his gaze was. "I'll do whatever you require of me to ensure you're around for a long time."

"Thank you," I said quietly. "Our next step is to find the piece my father had. The final pillar isn't lit up. Either he hid it and was killed, in part, for refusing to hand it over, or when Chariot learned of his betrayal, they acquired the scroll, but some high-ranking member who isn't one of the Ten secured it on their behalf."

Rafael placed the magazine back in the seat pocket. "For four hundred years Chariot and Jezebels crossed paths on the trail of the scroll pieces. Ever since Gavriella stole that third piece, there was never any evidence of Chariot seeking the final scroll. After what we learned today, I'm inclined to believe that your father got away with his con. Chariot doesn't know they possess a fake scroll. That's why they only ever endeavored to find the library. They believed they had two scrolls and wanted our other three."

"Did they ever succeed?"

"They got close. We've moved it a number of times over the years."

"Where is the library, anyway?" I got there via Rafael's father's ring, but wasn't sure where it was actually located.

"We have, as Attendants, never shared that information with anyone, not even our Jezebels. It's just traditionally not done," Rafael said primly. "Besides, what you don't know, no one can torture out of you."

I waited for him to laugh or indicate that it was a joke, but he didn't.

"Well, that's a motto for the ages. Thanks," I said, "for letting me know."

I spent the rest of the flight staring out the window, seeing nothing.

I stopped Rafael outside the Vancouver airport, right before we parted ways. "When you crack the code," I said, "I'm going to kill 26L1."

It was a stain on my soul I could live with. In finding my father, I'd sought closure and moving on, except I'd missed a salient point.

Moving on meant leaving something behind.

I may not have gotten revenge on Avi, and neither him

nor 26L1 would ever be brought to justice, but my father's death wouldn't be in vain.

"You can't," Rafael said. "He's one of the Ten and when we learn his name, we'll finally have the identity of one of the inner circle. We can use that to find the rest of them and reclaim the scroll that's in their possession. If you make him answer for his crimes, they'll replace him and we'll be no closer than we were before."

"He murdered my father." I kicked a baggage cart.

"Chariot murdered mine as well." Rafael fixed me with the same cold expression he'd worn when he'd shot Avi. "Tell me you won't kill him, Ashira. None of us get the luxury of revenge."

Rafael was right and I hated him for it. But there was nothing stopping me from killing 26L1 when this was all over.

I smiled grimly. "You have my word."

Chapter 25

"Dad's dead." I dropped down on Talia's couch, my black socks with the hole in the toe a stark contrast to her white plush rug.

Growing up, our home had been cozy and cluttered. It was a place that was well lived-in and well loved. Her apartment these days was ruthlessly maintained by a housekeeper. I'd never seen a speck of dust or a dish left out on the counter, and her furniture was the latest in high-end contemporary design, where comfort had somehow been left out of the aesthetic.

"Here." She handed me a piece of Scotch tape, measuring that she had enough wrapping paper to cover the box of dishes. "When I fold the paper over, tape it down for me."

"Did you hear me?" I said, waving my tape-covered fingers in front of her face.

"Tape it."

I secured the edges of the paper with the silver wedding bells on it together. "Who's getting married?"

"The Shulmans' daughter."

"Mazel tov. Dad is dead. Care to comment?"

"I'm well aware that my husband's dead." She ripped off another piece of tape, affixing it to the edge of the table, and spinning the box around to wrap the next side.

"How?"

"He never came back." Rip.

I took the tape away from her. "Yeah. That's what happens when people leave. But you couldn't have known for sure. Didn't you even wonder if he was still alive? Hope?"

"What was the point? He was dead."

"You didn't know that."

She slammed her hand down on the coffee table and I jumped.

Other than the crinkling of paper and the occasional rip of tape, we sat in silence.

"What makes you so certain?" she said at last, rolling the extra wrapping paper up.

"I visited Uncle Paulie. It led me to some information that confirmed Dad's death."

She caught her thumb on the edge of the tape dispenser and winced. "Paulie could have killed you. Whatever happened to him, that man is not the same person who snuck you M&Ms."

"True. He's broken. But he's not dangerous. At least, not to me."

The bag with the bows crinkled as Talia pulled out a silver one and stuck it to the package. "I don't want to know how Adam died."

"That's good, because I wasn't going to tell you." I systematically unraveled one of the frilly bows. I was a damn good private investigator. I got answers. I'd just never thought about how much this stuff hurt. People asked me to find cheating husbands, lying wives, missing kids, or delinquent relatives. I did, and then I always wondered why my clients where so upset when I got them the answers they already suspected. If you already knew on some level,

272

why did an outside source confirming it break you emotionally?

Now I understood. There was something to be said about people's tremendous ability to deny reality, even when it was right in front of them.

For our capacity to hope.

"I wasn't, you know, blind to your father's faults," Talia said, swallowing. "But he was just so damn charismatic." Some of her bitterness leached away as she added, "And he loved us so much."

"Then why weren't we enough?" My voice quivered and my body felt heavy and off-center. A black ball had settled into the pit of my stomach, making it ache.

"If I had a dime for every time I asked myself that, my retirement fund would be set."

"Do you know what he'd gotten himself involved in?" I wound the strings of the unraveled bows around my hands, snapping them tight like a garrote.

"No, but he wasn't sleeping. When he left, I thought, okay. He's in trouble, but it'll work out. He'll be back. Then the months passed with no trace of him and that was it."

"What if he'd stayed away because he didn't want to hurt us?"

"Oh, honey." She took my hands in hers. "You've never been in love like that. Not as a romantic partner and definitely not as a parent. Your dad was dead because he *couldn't* have stayed away. No matter what he'd intended when he left."

A lump rose in my throat. "But you've always been so angry at him."

"One doesn't negate the other. He didn't trust in our love. In us, no matter how hard that was."

I mulled that over, staring down the wedding bells on the wrapping paper like my life depended on them. "I'm dating Levi."

Dead silence.

"No one can know," I blurted out, barrelling on. "And I'm keeping the dog."

I shot her a glare, just daring her to fight back. Give me a target. I didn't need my family. I had my team. I'd survived without one parent. I'd be fine.

But Talia didn't deliver one of her usually scathing remarks. She didn't yell, didn't sigh disappointedly, and didn't give me the bullet-point list of the myriad of ways I was screwing up my life. Instead, she brushed a lock of hair out of my face and pressed a kiss to my forehead. "Okay."

I was so stunned I didn't realize my mouth was open. After a few tries to form sentences, I crossed my arms, blinked several times, and then said, "Maybe we could try breakfast again sometime. Patios are nice for the dog."

Talia smiled. "I think that could be arranged. Work talk stays at work."

"That would be good."

I didn't stay. I made it through the hallway and downstairs into the apartment lobby on autopilot before I realized: I couldn't go home. Priya was still mad and it wasn't fair to deny her space. But where else could I go? God, I didn't want to do this hiding out in my bedroom or office, all alone. And there was no way I could keep up a smiling face in front of strangers at a café.

Sunlight twinkled on the glass doors of the building. I had Levi. I could curl into him and he'd wrap his arms around me and it would make the finality of this revelation bearable.

Fuck. It was Tuesday. He'd be at work. Well, it was better than nothing.

Everything between Talia's apartment and finding myself standing in front of Veronica's desk was a blur.

Veronica barely glanced at me, cool and crisp in a pearl-colored sheath dress, her French manicured nails clacking against her keyboard. "Priya has your dog."

I pushed on my ribcage like that could help me pump air into my lungs.

Frowning, Veronica looked up and properly saw me. Eyes wide, she hit the intercom button. "Ashira—No. Levi. Wait. Damn it."

His office door was flung open so hard it bounced off the wall. Levi strode up, his body locked up with rage. "That necro fucker went after Mayan."

"Levi," Veronica said insistently.

I blinked at him dumbly for a second, willing my brain to switch gears. Then I shook my head at Veronica. "Is she okay?"

He motioned me inside the office and shut the door. "Yeah. He cornered her after work to see if Gunter had finished Alfie off. Mayan tried to go along with it, but Jonah figured out Gunter was gone. He flew into a rage, demanding to know how."

"Did she tell him about me?" That's all I needed. An angry necromancer with insider knowledge of my secrets.

"No. She maced him and fled." He rubbed a hand over his inky black hair, sending it into disarray. "She's safe now, but I want him locked up. Miles still can't track him down, so you'll need to follow up with Moran."

"Right. Of course. I'll…" My brain stuttered and went blank. The bolted cylinder lock and set of pick tools were on the coffee table, sitting on top of another Sherlock Holmes collection.

Adam, his large hands guiding my eight-year-old ones: *you've got to hold the tension wrench steady, little jewel.*

There was a ringing in my ears, but I smiled sunnily. "You're practicing. That's… good."

"Ash?" In an instant, all the fury drained out of Levi. He led me to the sofa. "Shit. Was it your dad?"

275

I opened my mouth, but no words came out. That ball of grief had spread into my throat like a cancer, choking me. Shaking my head, I curled into him, hanging on for dear life. The only sound was his heartbeat under my cheek and the silent scream in my head.

"Ah, bella," he said. "I'm so sorry."

Words were still beyond me. I leaned in and kissed him, trying to pour out my drowning sorrow, crumbling inside.

"Wait." He stood up and I grasped at his shirt. "I'm coming back," he said. He locked the door and returned to me. "Can you talk about it?"

I shook my head at him. I couldn't let it out. Not yet, when it threatened to consume me. I kissed him again, a soft brush of our lips. Longing and stark need whispered through me, banishing the grief and darkness back the tiniest bit. I clung to that flame slowly kindling to life, my kiss growing more desperate as I yanked him closer by his belt loops.

He wrapped a hand around the nape of my neck, his tongue tangling with mine. When he pulled back, his chest rose and fell in rapid breaths. I reached for him again, but he gently pushed me down against the leather sofa, pressing against me with his hard, lean body, and capturing my mouth in a kiss that stole the breath from my lungs.

Levi made his way down my body with hot, open-mouthed kisses that burned deliciously even through the fabric of my clothing.

My fingers bunched into the sides of the cushions. I felt like I'd willingly jumped off a cliff, tumbling faster and faster toward him, secure that when I landed, he'd catch me.

Levi popped the button on my jeans, stripping me in one fluid motion. "Forgot to do laundry again, huh?"

I was incapable of banter, turning stricken eyes on him. "Levi." His name was my anchor and my plea.

"I've got you, bella." He pushed my legs apart and I stuttered out a weak protest.

"If this isn't doing it for you…" I said.

He sputtered a laugh, his mouth vibrating against my inner thigh. "Beg to differ." He licked my clit, agonizingly slowly. "God, the taste of you."

I tensed up, flinging an arm over my face. A soft noise of pain escaped me. What was wrong with me? I should be grieving my dad, not getting off.

Levi tugged my arm away. Reluctantly, I opened my eyes. He gave a small shake of his head, no trace of amusement on his face. "Whatever you're feeling right now is okay. You're allowed to feel alive."

I gave a small nod, not sure I believed it, but needing it to be true.

He teased me, kissing and suckling along the insides of my thighs as I squirmed. Finally, I covered them with my hands. "Too ticklish."

Levi lifted his head. His hair was mussed and his eyes were enormous blue pools, but every ounce of focus was trained on me.

I dragged in a shuddery breath and whispered, "Keep going."

He licked into me again. Every slow flick of his tongue was a teasing rasp against my clit.

My face flushed, but the warmth on my cheeks was nothing compared to the molten flame stealing through me, a hot bright core lit up like the sun. No, the moon, breaking my grief up into manageable ice floes, swimming through the shadows within.

I fisted my hands in Levi's hair, wanting him to go faster, and felt him smile. Knowing Levi it was probably a smirk, but the sensation sent a welcome and interesting shiver through me, so I let him have it.

"Please," I whimpered.

His eyes met mine. They burned for me.

My nipples hardened into sharp peaks and I rocked

277

against him, thrashing against his iron grip, and desperately riding the torrent of desire cresting inside me, until I tipped over some unseen precipice and my body fireworked. It was that good.

I burst into tears. Huge, shuddering and snot-filled, I was helpless against them. I cried for my dad and my mom and all the days that could have been and weren't. My grief had zones: my stomach hurt, my back was cold, my hands felt swollen and hot, and my head throbbed. The dad-shaped hole in my heart bled afresh.

Levi gathered me to him, cradling me close and stroking my hair while I rode it out, a fresh supply of tissues at the ready.

The tears dried up like they always do, every last shard of crystalized grief excised from my chest. "My father is dead. Killed fifteen years ago by the assassin who stole his fake passport."

Levi winced. "On whose orders? 26L1?"

I nodded.

Levi took my face in his hands. "We'll find him and make sure he pays. I swear." He sealed his vow with a tender kiss. "I wish there was something I could do to make you feel better."

I leaned my head on his shoulder. "There isn't. But thanks."

"How about a date?"

I lifted my head to look at him. "Don't you have to work?"

"All I've got left is my training session with Miles." He flexed a bicep. "I'm such a prime specimen of manhood that it's really not necessary."

All kidding aside, my hyper-responsible boyfriend wanted to shirk his responsibilities just to cheer me up? I smiled. "A date would be perfect."

~

I INSISTED on going home to change and shower. The only instructions Levi gave me vis-à-vis clothing was to dress warm.

Priya wasn't home. However angry she was at me, Mrs. Hudson wasn't feeling the effects, since Pri had taken the pug from Levi this morning at work.

I bundled into a coat and gloves, and pulled a fleece cap low over my ears before going down to meet Levi.

He picked me up in a black Jeep with tinted windows that belonged to the House, refusing to say where we were going. I tried to figure it out, but by the time we'd reached the boundary between Vancouver and Burnaby, I'd run out of guesses.

He pulled up alongside Confederation Park, a huge green space running for blocks next to one of the library and community centers in Burnaby. During the summer, families would picnic here all day, while kids splashed in the water park or played at the sprawling playground. There was even a model steam train you could ride down in the far corner.

This evening, however, it was deserted. Levi took my gloved hand and led me toward trees at the east side of the park.

"Did I mention I'm not a fan of horror movies?" I said.

"Think more epic showdown, less slasher."

Lights up ahead broke the gloom. We'd arrived at the bocce ball courts.

It was packed with old men, not one of them younger than seventy, whose lined faces showed lives well lived, if not always easily so. They greeted Levi with an affectionate "Ragazzo!" and enveloped him in hugs, back pats, and kisses on both cheeks, all of which he enthusiastically returned.

My heart clenched. How starved had young Levi been for this kind of family?

"Shouldn't you have illusioned me?" I whispered when he tugged me forward to introduce me. I scanned all their faces, seeking a flicker of betrayal, a phone pulled out to snap a photo. More than ever, I was highly aware of who might be watching.

"I trust every single one of them," Levi said. "Being House Head, I've had to find places where I can be me without it hitting social media. This is one of them."

Trusting his judgment, I allowed myself to be introduced to the men, most of whom teased Levi good-naturedly about never bringing any friends with him before. I was hugged and given kisses on the cheek as well, which was initially overwhelming. I'd been an only child in a single parent home and was a loner by nature, but there was such goodwill and high humor to this encounter that I found myself awkwardly returning their embraces.

All while Levi watched me with an affectionate smile.

The goodwill, however, ended the second the bocce started. Competitive did not begin to cover it. Their smack talk game, uttered in a combination of English and Italian was superb. And the arguing? Every single throw stopped the game while five or six of them debated the move loudly and with much hand gesturing.

I'd never played bocce before, and while Levi had offered to have me on his team, he was waved away by the undisputed leader of the group, a stocky man who was eighty-five if he was a day, called Luciano.

Luce, as he insisted I call him, drilled the proper form into me like a Russian gymnastics coach, but he also mediated on my behalf, his fierce, bushy glower earning me a few points that I probably didn't deserve.

It was the most fun I'd had in ages. Especially with Levi lit up and joking around with an ease he rarely displayed. Between our turns he was always at my side, his arm around my waist or his hand resting at the small of my back.

My grief over my dad wasn't gone, but getting to be this way with Levi did much to banish it to a quiet muting.

Levi eventually said we had to leave and the group told me to come back any time. Even without Levi. He grinned, shaking his head, and said something in Italian that made them all laugh uproariously.

Luce motioned me over to his bench, since he rarely got up when it wasn't his turn. Arthritis, he'd explained earlier. He took my hand and kissed it like a benediction. "You're a good girl, bella. Take care of that one."

"I will," I said through an unexpected thickness in my throat.

Levi didn't speak until we were back in the Jeep. "Did you have fun?" he said, a tenseness at the corners of his eyes.

"I loved it."

He tossed his head smugly. "I knew you would."

"Uh-huh." I buckled up my seat belt. "What's next?"

"You'll have to wait and find out."

Our next stop was one of Vancouver's most popular pizza joints. It didn't take reservations and people waited for hours outside to get in. That wasn't Levi's way. Instead he knocked on the back door, which was opened by the famed pizza chef herself. After more kisses on both cheeks accompanied by a soft "Piacere," to me from the chef in a heavy Italian accent, she led us through the kitchen to a private back room where we feasted on amazing thin crust pizza that she made specially for us.

We talked about things that mattered not a whit in the scheme of good and evil but meant everything in terms of two people wanting to learn everything about the other. Then we laughed, reliving old memories of camp and who had hated who more.

The night ended at Levi's house, the two of us in bed. The curtains were thrown open to the stars, and the ocean lulled me into a relaxing trance as much as Levi cradling me in his arms and playing with my hair.

For a day that had started in shadows, it had ended in light. Moonlight, but the darkness made the glow that much more precious.

~

WE WERE WOKEN by Levi's phone buzzing.

"Take it," I said, with a yawn. "I should get dressed." I was fastening my jeans when Levi showed me the text with the red heart and crown emoji.

"Whoa," I said. "Richard Frieden was laundering money through Hedon? This is almost as good as finding out who in Chariot went after you and the Queen. I mean, it's not as cool as my all-access pass, but we both know she likes me more." I yelped as Levi threw a pillow at me, hitting me in the chest.

"That's only because she hasn't known me as long. I have it on very good authority that women adore me."

"Your mom doesn't count."

Levi tackled me and I shrieked as he buried his face in my neck and blew a raspberry. He rolled off me, a smug smile on his face. "Frieden did it in the same business venture connected to Jackson Wu."

"The allegations alone will rock the party."

"Jackson will be forced to step down and it'll send that damned legislation into limbo." Levi punched the air in victory.

"My mother's legislation." I sat down on the bed, my shoulders slumped. The legislation had to be stopped, but she and I were in the best relationship we'd had in years. Not for much longer.

Levi sighed. "Yeah."

I kissed him. "It's okay. I don't want it passing any more than you do. We'll get through it. Together."

He laced his fingers through mine. "We will."

It was my turn for a text from the Queen. Or Moran in her name. Hard to tell when the contact was an emoji.

Found the necromancer. An address in Vancouver's Marpole neighborhood appeared.

Levi sagged against me. "Thank God."

Me: *On it. Thanks.*

"I'll tell Miles," Levi said, his phone already to his ear.

"Hang on. Tell him to put his people in place outside the house, but I'm going in to cuff Jonah on my own. It's the only way," I said over Levi's protest. "If he tries to put a Repha'im in me, I'll take his magic. I'm the only one with a clear shot at him."

Levi nodded and made the call.

Miles' security team took up position along the sides of Jonah's place. Levi had not been allowed to come, but I swore I'd phone the second Jonah was safely apprehended. The house was a Vancouver Special, a style of architecture popular in the 1960s and 70s, characterized by its boxy structure, low-pitched roof, balcony across the front, and a brick or stone finish on the ground floor.

This was the first time I'd seen Arkady since Inferno. While Miles conferred with one of his team members, I thanked my friend.

"I really appreciate you flying all over the place for me," I said.

"Was it him?" Arkady yawned and rubbed his eyes. "Sorry. Too much travel in too short a time. Montreal sucks this time of year."

"Ottawa."

"Huh?"

"Didn't you go see your parents?"

"Yeah, but they were in Montreal with my grandmother. So? Your dad?"

He'd have convinced anyone else, but I'd spent years unearthing other people's lies and there was an almost palpable tug when I caught hold of one. My fingers twitched and I imagined his words infused with a deep rot.

"You're lying. Why?"

"Pickle, what would I have to lie about?"

"I don't know. But ever since we met I've been convinced that you moving in wasn't a coincidence. At first I thought Levi had put you there to keep tabs on me, but he didn't."

"You're being paranoid."

"Don't patronize me. I'll find out what you're hiding and I swear, if it impacts me or anyone I care about, I will fuck you up."

The genial expression that he usually wore fell away, leaving a shrewd calculation. "You've changed in the past couple days."

"I'm giving less of a shit," I said.

"Or more."

"It's a fine line. Well?"

"I'm not lying to you. Do with that what you will." He jogged over to Miles.

I'd been suspicious of him from the get go, and while I could pretend I'd become friends with him to appease Priya, the truth was, I'd wanted to be his friend. He was funny and he'd been there for me. I rubbed my breastbone. The Ash of two months ago would have beat herself up for it.

Even if he had betrayed me, I didn't completely regret befriending him. But how could I keep Arkady on the team if he was potentially working against me? That said, he'd done his job finding Avi, and I couldn't be everywhere at once. Nor did anyone else have his particular training and magic abilities. What should I do?

I'd spent so many years making all the decisions on

everything in my life that I'd forgotten that I didn't have to. Not on this. I could discuss it with the rest of my team and get their input. How times had changed.

Miles caught my gaze and nodded. Showtime.

I picked the lock on the back door and crept inside the kitchen. Drawers were being opened and shut from deeper inside the house. I tiptoed to the living room/dining room which was sparsely furnished with a table, a sofa and a TV set. I'd bet this was another rental.

Keeping to the shadows, I made my way down the hallway to the master bedroom where Jonah threw clothes into suitcases. There was a suitcase sitting closed by the door. I tested its weight. It was heavy enough for my purposes, so I flung it at Jonah, knocking him facedown onto the bed. Pulling out magic suppressing cuffs, I pressed my knee into his back and wrenched his arm around his back.

He fought back with a crazed determination, but I was stronger.

Jonah twisted his head around and his eyes widened. "You. Did you kill Gunter somehow?"

I snapped the first cuff on him. "Just lucky."

The air rent apart with a loud sucking noise. The room hung in two jagged pieces, separated by a chasm of swirling blues and purples.

The front door splintered with a loud crack, Miles yelling at his people to find me.

I struggled to clamp the second cuff on Jonah. I'd just snapped it around his wrist when I was sucked backwards into the chasm.

Jonah, meanwhile, seemed totally unaffected by the force that grabbed me and hauled me into the darkness.

The last thing I heard before everything went black was him saying, "Let's see how your luck holds up now."

Chapter 26

My eyes adjusted from pitch black to a dim gloom revealing that I stood on a faint dirt path in a desolate wasteland. I yawned, trying to pop my eardrums, but the silence that bore down on me like a physical force didn't change, and when I licked my lips, I tasted dust.

I spun around, frantic to find that jagged seam and claw my way out like a zombie from a grave, but it was gone. In my panic, my foot slipped off the path.

A mass of smudgy black shadows rushed toward me. I bit back a scream, scrambling safely onto the trail.

The Repha'im hit some invisible shield on either side of me, battering up against it again and again.

Oh hell. The realization sank into me with an icy certainty.

Welcome to Sheol. Population: millions of Repha'im, and me, Ashira Cohen, one living human who needed an exit strategy stat.

The ring! I slid the wooden ring off its chain and onto my finger. Come on. I visualized the library as perfectly as I could, willing myself out of here, but I didn't budge. The gold token didn't work either.

I didn't bother trying to attack the Repha'im. All of humanity's dead against me? No, the best I could do was stay on this path that stretched out endlessly in either direction and pray the shield kept them from devouring me. Replacing the chain under my shirt, I started walking.

Dust clogged my nostrils and scratched the back of my throat. I squinted, blinking furiously, my eyes watering as a fine layer settled over me.

I'd been trudging along for some time when I tasted freezing cold water. The world blurred, the path disappearing in favor of a murky current rushing past. The mouthful became a lungful and I coughed, clawing at my throat and fighting against the unseen hands that held me down. My magic was too sluggish to send into my enemy.

I was pulled up for one blessed moment, just enough for a final gasp of air, the hair almost pulled from my scalp before I was shoved under again. Drowning sucked balls. Icy panic suffused me, every breath a choking inhale of more brackish water. I flailed my arms, thrashing to live but to no avail. Death claimed me.

I came to back on the path in Sheol, curled up in the fetal position and hyperventilating. Without sound. My shoulders were sore, and when I touched one with wrinkled blue prunes of fingers, it was bruised. Exactly where those hands had held me down.

What the fuck kind of hallucination had that been?

Masses of Repha'im continued to batter up against both sides of the invisible shield, hard enough to rattle the ground.

I broke into a sprint, hoping to outdistance them, but I ran out of steam before there was even a break in their number. Panting, I pressed a hand against the stitch in my side. Best to conserve my energy, though dehydration would probably kill me first.

If I couldn't run to an exit, I'd have to think my way out.

What did I know about Sheol? It was the land of death, silence, and forgetting. Break it down, Ash.

Death. I continued along the dirt track, walking with the best posture I'd ever had, not wanting any part of me to touch the spirits that were just inches away. They were a pulsing force waiting for a single misstep to land me in their clutches so they could suck out my life essence in a futile attempt to rejoin the land of the living. For a bunch of dead people, their eager anticipation rolled off them in giddy waves.

Full up on the death part.

Silence. I was good on that front, too. People bitched about all the noise we lived with on a daily basis, wishing they could get away to the woods or out on the water and have some peace and quiet. Except our world was never truly silent. There was the rush of wind in the leaves, the lapping of waves, a bird's call.

This was true, pure silence and it terrified the shit out of me. With every passing second lacking sound, I became less and less certain I was still alive. My feet made no noise and my breaths were snatched away before they left my mouth.

That left forgetting. Except, I hadn't forgotten anything. In fact, I'd experienced someone else's death. Their memory? Was that key to getting out of here?

From one step to the next, the sky brightened to a hot glare, and the path morphed to sand under my bare feet that was a sharp burn. The thump of my heart kept time with the voice in my head screaming *Run!*

I clutched the scroll in my hand tighter. I'd found the second piece, tying us with Chariot. Not much further. My Attendant would be waiting and I'd be safe from the man with the portal magic.

Starbursts exploded behind my lids, a searing agony doubling me over. A blade stuck out of my middle and blood gushed out through my fingers onto the red sands of the Negev. If you ignored the part where my pink fleshy bits were hanging out, the crimson stain I made on the ground was kind of pretty, almost like one of the crown anemones that blanketed this area in February. Admittedly, I wouldn't bring this particular bouquet to a dinner party, but there was a certain fascination factor to seeing myself from this particular angle.

Pro tip: shoving your large intestine back into your body wasn't an effective use of your death throes. I launched myself at the man in the Bedouin robes, slapped my palm against the bloody ear hanging raggedly from his head, and sent my magic into his.

It tasted of dates and the sirocco. My pain ebbed away, his magic wrapping me in a gauzy haze that delivered me into the arms of death on angel wings. With my last vestiges of awareness, I snared his magic in the red forked branches I created. White clusters bloomed, decimating his powers for good.

The scroll tumbled from my hand onto the sand. I had one last glimpse of sunshine before darkness claimed me.

I snapped back into full awareness, traversing the same narrow path through the silent, gloomy land once more.

Jezebels. I was reliving Jezebel deaths. Fuuuuuck.

I pulled up my shirt with still-blue fingers. Sure enough, there was a gash across my middle, accessorizing my chic waterlogged look.

Two deaths. I was the thirteenth Jezebel. Was there an exit? And if I didn't make it out in time, would I die for real? I had no way of knowing, but I was damned if I was going to find out.

My third death was actually quite pleasant. There was a bed, for one thing, and my family was grouped around, weeping. Not fake cries either, where the intensity of their wails are in direct proportion to how fast they want you to bite it to ransack your jewelry box. They were really upset. Except they kept calling me Liya, which was weird.

Wasn't my name Sherlock? No, wait… Jezebel. That felt more familiar but not quite right either. Was it my middle name? I watched the flames dance in the hearth across the bedroom, and as I took my last wheezing breath, a chunk of wood crumbled into the flames.

Ashes.

I stood on the path once more, repeating my name over and over again. That was how this place got you. The forgetting part. I had to remember my name or I'd never get out of here.

But then my brain trumpeted a warning. Beware twelve.

I shook my head. Twelve what? What else had I forgotten here?

Between the third and fourth deaths, I tried using my magic to get out. There was nothing to send it into. No foundational magic to disassemble, and even if there had been, taking Sheol apart was not prudent.

The sixth time I died, the crack of gunfire echoed off the dense press of trees in the Black Forest. The shock of the bullet to my temple made me gasp and seize up. The world went tight and black and it was pretty much over. A total upgrade from death number five which had involved a rare poison and vomitus convulsions.

It was taking me longer to remember my name, but every detail of each death I'd experienced was burned into my brain. This place was not going to claim my identity—or my life.

I manifested a dagger and carved the word "Ash" into my flesh, a soundless scream tearing from my throat as the skin parted. Blood dripping, I kept moving forward.

While the eighth death was nothing to write home about, it beat the hell out of bursting into flame, which heralded my descent into the death of the ninth Jezebel.

Things did not get better from there.

Beware twelve.

Back on the path, I ran a finger over the jagged, blood-encrusted letters on my arm, wondering about the importance of the word "Ash." Faces flashed at me, swimming up as if from a dream. There was something so familiar about each of them: a pair of green eyes lit with laughter, a cocky grin and a flash of hair as black as a raven's wings. Even a puppy, its little tongue lolling out.

I teased out the knowledge. I am Ash. Maybe I needed the entire sentence on my arm. I tried to make another dagger, since I'd lost the one I'd had, but I was too weak and my blood had dried too much to write with.

I am Ash. I am Ash.

I stumbled, almost plunging headlong into the Repha'im, and only catching myself at the last second. I held my hand up to the side of the path. A Repha'im flowed up to meet my movements, close enough for me to feel the air vibrating between us.

I am Ash. I had the absurd desire to introduce myself to the Repha'im.

I kept walking, tricking myself into believing that moving forward was somehow accomplishing something.

Beware twelve. I turned the warning around and over in my sluggish brain, until the answer floated free. Twelve previous Jezebels, twelve deaths to relive.

The path still had no end, but at least the way out was clear. I'd have to relieve the deaths of the twelve Jezebels that came before me and if I survived, my identity intact, my reward would be a return to the land of the living. It had to be. I refused to entertain any other possibility. There was just the minor complication that after every death I experienced, I'd become more lost, forget who I was entirely and die anyway.

Nope, I had that covered with my handy name-engraved-in-flesh prompter. Skin. Was there anything it wasn't good for?

Three more deaths to survive. Fail and I'd die again. For good.

The tenth death was pretty much everything you'd expect from being crushed under a ton of rocks.

After the eleventh death, I realized the joke was on me. There weren't twelve deaths to relive before I either got out of here or experienced mine. There were thirteen. Gavriella had died twice, and I got to enjoy both.

The first one, when she was still Gracie, wasn't so bad. An electric blast of magic sent my heart into convulsions and then quickly stopped it altogether. It was no picnic, but in the scheme of things, it was one of the milder ones.

I trudged along the path in Sheol, fuzzy once more on my name, and who or what awaited me at my destination. Wherever that was.

Black shadows flowed along either side of me. So pretty. I pushed my hand through some kind of invisible shield to poke one and the little fucker leeched onto me, sucking on my soul hard enough to make my eyeballs feel like they were going to implode.

I tried to dislodge it, but it had bellied up to the bar and wasn't going anywhere. More shadows descended upon it. There was a tussle to drink me dry. Wow. I must be some kind of a saint with a primo soul.

The original shadow was dislodged and a fatter one took its place, crowding the rest out. Except I could taste this one. It was dusty, like everything else in this joint. If you're gonna drink me, I'm gonna drink you back, suckah.

A silky red ribbon flew out of me and into the shadow. Red forked branches appeared, and beautiful white clusters exploded. Whoa. Cool.

The shadow disappeared. Not shadow. I furrowed my

brow. Repha'im. And I am Ash... Someone. Madonna only had one name. Good enough.

Pain stabbed my chest. I sucked in a breath...

...bound by heavy chains to a chair. My ribs were cracked, blood caked my lashes, and my left arm hung at an awkward angle from the latest round of tortures. None of that compared to the stain on my soul. I, Gavriella Behar, had taken magic from innocents, used by Chariot to sow chaos, fear, and evil, and too cowardly to end my life and deny them this abhorrent act.

The chains loosened and I fell forward into someone's arms. The woman's features were blurred by the light shining behind her, like a halo, but my magic recognized hers and my breath caught. The missing Jezebel. She lived.

The world spun, my heart breaking.

Now I would condemn her to her fate. Another stain on my soul. I wanted to tell her I was sorry. That the road ahead of her was hard and lonely and in the end I wasn't sure we made any difference at all, but I was too weak. Or maybe too well trained.

I secured her promise to stop Chariot.

Poor girl.

Death reached its bony fingers toward me, cackling.

I came to on my knees in the dirt. The hands braced on the ground were mine, yet unfamiliar. Death surrounded me; I tasted it on my lips. So easy to stay here and fade away.

Ash.

The word carved into my flesh.

The woman who promised.

The Girl Who Lived.

Images assaulted me, my life rushing up to fill me with strength and power. It wasn't perfect, but it was mine.

I stood up. I might walk a path of darkness, but it wasn't this one. Not now.

"I am Ashira Cohen." I sounded like a rusty chicken, but

I made noise and it was beautiful. Forgetting was death, but remembering was life. "In the name of Serach, Tehilla, Liya, Catriona, Atef, Vasilisa, Thea, Rachel, Nikolia, Freyja, Vishranti, and Gracie Gavriella, I claim my life."

The Repha'im scattered, rising into the sky like a black funnel until they were lost to sight.

"In the name of the goddess Asherah, I demand passage back to the living." Head high, I stepped off the path.

And when my next step took me to the almond tree, back in the grove, I started laughing. I used the ring to get out of there. Fun as it had been to fall through the void and almost be hit by a car that one time, I didn't want to cheapen the experience by doing it too often.

Rafael dropped the book he was reading in the library. "Are—are you dead?"

"What? No, not currently, I think, though it's been a little touch and go lately." Granted my skin was bluer than it should have been, and I still bore traces of all the deaths I'd relived, but that was no reason to insult me. I picked at the scab on the "A" carved into my arm.

Rafael swallowed audibly. Heh.

"It bleeds. I'm alive. All good." I peered at the letters. "Geez. I really did that? Nice penmanship considering." The world went fuzzy, my legs gave out on me, and that was all she wrote.

When I woke up, I was lying on the library table, which had been cleared of all books and papers. Rafael wiped his brow. "Thank heavens. No. Give it a moment. I've healed you, but your injuries were extensive."

He was pale but bore no signs of arousal. Whew. Thank goodness for regular old healing magic.

I checked myself over. "Not even a scar. Much appreciated. I wasn't looking forward to going through life looking like Sally in *Nightmare Before Christmas*. You know, if she'd had a Thanksgiving mishap with a meat tenderizer and a carving knife."

Rafael stared blankly at me. "Are you quite sure you're all right?"

I shook my head. "We've really got to introduce you to our fine North American cinema, Rafael. There's plenty of time before Halloween. It'll be team-bonding."

"Never mind that, where did you go?" he said. My almost-death had blown away any of his remaining anger. Good to know.

"Let's just say if you're considering various holiday hot spots, I'd skip Sheol. The food is non-existent and the house-keeping leaves a lot to be desired." I brushed off some more dust.

"As in the Jewish underworld?"

"That's the one. The land of death, silence, and forgetting. Hence the fleshy reminder. Also, I've made great leaps into my knowledge of all previous Jezebels seeing as I just relived every single one of their deaths."

He blinked at me. "Aren't you industrious?"

"Right? It was like It's a Small World but replace the grand tour of countries with deaths. Also, less singing, because, silence. Long story short, the ride ended, I demanded passage back to the living, ended up in the grove where I'd first been tested as a Jezebel, and then it was a hop, skip, and a jump to the library."

"Oh," he said.

"Quite. Does anyone know I'm alive yet?"

"I called Priya, who was extremely distraught."

"Disappearing in the presence of a known necromancer tends to have that effect on friends and loved ones." I sat up, a little wobbly but mostly fine, and pulled out my phone. My call to Levi went straight to voicemail. I left him a brief "So that happened" message, hoping he'd call back soon. "If you don't need me, I should check in with Miles that Jonah is secured. Thanks, Rafael."

Then I was going straight to Levi.

"You're welcome," he said. "If you have any lingering symptoms, you know where to find me."

"Will do. Any solution to my magic problem?"

He shook his head.

"How about cracking the codename?"

Rafael made a discouraged face.

"Better and better. Want me to help with the second one after I check in with the others?"

"Thank you, but no. A cup of tea and some fresh air should be all I need."

"Good luck."

This time the ring took me home. Priya and Mrs. Hudson rushed me, Priya squeezing me tight.

"I'm sorry," I whispered. "Actual, full-stop sorry. I hurt you and then I doubled down with the dog. I apologize."

"Forgiven and forgotten."

When Mrs. Hudson nipped at my pant leg, I crouched down. "Who's a good girl? Who did mommy miss? Yes, she did." I gave the dog nose-to-nose kisses.

"Mommy, huh?"

"I'm keeping her. Yes, exactly like you said I would. Be smug at your peril because I will hurt you," I said in a cutesy voice to the puppy, who pranced in a circle around me, her sandy-colored tail wagging. "Who loves me more than the cow?"

Her ears perked up and she ran off in search of her true love.

"If I have to use the C-word, it better not be to describe a cow!" I yelled after the pug. I sat down on the couch. "I have a lot to tell you. Levi and I are a thing now. Yes, I owe you twenty bucks. Good luck trying to collect. Also, my father is definitively dead. Bummer, huh." I twisted my hands in my lap, kind of wanting another hug.

She didn't disappoint.

"I also have to tell you something." Priya bit her lip.

"Did Jonah get away?"

"No." She swore softly and made a phone call. "Miles, she's here."

Suddenly an unfamiliar woman stood in our living room, wearing the House security uniform. "Come with me, please," she said.

Dread snaked through me. "What's wrong? Priya?"

She dropped her gaze to her feet.

"Miles will fill you in." The woman took my arm and we disappeared, reappearing on the floor in House HQ where the isolation cell was located.

"We teleported?" I said and grabbed her arm. "Are the wards down?"

She shook her head. "I have clearance as a member of Levi's team. Miles?"

Miles blinked at her words like he'd been jolted out of a reverie, but he didn't stop pacing in front of the security room, a bleak look on his face.

"What the hell's going on?" I demanded.

"Jonah told us he'd sent you to Sheol."

"I swear to God, Miles, tell me what's happened or I will rip this place apart."

"We thought you were dead. Levi went ballistic. He's locked himself in the isolation wing with Jonah." If Miles rubbed his hand over his sleeve any faster, he'd be going at warp speed.

"You're worried he hurt Jonah? Killed him in retaliation?" Levi wouldn't regret his actions if I was dead, except they could cost him everything: his position, his freedom. The horrible irony was it would be for nothing, because I was alive.

"I don't give a fuck about that scum," Miles said. "Levi's torturing him with illusion magic. You know how he hurts himself when he overloads on his powers."

The hair on the back of my neck lifted and a shiver ran down my spine. "You think he's gone blind?"

"We'll be lucky if that's all that's happened. We can't get to him to help. Arkady tried. He lasted all of three seconds before the doors blew open. From the glimpse I saw? It's… madness in there. You promised me once that you'd save him from himself. Please, Ash." His voice cracked. "Save him."

Chapter 27

"Madness" could have meant a lot of things: Levi might have illusioned a pack of wild animals to rip Jonah apart or an ax-wielding clown to chase him.

My first clue that it was so much worse was when the woman with the Transporter magic put on a blindfold and industrial ear protectors before jumping us into the sealed-off wing.

"Good luck," she said and transported out.

I stood alone on a desolate moor. The moss, so dark green it was almost black, lay boggy beneath my feet, and fog striped the world like wraiths. A craggy rock face made up of jagged black boulders sticking up like crooked teeth barred my way to the right.

Deep red eyes borne of unspeakable evil moved across the crags as if tracking me, and an eerie howl rose in the distance.

I fell to my knees under the weight of a vast inconsolable loss and reached for my blood armor, but I no longer had magic. I was an insignificant speck and I was going to die here.

An enormous ghostly face appeared in the burning sky. It

rushed toward me and I ducked, screaming. The face swirled around me, ice crystals forming on my skin, and my teeth chattered.

It fired inside me like a spear, lifting me off my feet. I hovered in mid-air, impaled and shrieking. Suddenly, it jerked with an anguished cry and deposited me very gently on the ground. The specter swam around me again, but its touch reminded me of Mrs. Hudson seeking affection.

I swatted at it. I mean, I'd just survived Repha'im and my quota on all things ghostly were full up. "What do you want?"

The face hovered, two burning blue eyes trained on me.

My breath caught. Levi. With that thought, I pierced the illusion. No, that hadn't been me. I couldn't see through illusions, especially not one created by a level five Houdini. Levi had recognized me. He wanted me to find him. "It's me. Ash. I'm alive. Show yourself. Please," I added, because he was very fond of his precious etiquette.

The face disappeared.

"No! Come back. Show me where you are." Now that I was aware this was an illusion, I could use my powers. I sent my magic into the rocks, but it bounced harmlessly off.

Another howl rent the air, this one close enough to lift the hairs on the back of my neck. I spun around, certain of a hot breath of foul air and nip of fangs at my back.

"You asshole! Don't you dare *Hounds of Baskerville* me." It was kind of sweet in its own incredibly fucked-up way.

More sets of devilish red eyes blinked open in the rocks.

Think logically. I wasn't in a Sherlockian nightmare. I was in the corridor with the jail cell that nulled magic. Levi was here, but what stood between us?

I fingered the wooden ring on the chain. I could get out of here and wait for him to either black out and end this or come to his senses, but what if he was already out cold and that face was his unconscious cry for help? What condition was he in now?

"I'm coming," I called out.

The ground rumbled, knocking me to my knees.

More howls shivered through the fog, coming at me from my left.

I eyed the crag face—my only way out. I had to go through the boulders, but I couldn't make my feet move. Ninety-nine percent of me was positive they were illusions, but that other one percent was very insistent otherwise.

"We're going to have a little talk about waiting a suitable period of time to verify I'm actually dead before going all crazypants."

Calling up my blood armor, I marched determinedly up to and through a boulder.

That was the plan anyway, executed admirably except for the part where I bounced off the damn rock hard enough to crash onto my ass.

The ground rumbled again, a chasm splitting the rocks at my feet.

"You say I'm defensive?" I stomped my boot. "I swear to God, you are the most emotionally guarded man alive. Especially for someone who constantly puts himself out to protect other people. I'm trying to help you and you're so determined to be locked into your misery—a misery which is totally unfounded since I'm alive, by the way—that you're fighting me."

The world stilled into a watchful silence.

"Did you know you always touch me when you sleep, even if it's just my arm? And though you spent years on your pathetic need to one-up me, you let those old guys cheat if it earned them a point. Your love of anchovies on pizza is abhorrent, and I've never felt for anyone what I feel for you. So, fine, you big baby. I won't use my magic again, but I'm still coming for you, because you're not getting rid of me that easily."

Eyes closed, I rushed the closest boulder. Like Harry Potter, I escaped facial carnage, though there was no magical train waiting on the other side.

Arms askew, I skittered to a stop on a slippery rock ledge, knocking pebbles into the waterfall that fell from above me. They immediately burned up, as things do when the waterfall is made of spitting and hissing orange-red corrosive lava. My eyes watered from the stench of brimstone and hate.

It was the Reichenbach Falls on a bad acid trip.

"You. Need. Therapy!" I yelled into the wind that whistled like a tortured scream. I tapped my foot, seeking any other way possible to keep moving forward and get to my stupid boyfriend. There wasn't one.

"Damage me and you are paying for very expensive reconstructive surgery and a fuckton of drugs." Edging forward, I peered over the edge. My foot slipped on a wet patch and with a screech, I hit the rock on one knee, my other leg dangling over the chasm. I grabbed an outcropping of rock to keep from falling backwards.

My knee throbbed and tears stung my eyes, but I pulled myself to my feet, and cautiously leaned forward. The bottom of the falls ended in a frothing river of—surprise!—more corrosive lava. It was very far away. I gnawed on the edge of my thumbnail. It was just an illusion.

Ten minutes later, with two wet spots on my thighs from where I'd been wiping my palms on them, I hurled myself off the top.

Apparently, I only had the capacity to break one part of this very fine illusion, so while the lava didn't burn, I fell and fell and fell, screaming all the way.

At some point, it almost seemed pointless to keep screaming, except I was only halfway down, which was a good reason in and of itself to keep going.

I hit the river feet first, sending up a plume of lava. It still didn't burn, but I couldn't breathe under there. I kicked up as hard as I could, my enhanced strength barely giving me the edge over the racing current.

I broke the surface, grabbing onto a log rushing past. Then I screamed because it wasn't a log. It was Jonah.

He was charred and bark-like, his red hair patchy, but while unconscious and still cuffed with the magic-suppressors, he was alive. I didn't know if this was an illusion or Levi had actually fricasseed him somehow, but I was pretty sure that using him as a floatation device was not bucket list worthy. Since I couldn't help him until I found Levi, I released him and swam for shore.

Hauling myself out, I found myself confronted by a dense forest made of twisted metal spikes. Set into this impenetrable wall was a door barred with a rusted, heavy lock. I wrung an orange puddle of lava out of my shirt. "I played nicely with your ghost face and your stupid magmafall, but I'm done." I held up the ring on the chain. "Show yourself right now or I'm out of here."

With a creak, the spikes grew taller and more twisted.

"Yeah, you didn't protect me. Accept it and move on. This self-flagellation is getting old, Levi."

The ghost face appeared again, the eyes glaring at me.

I twirled a finger between the lava river and the spike forest. "Then this isn't you playing martyr? Okay, must just be you throwing a tantrum like a little kid." I rolled my eyes. "Jonah is a necromantic dick. I lived. I have a pretty good track record of doing that. Now punch him in the face and let's move on already. I'm hungry."

Jonah's body flew out of the river, once more unblemished. Well, until he flew face-first into some of the spikes and his nose shattered. I had a feeling that back in reality Levi had smashed him into the concrete hallway wall.

"Happy now?" I raised an eyebrow.

The lock banged against the door, still very present. Was this what he'd learned to do growing up, making more and more elaborate worlds to escape into whenever real life got to be too much? Was this still how he was spending his adulthood?

I swear, I was getting him some new hobbies when I got out of here.

I tried to break the weather-beaten lock with my enhanced strength, but I didn't even dent it. "Why are you making me work so hard? It's me." Manifesting lock picking tools, I set about opening it. It was so choked with rust that by the time I succeeded, my arms were aching and my hands were so sweaty that I almost couldn't hold the lock picks.

The sound of that damned lock hitting the ground was one of the sweetest ones I'd ever heard. I wrenched open the door and stepped through.

I found Levi less than a minute later. He stood outside the open jail cell door, his head thrown back and his eyes completely black, a whitish blue magic pouring out of him like he was an evil video projector.

While the cell was visible, the rest of the isolation ward wasn't. Levi was still surrounded by the metal spikes. His arms were outstretched as if he was conducting an orchestra, but his entire body shook under the weight of this illusion and corpses had rosier tints to their skins than he did.

I checked his eyes. They'd gone totally dead. There was no light to them, no awareness whatsoever.

"Levi?" I whispered. No response.

I repeated his name louder and more sharply but there wasn't even a flicker that he'd heard. He'd never been unresponsive before.

My heartbeat thrashed in my ears. I grabbed him by the shoulders shaking him. "Answer me, damn you."

Levi remained motionless, his arms frozen in what mockingly resembled a victory pose. This wasn't a win. I was down and out in the last quarter and I needed a Hail Mary.

The easiest solution would be to tug on his magic. Just enough to shock him to his senses. I licked my lips, anticipating the taste of scotch and chocolate, then stilled. What if I couldn't stop?

I rocked back and forth, my head buried in my hands. Sight, hearing, touch, all gone. That left taste and smell. If neither of those worked... I straightened up, my spine rigid. We'd wasted years dancing around each other. I wasn't going to lose him now.

Clasping his face in my hands, I rose onto tiptoe and kissed him. It didn't work.

"Fight, you stubborn bastard." I kissed him again.

His arms dropped to his sides.

Yes. Cupping the nape of his neck, I brushed my lips against his again, pouring all my feelings into it: trust, care, longing, need.

His eyes blinked open, his irises once more a clear beautiful blue.

The normal world flicked back into view.

"If this is how I can have you, then I'll take it," he said and rested his forehead against mine.

"Excuse me?"

He laughed and touched the spot between my eyebrows. "Did you know when you frown, your eyes crinkle up, and I want to kiss you? I did. Good thing, right? Or how would I have created that now?"

"I'm not an illusion."

"You're real to me. I don't care. Just don't leave."

"Is that supposed to be romantic? You idiot." I punched him. "It's really me. You think being sent to Sheol would kill me?" I made a raspberry noise. "Bitch, please."

"Don't mess with me." He paced the length of the hallway like a caged tiger, refusing to meet my eyes.

Dread skittered through me. "I'm not."

Pain flashed over his face. "You got locked in Sheol. The real Ash got herself out of a lot of impossible scrapes, but even she couldn't do that."

"You're right. This is an illusion, but I'll never leave you, baby. How could I? You're perfect and you'll always protect me."

He stopped pacing.

"Also, I think Miles and I are going to be great friends for the rest of our lives."

He warily inched closer.

"You should also really give Veronica a raise and—"

Levi crashed his mouth on mine. I wrapped my arms around his waist, relaxing as his scent enveloped me.

"I believe you," he whispered and kissed me again. Sweet and slow, it lit me up like a thousand fairy lights riding through my veins.

Somewhere in the distance, shouts and thudding feet got louder. Miles sprinted into the room and we broke apart, just before he crushed us all back together in a bear hug.

"Okay. That's... Yeah, no." I wriggled out of it, but Levi held fast on to my hand, while he proceeded to apologize to Miles for the trouble he'd caused him.

"Shut up, Levi, and let your girlfriend take you to the infirmary."

"Lovah," I said.

Both men grimaced.

"Jonah has been secured," Miles said. "I trust you'll leave him in my care now?"

"He's all yours," Levi said, holding tightly to my hand. "I've got everything I need."

We ended up with two paramedics as escorts, asking Levi all kinds of questions as we went to the infirmary. He was remarkably lucid, though he moved slowly, wincing every now and again.

I sat quietly by his side while he was given scary shots and vision tests and hooked to a heart monitor.

Levi didn't say much, nodding abashedly while the House medic admonished him that he was going to do permanent damage if he ever invested that much of his power into a single illusion again. I'd have chalked it up to post-illusion fatigue if the expression on his face hadn't grown more and more pensive.

The doctor finally finished all the tests. He gave Levi some pain meds for his fractured ribs and a couple of sports drinks to combat mild dehydration, but at last Levi was told that he was good to go home and rest.

"I want someone to stay with you," the doctor said.

I raised my hand. "That would be me."

Levi gave a wan smile.

I waited until the man was gone and Levi was putting his suit jacket on with slow, careful movements. "What's on your mind, Leviticus?"

"Nothing." He wrapped his tie around his neck, tying it tightly. Oh boy. Locked-down mode in full force again.

"Bullshit. You thought I was dead. I'd have been miffed if you hadn't gone all dark side."

"It isn't funny."

"My darling Levi, you're a monster. This is not news to either of us."

"Not this monstrous," he said. "How can you be okay with this? I didn't even think twice about what I was doing. Jonah had killed you and I wanted him to pay. No matter how I came off or what it cost me. All my years of being in control and I threw it away in a heartbeat."

"Because of me." I took a step back. "You're worried I'll do something and make you lose control again when I get hurt."

Not if.

"No. Ash. Fuck, I'm making a mess of this." He raked a

hand through his hair. "I've always known exactly how deep my darkness runs. That's why I've always kept the worst of it in check. No one who truly mattered was ever supposed to see it."

"You're forgetting how bright your light is. You only have this darkness because you care so much. What we have might be new, but if our positions were reversed? I'd have ripped that fucker's magic out in the most painful way possible. We are who we are, and you're the *only* one I trust to see it."

The tension drained out of his body and he hugged me, burrowing his face in my neck.

"Do you want to still come home with me?" Levi said, and handed me my jacket.

"Yes. So long as we can stop by my place to get clean clothes, because I need a shower like nobody's business. Then you have to feed me."

"You know, most women would want to take care of *me* after the ordeal I just went through."

"The one of your own making?"

Levi tugged on my hair. "Be nice."

"I'm always nice. Also," I said, "as we've established, I am not most women."

"No," Levi said. "Most women induce ninety-seven percent less heart attacks in me."

"Where's the fun in that? Hey, Leviticus?" I caught his hand, swinging ours together.

"Yeah?"

"Dead people, psycho illusions, I don't care. I'm happy."

His eyes danced and his smile was sweet and all-mine. "Me too."

Rafael sent me a text ordering me to meet him immediately at the library.

I got a sour taste in the back of my throat.

Me: *Unconscious. Sorry. Try back tomorrow.*

I'd promised to stay with Levi. Moreover, I'd only barely

convinced him that he could share all sides of himself with me and I wasn't going anywhere. I couldn't run out on him now.

I wasn't going to add another scar to the ones he bore.

Attendant mine: *Your Jezebel duties come first.*

The words sat there, heavy, black, and immutable, reminding me that before Levi, I'd made a promise to serve the greater good. I'd accepted all of Levi. Would he do the same and not get tired of a girlfriend who couldn't take one night to put him first?

"I have to go," I said, my voice heavy with regret. "Rafael wants to see me in the library. A.S.A.P." I tried to slide my hand from Levi's, but I couldn't make myself let go.

A tightness flashed over Levi's face and he pulled free of my grasp. "I'll ask Miles to stay with me."

Fuck it. I pulled out my phone to tell Rafael to wait until morning, but another text came in before I could.

Attendant mine: *Now, Ashira!*

Rafael was not an exclamation point kind of guy. Maybe an ellipsis in extreme circumstances, or in the event of the zombie apocalypse he'd forgo a period, but such profuse emotion? In a text? Horror.

"Rafael must have…" My legs gave out on me and I dropped heavily onto a chair.

"Must have?" Levi prompted.

"He must have cracked the codename."

I still harbored revenge fantasies around this person for ordering my dad's execution, but this interlude with Levi had dampened my enthusiasm somewhat. There was a lot to be said for being happy. I had never truly understood that before. As soon as Rafael said the name and set us on this path, that part of my life might become a distant, if precious memory.

Shit was about to get very real.

"I'm not sure I'm ready for this," I said.

"Let me come with you."

"You can't. He's at the library. And, I think I need to face this myself. But can I come over right after?"

"If you want to go home," Levi said, "be in your own space, be with Priya, someone who's been there with you all these years in dealing with Adam's absence, I won't be hurt."

"I want to be with you." I kissed him quickly, but he hauled me back against him, taking his time until I clutched dizzily at his shirt front.

"Now you can go," he said smugly.

"You're a bastard."

"Good. When you get back, we can fight about that fact and then have really good make-up sex."

"Get real. I'm not forgiving you that easily. We'll have really good hate sex first."

He lay his hand on my cheek. "Thank you for not being dead."

I smiled at him. "Thank you for breaking Jonah's face. And take Miles home to watch over you."

I slid the ring on my finger and disappeared.

Rafael was practically levitating, he was so excited. His eyes sparkled behind his slightly askew glasses, his short hair sticking out in tufts as if he'd been pulling at it.

The library looked like a bomb had gone off. There were Attendant records strewn all over the table, from the very ancient to the most modern, along with reams of loose leaf paper and a variety of colored pens.

He dragged me over to the table and pushed me into a chair. "I did it."

"Can I get some tea?" I said.

"Pardon?"

"Tea? Generally served in one of your frou-frou little cups, preferably with something sweet to accompany it. Your host skills were subpar on that front last time." I didn't give a damn about the tea. I was stalling.

Rafael glanced about him, bewildered. "You really want tea? I don't have any here and I can't remember what I have at home."

I sighed. There was no putting off the truth. "What did you find?"

He rummaged amongst all the books. "I got to thinking. Chariot took its name from the Old Testament. What if the members took their codenames from there as well? I found…" He picked up an older leather-bound volume. "Right. Here it is. Remember I mentioned how we had another codename? It's 34E13."

"Yes. Number, letter, number. I don't see what it stands for, though."

"Ah, but throw in the Old Testament." He bounced on his toes.

"Still not following."

"The five books of Pentateuch. It occurred to me that the letters might correspond to the various books. Thus the E in 34E13 refers to Exodus."

"And the numbers?"

"Quotes. Generally when a passage is cited it would be written like this." He grabbed a red pen and scrawled Exodus 34:13. "They rearranged it a bit. If you were going to use it as a codename, you wouldn't want to be obvious about it."

"Heaven forbid. Okay, lay it on me. What's the quote?"

"Exodus 34:13." He cleared his throat. "'Break down their altars, smash their sacred stones and cut down their Asherah poles.'"

I slammed my hands down on the table. "You. Are. Shitting. Me."

"I'm not. I assure you. This has to be the key."

"It does. But does it give us their identity?"

He frowned. "I'm still working on that part."

"You're doing brilliantly. Truly," I said. "What's the quote corresponding to 26L1?"

"Ah. That one comes from Leviticus." Grinning, he pushed his glasses up his nose, totally unaware of the tsunami he'd unleashed with the word Leviticus, now barreling toward me to upend my life.

He babbled on as he found the correct passage. I tried to shut him up, but I couldn't get anything other than a faint squeak out.

"Aha!" Rafael said. He didn't notice me frantically waving my hands. "Leviticus 26:1. 'You must not make idols for yourselves or set up a carved image or sacred pillar, or place a sculpted stone in your land to bow down to it, For I am the Lord your God.'"

The quote on the clock.

A pained sound from deep in my belly escaped me as I bent over, my fists pressed into my stomach. I gagged on the taste of bile, then jumped up, barely making it to the trash can before I vomited.

Rafael stared at me, the book forgotten in his hand. "Ashira? Are you still injured?"

I wiped my mouth. "26L1 is Isaac Montefiore. Levi's father."

Chapter 28

Hope is a funny thing. It forces parents to sit by the phone years after their child has gone missing, just in case. It causes spouses trapped in loveless marriages to have a baby—like that can save them.

It found me cramped in an economy seat, flying back to Antigua to see Paulie, seeking a miracle that would make this nightmare disappear.

I'd been too cowardly to talk to Levi, texting that I'd been wrong. Rafael desperately needed my help breaking the codename and we'd be working late into the night. I used my own funds to buy the ticket.

Levi had barely just been saved. He'd been willing to go to his darkest place when he thought that I'd died, and I'd only started to mean something to him. Isaac, for all his many faults, was his father.

Even if I could convince Levi not to go after Isaac in retaliation for killing Adam, Levi wasn't a fool. He'd know immediately that his dad wasn't merely supporting a party that intended to impose legislative control on all Nefesh. The rumors around the vials, the virus, abducting kids in Levi's home territory—Isaac was engaged in a systematic and ruthless takedown of his only son.

The darkness Levi had unleashed in the wake of me going to Sheol would be mild cloud cover on a summer's day. He was going to destroy Isaac and in the process, destroy himself.

I'd been kicked when I was down before, but having to be the voice of reason on why Levi shouldn't kill Isaac was an all-time low. I wanted to cheer him on and bring the acid and the bathtub for the body disposal party.

No, it wasn't just that. I would do anything so that Levi didn't end up with that blood on his hands.

I pressed my phone with Levi's text of "I miss you. - Your happy lovah" to my heart like it was the only thing powering me.

Penned in the middle seat between a snoring man and his restless sleeper wife, who'd had no desire to switch seats with me so they could sit together, I ignored my shitty overpriced sandwich and concentrated on happy thoughts.

I clung to them for the entirety of the flight, the drive in to town, and the time it took to find Jacques and convince him to take me back to Inferno. He took one look at my face, negotiated a price that was only slightly extortionist, and didn't try anything funny on the way over.

He must have alerted the crew on the island because Unibrow was waiting with some other security people in another speedboat, even though it was the middle of the night.

"Turn around," Unibrow said. "You get one warning."

I hopped out of the back of Jacques' boat.

Red laser dots appeared on my arms.

I stopped, a curious calm descending over me as my armor fell securely into place. "I'm going to see him."

"Cute trick," Unibrow said, "but there's no magic on the island."

"True, but my armor will repel your bullets."

One of the guards fired off a burst which pinged harmlessly off me.

"Told you." I walked toward their boat. "Want to see what I can do to you when I climb aboard?"

"You want to see Caligula, you'll have to go on the island," Unibrow said. "We'll wait."

"Ah, but if you shoot me you'll have the Head of House Pacifica to deal with."

Unibrow laughed. "Oooh. Big deal."

"And the Queen of Hedon."

That gave him pause. "You're bluffing."

"Let's find out. Do you have a way to contact Moran, her second? Wears white, pretty good with a sword?"

The guards checked in nervously with Unibrow who gave them a signal. They lowered their guns.

"Smart thinking. Now, who's going to escort me there?" I brandished my hope like a shield.

Paulie waited for me on his front steps, bleary-eyed and dressed in silk pajamas. "Ash? Why are you here?"

Tree frogs chirped loudly and the waves were a distant murmur.

"Is 26L1 Isaac Montefiore?" I said.

"Adam never told me."

"You knew every other detail of my father's plan. You've tortured yourself remembering it. Built a fucking prison on this island to death wish yourself into penance." I advanced on him. Again with the red dots.

Paulie called his guards off and they dematerialized into the jungle.

"Now, I'm going to ask you one last time," I said, one foot barely separating us. "Did Isaac Montefiore order the hit on Dad?"

Paulie sat down heavily with a nod.

No sound penetrated my numb haze. It was almost as if I

was back in Sheol, except that would have been a million times better because then I'd have been able to forget.

Paulie patted the knotted wood next to him.

I stood, my arms crossed, waiting to speak until the haze had dissipated, if not the numbness. "Why did you lie to me?"

"Because sometimes I can convince myself that it didn't happen that way." He pressed his fingertips into his forehead so hard they turned white. "That it wasn't my fault."

I gasped. "Did you sell Dad out?"

"What? God. No. Never." Paulie rubbed his thighs, agitated. "Adam never told me his boss's real name. But Isaac came by the shop on totally unrelated business while I was making the Avi passport. He threw me odd jobs every once in a while for that cybersecurity business of his. He saw Adam's passport photo and he got this crazed look in his eyes. I'd never seen such a burning hatred, especially just switched on from seeing a photo. Adam was supposed to meet his mysterious boss before he left Thursday night, and when he never contacted me with our code to say he'd made it wherever he was going safely? It had to be Isaac." An ant ran along the top stair and Paulie redirected its path with his finger. "Your dad planned to bring you both to him. When things died down."

I leaned on the porch railing, my head on my arms, my eyes dull and wet. Mom had been right. He hadn't planned to stay away.

Dad had died not for pulling the con of all cons, but for daring to leave.

I clenched and unclenched my fists. Isaac had the gall to then blithely support my mother's legislation, knowing what he'd done. Did he get a little thrill when he spoke with us, cherishing his secret of how he'd ruined our lives? Did he long to see our scars that proved his power, just like he'd once seen Levi's?

316

Was his behavior that of a narcissistic psychopath or was it misdirection? After all, he'd learned from the best.

I gripped my uncle's sleeve. "Where were Adam and Isaac to meet?"

He shrugged helplessly.

"Please, Paulie. You have to remember." Dad never made the meeting with Gavriella, and Chariot didn't have the scroll.

He tapped a finger against his forehead as if needing to physically trigger the memory. "Um. Isaac's house?"

Had Isaac had the balls to look him in the eye and tell him? Or did he take the coward's way out and let Dad leave believing he was about to meet Gavriella and then skip town? That he was home free? Except my paranoid, people-intuitive father would have known his luck had run out and even if he'd tried to charm Isaac out of it, the assassin would be immune.

Avi genuinely hadn't known about the scroll, which meant Dad had pulled one final con. Hidden in plain sight.

I kissed the top of my uncle's head. "I absolve you, Uncle Paulie. Get your shit together and sell this dump."

"But—"

I glared at him until he shook his head and laughed.

"You're just like your father."

It was the sweetest thing he could have said.

When I got back to Vancouver, Rafael and I waited until night to break into Isaac's house. I'd continued to avoid Levi. Priya, too. We killed time in the library while I fobbed them both off with texts about how close Rafael and I were and thanked Priya profusely for watching the dog. At least I'd had a shower and was dressed in new black clothes perfect for the modern cat burglar.

"You have to tell Levi the truth about the hit," Rafael said. "You work for the man. You're dating him."

I picked mushrooms off of my slice of pizza. "How do

you see that conversation going? 'Hey, Levi. Isaac is one of the Chariot Ten. He hired my dad to find one of the scroll pieces, possibly with the promise of immortality. Dad freaked out and left his family when he realized how dangerous this job was. All would have been well except I crashed a car and got this crazy Jezebel magic and he decided to con Isaac. Oh, don't worry. That didn't kill him. The con of the switched scrolls stands to this day. No, on a totally random fluke of poor luck, Isaac saw Adam's fake passport photo. Isaac's abandonment issues went haywire and he hired an assassin to kill my dad. But LOL, laugh's on him because Dad hid the real scroll in Isaac's house, right under his nose.'"

Balled-up cheese and pepperoni joined my pile of mushrooms.

Rafael grimaced. "Perhaps not phrased exactly like that."

"Perhaps not phrased like anything. I don't want to hurt Levi."

"You aren't."

My deconstructed pizza had all the appeal of boiled pig's feet. "I don't want him to experience any more hurt, Mr. Literal."

"That's simply impossible. He's part of this, Ashira."

"And I'm trying to keep him out of it as long as possible." Giving up any pretense of the Great Pizza Reassemble, I wiped off my hands, my appetite gone.

"Ironic, since you yourself take issue with that very behavior."

Our fathers were our own personal nuclear missiles. The desolate wastelands they'd created in their kids had burst into a glorious radioactive bloom, but I was damned if Levi was going to view me as his own ashy holocaust.

"This is different. Drop it."

Our plan to wait for nightfall and silently slip inside was

"She didn't. I suggest you take more care this evening."

"Again," Rafael said. "Apologies."

"Thank you," I mouthed.

An unreadable expression flashed across her face.

"See, Isaac," she said, returning to the office. "No need to terrify the help."

She shut the door with a firm click.

I allowed myself one second of sagging in relief that this hadn't gone totally tits up, then we crept past the office.

Silently, we opened and shut all the doors until we found Levi's old bedroom. We snuck inside, shutting the door behind us with a soft click.

There was a double bed with a blue bedspread, some sturdy wood bedroom furniture, and tons of trophies. Academic, athletic, you name it they crowded his shelves. My heart wrenched for young Levi, trying so hard to prove his worth.

"Where do we begin?" Rafael whispered. "'Hiding spot' is pretty vague."

"You take the closet. I'll check for fake drawer bottoms. Just do it quietly." I methodically searched through Levi's dresser. "I don't sense anything. Maybe it's not here."

"Or the scroll is sealed in something which prevents its detection. The pillars aren't anything special in terms of containing the magic. They're virtually impossible to break into, but they aren't warded up, either. A good waterproof container might be enough to keep you from detecting the scroll's presence."

"Maybe the Tupperware dream is alive and well and your day will be made."

Rafael grinned at me.

We'd searched about half the room with no luck when I asked Rafael to help me lift the mattress. We hefted it up, but there was nothing hidden in the slats.

We dropped it back into place and I jumped.

Levi stood against the closed door, his arms crossed. "Care to explain?"

"Not really," I said.

"That wasn't actually a request," he said, "though I guess I would be somewhat loath to talk about why I was lifting my boyfriend's mattress with some other guy, visiting his parents' house without letting him know, and, oh yeah, avoiding him."

I planted my hands on my hips. "How did you find us? Did you have Priya track us? I don't believe this."

"You ghost me for two days, search my room, and then have the audacity to get indignant?"

"I'll just…" Rafael pointed to Levi's trophy shelves, getting very interested in one with an archery symbol on it.

"The two hundred pages of Google results on you were pretty superficial," I said, "so I figured I'd check out your old bedroom to get a sense of the man I was dating." I pointed at a small trophy. "Spelling bee, huh? What was the winning word?"

"Mendacious," Levi said in a flat voice.

I swallowed. "Walk away, Levi. I'm begging you."

He stood in front of me. "Whatever this is, we face it together. Remember?"

"I don't want you to face it."

He brushed his thumb under my eye, looking at the smudged tear. "Bella, please. You're scaring me."

I looked away and Levi made a frustrated sound.

"You told Ashira's father about your hiding place, correct?" Rafael said.

I thunked my head against the wall.

"I did," Levi said. "Are you looking for something in particular?"

"No," I said, just as Rafael said, "Tell him."

I sighed. "The missing scroll piece."

Levi frowned. "Why would it be…" His face twisted. "No." He stepped back, turning away from me.

I closed my eyes. Please let me be wrong. Pull me close and tell me not to worry. Tell me that we're not our fathers.

"Levi." I reached for him but at the last second, I dropped my hand. "Isaac is one of the Chariot Ten," I said. "That's who my father was working for."

Levi blinked at me, his mouth slack. "He's Mundane. He despises magic."

"Despises or covets?" Rafael said.

"Not helping," I hissed.

"He supports the Untainted Party," Levi said. "He can't be Chariot. They want immortality. He wouldn't back the legislation if that were the case."

"There's an argument to be made that immortality is different from magic power," Rafael said. "Actually, one of the Attendants from a hundred years ago had some fascinating—"

I glared at him. "Show us the hiding spot," I said. "If the scroll isn't there, then we have this all wrong."

That was a logical argument, right? If X, then Y. If I said it enough times, it might become true.

Levi lifted up a tile in the ceiling and pulled out a large shoebox.

Rafael and I crowded around it, barely breathing as Levi flipped it open.

It was empty.

"We were wrong." I said it, but I didn't believe it.

"I wasn't," Rafael said. "It's Isaac. The codename matches the quote on the clock."

Levi buried his head in his hands with a low moan.

"Levi." I placed my hand on his arm. He was so stiff.

"Misdirection." His voice was flat, his expression bleak. I had the scariest feeling that he'd gone away and that this Levi was just an illusion. "Hidden in plain sight, right? That was Adam's thing."

"The box is empty." I rubbed his arm, trying to get some look or action to prove that my wonderful boyfriend was there and not this shut-down automaton.

"It shouldn't be," Levi said, and walked out the door.

Rafael and I scrambled after him down the back stairs and into the kitchen.

"Mom," Levi said.

Nicola turned, her entire face lighting up at the sight of her son. "Levi. What are you doing here?"

He took her elbow and led her outside. Rafael and I weren't invited, but we followed and Levi didn't protest. He didn't register us at all.

"Remember when I was younger, I had that hiding spot?" Levi said.

She smiled. "Sì. Where you used to put your special toys and books." She glanced at us.

"You can speak in front of them," Levi said.

"Va bene. Anything you didn't want your father to know you cared about."

"Yes." Levi pressed his lips together, looking heavenward.

I wished I could wrap my arms around him, but he had to face this on his own. Only that way would we be able to deal with it together.

"The things that were in the box, what happened to them?" he said.

"I packed them with all your other belongings. You remember." She used her hands as she spoke, a trait that I found terribly endearing. "You came and picked them up a couple weeks ago. I told you that you had to go through it all." She wrung her hands together now.

Levi kissed her. "It's okay, Mom. I will."

She grabbed his hand, a fierce expression on her face. "I despised him for how he treated you."

"I know. He won't hurt either of us anymore."

All the damage had already been done.

Levi spent the drive to his house in his Tesla white-knuckled and tight-lipped. I tried talking to him, but he didn't respond to any of my pathetic icebreakers.

Levi unlocked his front door, motioning for Rafael to go on in. He stopped me before I could enter. "Did he kill Adam?"

"He ordered the hit."

Levi spun away from me and marched down a set of stairs off his kitchen into his basement. There were no biscotti, just a cold empty room that I wondered if I'd ever see again.

I stopped Rafael. "I'm going to stay up here."

"Good idea," he said, and headed downstairs.

I strained my ears for any sign that they'd found the scroll. Then out of nowhere, sandstorm and hot wind snaked up into the kitchen.

Rafael snapped at Levi to "seal it up," while I clutched the doorknob upstairs to keep myself from moving.

"Ashira?" Rafael called up. "The scroll is sealed once more. Are you all right?"

"Give me a minute. Let the magic fade." The doorknob splintered under my tense grip, but I didn't move and slowly, the tantalizing magic dissipated.

"I'm good." I was, too—until they came up the stairs and stepped into the kitchen.

The scroll's magic engulfed me, the guys' voices becoming Charlie Brown wah-wah-wahs. That ancient magic wound me in its loving grip, spiraling me higher and higher.

"Ash?" Levi frowned.

Rafael waved a short plastic tube at him. "It's leaking. Get another container."

"Don't worry," I said to the Technicolor pixels of the two people standing there. "Everything is perfect."

I rode the magic out to the edge of the cosmos and when it demanded I fall into the darkness, I was helpless to resist.

I didn't want to resist.

The taste of water slid down my throat. When I snapped into full consciousness, I had Rafael pushed up against the wall and was pulling smudgy magic out of a gash on his chest that I gulped down. In my eagerness, I'd pressed bruises into his skin, but that refreshing magic flowed into me, restoring me. The symptoms fell away, the floor firm under my feet. My urges died down, the song in my head quiet once more.

"Rafael?" I said.

His head was thrown back, his pupils were blown out, and his breathing was ragged. He shot me a besotted smile.

Levi stared at us with cold, flat eyes. "You left a few details out about what your Attendant does, Ash."

I scrambled back from Rafael, who reached for me. His magic was still on my lips and in the back of my throat and I clutched him back, only releasing him when Levi flinched. "These aren't my finest moments," I said lamely. "Rafael." I slapped him lightly across the face. "You need to take the scroll to the library. Can you do that?"

He slowly blinked into awareness, closing his eyes with a grimace. "I'm so sorry, Levi."

"Don't sweat it."

"I'll just… Yes." He snatched a large Tupperware off the counter and disappeared.

Then there were two.

"I can't do this," Levi said.

"Because of the magic thing? It's a healing remedy. That's it."

"Is that what you're calling it?"

No. I wanted to scrub the taste of Rafael's magic from my mouth, because it turned my words to lies. With everything laid bare between us, we needed truth.

"I was scared to tell you, okay?" I said. "I feel like I'm betraying you and I don't ever want to be that person. We tried to not do this after the first time, but it's the only thing that brings me back from the brink."

"I saw your faces." Anguish flashed across his features and I wondered how we'd looked, Rafael and me, curled up together. My stomach turned as Levi's mouth twisted. "Or was I just imagining things?"

"I'm not going to lie. It's an incredible connection when it happens. It quiets my urges and the magic bump is amazing. But it's completely hollow next to what you and I have. I've trusted you with all of me. Not even Priya has gotten that. I'm all in. Do you understand?"

"I do. And if that was all it was…" He reached out to touch my shoulder, but stopped himself before making contact, and took a step back. "You said you'd kill 26L1. Hell, I swore I'd support you in that, Ash. But my own dad?" His voice broke on the last word. "And how do I look you in the eye every day given my father murdered yours?"

I stared at the distance between us, an odd buzzing noise in my ears. "That's them. Not you and me." My words were even. Measured. They were calm and a far cry from the scream lodged at the back of my throat, eager to come out. "You've already suffered so much at his hands. Are you going to let him ruin this for you? Ruin *us*?"

Levi bowed his head, gripping the doorframe. "It is us. Our pasts don't exist in a vacuum. How are we supposed to be together in the face of all of that?"

The truth shall set you free. I'd steered my life by this sage wisdom, only to find it was a crock of shit. The truth had cost me Levi.

"You're a coward." I blinked back tears. "Go hide behind your illusions. I was ready to face this awful truth. With you. Let me know when you're ready to do the same and fight."

"Please go." His words were barely audible.

On the way into Hedon, I'd told Levi that he had to be prepared to destroy whatever secret desire he harbored. Guess he'd taken that to heart. I couldn't even blame him. I mean, I could and I did, but I understood. That's why I walked away without a second look back, my heart in pieces at Levi's feet.

Rafael was wrong about revenge. It wasn't a luxury. It was my life's mission. And Isaac Montefiore and Chariot were going to burn.

~

THANK YOU FOR READING SHADOWS & SURRENDER!

Get ready for the final chapter of Ash's story! REVENGE & RAPTURE (THE JEZEBEL FILES #4).

Ash is tightening the noose on her enemies…

…and praying the rope holds.

Ash's revenge plans for Chariot and Isaac Montefiore take a surreal turn when Isaac's wife hires Ash to find an item that Isaac is obsessed with. Ash takes the job, but this quest throws her back into Levi's path and puts Rafael in grave peril.

Meanwhile, Ash's search for a rare type of magic once again pits her against the Queen of Hearts. A little knowledge is a dangerous thing, but too much might prove fatal.

To top it all off, Ash's mother is being blackmailed by someone threatening to expose Ash as a Rogue unless Talia resigns from her political career for good. Talk about putting the "fun" in family dysfunction.

Secrets, vengeance, and magic collide in the final chapter of The Jezebel Files. With love, family, and her enemy's immortality on the line, a con set in motion fifteen years ago comes to an explosive conclusion, and Ash only has one chance to come out alive.

Get it now!

Every time a reader leaves a review, an author gets ... a glass of wine. (You thought I was going to say "wings," didn't you? We're authors, not angels, but *you'll* get heavenly karma for your good deed.) Please leave yours on your favorite book site. It makes a huge difference in discoverability to rate and review, especially the first book in a series.

Turn the page for an excerpt from *Revenge & Rapture* ....

Excerpt from Revenge & Rapture

Vancouver was burning.

Outside my office window came the sound of breaking glass followed by a wailing alarm, while loud angry voices yelled ugly taunts. The simmering tension of the past couple months between Nefesh and Mundanes had exploded on this June night.

Sirens shrieked nonstop and the smell of smoke drifted in through my shut window. Every cop in the city must have been on patrol.

Inside, all was still, the air sharpened to a pointed focus. I scanned the wall that I'd turned into a link chart. At the top were photos of the four scrolls of the *Sefer Raziel HaMalakh* held by Team Jezebel, along with facts such as the place of their capture and any encounters with Chariot in obtaining them. Pieces of string ran between connected information. I'd rejigged the chart numerous times but had yet to find either the one piece of the *Sefer* still held by Chariot or any more of the Ten's identities.

My phone buzzed and I distractedly stabbed the answer button. "Stop waiting up for me, Pri."

"They've closed the bridges in and out of downtown," my best friend and roommate said in a tense voice. "And it's uncertain how much longer they'll keep Hastings Street open. Come home or you'll be stuck there."

"I'll sleep in my chair. I spoke with the company who bought the party warehouse where the golem was patrolling. Totally legit local developers are turning it into condos." I fired a dart into a photo of Isaac's head, half-turned away from camera. "Another dead end."

"Cut yourself some slack. Jezebels have been fighting this for four hundred years. You've barely been on it four months. You need to sleep."

"Saving the world comes first," I said.

"Is it about saving us or beating them?"

"Does it matter so long as they're stopped? I'm doing my job," I said. The noble cause of dispensing justice warred with my desire to destroy Isaac Montefiore so comprehensively that his life would be a smoking ruin, my signature writ large in the ashes like a painter signing his masterpiece. Work goals were important.

"It matters a lot," Priya said gently. "Your dad was murdered. Don't you think you should get help? This isn't healthy."

"I had enough of talking out my feelings when I was thirteen. Taking Isaac down is the only therapy I need," I snapped.

Mrs. Hudson, my pug, lifted her head from her doggie bed in the corner and whined softly. She hated when her mommies fought.

"That's exactly what I mean." Priya gave an aggrieved sigh. "This isn't about Chariot anymore for you. It's all about Isaac. He's cost you two men you loved and—"

I hung up on her.

Her words lodged under my skin like a splinter. I rubbed

my eyes, nearly blinding myself at the boom that rocked the building. After a second boom—someone ramming the front security door downstairs—came the joyous cries of emboldened rioters entering and looking to mindlessly pilfer.

Not on my watch.

Become a Wilde One

If you enjoyed this book and want to be first in the know about bonus content, reveals, and exclusive giveaways, become a Wilde One by joining my newsletter: http://www.deborahwilde.com/subscribe

You'll immediately receive short stories set in my various worlds and available only to my newsletter subscribers. There are mild spoilers so they're best enjoyed in the recommended reading order.

If you just want to know about my new releases, please follow me on BookBub: https://www.bookbub.com/authors/deborah-wilde

Acknowledgments

Enormous thanks to my darling daughter Kiki for the idea of emotion perfumes and for having a serious conversation with me about "What does paranoia smell like?" How clever of me to have trained you so well in matters of storytelling.

Alex Yuschik, my incredible editor, you continue to inspire me with your brilliant insights. It brings me insane amounts of joy to work with you.

The last edits on *Shadows & Surrender* were done during the early days of self-isolation. Sure, I always work from home and regularly make jokes about being misanthropic, but my life these days really hammered home how important human connection is to me. Thank you to all of you in my FB group and on my mailing list who have reached out. You have been an incredible source of comfort during these strange days. xo

About the Author

A global wanderer, former screenwriter, and total cynic with a broken edit button, Deborah (pronounced deb-O-rah) writes funny urban fantasy and paranormal women's fiction.

Her stories feature sassy women who kick butt, strong female friendships, and swoony, sexy romance. She's all about the happily ever after, with a huge dose of hilarity along the way.

Deborah lives in Vancouver with her husband, daughter, and asshole cat, Abra.

"Magic, sparks, and snark! Go Wilde."

www.deborahwilde.com

 facebook.com/DeborahWildeAuthor

 instagram.com/wildeauthor

Made in the USA
Coppell, TX
29 March 2024